Starburst

Warriors of the Elector Book 3

Featuring bonus novella

The Star of Eternity

Contents

Acknowledgements

I'm sitting at the dining table finalising the print version of this book, and thinking how much has changed in the 7 years since I first penned Starline & The Star of Ishtar. Now the story arc is complete with the introduction of The Star of Eternity (which is the featured novella in this title.) All our couples are happily communed and peace reigns in my futuristic universe and it's time to thank those who've been involved along the way.

So many people help in the production of books and it's honestly hard to remember everyone! So, first and foremost thank you to my wonderful Editor - Sassie. When I mentioned we needed to hurry this along, she gamely hooked in and finished it in record time. Thank you also to Willsin for his awesome cover work. I mean, without his efforts the cover wouldn't be half what you see. Also to Pamela from Beachwalk Press who took the series on in digital format but allowed me to retain the rights to print so I could do what I'd dreamed of from the beginning— release the entire series in paperback.

Thanks to JL for reading the original manuscript.

Tracey (my super duper Beta Reader & friend… No words can adequately thank you for what your help means to me.)

My family, including those who also read it at the last gasp making sure everything was right, also to Cocoa Bean, Super Pup and Galilee. Trust me, they deserved their entry here!

Finally, to you, my readers. Thank you from the bottom of my heart for taking a chance on a once 'New to You" SciFi author! Every email, every review and every message on Social Media reminds me daily of why I write.

Imogene

STARBURST

Prologue

The door burst open, and Chowd watched, wide-eyed, as his mother moved into the room, her graying hair in disarray, her face filled with joy, and her brilliant blue eyes shining.

"Quickly, son, we don't have a lot of time. Your half-brother Vi-Hal is dead, and while he's busy—" Chowd couldn't mistake the hatred he heard in her voice. "—we have an opportunity to get away. Grab the bag you made ready and follow me." Her words stumbled over each other.

His mother vibrated with excitement at their imminent escape, and he felt it wash over him. The bruises on her back and neck once again prompted an acid sickness to crawl up his throat, but he controlled himself and the burst of anger that bloomed at the sight. She cracked open the door, scanning quickly here and there, then with a hard pull they entered the cold, long, and soulless corridor, sliding along the walls that led them to the open shuttle bay.

Eerie quiet filled the gloom, and his mother pushed him toward the ship he knew how to pilot. The one she had given up much to gain access to. The small, battle-scarred shuttle sat at the far end of the bay, but they had prepared it, stashing food and necessary supplies within. It also hid a secret. He had watched as she used her considerable knowledge to make carefully hidden additions to its original specifications.

He moved quickly. His sturdy, late-teen frame with extra musculature, part of his human legacy, gave him a burst of speed. His feet tapped on the surface of the bay, the occasional slip and slide of the metallic surface impeding his progress slightly as he heard sounds of pursuit from outside. His heart rate increased with the burst of adrenaline that followed.

The base on Otega had housed them for the last several cycles, but he hated the lunar-style landscape. He detested the cold silence of the planet's rocky terrain and the dull dun-colored hills that surrounded the ugly military-type base. He hated everything about the lifestyle here, especially the way his father regularly used the women he collected—human, Ru'Edanian, or any other species he subjugated. Rage clawed at his insides when he considered Crick Sur Banden's treatment of his mother, who was no more than a convenient punching bag, bed warmer, and possible incubator when his needs arose. Chowd had no recollection of Crick ever treating the females with the respect they deserved.

Crick had made it clear that he only tolerated Chowd as a lesser son with his impure breeding. Not that Chowd had ever expected any chance of a real familial relationship with the maniac who sired him. It had become worse since the ceasefire with the humans though, as he remained a constant reminder of the potential alliance between humans and the Ru'Edan Senate. Crick despised humans and saw any concept of peace as a weakness in a strong warrior race. Since the followers of Crick Sur Banden and his rogues had been outcasts before banding together, now they followed his lead in every possible way, including their sexual appetites for the women they kept captive.

"This way." She tugged him forward, cutting through the rambling thoughts. Chowd and his mother reached the shuttle as the klaxon started its strident wail. He pushed onward, making it to the ramp and heading up the bouncing board, praying they could move fast enough to get inside the shuttle before their followers entered the bay.

The *fzzt* of a laser whined behind him, and he turned to see his mother standing in front of him. She shielded him from the beam of light—which could cut through flesh and bone— fending off the first of an advancing number of pilots and warriors coming toward them. They'd obviously been alerted by the sudden computer-generated siren that rent the air.

Laser fire split the air again, once more missing them. He saw his father's closest men at the entrance to the bay and, beyond, the angry face of Crick Sur Banden himself. The harsh lighting illuminated the gray of his skin and the glint in his eyes.

"Come on, Mother!" he cried out to her just as a laser blast found its mark. He watched, shocked, to see her eyes glazing with pain as she half-turned her face toward him. He noted the jolt of her body and the seeping red blood that escaped from the point of impact at the center of her chest. Everything moved slowly, as if captured in resin. He heard his voice, harsh with grief, cry out.

"Go, my son. Go! Take the chance and escape."

He hovered anxiously for a second. His mother would die; he could see it as she slumped to the floor, her face a mask of agony. He made his decision in an instant. He had to go; there was no choice. She would die and he had to escape, had to get to his uncle. His mother had given her life to allow him to flee.

He lurched into the shuttle, slapping his hand on the emergency lockdown button, which

also turned on the improved shielding around the pitted and scarred metal. As the ramp rose he shouted commands to the computer, the one his mother had carefully reprogrammed. "Secondary shields online and complete exterior lockdown sequence initiation. Sequence beta-beta-zulu-omega-fiver-niner-gamma." He breathed heavily as he ran toward the cockpit, yelling to the computer, "Initiate automatic launch sequence and lay in the course gamma-alpha-two."

The engines roared to life as he reached the command seat, buckled in, and brought the rear vid-feeds online. His mother lay lifeless on the ground as his father reached her. The rise and fall of her chest had ceased, and pain filled him as reality hit home. His eyes welled with burning tears, which he ignored. Crick's foot aimed a vicious kick at his mother's body, the contact making it jerk even in death.

Chowd punched the thrusters. Crick lurched back, but not before the heat seared him. Chowd saw him slump to the floor, jerking in agony, as the body of his mother ignited.

Pain slashed through him, and he dashed away the tears blurring his vision as he slapped off the feed. He could feel the shuttle begin to ascend before it shot forward, the forces thrusting him back in his seat.

The radar wailed as other ships set an intercept course, but his mother had taught him well. Her skills as an engineer with the Admiralty had been carefully instilled in her son, together with his knowledge of flight. Chowd brought the radar dampener on line as the ship, which looked old and worn, climbed through the atmosphere at a speed beyond its normal specifications, leaving the craft rocking and groaning under the pressures.

He closed his eyes, saying a quick, silent prayer for the safety of his mother's spirit into the afterlife of Re'Ven'Har, the goddess of the Ru'Edan people. His stomach clenched as the ship punched through into space, accelerating as it prepared to jump to hypersonic speed.

The bleep of the comm signaled, and he opened the link, but he already knew what his father would demand. "Return to base, or I will instruct my fighters to shoot you down like the half-breed dog you are." His father—so loving in their every interaction, he thought with bitter sarcasm—bit out the words between halting pants.

Crick's gasping breath reminded Chowd of his injury, possibly mortal, but he could feel no remorse at the thought that his father could die. Instead, something within him rejoiced at his freedom. But then another part of his psyche reminded him that he'd lost his beloved mother, the only one who had showed him nurturing love.

He turned off the comm. "I wouldn't give you the satisfaction of a response." He hurled the words at Crick Sur Banden, knowing he'd likely never hear them. Crick might be his biological father, but he felt no familial connection. Crick held no importance to Chowd apart from that of enemy.

Chowd knew what he needed to do. Entering the coordinates into the system and rerouting every possible ounce of power into the drives, just as his mother had taught him, he watched the blip of Otega spin away.

The pain was excruciating. Crick pushed another Xeradax into his mouth, waiting for the tingle, and the pressure and pain in his burned limbs retreated. "Chowd Sturat Sur Banden is a traitor." He considered how best to deal with such a dangerous youngling.

Chowd had reached the edge of human space before they could catch him, and the fury within Crick rose. Chowd and his mother had altered the old shuttle somehow and already the youngling traveled outside the borders of his control. Crick knew the traitor had traveled too far away for him to exact retribution. He cut the thought off as he heard the tapping of feet heading toward the infirmary. He quickly secreted the vial of Xeradax tablets that one of his men had liberated for him from the locked pharma-room.

"You are doing better, My Lord. Perhaps in a few days we can release you to the care of your concubines, though I am concerned that even with the weaning of drugs, there seems to still be more than you require in your system." The medi-tech wrung his hands nervously. "There is also a small matter of some drugs missing from the pharma-room. My Lord...do you by any chance...have access...to a source of Xeradax?"

The medi-tech knows about the Xeradax. He assumed his most menacing pose, and the tech wilted before him. "No."

The medi-tech shifted slightly, and Crick wanted to roar. He held onto his composure by the thinnest of threads. *I am the leader on this rock, and my will is the only one that's important.*

"Sir, Xeradax is highly addictive and has a number of side effects, each becoming progressively worse over time."

The sniveling tech. If Crick didn't still need him, he would have the man shot down and his body left outside as carrion to the Vrai. "And you are telling me this...why?" His voice conveyed his disdain, waiting expectantly for him to cross the line into traitorous speech.

"Ahh, My Lord. Indeed." The tech backed away, just one

step, but it was a sign of weakness, and he smiled. "I just wanted to assure myself that you were aware of any side effects and the reason I am seeking to wean you off them." The youngster before him had paled and now he wobbled with fear. There wouldn't be any more lectures. At least for now.

He would keep this one a little longer, until he personally had no need of him. For now, though, the most pressing duty remained the appointment of his successor. An heir and second who could be trusted must be chosen, since the loss of a son left him with no alternatives.

Chowd, the traitorous offspring, needs bringing to heel, or will need to be disposed of.

He lifted one blistered hand and flicked it, dismissing the shaking medi-tech from his sight, controlling his response to the pain that rocketed through his body with some effort. The older medi-tech would soon begin graft therapy, taking the skin from his most trusted soldiers to repair the damage to his and covering the damaged nerve endings.

Crick turned his mind from the pain. He needed to plan how to deal with the humans causing him so many problems. Plus, he needed to find a way to deal with the cowardly Senate. Most of all though, the issue of how to make his Ru'Edan warriors fitter and more capable continued to badger him. How could he could swell their ranks? Problems, questions, and conundrums filled his mind.

The Xeradax kicked in, and he felt the quietness he craved lifting him from the pallet where he lay as the pain disappeared.

Chowd's uncle waited in the office beyond the wall. With him waited his second-in-command and another senior commander. Neither had spared Chowd a glance as they entered the office area. Duvall McCord and Grayson Myatt. Chowd already knew their reputations as strong, driven officers, totally committed to the Empire.

"You've got to be joking, sir! He's..." There was anger and frustration in the words, and while Chowd wanted to wince, he didn't. Instead, he stood at attention, listening to the raised voices beyond.

"That's an order, Commander McCord!"

Once more he would be subjected to derision from these people who knew his background, but he held fast, even as his muscles tensed, not looking forward to the encounter that lay ahead. He reminded himself gratefully that the slight gray tinge had slowly disappeared from his skin over the last few months. The color of his eyes had changed significantly too since he'd become a test subject for the radical gene therapy his uncle, Fleet Captain Elphin, had suggested might help.

For many years, his mother had spoken of her younger brother, Gustav, a man set on achieving a larger and more powerful ship since he'd attained his rank of captain. But Chowd hadn't expected to find that he was a fleet captain. His mother would have been so proud, but she hadn't lived long enough to experience a reunion with him. He turned his mind from the thoughts that threatened to overwhelm him, bringing himself back to the now.

The door slid open quietly, and the voice of his gruff uncle, prematurely aged from his command and the concern over his sister, came from within. "Chowd, could you come through, please?"

Chowd's uniform rubbed his skin, and the scent of new material wafted into the air, assaulting his senses, something he now understood came from his Ru'Edan heritage. He stepped into the office, the atmosphere surrounding the two openly hostile men leaving him bristling. He worked to release the bunched muscles. A cold pool settled in his belly.

"Chowd, meet Duvall and Grayson. Both are commanders that I respect and personally would call friends. They've been apprised of the need for you to be stationed aboard the *Star of Ishtar* with me. Grayson here will be in charge of your training and your day-to-day integration into the crew. I've discussed your background and the training you've told me you received, with an emphasis on engineering and security." His forehead creased as he sat back in his chair and steepled his fingers.

"Commanders," he greeted. He refused to hold out his hand, though, until either of them made a move. If they wanted to play power-control games, then let them, he thought sourly.

"How do we know you aren't a plant from Crick Sur Banden, given you're his son, according to the captain." The blond man, Grayson, his uncle had called him, leaned forward as he spoke.

Irritation and anger washed over Chowd. "If I was a plant, do you honestly think that I'd be prepared to undertake the gene therapy my uncle suggested? You sure wouldn't know anyway." He stopped, taking a deep, cleansing breath before continuing. "I'm here because my mother died giving me the opportunity to get away." The burn in his belly grew. How in *Eshra* did they expect him to prove his allegiance to the Empire when no one would let him show what he could do and what he knew? When no one allowed him to show his allegiance?

He took a step forward as the dark-haired man, Duvall, raised his chin. The silent question flowed between them. Would he try to take Duvall McCord on? He sure wanted to, but his uncle had warned him of the need to accept the pre-determined and imagined offences against him based on his mixed parentage. He let his anger subside to a place at the back of his mind where he could control it.

He stepped back a pace. "Commander, my mother was the sister of Fleet Captain Elphin. She died getting me onto that shuttle and giving me an opportunity to escape. As the lesser son, I was little more than dirt under Crick Sur Banden's boots. With the death of Vi-Hal, there was danger that he would choose me as his successor." He sucked in a deep breath. The next words could make or break his future with the Empire. He weighed them carefully. "I didn't want that, and I still don't. Neither did my mother. I've given my uncle the information pertaining to the whereabouts of his base on Otega and all the information I have concerning his alliances that I know of. I have shared every piece of information I have, including maps and details of his strengths and weaknesses. I'm happy to share the same information with you. My first loyalty, however, is to my uncle. It always will be." He stood quietly, waiting for the sneers and condemnation.

Duvall nodded while the blond-haired man, Grayson, watched him in silence, taking in every aspect of the conversation as if scoring the emotional response of each participant.

Chowd looked toward his uncle, who also watched silently. He knew he had to make his own way, but something inside him ached. Perhaps it was his humanity, the one his mother had nurtured. *Why can't anyone accept me at face value?* He already knew the answer to that question. They were at war. No matter that a fragile ceasefire between humanity and the Ru'Edan was in place. Until his father was brought to account for his crimes, nothing could be simple for him. And even then, simple was highly unlikely.

"Welcome aboard then." Duvall McCord smiled, his face softening from the tight mask as he offered a hand. "I had to be sure myself before we gave you a chance."

Chowd looked at him, uncomfortably aware he had passed some kind of unwritten test. He felt something unfurl inside him. He shook the hand Duvall extended.

"Welcome to the *Star of Ishtar*," Duvall said.

Chapter 1

The ship was silent as Chowd brought up his personnel files. "Show the senior crew of the *Elector* and their partners." He picked up his coffee, a beverage he preferred to most alcoholic drinks available, and took a long, slow draught, savoring the taste of the hot, bitter brew.

Aching tiredness pulled at him while his eyes burned, but he pushed aside his discomfort. He needed the memory of why they had come here, why he fought what some would say wasn't his battle.

In the last few years so many changes had taken place, both for himself and on the *Elector*. Members of the crew had come together, first in the knowledge that the *Elector* had become the first of her kind then tested in the heat of battle. The successes of the new stealth ship had given the Admiralty hope that one day they would overcome the scourge of the Ru'Edan rogues and, even more importantly, Crick Sur Banden.

"I can only hope so," Chowd muttered.

Since the day the ceasefire had come into existence, the Earth Admiralty had worked tirelessly to find the one person who continued his private war against humanity. The Ru'Edanians had a similar mission, though neither had shown signs of working in harmony with the other, so each found their own way to undertake the task.

"Damned fools." He scanned the journal entry file he had on the screen alongside the personnel files.

The problems remained. Neither race could find political gain in forgiveness, resulting in unsuccessful peace negotiations following the ceasefire. Many privately agreed that the capture and defeat of Crick Sur Banden would go a long way to healing the rift that continued to exist between them. It hadn't happened yet.

The Admiralty had taken a chance, placing a new captain

in charge of their greatest weapon to date, yet Duvall McCord had pulled together a crew, consisting mainly of those he trusted and knew and others with links to his senior staff. Duvall's second, a long-term friend, had also committed to the cause whole-heartedly. With Grayson Myatt had come the amazingly talented Elara Sudonne, his chosen life partner and a more-than-capable SurgiTech.

On their first major mission together, involving traveling through the time portal to Earth's distant past, the crew had expanded when Duvall had saved and fallen in love with Mellissa—a woman from the past, yet she'd settled in quickly and held the post of researcher aboard the ship. As with the other members of the senior crew, she'd become important to Chowd, and he had added her to his circle of family. They'd nearly lost her in the skirmish against the insurgent Corbin Jard, and as a result of his untimely death, they'd added Raven Fraser to their crew.

Raven. He smiled, thinking of the charismatic man. Chowd found him easy to work with, watching as he fought with the ghost of Jard's damage to the *Elector*.

The *Elector* had traveled back to the past once more, bringing with them a number of prisoners as well as the beautiful, but damaged, Jemma Cardnew. When her picture appeared on the screen, he let loose a laugh as he recalled the uproar she'd caused with her wild and unpredictable ways, but now she was a valued member of the crew. His mirth died away as the memories flowed.

"Jemma, such a sad, young woman you were, but not anymore."

Chowd knew of the stress these crew additions added to Duvall's worries, but he applauded the man. He made life-and-death decisions, and his intent with saving Jemma from what would have resulted in certain death, had been morally right. Once returned to their own time, the Admiralty had placed her in the academy for her own safety, and Raven had taken on the thankless task of protecting her—at least until she'd entered the combat pilot program. Chowd snorted at the memory of the faces of Raven, Mellissa, and Duvall on hearing the news. But she'd proven herself time after time.

With Jemma, he felt a kinship he'd experienced with no one else aboard the *Elector*. Her difficulty integrating and her damaged psyche emphasized for her that she didn't belong in either the past or the future, something she and Raven were working on together with help from Elara. It reminded Chowd how he didn't belong with either humans or the Ru'Edan. Until Jemma had come to terms with her chances and choices and made a decision, the one where she accepted Raven, she'd fought everything and every decision taken to ensure her safety.

He let his fingers flick to the next image, playing through the images as they scrolled across his screen. His private pleasure in the fortunes of his friends calmed him as nothing else could. He smiled, looking at an image of Jemma, taken at her graduation. Not that she knew he had it.

Jemma had finally found her place on the *Star of Ishtar*, where so many of them had also begun their career with the Admiralty, and her first job as a combat pilot meant acting as escort for the *Elector* on the way to the Alpha Star Colony. The battle for Alpha Star Colony had only taken place days before, but it seemed like forever. Even before that, though, her presence had loomed large. Her volatile nature had meant she struggled to come to terms with her changed life.

His friend Raven had watched Jemma for some time with an intense connection, he'd claimed. One that had slowly evolved into the promise of forever. They had almost lost Jemma when she'd put herself before them all in her attempt to save the souls on the *Elector* from the Phobos pirates. Chowd's heart still thudded at the memory of Raven shouting as he sought a way to save her and his own wild effort, which had, thankfully, paid off. They'd made the colony in good time from there, and she'd once more shown her mettle in battle, saving so many, and particularly the Admiralty's own infiltrator that the Admiral, Chowd's uncle, had shown great concern for.

Jemma currently resided in the SurgiTech suite, recovering from the damage a laser pistol had wrought on her body while attempting to save the man she loved, and while Chowd had protected Meredith, Duvall's sister.

"Another strong woman." One who called to him like a siren of Earth's mythological past. "Why Meredith, and why now am I so driven to be with her?"

Barsha! Her proximity remained a distraction from his tasks. Totally unacceptable for one in his position, but now she was there, on board, helping with the ongoing decoding of messages. Duvall had indicated that she would remain with them for the foreseeable future. Chowd had a suspicion the Admiralty would soon inform them of the new mission. He sighed over the thought as his body once more produced a jaw-popping yawn and the fatigue that clawed at him called again. He fought against it, just as he always did.

"Computer, run scans of known accomplices of Crick Sur Banden located in this system." He sat back while information scrolled across the screen and picked up the coffee once more, frowning as he realized, for the first time, the cup and beverage had now cooled. His eyes drooped as he stared at the screen.

He stank of sweat. The damp stickiness coated his skin as he shrugged out of the ship suit, letting it drop to the floor. Chowd sighed, rolling the tight muscles in his shoulders. A good workout helped, but still, he felt the coil of desire burning in the pit *of his stomach. Since she had come on board, it never went away.*

He snatched up the tube of water, letting the cooling stream slide down his throat, not quite quenching his thirst. His nudity didn't worry him as he padded through the office to his sanitary unit and gave the order for the showerhead to engage at full spray, the steam rising upward as he watched. Stepping beneath the stinging, hot spray, he splayed his hands against the cool wall, feeling the flow of water down his body, and considered the latest situation.

Crick Sur Banden had escaped in the mess of the operation on the Alpha Star Colony. They had managed to get Jemma out in time for Elara to save her, though it had been touch and go for a while. The operative—Kera—that his uncle, Admiral Gustav Elphin, had ordered them to rescue had been saved, but the mad dash for the shuttle at the end had angered him. Somehow, Crick Sur Banden had slipped through their fingers once more.

This time they had the majority of his forces from the Alpha Star Colony base held in detention. The women they'd released had started putting the pieces of their lives together and giving information to the Admiralty officers. They'd also seized Crick Sur Banden's tactical plans. Their location, in what the teams surmised were his private rooms, had been unsurprising in hindsight, though Chowd had thought many of the installations abandoned. After he'd joined the Admiralty, they'd sent a strike force to the locations, only to find them empty.

*"Water off," he growled. The near loss of Jemma had worried him, reminding him that every member of the crew remained in danger. Including Meredith. Ahh...now how he wished he could con*tinue to avoid thinking about that possible outcome.

He breathed deeply, letting the emotions drain away, the heavy beat of his heart once more slowing to a steady life-affirming rhythm. He opened his eyes and sought the mirror. She stood behind him, waiting silently in the half-light, watching him with gleaming eyes.

His body firmed and sizzled with pleasure, his cock erect like every time he saw her. Chowd turned, looking at her, watching as her gaze trailed over his nakedness. He made

no move to collect the towel from the rack beside him. He knew she liked the view, as her eyes dilated with desire and her soft pants betrayed her arousal.

"Is there something I can do for you, Meredith?"

Her eyes glazed with passion, and he watched, fascinated, as a red flush crept up her cheeks. She licked her lips, sending a surge of awareness through his body.

"I, um...I came to see how you were feeling." She spoke nervously, her gaze darting here and there as if she didn't know where to look, and he smiled, feeling triumph roar through him. He had guessed—well, rather hoped—that she too felt that quick spark of lust. His experience remained limited to vids and reading, so he hadn't been totally sure. At least, not until now.

She stepped forward, a shy smile appearing at the side of her mouth, and his knees trembled. Her hand reached out—

The buzz of the alarm woke him with a jerk. His arm flew and hit the side of the desk screen with an audible thud, and his head snapped up. *Barsha!* He'd dreamed about her again. Chowd raised his hands from the hard surface of the desk, and he scrubbed them across his tired and aching eyes, gritty with the lack of sleep

The buzz cut through the silence once more, and he knew it emanated from his communicator. He groped for the communicator, woken by the insistent wail. "Yeah?" he answered with a groggy voice as he willed his tired mind to respond.

"Chowd? Are you free right now? New orders have been received and I need the command crew in my office immediately." Duvall's voice filled the air, the tinny value of the communicators something that continued to irk him. They could travel through space but not get the sound quality of communicators right.

He rose slowly, feeling the ache in the muscles of his back from the cramped chair and desk where he had found himself involuntarily napping. Not to mention the ache in his arm from that sharp crack.

"On my way." He flipped the communicator off and moved around the desk, working to clear the fog from his mind, hoping he didn't look like the wreck he felt. Short naps never powered him, but after thirty-nine straight hours, his body had shut down in retaliation of its abuse. Since they'd returned from the mission on Alpha Star Colony, the entire team had worked every possible hour to track the movements of Crick Sur Banden.

His stomach rumbled, and Chowd hoped Duvall had remembered food for this meeting. His hands met the rough stubble on his cheek as he moved quietly down the corridor of the ship, passing by others moving swiftly along the metal walkway, until he came to Duvall's door. He touched the palm reader that allowed him access.

The long table was almost full. Raven looked with sad eyes at the empty spot next to him where Jemma usually sat. Chowd grimaced slightly, remembering the last time he'd seen her, and noticed Meredith and Elara's absences. Silently, he moved to the seat he usually filled, lowering his body down into the welcoming cushion and resisting the urge to sigh. The softness of the gel molded around his aching body and warmed his muscles slightly.

Duvall stood, looking as tired as the rest of the crew slouching around the silent table. "Food will be here soon. Mellissa has organized refreshments to be served after the initial briefing. For anyone who isn't aware, Elara has released the operative—Kera Aarens—from the SurgiTech suite, and she should be boarding the freighter, the *Merry Darling Girl*, anytime now, carrying back information we cannot send via our usual communications channels." He looked around the table, his gaze briefly resting on the empty seats. "I've been informed by Elara and Raven that Jemma is making a slow but good recovery. We expect she should be released today or tomorrow, depending on the scan results. Meredith is working on decoding the tactical plans we found on the Alpha Star Colony and is expected to join us momentarily. Elara has indicated she hopes to be here soon as well. Lastly, we've been informed that new orders will be received via holo-transmission and we are all required here to accept them." Duvall finished his monologue by scooping up his coffee cup and taking a long draw.

No one spoke as the briefly outlined information filtered

through their tired brains. Duvall sat down heavily. Mellissa laid a soft hand on Duvall's arm, and Chowd felt a stab of envy, a swift jab straight to the region of his heart, shocking him in its intensity. He grimaced. He focused on ignoring that abused part of his anatomy and instead looked around the table, away from the intimate tableau unfolding at the head. Grayson reclined in his seat, and Raven rubbed a shaking hand over his face, the stubble not usually associated with him standing stark against his pale skin.

The entire team had been rocked by Jemma's near death, she'd slowly become an integral member of the crew as well as Raven's lover. That she'd come so close... It didn't bear thinking about.

The door chimed, and they all looked up. It slid open to reveal a pale and shaky Jemma, relying on Elara's stabilizing arm. Raven half-stood, and Chowd watched, fascinated, as Elara waved him back down to his seat. Jemma advanced, dropping with a sigh into the chair, and

Elara slipped around the table to seat herself beside Grayson. "Are you okay for this?" Raven asked in a low tone.

Jemma nodded slowly. "Yeah, Elara released me just now, so long as I don't do anything too energetic." Raven opened his mouth, and Chowd grinned at Jemma's next words. "No, it won't push our communing ceremony back."

Chowd let his head turn back to the end of the table, and Duvall and Mellissa both sat smiling as the alarm for the holo-transmitter beeped with imperious ferocity.

"Duvall. Ah, yes, I see the rest of the crew are there. Right, let's get started. Good work on releasing Aarens. I take it you've expedited her transportation?" Something in his uncle's voice had Chowd wondering about the importance of this woman. He continued watching intently for some sign confirming what he thought, but his uncle gave nothing away, so Chowd pushed the thought to the back of his head for later consideration.

"Yes, sir. We have her moving onto the *Merry Darling Girl*. It will be meeting with a shuttle two days out from Aenna and will allow her to be back there in some four and a half weeks. Given we had no transport heading in that direction from here, it was the fastest we could arrange at short notice. However, we were able to spare a couple of long-range fighters to remain with the ship until they reach the outskirts of the galaxy, where they will join a convoy."

"Excellent." Chowd's uncle paused, rubbing a hand over his forehead. "You will send through the medical report?"

"Admiral, I sent the required information just a few moments ago to your secure palm screen. Obviously, some information had to be withheld for privacy reasons, but I've included the rest in the report. It should be enough to allow you to work with her current status," Elara responded firmly, and Chowd smiled. He could always count on her to act like the consummate professional.

"Indeed. Thank you, Sudonne. I will peruse the report later." The Admiral pressed a button, and an image floated over the holographic unit. "In a few hours, once the all-clear has gone out, you will be redeployed from the hunt for Crick Sur Banden to act as secure transport for the Earth ambassador to a Ru'Edan ship, which will transport him to the location of the talks. A number of your members will be required to travel with the ambassador, offering him a secure guard for the duration of his discussions. At the same time, we're expecting the Ru'Edan ambassador to be delivered to our nearest secure facility on Paduran IV. You will offer security assistance until such time as our ambassador has concluded his talks with the ruling Senate and has been returned to the *Star of Ishtar*. Once that mission is completed, you will recommence your primary objective of finding Crick Sur Banden and neutralizing the threat to the Earth Empire and the peace negotiations."

The silence of the room grew stifling, and Chowd felt the blast of heat from the angry members of the crew. It felt like a knife-edge, sharp and uncomfortable, as the wave moved around the table. He felt the anger of the crew at being pulled away from their substantive mission to play a babysitter role to a civilian. He could understand their feelings. No one wanted to deal with the threat of Crick Sur Banden more than he did, although he certainly understood the necessity to undertaking this mission.

The door chimed once more before sliding open to reveal Meredith, her hair tucked behind her ears, her brown eyes deep in concentration as she entered information into a palm screen. Her head flicked up to see the holographic image. "Oh, I beg your pardon, Admiral. I would have been here sooner, but I was caught up dealing with a possible new code we believe Crick Sur Banden is using."

"Gentry. I have just informed the captain and crew of their new mission. You will also remain aboard the *Elector* in case there are any transmissions or discussions that require immediate translation. You will continue working on the tactical plans, act as personal translator for the ambassador, and report back as necessary."

She nodded while her hands continued to work at her palm screen, and Duvall leaned forward to speak. "Admiral, I believe another ship would be best for transporting the ambassador—"

The Admiral cut Duvall off, shaking his head. "No, Captain McCord. In this instance, we need something light and with speed, maneuverability, and most of all, a calm head to ensure this mission is successful. I need someone I can trust implicitly spearheading this task. In short, we need you to transport the ambassador and ensure his safety at all times. Stand by for his arrival within the next twenty-four hours. Further detailed orders will be forthcoming within the hour. Elphin out."

The holographic transmission winked out suddenly, and Chowd released the breath he unconsciously held. The expulsion of air loosened his mind as much as his tongue. "Captain, do you wish to give us any further instructions, or would you prefer to reconvene this meeting?"

Duvall shook his head. "We need to make adequate provision for the ambassador. Chowd, I'll need you to arrange a twenty-four-hour security detail, whatever it takes. Put together a possible team for the safe transportation of the ambassador. Grayson, arrange for accommodation." Rapid-fire instructions and plans flew around the table, stopping only once the refreshments arrived. The room grew quiet as assorte

To Meredith's eyes, the crew looked exhausted, and Jemma drooped visibly in her chair. They settled into eating with quick snatches as their hunger abated. But Chowd caught her eye, as he always did. Every time she had seen him since that first meeting in her parents' home had increased her fascination. Some indefinable quality captured her attention when he was around her.

His fine features and sensuous full lips, high forehead, and dark eyes, with just a hint of gray in his skin tone, told of his heritage, no matter how he tried to disguise it. He wore his black hair long and tied back, slicked away from his almost feminine features. His high-slashing cheekbones and finely chiseled chin attracted her physically, and as always, her body quickened. She knew just how fast and dangerous he could be. His hand-to-hand skills were legendary, and he had a reputation as a man not to cross.

She liked his height, well over six feet, and it made her feel petite and feminine. It wasn't that he dwarfed her so much as the sense of protection his nearness always seemed to bestow on her. She knew he considered himself exceptionally tall for a Ru'Edan, and put it down to his human heritage.

She shifted in her seat. She wouldn't describe him as muscular like her brother or Raven, but from what she'd seen, he had no issues with definition of his muscles. Chowd also carried an air of command and confidence about him. His physical body was only one aspect of Chowd.

Meredith knew he didn't participate in any shipboard romances. For that matter, in the whole time she had known him, not so much as a whisper of his partners had been hinted at, and she found that interesting. More to the point, the concept that he might be asexual intimidated her slightly. What kind of man showed no interest in a relationship? Either that or he kept everything incredibly discreet. "Stands to reason."

Elara threw a glance in her direction and she colored, dipping her head. *Get your head in the game.* When her gaze settled on Chowd again, she realized he was watching her. What did he see behind that shielded gaze?

Did he realize she prized such discretion? Probably not, but she'd taken great pains to keep her dalliances off radar. She'd only indulged in a single liaison while at the Academy, and since then...nothing. Initially, because she had focused on learning her job, she had shied away from entanglements, intent on proving herself.

Then after she had met Chowd...well, somehow no one else drew her like he did, and the lack of attraction to any other man had weighed heavily against any romantic entanglements. A sigh rippled out of her lips before she could restrain it, and he looked at her with a question in his eyes.

"Meredith? Do you need something?" His words slipped like silk over her, and heavens above, she felt the familiar pull of arousal with just those few words.

"No, thank you, Chowd. Though perhaps there will be time in the morning for you to look over some of the work I've accomplished. No one else could really get into his head the way you could." The instant she said the words, Meredith cringed, wishing she could call them back.

His eyes turned dark and flat. All the warmth in his face leached away. "Indeed." "Chowd, I didn't..." *...mean it as it came out.* But he'd turned away, dismissing her, and she wanted to close her eyes. *Barsha!* She should have thought that over before she opened her mouth. She always seemed to say the wrong thing to him.

Meredith twisted the napkin in her hands, tormented by once more saying the wrong thing. If she kept this up, he wouldn't even want to know her socially, or, she reminded herself, sexually either.

Communicating with Chowd always seemed to present a challenge for her. The pressure building in her chest swelled larger than before. Suffocating.

Meredith remembered meeting him for the first time over a year and a half ago, when Duvall had first brought him, together with Elara, Grayson, and Mellissa, to their home to discuss what had happened at the Admiralty base on Aenna and needing her skills and abilities. Her brother had told her about him and their experiences over the years.

After that had come the announcement made to the crew before leaving on a mission to the Alpha Star Colony of who he was. While it would have been a shock to the crew, she had already known because of the transmissions she intercepted and decoded for the Admiralty. She refused to let his origins become an issue for her, but for him, it still remained a sticking point. She took a deep breath. "Chowd?" She waited for him to turn around. His brow quirked up slightly, and she screwed up her courage. "Would you meet me in my quarters after this meeting breaks up? There is something I would like to talk to you about."

More than eighteen months of procrastination would end today. She considered herself intelligent, witty, liberated, and capable. She could ask him if he was interested in an interlude with her. Perhaps once she had that ticked off her list, she could focus on her work and not feel so excited each time he walked by her.

"Of course, Meredith." His words may have been cool, but heat stirred within her.

Stars preserve her! She wanted to lean in—in front of the entire crew—and kiss those full lips. The need to taste him nearly overcame any sense of self-preservation she clung to. Meredith restrained herself and nodded stiffly, starting to look at the behavior he exhibited to see if she could detect a clue to his feelings.

Oh, for stars' sake! You've got work to do, Meredith. Go

do it! Get out of here before you do something incredibly foolish. Meredith pushed her chair back slightly, catching her brother's eye. "Captain, would you excuse me?"

He nodded quickly, and she stood, stepping lightly around the chair, in the process brushing against Chowd who'd stood to move a platter to the table behind her. An electric current ran through her, and Meredith sucked in her breath at the shock, which reverberated within her body.

"Apologies," she muttered, stepping away from the table and heading to the door. "Wait. I'm finished and can come with you now."

Visions of them naked and writhing on a bed filled her head. She gulped. Her libido was seriously getting out of hand, and she felt the warmth of her blush rise over her cheeks and neck.

"Sure." She didn't turn around as she muttered the word. If she did, he would see, and so would the others. Not something she really wanted to broadcast at the moment.

The door opened, and she stepped into the corridor.

Chapter 2

Chowd followed Meredith down the corridor, watching the sway of her hips, the way the dark cloth clung to her backside. *Barsha!* His erection, which had once more made itself known during the meeting, stood uncomfortably erect, brushing against his pants, and he hoped she wouldn't notice it. He lusted after her, but reminded himself of her off-limits status. She always made it clear with comments like the one just before. Comments that reminded him she knew he was Crick Sur Banden's bastard half-breed son.

As the beautifully talented younger sister of his captain, Duvall McCord, Meredith continued to stir his senses as no other ever could. Duvall might be one of his closest friends, but it caused an emotional quandary for Chowd.

In all honesty, though, it wasn't her status as Duvall's sister that concerned him. The woman herself upset his equilibrium.

Even as he reminded himself that she was Duvall's sister and knew his dark heritage, his fingers itched to touch her soft skin, to bring her ripe mouth to his, and to delve into her body, seeking release. His chest ached at the effort of keeping his breathing normal, and he concentrated on the length of hair in front of him.

They reached her cabin, and she swiped her hand over the palm reader. The door slid open, and she stepped inside with him following.

She groaned and moved forward quickly, gathering up clothing articles from the desk screen and bed, but not before he noted the sexy black underwear. A discarded flight suit sat on the floor next to the bed, and a damp towel hung off the back of the chair.

His knees locked as the visions of her wearing the flimsy creations spun through his head, causing him to start reciting security protocols, taking his mind off thoughts of stripping the material from her body.

She gathered everything up and threw them into the sanitary unit with a small laugh before pulling the door closed. "Well, that was difficult." Her muttered words made him want to smile, but he cautioned himself to keep his amusement private.

"Don't be concerned. The last few days have been quite unnatural for all of us with the mission, Jemma, and now trying to decipher all the codes." He smiled in an understanding manner, or so he hoped. *But I'm an alien, when all is said and done. Sometimes these more human behaviors are beyond my ability to decode and understand.* He shrugged mentally.

"Please, make yourself comfortable."

She turned to face him, and his breath caught as the lights picked up the shine in her hair. A slight tinge of pink highlighted her high cheekbones. He let his gaze roam over her dark-brown, velvety eyes and lush, pale-pink lips, all framed by her pixie face, angular and small in shape. *Perfect in every way.* He swallowed the lump that lodged in his throat as she smiled at him.

"Would you like a drink?"

"No, thank you, Meredith. How can I be of service?" Her eyes rounded, and the color leached from her face.

"Is something wrong?" Chowd took a step forward, his gaze darting around the small room, looking for danger.

"Ahh, no. Nothing's wrong."

He relaxed and watched as she twisted her fingers together. Fascination filled him, and he scanned her face. Meredith never seemed nervous, so what caused this response in her now?

What on Earth does she want from me that she can't just come right out and request?

Meredith sat down with a jerk on the edge of the narrow bed, and he took the seat by her desk screen. Her cabin, a tiny room suitable for visitors, left him with his feet nearly brushing against hers. "So?"

"Look, this is probably stupid, but..." She turned her face away, flaming pink creeping up her long neck and cheeks, and stars help him, he wanted to go over and touch her. Whatever was concerning her, she was clearly discomforted talking about the situation.

"Meredith, I can't help you if you don't tell me what is wrong." He leaned forward, elbows resting on his knees.

"Oh, stars! I can't believe I'm about to do this..." He could clearly hear the embarrassment in Meredith's voice as she turned back to him. "Look, let's not worry about it, okay?" She stood and moved toward the sanitary unit, her movements disjointed and jerky.

"If I can help you, I will, Meredith." He kept his words calm and comforting, all the while his stomach churning like a seething mass. What could be upsetting her equilibrium this way?

"Oh, I didn't really think this through!" Her voice sounded strangled as she looked away, and she exhaled slowly, obviously seeking some inner calm, before slowly turning back toward him. She stepped forward and looked into his eyes. "Will you kiss me? Please?"

"What?" His heart stopped beating in his chest, and the warmth in his body seemed to flutter away. "Will I *kiss* you? Meredith?"

She turned away, and he knew why...because of his father's identity.

"Meredith, I thought better of you than that." Chowd's hoarse words escaped while his heart shriveled in his chest, and he stood, stepping back toward the door.

"Please...don't go." Her words were almost silent, and he strained to hear her.

The crushing pain weighed down on him. She would laugh behind his back—never to his face, he knew that wasn't her way. No doubt she would think it funny, that she thought he would laugh along with her, but right now, it didn't seem quite so humorous.

"I need to leave." Chowd reached his hand toward the palm reader as her soft hand reached out to him.

"No, please. Chowd. Please kiss me."

Her pleading stopped him in his tracks for an instant. Then Chowd turned, ready to share his distaste at her request, but her face had paled, a tear shimmered on her eyelash, and he felt a responding squeeze in the region of his heart.

"Don't cry, Meredith." Chowd took one step then another until finally they stood so close together he could feel her breath. He wanted to open his arms and enfold her in them, and he clenched his fist against the urgent pull that told him to claim her.

"It wasn't inappropriate, Chowd. We could die anytime, now that we are going to be shepherding the ambassador, and I refuse to die without kissing you, at least once."

He closed his eyes at her husky words. Dear stars! How he wanted to kiss her, but he needed distance. "Meredith, we'll come through this, and you'll laugh at your thoughts one day."

He heard movement but reacted too slowly to escape the soft lips that met his. So sweet and so warm. The thought flashed through his brain before it shut down with sensory overload. They felt pliant and opened over his as he moaned. The pressure in his chest exploded with his tenuous control, and his arms moved around her, crushing her to his body.

At last! His body cried out at the feel of her soft curves against his chest, and he opened his mouth slightly to feel a tentative flick against his lips before her tongue dipped into his mouth.

His body electrified at the feel of her. He opened his mouth wider. Never had he felt such emotions or sensations. His chest thudded harder than ever before.

She pulled back. "Oh, Chowd! You do taste so good," she whispered, and he sucked in a deep breath.

"*Barsha*! We shouldn't be doing this. You're—"

"I am a woman who knows exactly what she wants." He heard a touch of asperity in her words before her voice softened once more. "Chowd? I mean, you do find me attractive, right?" Her voice ended in a high squeak, and Chowd felt an instant of horror. That she didn't think he wanted her amazed him.

"Meredith. I'm not a man. I'm an alien hybrid. Nothing more than a—"

She stopped his words with a soft finger across his lips. "No more than a what? You *are* an exceptional man. My brother describes you as loyal, strong, and caring. Don't let anyone tell you differently." This time her fierce words married with the glowing light he saw in her eyes. Once more she reached up, her hands now resting on his shoulders, and she moved closer.

He closed his eyes, waiting for the pleasure to once more fill him. He was almost ready for the shock of her lips across his, slanting and soft, while her tongue invaded more forcefully this time. *Stars!* He held her close, luxuriating in the silken feel of her mouth, tentatively allowing his tongue to touch hers and groaning into her mouth, pulling her closer.

They pulled away, their chests heaving for oxygen. He wanted her so badly his entire body ached. But they had work to do. He wanted to shake his head, to clear away the fog that invaded his brain and wouldn't allow his body to move. He couldn't show weakness now; otherwise, *Eshra* help him, he'd start stripping the clothes off her and finding out the joys of loving this amazingly strong woman. But then, neither of them agreed to that or could even remotely call themselves ready for that, he suspected. Not yet.

Chowd stepped back. "I won't apologize for that, because you wanted it as much as I did." He smiled, knowing that she had wanted to kiss him. After all, she initiated it. "But we don't have time for any of this. Our priority must be our mission." He let the words trail away.

Meredith is a beautiful woman, and she wants to kiss me. Why? That he couldn't understand. Here stood the unwanted son of Crick Sur Banden, the known universe's most vile mass murderer, who believed it was his Goddess-given right to crush and kill at will. Even his evil father hadn't wanted him, hadn't seen a feature he thought worth keeping, but this beautiful woman did somehow. It didn't make any sense to him. So he would work, he promised himself, and investigate these emotions until he understood them. The same way he did everything else.

Then, if luck holds, we might forge something together. Maybe.

Meredith stepped forward, her hand brushing over his face. "I want to know more about you, Chowd. I know we have a dangerous mission ahead, but it didn't seem right to let the opportunity go past without seeing if you wanted me the way I want you. Now I have the answer. I can start work, knowing that sometime down the track, we might just find out if there is more than just attraction between us." She smiled softly.

She must have read the uncertainty in his face, as she pulled back.

"I know. Right now we have work to do. I just wanted to make sure you knew. I've watched you ever since I met you. I could only hope you thought I was... Darn, this is so much harder than rehearsing it was."

He nearly laughed then, but she looked so flustered that he didn't dare.

"I had this all planned out in my mind." The last words died away to a mutter. He was fascinated by the way she carried on her internal dialogue so openly.

Her hand covered her eyes, and she breathed in, her chest rising and falling with the action. He watched the movement of her breasts through the suit. He couldn't help himself. Though small, they were just the right size for his hands, and he struggled to clear his mind.

"What?" Her voice sounded tart as she looked at him, startling his from his thoughts. "You act like you've never seen breasts before."

"Well, I haven't. I mean..."

She gaped at his admission, and how he wanted to call it back. The tide of red tingeing his cheekbones burned him. He could almost hear her thoughts—*He's a virgin? No way!*—and he cringed inwardly.

She smiled, reaching out and grabbing hold of his hand. "I won't tell if you don't." He smiled through his embarrassment.

"Yeah, well. Maybe we should just get to work.

You know, concentrate on the threat to the *Elector* and the ambassador." But now she knew the truth in all its innocent glory, and he wasn't sure how that made him feel.

Images flowed across the screen, and Meredith rubbed her tired eyes, feeling the sting and ache as her abused body chastised her. How she longed to crawl into bed and curl up. She cast a look at the empty bed behind her, but she hadn't achieved her self-imposed quota of work.

She needed to finalize this one passage before she could rest. Something about it told her that within these pages lay the key. She entered a keystroke and watched with dismay as the work unraveled before her, the unfamiliar characters filling the viewscreen once more.

"No! Don't do that!" She slapped her hands to the desk in frustration, her hands smarting as they met with the cool and hard metal of the table.

Carefully, she tapped in the command to undo the last action before pushing away from the desk, the chair squeaking in protest. Perhaps a quick meal would help. Her aching legs and back reminded her of the hours she'd spent hunched over the desk screen in the tiny cabin. She wondered if there was a free desk somewhere—perhaps one with a bit more space to work.

She exited the room and gave the lock command before swiftly moving through the empty corridor, heading in the direction of the mess hall. The clank of her feet on the metal flooring echoed through the silence as she hurried up the stairs. Her stomach rumbled and her gut churned painfully as vertigo hit, and for a moment, everything swayed in front of her. She reached out a hand, looking for support. *Barsha! It's either later than I thought, or earlier.*

"When did I last take a break or eat?" She glanced at her wrist chrono. Just after 0300 hours. *I should have eaten earlier, when Duvall beeped.* But she had been in the middle of breaking an encryption on some data and refused the invitation. That would have been some seven hours ago.

Meredith carefully placed one foot in front of the other until she reached the top of the stairs and entered the silent room, continuing toward the dispenser. Her weariness blurred her vision as she scanned the choices, and she squinted slightly, waiting for the words to finally clear. A hearty broth and coffee sounded good. After placing her order, Meredith grabbed a tube of water and gulped it down while she waited for the dish to appear. The aperture appeared and her food slid out. With quick, efficient movements, she stacked the food onto a small tray then carried it in the direction of a table.

"Here, let me help you." The words startled her, and she lifted her head. Chowd reached out, taking the tray and leading the way to a booth.

"What are you doing here?" She knew her words sounded terse.

"Probably the same as you. Grabbing a late meal—or early—then heading back to my cabin to sleep. We only have a couple of hours before we're due back in Duvall's office for the briefing."

The heat of his eyes seared her, warming the cold recesses within her, waking her up enough to let her focus on the empty room and the man opposite her. He shifted his empty food container to the end of the table, making room for her tray.

"I needed to take a break from decoding the message. It just isn't working though." She picked up the spoon once she had lowered herself into the seat and took a taste of the meaty soup. "Aahh, this is good." The smell of the food filled the air, succulent meats and the hint of herbs enticing her taste buds.

"Yes, it is good. But you need to rest. You won't be able to focus in the meeting otherwise."

She heard the concern in his voice and stopped her hand

in midair, considered his words. "I know. I'm thinking maybe the best thing I can do is take a break, grab some sleep, then look at it again in the morning. But something about this particular code is just eating at me." She shook her head, tendrils of hair whipping around her face.

The glint in his eyes caught her attention, and she drew an unsteady breath. "What?" she asked.

"You look so...innocent...sitting there with your hair curling slightly and the bowl of soup. I've just never seen this side of you before."

She grinned. "There's always a first time, Chowd."

She took another spoonful and swallowed it, letting it fill her stomach, calming the rippling sea that the hunger had aroused. With quick moves she made her way through the bowl until only a thin layer of liquid covered its bottom. She grabbed the hunks of bread on the plate and mopped up the juices.

He snickered at her, and she grinned. "I know. My mother hates it when I do this at home. But it just seems a shame to waste what is left."

"Can I help, somehow? With the code?"

"I don't know. When would you like to take a look?"

"Well, I was about to turn in now, but I can take a look after the briefing if that suits you."

Meredith cocked her head as if weighing his suggestion. "Sleep is the best thing for now.

After the briefing will be fine."

She smiled up at him and noticed that the intense look she associated with him was missing. Instead before her sat a man open, if a little vulnerable. She gave in to the urge, reached out one hand, and let it touch the planes of his cheek, surprised when he nestled into her hand with a smile and covered her hand with his before turning his head and planting a soft kiss on her palm.

An explosion of feeling erupted like a wildfire coursing through her blood. In the depths of his eyes, she detected a fiery passion.

"One day, beautiful Meredith. Perhaps." He released her hand and rose smoothly from the soft seats. "But for now, let me escort you to your cabin."

She took the hand he held out and rose. They walked out the door of the mess.

Chowd tossed and turned. Thoughts of Meredith filling and warming him, almost as much as the conversation he'd had with Duvall and Raven before meeting her in the mess gave him hope.

He'd returned to Duvall's office after the initial briefing with the Admiral. His discussions with Raven and Duvall had swiftly turned personal though. Facing her brother had seemed an impossible task, but he had no choice given Duvall's status as his commanding officer and provision needing to be made for the safety of the ambassador.

When he arrived in the office, he knew they'd picked up immediately that something had transpired, and he wondered if the tide of red on his face had given him away. The discussion had started off in the usual vein regarding the tactical needs of protecting the ambassador, but no matter how hard he concentrated on the discussion, his thoughts returned to that moment when she had pressed her lips against his.

No matter how hard he hoped fate would throw him a lifeline and let him out of there without the discussion he dreaded, it came at the end of the meeting.

"So, Chowd. What happened?" Duvall's voice caught him by surprise, and his head rose sharply.

"What do you mean?" His body stiffened, alert and prepared, while he waited for the argument he knew would come.

"Meredith. She finally cornered you?" The mirth in Raven's voice upset his equilibrium, as Chowd couldn't see anything funny in the comment. Of all people, Raven should understand. "I will not discuss it." He kept his words stiff as he narrowed his eyes on Duvall and

Raven.

The slap on the back took him by surprise as Raven laughed. "My sister has had a thing for you for the longest time. And while I doubt anyone would ever be good enough for her, she's grown up enough to know what she wants and how to get it. I'm big enough to let her take the chances on finding happiness." Duvall looked him in the eye as he delivered his thoughts on the matter.

"Duvall, I would, but—"

"But what, man? Are you going to spend your entire life letting *his* actions stop you from having a life? A woman who wants you badly enough that she will make the first move isn't enough?"

Chowd absorbed Duvall's intent, but it felt... He struggled to find a word that adequately summed up the mass of emotions that swirled within him before finally settling on *confused.*

"You're better than that, or I'm a terrible judge of character." Duvall paused. "I would trust you with my life, which I do on a regular basis anyway. I trust you with Mellissa." Chowd didn't know where to look. "I trust you with Meredith."

Chowd didn't know how to respond, feeling like someone had just given him the world and the stars. But he couldn't hope. Not until they remembered everything that kept him apart.

"Duvall, I'm not even human."

"You are more human than most humans I know."

The words created a warm bubble of emotion within his chest. *Acceptance.* Duvall accepted him as a potential partner for his sister.

He looked up at Raven, who stood unsmiling, watching Duvall. "So you did learn something from your outburst when Jemma and I finally got together?"

Duvall nodded. "Yeah. I did. And now I'm using that to make sure you—" He spun back and pointed at Chowd. "—

don't mess up with my sister. Hurt her, and you'll be sorry."

Raven smiled. "I need to get back to Jemma. With the *Ishtar* arriving, we have things we need to attend to, including getting her personal items transferred and arranging a communing ceremony." A broad grin appeared on Raven's face. "Oh, and wait 'til I tell her what you just said."

For just a minute, Chowd felt the bite of jealousy. Would he ever experience that joy? Better not to hope than to let it grow and see it dashed, he told himself, but somehow, that bubble remained, filling a part of the emptiness in his chest.

Raven left, and Chowd looked at Duvall. "I won't hurt her. At least, never intentionally, and I will protect her with my life."

He needed Duvall to understand. He and Grayson had known exactly who and what he was since the beginning of his association with the Admiralty. They were both aware of how hard he'd worked to fit in with the crew. Raven had entered their circle later, but now had integrated, becoming just as much a family member to Chowd as anyone ever could be.

"I know, Chowd."

Duvall's quiet words rocked him. He stood still for just a moment longer before he, too, left the office, making for his cabin and letting Duvall's words filter through his mind as he fought to make sense of them.

He didn't usually consider himself indecisive, but this time his actions would have such wide-ranging impact. Its importance burned into his heart and mind so that by the time he had reached his cabin, he knew what he had to do. His very soul depended on taking the chance.

He needed to shower before going to her, but when he checked his chrono he saw it was past 1100 hours. She was likely resting. So instead he showered, powered up his desk screen, and began the planning work. Hours later, though, hunger roared through him, and he had headed for the mess where he met her. Their conversation captivating him and leaving him confused. When she caressed his cheek, he couldn't help himself. The need to touch her grew by the moment.

It was the wrong time and the wrong place for a life-changing conversation, so he walked her back to her cabin, not touching her in any way, though his soul screamed for more, before heading back to his silent and empty cabin.

His stomach clenched as he threw scenarios up in his head as he stripped down and climbed between the cool sheets. When to make a move? What to do? Not for the first time, he damned his own inexperience, flinging his arm over his eyes. He needed to sleep, but it took a long time for his eyelids to lower.

The senior staff waited in the cold landing bay, impatient in their formal uniforms as the ambassador prepared to disembark from the larger shuttle sent from the *Star of Ishtar*.

Meredith wanted to scratch the irritated skin under the itchy wool of her uniform, or at least peel the scratchy layers away, but she curled her hands in their formal white gloves instead.

The ambassador exited the shuttle, followed by a blonde woman, who had a large bag slung over her crooked elbow. They had been informed that the ambassador was bringing his personal assistant, Ms. Portia Delfray, but Meredith hadn't foreseen that she'd look like this. The woman was all angular points with a precision-perfect nose and tilted, almond-shaped eyes, hinting at either a far-removed Asian heritage or the help of an excellent facial-construction surgeon. She smiled broadly as she clattered down the steps, showing perfect snowy-white teeth and her impressive bosom—which Meredith felt sure wasn't uplifted with the help of nature alone—barely contained in the tight, flimsy white blouse. She wore what Meredith guessed were at least nine inches of spiked heels.

If Meredith didn't know better, she would think the woman considered this akin to a career as either a vid star or model. She nearly growled at the sight of her wiggling in her tight, molded skirt which flaunted miles of perfect legs. "Stupid woman."

"Did you say something, Meredith?" Chowd spoke quietly, and Meredith started.

"Oh, just a comment that she might need to be careful where she steps." Meredith's tone dripped with mock sweetness, and if she didn't mishear, she was sure he stifled a tiny laugh.

Refocusing on the meeting of Duvall and the ambassador, she controlled the irrational dislike.

"Captain, it's an honor to be here."

"Ambassador, the honor is ours. Welcome to the *Elector*."

"I've heard so much about this ship and your missions to date," the ambassador said. The woman standing behind him all but tapped her foot and the ambassador shot her an indulgent smile. "Allow me to introduce my assistant. Portia Delfray."

Ms. Delfray looked at the women with a wide though rather forced smile, then she turned her attention to Duvall. "Captain? Captain McCord? I've heard much about you," she cooed, extending a hand, and Meredith wanted to cringe at the little-girl voice.

Meredith looked back to the ambassador, assessing the man who smiled the quintessential politician's smile, noting that it didn't reach his eyes. He had to have achieved at least his fifth decade or even entered his sixth, judging by his salt-and-pepper hair, perfectly styled against his casual, blue flight suit. His carefully groomed eyebrows and hairless chin were in perfect proportion with his face. Clearly it had been surgically sculpted, and it remained line free in spite of his obvious middle age. Meredith considered the chances that his body had benefited from the use of a constructive surgeon, as nothing jiggled or drooped the way nature would have intended.

The ambassador watched the woman as a tiny smile lit his pale-blue eyes, his lips curving at his personal assistant's antics. *I wonder what their relationship is outside of the office.*

"Uh, yes. Ambassador Vierghent? Allow me to introduce

my crew." Duvall's voice was tight, and she felt amusement at the subtle hint of distaste in his tone. *Good to see Duvall isn't taken in by her fatuous fawning.*

The ambassador stepped forward, shaking each crewmember's hand. Meredith noticed the woman beside him grimaced when introduced to Duvall's wife and partner, Mellissa. As each male member stepped forward, her eyes widened and she flushed prettily. *Probably all those rampant hormones.* Meredith allowed the nasty thought to linger for an instant before brushing it aside.

As each male officer introduced their partners, her face grew cold, the look becoming increasingly frigid as if she took personal affront to the lack of unattached males in the senior ranks of the crew. *What does she think this is, some kind of luxury resort?*

Finally, Portia stepped in front of Chowd, and Meredith tensed slightly as the woman grasped his hand, smiling once more with that vacuous little-girl look as she batted what Meredith would bet were false eyelashes. Chowd exhibited a deer-in-the-headlights expression as she turned on the charm.

"My sister, Warrant Officer Meredith Gentry. Meredith is the Chief Admiralty Cryptologist with advanced degrees in the study of the codes of Crick Sur Banden. She's currently working on decoding the intercepted transmissions and ensuring we can understand the tactical maps and plans left behind on the Colony."

The woman dismissed her with a quick, impersonal smile, and Meredith tensed again as the ambassador smoothly moved forward to take her place.

"My pleasure to meet you, Officer Gentry. May I call you Meredith?" His voice sounded warm and silky smooth, and she was sure it had been perfected over the years. She considered it well greased, like a squeaky political wheel.

She really didn't want to give him an inch—something about him said *smarmy* and *slimy*—but what could she do? Rather than answer him, she smiled and simply said, "Ambassador, it's a pleasure." She kept the tone neutral and nearly gasped as he reached for her hand, the look in his eyes warming.

"I would be honored if you would show me the ship." His words bordered on intimate, and the smile he bestowed on her made her want to recoil.

"Uh, there are others who know the ship much better than I do, Ambassador. I've only been on here for a few weeks." She let her gaze flick to Duvall and noticed his frown and the small shake of his head. *Oh no! Say I don't have to show him around?*

She snuck a look at Chowd, who scowled at her under the fawning attentions of the woman. For the life of her, she couldn't work out why he'd be cross with her. She was as stuck with the ambassador as he seemed to be with the octopus-like Portia.

Meredith glanced back to the man waiting expectantly before her. "Of course, it would be my honor to do so." The words stuck in her throat, but there was little room to maneuver right now.

The formalities completed, he took her hand, and a shudder almost broke through her composure. The touch of his cold skin on hers was more than unwelcome.

She led the way, listening to the clank of the floor and answering his questions about the ship. She tried to avoid the myriad personal questions, queries of the length of her deployment, her connection to the ship. He tried to get a look at the inside of her wrist below the dark-blue flight jacket she wore and above her regulation-white glove. She worked hard to keep her wrist hidden. He was looking for communing marks, she bet.

They ushered Portia—Ms. Delfray—to her cabin and waited while she inspected it, making pains to ensure the ambassador's assistant found her cabin adequate. Then they continued to a larger cabin next door.

"This is your cabin, Ambassador. Your sanitary unit can be found through there." She indicated the small room, stepped him through the addition of his palm print to the door security system, and started to back out of the room.

"Will you stay and take a refreshing tea with me?" His face looked hopeful, and a cold feeling flashed through her system. All indications pointed to a problem if he was expecting some kind of companionship. *I need to raise this with Duvall.*

"I apologize, Ambassador, however, I do have work to complete. Should you need anything..." Meredith started backing out toward the door. "Of course. You are near my cabin?"

Oh no! Please don't ask where my cabin is...

"No, Ambassador." She temporized, hating that she might get caught in a lie. "However, should you require assistance, we can all be reached via communicator." She handed him the one Duvall had passed her as she left the cargo bay. "You'll need to keep that near at all times." She smiled and turned, making once again to leave the cabin.

"Then join me for dinner?"

Now she really had a problem. He was going to be persistent, and that level of persistence in a man was something she didn't want. She pasted a bright smile on her lips and hoped the panic that boiled within didn't shine through.

Turning her head toward him, she kept her voice even. "Ambassador, I do have a role that keeps me very busy. My duties for the Admiralty are extensive and time consuming. I would imagine the captain will make provision for meals, and I understand he has a formal dinner planned for tonight, with yourself and your assistant due to attend. Security officers will escort you at the appropriate time. Now, I really must go."

She bowed low as she said the words and made her escape, watching as the door shut behind her and taking a deep breath.

"Duvall? Do you have a moment?" Meredith headed in his direction as he answered the hail.

"Meredith?"

"I have a problem and may need your help. Are you in your office?" "Yeah. Come straight along."

"Excellent. I'm on my way." She needed to stop this

debacle before it ballooned. For a moment she hoped Chowd understood her fears otherwise—and she stopped, sucking an unsteady breath in—he'd likely back right off, again. She refused to let that happen and spoil all her good work.

She moved swiftly through the metal corridor to Duvall's office.

Chapter 3

Chowd walked down the corridor. The blonde woman reminded him of a man eater; someone best avoided, he knew. He hid out in the security offices waiting for a clear run. And the man, the ambassador? He had all but slobbered over Meredith. The thought made Chowd's gut burn as he headed to Duvall's office. He swiped his hand over the unit, and as the door opened, Duvall and Meredith lifted their heads.

"Oh, thank *Eshra* it's you, Chowd." Meredith's voice betrayed her agitation.

His instinct to protect her kicked in. "Meredith? Are you okay?" He moved swiftly to her side, and she smiled at him, warming him.

"Oh yeah. But I think I have a problem. The ambassador is...well, in not terribly technical terms...lecherous. He wanted me to stay and have a drink. He wanted me to join him for dinner." Deep rose colored her cheeks, and the glint in her eyes both made him feel angry that the human would upset her as well as relaxed the nervous tension that had filled him. *She isn't interested in the ambassador, but she wants me.* He grabbed hold of one of her hands, feeling instinctively that she needed support.

Duvall glared at the door before exhaling heavily. "Okay, well, the only thing I can do at the moment is either move you to the command post—but chances are he'll track you down and spend a fair bit of time there in the next few days—or you can move into the security sector with Chowd, during your working hours. We can't afford to upset the ambassador or his assistant, but you need clear air to do your work. Chowd?" Duvall cast a look at him, letting him know that he had his captain's full support, whichever way he chose to act.

Anger, hot and acidic, burned inside him. He knew that this would only offer her some small amount of freedom. If the ambassador truly were that intent on following her, then he'd look for her in her private time. He ran tight fingers through his hair, his mind working overtime. "I believe that would be appropriate. In fact, in the interests of keeping a lid on any advances he might make, we should move Meredith into my cabin until the ambassador is safely returned to the *Star of Ishtar*. I will, of course, sleep in my private office." *Though, the stars know, I will probably sleep badly with her so close by.*

Duvall watched him with assessing eyes. Chowd knew he'd been in this position before and was obviously assessing Chowd's behavior before allowing it.

He stood quietly, waiting for Duvall to reach his own conclusions. In his own mind, he had no question over his actions. Meredith didn't want the ambassador's attention, and he would move all the stars in the galaxy to ensure she didn't have to endure it.

He knew Duvall could argue the anti-fraternization rules the Admiralty had set in place, but the *Elector* was a place where people made decisions that worked, whether or not it broke any other rules. He snickered to himself at the thought.

The silence grew before Duvall nodded. "Fine. That is probably the best outcome. I also need you to take on training with Meredith. Keep her skills current so we can ensure her safety during this mission." He looked rueful for a moment before continuing. "Not just because she's my sister, but she's also a valuable asset to the Admiralty."

Meredith opened her mouth, but both Duvall and Chowd raised a hand. "No, Meredith. Trust me."

Chowd watched her face until she nodded. "Fine, I'll train. Anything else?"

Duvall looked at them, shaking his head. "Is there anything else I need to be aware of?" His words sounded heavy.

"No, not really. Meredith and I will head to her cabin and retrieve clothing and files, then I will relocate her to my cabin." He bowed slightly, Meredith grasped his hand, and they waited for the door to open.

They stepped through together, and Chowd looked around, making sure no one saw them, then without a word they headed to her cabin. On one level, he didn't want the added problem of the ambassador finding them just yet, but he also saw the positives in him finding out now what he wanted him to think.

At the door to her cabin, Meredith pulled off her glove, waving her palm over the scanner, and the door slid open. The silence between them grew as he watched her pull clothes from the drawers and small cupboard beside the sanitary unit door.

"Do you need any assistance?" He indicated to the large carrier she tugged onto the bed. "Uh, no. This shouldn't take long."

Meredith worked methodically, placing large items into the bottom of her bag, uniforms followed by the few more casual clothes, including a single workout suit then underwear. She had attempted to shield the red, blue, and black underwear, but the lacy pieces of fabric caught his eye.

He swallowed deeply as heat traveled through his body at the thought of her dressed in those flimsy scraps of lace. What would she look like? The rattle of her moving to the sanitary unit, snatching up toiletries and shoving them into a small bag, brought him back to reality.

Meredith fastened the bag with a firm pull and the ripping sound of a zipper echoed. Meredith turned to him, swiping a stray strand of hair from her face. "I need that desk screen downloaded to my personal unit. It'll only take a minute or two, then I will initiate a level five wipe."

Level five, huh? That meant a total re-write of the operating system, making the information irretrievable by anything but specially prepared software, with the correct codes.

Meredith moved toward the machine, engaging the connection between desk screen and palm-sized unit. The beep as the unit completed the programmed download filled the air, and she entered the command sequence to the desk-based unit. Her hands moved with precision as she typed the overriding passcode into the machine. It whizzed and whirred, and he waited in silence as she worked.

"That should do it." She stood upright and smiled at him. "Okay, we better deposit all of this in your cabin, then you can take me to your working office and you can track down a machine for me. You do realize I need an off-system machine?"

Her nervousness amused him. She knew well enough that he'd get what she needed. He answered with a dry, "I was aware."

She blushed. "Okay, so you already knew that. Come on, let's get out of here before I get cornered again by the ambassador." She waved her hands over the unit nervously, and he grabbed the bag, following her.

She stopped still in the doorway, as if something blocked her way. A glance over her shoulder was all it took to work out her sudden stillness.

"Ambassador? Can I help you?" she asked, sounding surprised, as she looked at the man standing before her.

Chowd felt a greasy emotion fill his stomach. *Is this jealousy?* The new emotion left him feeling angry and confused and somehow threatened. *Barsha*, the man was going to be more of an issue than they thought. She's mine now, his mind screamed, and he allowed the thought to settle him as he slipped behind Meredith.

He saw the way the ambassador's eyes narrowed when they settled on the bag in his hands before his gaze darted to Meredith's. Chowd grabbed her hand, the small contact giving him an emotional boost and reinforcing the message that she was taken. He felt a tiny measure of satisfaction as he nodded deeply.

"I, uh... I came to ask a question, but now isn't really appropriate, is it?"

"Ambassador? Meredith and I have some work to do, so maybe she can help you later?" The ambassador's lips tightened, a white tinge appearing. "Maybe later." The man

nodded stiffly and moved to the side.

Chowd mentally made a note to discuss the ambassador's perambulations with the security detail. He wanted a warning of the ambassador's location if he came near Meredith. For now though, he steered Meredith toward his cabin.

At 1700 hours, the senior crew of the *Elector* sat at the table, waiting for the ambassador and his assistant to join them. Subdued discussions filled the room. They had already discussed the issue of the ambassador's immediate attachment to Meredith, and Chowd outlined the plans they'd made to head off any further issues that they may experience. He wouldn't call himself happy, but at least they had a plan, and hopefully it would work.

His communicator beeped, and he stood, moving away from the table. "Chowd." "The ambassador and his assistant are on their way. Apparently she couldn't find the right ensemble." His second said the words with a caustic tone, and Chowd wanted to roll his eyes but refrained from the unprofessional conduct. No doubt this sort of event could be classified as usual in the diplomatic corps, but never aboard an Admiralty ship. He wondered how this could be broached before deciding to ignore it.

"I see."

"Sir, she brought four bags and is complaining that her cabin isn't big enough for her to access all her clothing. Apparently that was the reason she was unable to accessorize and find the right shoes."

"Shoes, bags, and clothing. Right. I'll let the captain know." He tapped the communicator off and turned. Every eye seemed focused on him. "They're on their way. It seems the right pair of shoes must be found for an official welcome dinner." He moved beside Meredith, thankful for the regulation-seating layout which placed the ambassador beside Duvall and

Mellissa, leaving Chowd and Meredith together.

Unfortunately, the assistant's seat would be beside him. He'd already suffered a dose of her cloying sweetness and knew, even with his very limited experience, that his taste ran to women with strong and useful minds who didn't feel the need to exaggerate their assets. Women who knew manners trumped the right pair of shoes. He knew beyond a doubt that the one woman for him had to be Meredith.

The door chimed, and they turned as the ambassador entered the room wearing a casual purple suit, once again impeccably groomed. He smiled as he looked around, his gaze darting to and fro until it settled on Meredith. The smile on his face turned intimate.

"Not happening," Chowd muttered.

Meredith squeezed his hand. "No. I second that."

On the ambassador's arm was none other than Ms. Portia Delfray. She sashayed into the room with her tight, hot-pink pants and low-cut, silver-spangled top. It showed her cleavage to advantage—and in that department, she had more than ample assets, he reflected before looking away from the swell of rounded breasts rising over the top of the cloth. Her 'perfect' shoes turned out to be silver and pink with impossibly tall heels. Unsuitable for the ship, Chowd thought. Her blonde hair swept up onto her head, revealing large, sparkling earrings. He knew many would consider her beautiful, but her outward glamour left him cold.

Duvall seated his guests and requested the immediate service of the meal. Ms. Delfray laughed gaily, constantly chattering, her hands moving here and there. Every now and then she would touch his arm, and he felt uncomfortable with her less-than-discreet advances.

"Oh, Chowd, I was wondering if there was any chance I could find another cabin. I believe there is one next to you that is larger and available?"

He blinked, momentarily stunned by the barely veiled suggestion, then shook his head. "No. I'm sorry, those cabins are for executive crew only."

She frowned, her lips dropping at the corners before she heaved a sigh. "Well, if that's all there is to it..."

Chowd looked away, and Portia engaged Raven on her right to an animated discussion. Chowd breathed deeply while his free hand rested on Meredith's thigh, out of sight. He worked hard to ignore the glare that Jemma aimed in his direction.

"Not sure that you put her off for good," Meredith muttered against her glass, and he smiled.

"Maybe not. But when needs must..."

A tinkling from the head of the table drew everyone's attention and Duvall stood. "Tonight we welcome the ambassador and his lovely assistant. As you are all aware, the *Elector* is to journey deep into Ru'Edan territory where we will meet and transfer the ambassador. A number of our crew will be escorting him and ensuring his safety. But tonight... Tonight is about breaking bread and being thankful for what we have and what the future might hold." Duvall toasted the ambassador and Ms. Delfray and those assembled raised their glasses.

The ambassador cleared his throat. "I'm very pleased to be aboard the *Elector*. I've heard... We've heard many good things about both the ship and her crew. This mission is as much about strength as it is about the spoken word. It is my hope, once this mission is concluded, a new and stronger accord can be forged between Earth and Ru'Edan alike. The *Elector* and her crew are central to that happening. I, for one, am pleased to be associated with this new beginning."

Cheers filled the room, then Duvall gave the order for the ship to proceed. The vibrations of the engines rippled through the air. The ambassador proposed a toast, and they joined him.

The view from the ports which dotted the captain's dining room-cum-office showed that the ship made immediate headway, moving away from the Alpha Star Colony and into the nether regions of the Border Planetary Zone, where ships didn't travel without a convoy or authorization.

Chowd felt a thrill at the same time as a sense of

foreboding, but he pushed it away as fanciful. They had the official insignia of both the Earth Admiralty and the ruling Ru'Edan Senate. He also knew that the ship would remain flanked by not one but three fighters, not including the small craft Jemma would command, so they remained adequately protected from any incursions.

Ms. Delfray's voice tinkled in the air, cutting through his thoughts. "Well, Chowd. You must be terribly busy."

"Indeed." *What does she want?*

"Perhaps, when the formalities are concluded, you could—" She breathed deeply, enhancing her already impressive cleavage, and leaned closer. "—show me the hidden places of the ship." Her voice dipped at the same time her hand did below the tablecloth to find his thigh.

She glanced under her thick lashes as him, her ruby-red lips partially open, her hand questing higher toward his groin.

It felt like the movements of some eel slithering over his body, and he worked to stop the shiver of revulsion that overwhelmed him. His stomach curdled at the thought of this... predator...touching his skin. He gripped her hand under the table, returning it to the white-covered top, and smiled as blandly as he could. "I fear I have other duties that are pressing."

She scowled slightly. The calculating hardness in her eyes that lay beneath her party-girl facade showed for an instant then disappeared in a flash. He had to work hard to remember what he'd seen there. He would need to watch her with not some little amount of concern. She could and would cause trouble.

Chowd was thankful to see the elaborate cream-coated dessert, flaming on a silver tray, now carried in by the ensigns in dress uniform just as his communicator badge beeped. He looked quickly at Duvall, who nodded infinitesimally.

He stood and moved slightly away from the table. "Chowd here."

"Chowd, can you bring Gentry to the security offices?" His second didn't make such requests without good reason, and he could hear the strain in his voice.

Chowd nodded once more silently to Duvall, who watched while he indicated to Meredith that she should also go. She stood gracefully, placing the napkin on the table, and smoothed down her uniform. Even in the midst of his concern, the pull of arousal tugged at him.

"On our way," Chowd said to his second, then he snapped the small communicator closed.

Ms. Delfray stood, wobbling slightly on her silly thin heels, an almost winsome look on her face. "Chowd? Can I come?" Her attitude seemed as inappropriate as her footwear.

"Ms. Delfray, forgive me, but I cannot grant your request, as something of the utmost urgency has arisen." He bowed stiffly before continuing. "Now, if you will excuse us." They stepped through the exit together, moving swiftly toward the security offices.

Others sidestepped to clear the way as they marched along the decking. When he entered his office, he breathed a sigh of relief at the sight of the familiar red panels.

His second, Ah Run, waited, palm screen in hand and smiling slightly with relief as he handed the unit over. "We don't know what to make of this. It's obviously a transmission of some sort."

Chowd indicated they should sit at his desk. "Meredith?" "Pass it here. It might be something simple to decode."

He handed her the unit with the glyphs on it, and she sucked in a breath.

"Yes, I know this particular code." She dug around in her pocket before pulling out her personal unit. "This may take me a few minutes. Can I get a coffee while I work?"

He knew the tone now, she needed to talk to him. *Privately.* "Sure. Ah Run?"

His second nodded, asking only if she preferred cream or sugar before heading off to grab the drink.

Chowd turned back to her. "Now what can't you say in front of my second?"

"We're about to be attacked. See this glyph here? That is

attack. I think the next one is wait, but I can't tell what this last one is off the top of my head." She squinted at him. "But why can't you decode this anyway?"

"I only learned what I needed to know. Crick... He never thought it was important that I should be able to follow the written language. My mother insisted I read and write the basic standard language of Earth, but..." He shrugged.

"I'm sorry. I shouldn't have—"

"No. You needed to know." Emotions swirled deep inside him.

When she opened her mouth to remonstrate, he laid a finger against her lips and shook his head. She subsided.

His gaze dropped down to the glyphs in front of her. *Damn.* He reached for his communicator. "Duvall? We have a situation. Can you get the guests to their quarters and meet me in security?" He heard the affirmative as the first explosion rocked the ship. "Where in *Eshra*'s name did that come from?" Chowd thrust out a hand to the wall.

The ship rocked and bucked, and he grabbed hold of Meredith's hand as she reached for the table for support. Another explosion rocked the *Elector* as klaxons wailed and the lights turned red.

The first explosion rocked the *Elector*. The second made her shudder like an addict coming off a high. Meredith, unable to stay still, found herself thrown against the table, the hard surface cutting into her flesh, and she cried out at the sharp pain. Chowd's hand found hers as he steadied himself against the rocking motion of the ship.

Something had gone seriously wrong. The wailing klaxon warned her of their status— under attack. *But how?* Why now and how could they not know these enemies were close enough to fire on them?

"How did we miss the enemy ship coming up on us?" She couldn't help blurting out the question.

Lines of concern bracketed Chowd's mouth and forehead while worry clouded his eyes. "I don't know, Meredith."

She sighed, knowing her role right now was to decode this message and get the information to Duvall and Grayson. "I should deal with this, and you need to do your thing. I'll be fine here, you go." Her words were breathless as she righted herself, rubbing on a sore spot with one hand while the other started the process of the decoding.

For just a second the air felt thick with emotion before his "Stay here" filled the air.

He called together a team and headed out, and Meredith rubbed her hand over her aching eyes while listening to the creaking and groaning of the damaged ship. The noise in the background grated on her nerves, but she concentrated on digging deep within herself. *Exhale. Inhale.* Clear your mind, she told herself, finding her center. Then, opening her eyes, she scanned the message.

Her hands flew over the small screen as she instituted the protocols necessary for the decoding, uploading her software and watching the screen highlight glyphs. She checked each individually, cobbling together the message from the ones she knew and checking for details of the ones she didn't.

"This can't be right." The message didn't contain Ru'Edanian markers.

The knowledge hit like a blow as it descended on her consciousness. Their attackers were Phobon. "Dear *Eshra*." The message flowed across the screen. Two glyphs stood out.

Cloaking.

Opportunity.

"They have cloaking technology?" Her voice sounded like a croak as she realized they'd attacked the *Elector* because they found an opportunity. The twin realization made her sick to her stomach, and she doubled over, nearly retching.

Meredith pulled herself together with great difficulty

before continuing to double-check the message, her stomach churning wildly.

"I need to..." She printed the decoded message, the *rat-at-at* of the machine filling her senses. Meredith reached a shaking hand to her communicator. "Duvall? I have the message decoded and am heading to your office now. You're going to want to see what I have."

"Not the office. The bridge. I'm there now." His voice was strained.

She rose, making her way across the floor. The ship still shuddered and yawed in space while acrid, oily air filtered through the room. The lights on the ship glowed a reddish orange as the ship changed security status.

People moved throughout the ship swiftly but calmly. Meredith saw a few injuries as she made her way to the front of the ship, their bodies coated in a black, sooty substance. Members of the engineering team had stationed themselves at various locations, mainly with spanners and screwdrivers in hand, though some carried large black bags, the contents of which she could only guess at. The increased security presence stood at attention, armed and ready to offer support where needed.

Upon entering the bridge, she noted the ambassador sitting still and glassy-eyed in a chair near Duvall. Every now and then a trembling betrayed his fright, and she quirked a brow at her brother. He shook his head. She skirted around to his vantage point behind the command chair.

"What did you find out?" he asked.

"A few things. Firstly, they are Phobons—Phobos pirates. The attack was purely on the spur of the moment. They considered the *Elector* a first-class prize, and with the dual authorizations and insignias on the hull, they knew we were transporting something or someone of importance. But that isn't the most concerning aspect. They have new technology. It's some kind of cloaking, a sort of stealth mode that we haven't detected at any point in the past. There hasn't even been a whisper of it." Her voice wavered. She tried to keep her voice down, but someone must have heard them.

"Cloaking stealth mode? Sweet stars, we don't stand a chance." The voice was choked, and she looked around to see a young ensign behind the captain. The deck went quiet at his words.

"Oh *Barsha*, Duvall. I'm sorry." She felt ill with greasy waves churning in her belly at the young man's words. *I should have looked before I started my report.*

She looked into her brother's tense eyes. "Come on, Meredith. Show me what you have."

He gripped the palm screen she handed over and scrolled through the decoded message, grunting as his mouth tightened to a white line. He finally nodded, handing back the compact unit. "I'll get Raven onto looking for some sort of emission trail that we can use to keep an eye out. For the moment though, we have another immediate issue to deal with."

She raised her eyes to his. "What could be as important as this?" "The ambassador's assistant, Ms. Delfray, died in the attack."

She started at his words. "What?" She hadn't liked the woman, with the way she had looked at Chowd like a commodity for the taking, but she never would have wished her death. And now they would have to contend with the issue of a diplomatic assistant dying on the *Elector*. Thankfully, it hadn't been the ambassador, but still...

"They were making their way back to their assigned cabins when a light fitting broke loose from its moorings, hitting her in the head as it fell. In front of the ambassador. He isn't coping so well, but Elara's just too busy at the moment dealing with the injured to work with him. Under the circumstances, we felt it was better to have him here, under guard, rather than left to his own devices in his cabin by himself."

"Were there many other injuries?" She needed to know just how badly her failure had impacted the crew. Her stomach curdled at the knowledge that she should have known. If she had found the key to the documents, she could have warned Duvall and the crew. Her head ached, and she lifted a shaky hand.

Duvall sighed. "Thankfully not. A few broken bones, a burn, and some cuts that needed immediate attention. Ms. Delfray was, unfortunately, the worst of it, but I need to get Raven working on finding a way to pinpoint them before any further incursions, unless you have found something in the transmissions?" His voice sounded hopeful, but she shook her head.

"No. Sorry, Duvall. If I find something, I'll let you know."

Once more he became the captain, his voice brusque. "You know it's not your fault, don't you?"

She shook her head. "If I'd managed to..." The words petered away. Her failure...her guilt...all weighed heavily on her soul.

"Meredith, you did what you could with what you had. It's not your fault." She opened her mouth to disagree, but Duvall pinned her with a firm expression. "No. You're only able to do what you can. Don't take on a responsibility that isn't yours. Now then, we won't discuss this again. Can you get back to security by yourself, or do you want me to call Chowd?" He smiled slightly, and for the first time since the first explosion, the knot of anguish that lodged in her chest loosened.

"No. I'll be fine. You get back to your work."

He nodded, dismissing her, and she made her way past the ambassador, who looked sightlessly around the bridge. "Ambassador..."

The sightless gaze he bestowed on her reminded her she had nothing to give him. No offer to make things better. And, her mind chimed in, even if she did, he might construe something that wasn't there.

"I'm sorry." The inane words were all that came to mind.

He blinked owlishly and she retreated. She would be more useful to the crew decoding the messages, she reminded herself. The thought kept her going.

✪ ✪ ✪ ✪ ✪

He ached. Every inch of Crick Sur Banden's body burned with fever, and he hated the way they stood around his bed, staring at him. Hot anger roared through his veins. He sweated and stank but didn't care. He needed the relief of his Xeradax, and all would once more be well. His vision swam, and he shut his eyes against the vertigo. He reeled back, letting his head roll slightly as he caught an unsteady breath, trying to focus on those around him once more.

"Give me my drugs." Even to himself, the words sounded slurred and loud. His head felt heavy, as if his neck couldn't support the weight.

"My Lord. We don't have any Xeradax here. We are trying—" The small medi-tech hovered close. Too close.

The voice stopped as Crick's hand extended swiftly to grasp the doctor's throat. The soft flesh beneath his fingers gave under the pressure, the face purpling before Crick's gaze as the man tried to squirm out of the deathly hold. He felt a small punch of pleasure at the feeling and kept the pressure on, until a gargling sound filled the air, then he released his grip.

He stared at the fool kneeling on the ground beside him and took pleasure from the purpled skin tone and bulging eyes. They'd tried to take away his simple pleasure. *They will learn. They will all learn.*

"I will have my medication." His grunt was forceful and the one on the floor flinched away.

"My Lord. I am working now to source a new supply for you. If you could stop terrorizing the medic? I am making for a planet nearby that assures me they have some in stock. Enough to at least give you some immediate relief from your present discomfort. There should even be enough to last until we reach Otega." The voice of his second-in-command filled the air, and the pocket of fevered worry subsided within his chest.

"See? He is so much better than you." He spat the words at the cringing coward and watched as he scuttled away on hands and knees, just like some kind of bug, Crick thought with pleasure. That they would make him give up his Xeradax was unacceptable. "Take us there immediately."

"Yes, My Lord. I am arranging for the necessary adjustments to be made in our heading now." His second bowed low, subservient under these trying circumstances.

Crick Sur Banden liked that. It made him feel superior even as his body refused to accept his exalted position, letting him down as he drooled slightly from the side of his mouth. He hated the weakness but took comfort in the knowledge that this would soon pass.

"My Lord...there is one thing. The Phobos pirates have used their stealth cloaking on the *Elector*. They have stated they've achieved some minimal success. They have also reported that the ship is traveling under dual authorization—Ru'Edan and Admiralty."

Crick felt no concern at this trifling intelligence. His Xeradax would make him feel better, then he could concentrate. But something about the *Elector* elicited a strange feeling of hate. For just a moment, the answer danced beyond the tip of his mind. Then it snapped into focus.

Chowd. Duvall McCord. The *Elector*. A pulse leapt in his throat as he felt the anger and hate grow inside him once more.

He roared in anger. "Kill them! Kill them all, but I want Chowd. I want Duvall McCord. I want to tear them limb from limb." His arms moved, mirroring his words, and he saw horror in the eyes of his cowering medics. His second watched him with a grim look on his face. He must have moved or made a sound, as his second hovered over him for an instant before stepping back away. "Wait!" Spittle flew as he demanded obedience and once more a wave of dizziness hit. "Wine. Bring me wine."

"My Lord, will you take some sustenance too?"

"No. Just the wine." He lay back down, feeling the soft bedding beneath his aching frame. "And turn down the temperature."

"My Lord, it is already as low as we dare—"

"I don't care! Turn it down now!" His voice filled the air, and he caught a quick exchange of glances between several of his men. *What? Why? Do they think to mutiny? I will see to that. After my Xeradax and my wine.*

A goblet of red wine found its way into his hands, and he lifted it to his mouth with shaking hands, uncaring where it came from, drinking deeply then noting the tart taste with a hint of bitterness. *Bitterness?*

"What did you put in this?" he growled as a fog descended on his mind. He fought against it, but darkness crept into the corners of his vision. The need to sleep, heavy and dark, filled him. "You drugged me..." The words skittered away as his lids closed over his eyes.

Chapter 4

Chowd scrubbed his tired eyes and glanced toward the dark cabin beyond, where Meredith had retreated in the early hours of the morning. He'd found her in the security offices, head bent over a small desk screen, going through transmissions, looking for similarities to help her break the codes. She'd been drawn and pale and he tugged her away in spite of her protests that she was fine.

The ship settled into an edgy kind of quiet routine, and while his whole body craved relaxation, his mind was alert to even the most minute action that would chip the brittle veneer of his control. He rested his head against the back of his seat, taking a deep breath, hoping to calm the agitation that threatened to overwhelm him.

His chest expanded as he filled his lungs, and he imagined the place his mother had always spoken of. A lush, green garden filled with fragrant flowers. *Exhale*. It calmed him, the sense of quiet he always experienced once more filling him. The stiff muscles in his shoulders, arms, and torso releasing the pent-up tension.

A rustle alerted him, and he opened his eyes. Meredith, in a lacy, flimsy gown, stood before him.

"Chowd?" she said uncertainly.

The gown settled on her frame, showing her perfect form. Small, pert breasts with peaked buds and a hint of those pink nipples barely hidden under the light covering called to his gaze. She swallowed, and he rose, his body moving without conscious thought.

Chowd concentrated on her as he moved forward, seeking a sign of welcome. His hands clenched and released convulsively at the thought of touching her delicious skin. Of kissing those soft, pink lips. Of joining his body to hers.

Sweat beaded his upper lip. His legs felt like vats of

noodles, and his body shivered at the invitation he hoped this represented. "Meredith?"

"Come to me?" Her luminous eyes shone in the half-light, and his breath caught at the back of his throat.

What she was offering... His mind splintered, his deepest desire rising in his chest. "Are you sure?"

She smiled lightly, nodded, and—bless the stars—moved forward. Her slim hands rose to his shoulders and touched lightly, but the heat her fingers generated burned him.

"We can take this slowly if you prefer." Her words came out a mere whisper, and he felt the warmth of her breath against his skin. He shivered anew.

Sensations burst like stars within him. He leaned in, and she met his lips. His hands snaked around her waist, pulling her closer against his body. The feel of her against him... Tiny zings of electricity rippled under his skin as nerve endings reacted to stimuli.

She shivered as his tongue dipped into her mouth, and the moan he swallowed excited him further. She moved against him, and his body cried out for skin-to-skin contact. Her hands tangled in his hair, and...dear stars! He had to close his eyes as he accepted the onslaught of sensations.

Chowd felt her pull back slightly. "What did I do wrong?" *Have I gone too fast?* Fear and confusion welled while his heart stuttered in his chest.

She shook her head, smiling slightly, and reached for the buttons of his ship suit. "Let's make you more comfortable." Her voice wobbled a little, and the touch of her fingers at his chest filled him with wonder.

Inch by unbearably slow inch, she revealed his skin. Finally, the last button gave, and his whole bare chest was exposed to her. He started to lift his hands, but she brushed them away.

"Not yet," Meredith whispered, her breath caressing him as she dipped her head forward to touch his skin with her petal-soft lips.

He jerked as her lips made contact. Chowd held himself rigid, feeling the swamping emotions, all the while burning for her touch. Meredith's fingers skimmed over his skin, peeling back his shirt. His shaking hand rose to the small strap sitting across her collarbone, but she danced away from him.

"Not yet." A shiver worked through her body as she whispered the words.

He wanted to hold her. Touch her. His body raged with the now-familiar desire, but this time...this time it was returned. Chowd felt his body tighten, hard and aching, with a need he'd never before experienced.

Meredith moved back to him, a teasing smile on her lips as she slipped the shirt off his shoulders. "So beautiful." Her hands caressed his shoulders, smoothing over muscles very few had seen and none before had touched. His breath hitched.

Her warm fingertips slipped down his chest, finding the small, brown nipples and toying briefly before returning to their downward track. He shuddered as they found his flat stomach, his navel, and he felt one finger dip within slowly, swirling before moving onward. His muscles clenched involuntarily, his body burning hotter than he had ever experienced before.

"Let me touch you." The guttural words resonated through his burning body.

"Only if you follow me." She smiled, holding out one small hand, which he gripped, and she led him toward the dark cabin beyond.

Meredith shivered with anticipation, knowing deep inside her that the wait was almost over. Her belly warmed and filled her up with a long, slow curl of delicious heat, and excitement zinged through her veins. His hand entwined in hers, fingers locked as they headed toward the cabin in silence.

She turned to look at him. Her nipples tightened to buds

of desire. She wanted this man so badly. Moving closer to him, she smiled in the half-light, his face shadowed and mysterious. "I want you, Chowd."

She placed her hands on his bare shoulders with a light touch, glorying in the feel of his skin, silky soft and so warm. He moved closer as she did, and their lips met and clung while their bodies touched at breast and thigh.

When he granted access, she investigated his sensuous, full lips with her tongue. A moan of desire rose in her throat and robbed her thoughts as he touched her waist lightly. What started as tentative became more sure, as if he understood her need.

"Yes, touch me there." She had to remember he'd never done this before and scrabbled madly against the burning need that ratcheted higher and tighter within her body, but the thoughts skittered away once more beneath his careful caresses.

His mouth lifted from hers, and she mewled softly at the loss of such drugging pleasure. "You're so beautiful, and I want to make you happy." He settled his lips to the tender skin of her neck and kissed her.

His long, open-mouthed touches sent shivers rocketing through her system. She arched backward, giving in to her body's desire for his touch. Firm hands inched up over her rib cage, and molten fire followed. Her heart rate increased as his fingers rested just below her breasts.

"Meredith?"

"Please..." she moaned.

His hands snaked upward to cup her aching breasts, and she shivered. He hissed out a tight breath, and she groaned.

"Come. Come with me..." Meredith stepped back, her body ready for this next step. She slipped the hands under the straps, but he stopped her.

"No. Let me." His voice, deep and liquid, whispered against her skin as one finger slipped beneath a strap, tracing a light circle before pushing it from her shoulder.

Then the other strap fell free, the soft material sighing

as it dropped, catching briefly on her breasts. She watched the incandescent glow in his face as her skin was bared to him. He reached out a tentative hand, pushing the fabric away. It dropped to the floor soundlessly.

"You're so amazingly beautiful." His shaking hands once more clasped her waist, and he lifted uncertain eyes to hers.

"Touch me."

His hands slid upward, cupping the supple flesh, soft fingers tracing the nipples, and she rocked slightly. Then he molded her flesh as she cried out with pleasure at his gentle grazing.

"Is that..." He stopped, uncertain once more.

"It's perfect. You're perfect." She reached out, touching his hand, and his face cleared once more, his full lips twitching slightly.

She fumbled with the buttons and clasps on his pants until she finally freed him from their confines and felt his hot flesh beneath her hands. She trembled, then dipped her gaze, seeking the sight of him. *How can I not?*

No underwear. Her mouth dried as she took in the erection jutting proudly up from his body, nestled against his belly.

Fascination wound through her. "Your skin. It's bare?" "It's natural for the Ru'Edan."

Her belly quivered as she slid her hand down the silky flanks of his thighs. "You're truly amazing."

Then she leaned in, skin to skin, her nipples barely touching his chest, but the feeling...

Oh my! The feeling is electric. Meredith's lips met his and clung in an exotically hot, dark kiss. When he retreated for air, she gathered her scattered senses. "Take me to the bed." They moved together, and he nearly pulled her over as their feet caught in the tangle of discarded clothing.

"*Barsha*!" His growl made her smile as he bent and removed his offending clothing and boots. They flew through the air, landing with a thud against the wall. She giggled, and he glanced up, his lips quirking.

Meredith stepped delicately away from her gown, watching him before she sat down on the bed and patted the side. "Come join me."

"What about..." He stopped and swallowed.

"Pregnancy control? Not a problem. I have an implant." She smiled broadly as he moved like a dangerous predator to her side, and the bed dipped under his weight.

Meredith felt his hands, the soft touch on her shoulder, and she turned into him, lifting her legs to the coverlet as he rolled her to her back, leaning over her slightly. They kissed again. His hands roamed over her body, learning the dips and swells, as her fingers traced the muscles of his back. She lay back, watching him investigate. A feeling of deep satisfaction built that it was she he would learn this lesson with.

Even as that exultation flowed through her, another emotion took its place. Emptiness welled inside her, and she cried out as her body responded to him. "More. Oh, dear stars! More."

Her throaty moan propelled him into action. His fingers found their way toward the downy hair that hid her heated core, slick and damp with need for him and his touch. He fondled her, and she writhed beneath him.

"Tell me what you want. Tell me." He whispered the words against a breast before opening his mouth over the hard nub and suckling.

"Fill me. Touch me. I want you inside me." Her words were broken as she wound the fingers of one hand in his hair while guiding his other to the places she needed him to fill. His fingers slipped between the damp skin folds.

She bucked against him. She pulled her hand from his head and ran it down his back, savoring the damp slickness of his skin. Down to his rounded buttocks that quivered beneath her fingertips, slipping over the skin of his flank and inexorably working toward his cock. Meredith grasped him firmly, and her reward came with his harsh grunt of pleasure. He bucked as she pumped him gently, feeling his satiny hardness in her hand, the soft roundness of the head.

His fingers moved faster and harder, slipping within her body as she pumped him. Both of them shuddered with pleasure, and their bodies moved urgently.

"Not this way. Not now." Her mutter broke through the welling pleasure, and she gulped air.

He wheezed and she framed his face with one hand, slick sweat coating her palm. "Meredith?"

"Wait." Meredith pulled his hand away, letting go even as she made to pull him over her body. His eyes glinted in the half-light as he positioned himself at the entry to her core, the burning tip calling to her urgently. "Chowd."

His head dipped as he pushed into her, and their mouths fused once more, her legs rising to wrap around his waist, flexing slightly as she welcomed him within her body in one surge. His body stiffened for just a second then began the ancient rhythm. They moved together, slowly at first, letting the pleasure build to a higher peak.

They moved faster, harder, and higher. Sighs of pleasure filled the air, and fingers gripped tightly as they clung to each other's sweat-slicked skin.

More. Faster. Harder.

The pleasure that continued to build within her body ached to be completed. She moved toward it, and finally the orgasm hit her like a wave, her cry captured within his mouth as he shuddered with completion. The feel of his jetting seed almost overpowered her as she floated in a sea of sensual ecstasy.

Slowly their heart rates dropped, and they moved together, his front nestled against her as he caressed her hair. The feeling inside her chest grew to bursting. She lay supine in his arms in the dark.

"Thank you," he whispered against her hair, and she sighed.

"I hate to tell you, big boy, but I got as much out of tonight...this morning...as you did." She deliberately chose a light tone. He was sensitive in so many ways, and the gift he'd given her was immeasurable. Fragile, like his ego, she thought silently. "Besides, I'm thinking we could practice again later." She pulled his arm around her. "But for now, we'd better get some sleep. We have a number of things to do in the next couple of hours and need a little rest for our weary bodies."

"Sleep then, my beautiful Meredith. I will wake you in the morning."

She rested against him. Quiet filled the air, and she listened to the thump of his heart beneath her ear as she drifted off to sleep.

Chapter 5

Meredith liked coffee. And small pastries filled with fruity fillings. Chowd knew she snuck them from the mess hall on occasions, when she thought no one watched. Chowd arranged the ones he had appropriated on a plate, wondering if he should have grabbed one of each, not just the four varied fillings.

He checked the chrono and worried. *How will she react if I wake her?* He mentally cursed himself for his vacillations before heading into the room, where she had already begun waking, saving him any more to-ing and fro-ing with himself. She stretched in the bed like a well-fed cat, and he watched, entranced, as she slowly realized he stood there.

"Good morning. You look like you've already been up for hours." Her hair was mussed and sat like a halo around her pixie face. A small smile crept across her perfect pink lips, and a light, telltale blush colored her cheeks as she focused her sleep-heavy eyes on him.

"I don't need much sleep. I have breakfast in the other room if you would like." He indicated the other room with a languid hand, attempting to hide the tension within him. She looked at him, surprised, and he grinned at her reaction.

"Can I shower and dress first?" She rose, allowing the sheet to fall and showing her glorious body to him.

Heat flooded his body together with the adrenalin caused by his sudden arousal. He remembered the feel of her against him and swallowed.

"You could share with me if you like." She smiled sweetly, filling him with heat, and he knew she was flirting.

He felt flustered, and while his body urged him to agree with the proposal, his mind tried to weigh up the positives and negatives in taking up her offer. It must have shown on his face, since she sighed.

"If I do, I fear we'll be in there for far too long. When you're finished, come through to the office." *The best way to deal with this is to remain on task.* He nodded at his thoughts. They seemed wise.

"Chowd?" Her voice now sounded a little unsure, and he felt like something had hit him hard, the warmth he had just experienced evaporating and leaving a cold hollowness lodged in his chest.

"What?" he asked. A small frown marred her face. "Meredith?"

"I...last night? I wasn't too...forward, was I?" Anxiety lit her face as her words filled the air, and the knot of panic in his chest released. The air in his lungs expelled with a hiss, and he lurched forward.

"No, Meredith. Last night was perfect." He looked for signs that she didn't believe him. She smiled tremulously. "I wasn't sure. Maybe, then, I could have a good-morning kiss?" Realization dawned. *What an idiot I am!* He moved toward her and enveloped her in his arms. His lips met hers. The kiss warmed the empty spots inside him, and he had to push away when arousal once more reared its head, tempered this time with tenderness.

He ran a light hand over her tresses, feeling the silky length beneath his trembling fingers. "Now, go and shower. Otherwise your breakfast will be cold."

He turned and left her but kept an ear on her movements as she showered and dressed, the whole time weighing and measuring his responses and actions. His usually calm exterior in disarray, he struggled to regain control of the constant see-saw which left him feeling confused and uncertain, an experience totally foreign to his usual pattern of behavior. He didn't know for sure if it could be considered a normal reaction or some aberration that he should report to Elara. He didn't have anything much in the way of data to fall back on.

Meredith appeared in the doorway, uniform in place, and joined him in the room. She raised an eyebrow as he handed her the plate. "Pastries?"

"Your favorite, I understand."

She smiled conspiratorially. "Just don't tell anyone. Duvall always teased me when I was younger about my sweet tooth." Meredith bit into the treat, her eyes closing as she savored the taste.

She really is a woman of many facets. She allows herself to indulge her sweet tooth, yet she's sensual, with a brilliant mind. She's witty, and yet still so shy.

"You said you don't need much sleep?"

He blinked away his thoughts and reached out a hand to capture a tiny crumb which sat on the corner of her mouth. His gaze clung to hers as he drew it to his mouth. She visibly shuddered as did he, and his breath caught at the hunger he detected in her gaze.

He shook himself free of the sensual haze and considered her question. "Ru'Edan usually sleep for around four hours in every forty, unlike humans, who usually require eight in every twenty-four. As a hybrid, I can manage six over about thirty-four but find longer hard to manage. I believe it's a genetic difference on the DNA level, though there aren't a lot of differences between humans and Ru'Edanians, which is why we can impregnate human women, and it is generally believed human men should be able to do the same to Ru'Edanian women. Not that I've heard of any such pairings before." He shrugged, uncomfortable with the conversation, but he knew they had to have it.

"Chowd? I know who and what you are. It makes no difference to me." Her soft words had him looking up to see the compassion and some deeper emotion in her eyes.

"It should." His harsh outburst spurred her to stand, wide eyes betraying her emotions, before an angry look crept over her face. She poked a sharp finger at his chest.

"No. I know who you are. Deep inside is what counts. Every time you've had an opportunity to go back to him, you've stayed steadfast and loyal to your uncle. To Duvall. To the ship."

He didn't know how to respond to her sudden outburst

and when her voice quieted, tiny pricks of heat started in his eyes.

"Don't belittle what and who you are."

Her passion warmed even the coldest recesses of his soul.

She turned away jerkily, placing the plate on his desk before she swung back to face him. "I know you also underwent genetic therapy, cutting edge and unheard of beforehand, so that the differences weren't so noticeable, affecting a change to both your eye color and skin tones, and possibly other internal organs and musculature systems. You want to belong, and I want that for you. But in order to do so, you need to allow yourself to be what you are. Who you are, deep inside. Until you do that, you will always feel like an outsider to some extent." Her voice softened. "And I like who you are." She rose on tiptoe and placed a soft kiss on his mouth. "Now, pass me a denta-tab and let's get up to the bridge before they start without us."

He did so wordlessly, thinking about her words and the passion in them. She made him feel like he belonged. A dangerous thought, he conceded, but one he wanted to accept at face value.

She grabbed his hand, dragging him through the doorway and along the corridor. Together they made their way to the bridge, silent except for the sound of their feet clanking on the decking, ready to witness the union of Jemma and Raven. The time they traveled in quiet hyperspace was the perfect opportunity for a communing ceremony. He felt buoyant and happy for the first time in...well, he couldn't actually remember when he had ever felt quite like this.

Both Raven and Jemma waited on the bridge, smiling, for the friends and family that made up the crew of the *Elector* to gather around them. Meredith had shown surprise that neither had chosen to wait for Raven's family, but they both explained they felt those most important to them were present already.

During the ceremony, Meredith dabbed discretely at tears as they made their commitment before Duvall. Chowd offered her a cloth to wipe her tears, feeling pleased that two of his friends had found a profound love, one he would probably never experience. A section of his chest ached at the realization that he'd found a temporary surcease from his loneliness with Meredith. Even so, he had to work hard not to rub at the physical pain that came with the thought that, one day, even that brief but satisfying connection would end.

He cast away his negative thoughts. They didn't belong there today.

Today was a day to celebrate, even after the incident from the night before. He knew Duvall, Raven, and Jemma had discussed postponing the ceremony. In the end, everyone had agreed that given they were in hyperspace and that there was a brief period of quiet, it was the best time for it to take place until after they'd finished the negotiations.

So the ceremony continued as planned, and afterward, the senior crew retired to Duvall's office, the ambassador having cried off, citing his distress at the death of his assistant.

Chowd had found the woman cloying, but he understood the feeling of loss, and he empathized with the ambassador and understood his need to retreat. Today they had celebrated a joyous occasion, and no one could find anything in his absence to concern them or dampen the mood.

In the hours since the celebration, Meredith worked at the desk screen, her eyes now dry and achy from the strain of reading glyphs that appeared on the shining monitor, while the recycled air dried the sensitive tissues. She stretched her back, thinking longingly of the conformable seat in her office on Aenna. She loved the work of cryptology and translations, the working of algorithms, and the quick thinking, but the long hours and constant mental requirements were sometimes physically exhausting. The Admiralty had made efforts to meet the needs of its specialist staff with careful choices of furnishings in the offices. Those comforts were sadly lacking on the *Elector*.

She tugged at her ear in frustration. The glyph in front of her made no sense. She shouldn't have trouble decoding this one. She'd seen it before but couldn't remember where or when. *I have a sneaking suspicion this one has passed me by somewhere, making the meaning incomplete.*

"You'll pull it off doing that."

Meredith jumped. "Chowd, you startled me! Don't do that again," she snapped, and instantly regretted her reaction. "Oh, stars! I'm sorry, I shouldn't have snarled like that. I just can't see the logical progression here." She scrubbed her hand across her aching eyes once more.

"Want me to have a look?" He peered over her shoulder.

Meredith's hand dropped as she turned in the seat. He had a tick in his left cheek, and his full lips firmed while he scrolled the screen through the images.

"There." He pointed to the glyph that had irritated her earlier. "That one? It's one I don't know."

He looked at her, an eyebrow raised and a slight smile kicking up the corner of his mouth. "You should. It's Chowd."

"Oh my...then he knows you are aboard." Her hand touched the screen, tracing over the glyph. She opened her mouth to command it to find all such glyphs, but before she could say a word, he moved his hand in front of the screen, obscuring her view.

"No. You need to eat and sleep. Not necessarily in that order though. You haven't slept properly since the ambassador boarded." He placed a tender hand under her elbow, levering her to a standing position. "And I noticed your discomfort, so perhaps you'll forgive me being so forward." He smiled, softening the impact of his words. But she knew it was a caring command, making her insides turn gooey at the warm feeling curling through her once more.

"Then just let me sync this and I'll head along to the cabin with you." She gave the command and watched the download progression. It beeped once, letting her know the task had concluded. Meredith gave a final lock command on the information she had decoded and stepped away from the desk. "Okay, let's go."

They moved slowly out of the security section and into the corridor, the silence between them companionable. Neither touched the other, but she remained hyperaware of his closeness, the brush and sighing sounds his uniform gave, as well as the distance between them.

He opened the door to his cabin. "Would you like to change?" he asked as the door shut behind them. He seemed uncertain again in the way he stood back.

"Well, yes, a shower and changing would be nice." She grinned and stepped closer, inhaling his musky scent. "But first I would like to do something else." She laid her hands on his shoulders, reaching up to kiss him fully on the mouth.

He groaned and opened to her, and she felt the almost familiar spurt of pleasure, letting him deepen the kiss this time. His arms surrounded her, and she felt the heat of passion once more rising within her. Triumph that she'd taught him this roared through her system. Chowd's mouth left her lips to travel to her throat, and she arched against him, allowing him access to the soft skin, feeling the throb between her legs as blood rushed like a wildfire through her veins.

"Chowd, I love the way you touch me."

He pulled away slightly. Desire glittered in his hooded eyes, and she shivered with anticipation once more. He reached for the buttons on the front of her suit.

His communicator blared into the heavy silence. "*Barsha*!" He thumped his hand against the communicator. "Chowd." The fog of arousal slipped away, though she noted the ruddy glow of frustration staining his high cheeks.

"We're about to have dinner in the mess. Want to join us?" Duvall's voice filled the air, and a bubble of laughter rose in her throat, one she quickly contained. If only he knew what he had interrupted.

Chowd cast a questioning glance toward her, and she

nodded. The mood had dissolved...for now. "Tell him I just need to change first," she threw over her shoulder as she headed for the room beyond.

She listened to the undertone of his voice through the wall as she mentally sifted and sorted through the few clothes she had brought with her. *Perhaps the black exercise pants which hug my figure? No, they make me look too much like a boy. What about the pale-blue ship pants and its matching top?*

She stopped in her tracks. Worrying about clothes hadn't ever been important before. She'd always risen above those sorts of discussions in school and later at the Academy. It had always seemed so much more important to carve her career with Admiralty and follow in her brother's footsteps.

Meredith bit her lip as she considered this unsettling development. Sure, underwear had been a guilty secret, her longing for lace and soft fabrics close to her skin, but outerwear? She shook her head. No. This wasn't the normal her. She sighed, reaching for the fastenings on her uniform and stripping down. Meredith grabbed the blue outfit before tossing it to the bed and finding the light-colored shoes she had packed for non-working hours to team with them.

It would do, but she needed to break herself out of this thought pattern before it became a habit. Knowing that she currently suffered from such confusing emotions and vacillating behavior scared her...a lot.

She turned in just bra and panties to see Chowd backing away as quickly as he had obviously entered the dark room.

"I'll just give you some privacy."

She grinned at his discomfort. *He's still so innocent.* "Chowd Sturat Sur Banden, aren't you intending to change?"

"Well, yes, but..." The heated glow on his cheekbones returned. "Then hurry up."

A sheepish expression spread over his face. "I thought you might want to change privately. I was respecting your need for—"

For the first time a spurt of irritation welled. "Well, I

don't. We're more than just a casual one-night sex fling thing... aren't we?"

His startled look answered her question, but he needed to say it just as much as she suddenly needed to hear it. "Of course, Meredith..." His words trickled away.

"Then for the time we are together, unless I specifically ask, you don't need to leave when I change. This is what lovers do."

He gave her a grave nod. "Yes."

Meredith dropped down to sit on the bed and enjoy the view as he dressed. His nudity didn't seem to worry him, and that pleased her. *He's a man of many contradictions.*

Chowd grabbed clothes without any seeming concern for style or cut and pulled them on quickly. Happily, she noted he wore no underwear again, and a shiver of arousal zipped through her system. It could quickly become a normal aspect of her nature around him, she thought with a silent giggle. After he dressed, Chowd held out his hand, and she rose to take it.

They left the darkened room behind and moved out of the office, heading toward the mess. Meredith grinned, knowing Duvall may or may not understand the connection of the clasped hands immediately, but Jemma, Mellissa, and Elara certainly would.

Chapter 6

The soft rumble of Chowd's breathing beneath Meredith's ear woke her, and she smiled. "I could get used to this."

In the three days since the communing of Jemma and Raven, she and Chowd had slowly worked at finding their way forward as a couple. Of course, neither of them would let this connection impact their roles within the *Elector* and Admiralty, but something definitely continued growing between them, blossoming in the midst of a dangerous mission. She knew Duvall had noticed, judging by the slight narrowing of his eyes when they joined the other members of the crew for supper after the ceremony and afterward at the informal reception.

If it hadn't irked so much, she would probably laugh it off, but with this—she hesitated to think of it as a relationship just yet—thing budding between them, she remained protective of the growing connection and of Chowd. She nearly groaned at the introspective psychobabble but realized that would wake the man lying beside her, so she kept her response to eye rolling.

Since then, she'd worked studiously, decoding the messages they had intercepted just before the attack and decrypting the information they had found on the Alpha Star Colony. Meanwhile Chowd made plans, trained with his men, and pored through layouts of the station where they would protect the ambassador during the talks.

Meredith rolled onto her back carefully, and Chowd shuffled forward, moving closer to her. She grinned, though it quickly died away as she realized that, even in his sleep, he needed the reassurance of her touch. That alone drove her anger at Crick Sur Banden to great heights.

With careless disregard, he'd damaged Chowd's ability to trust and accept any sort of relationship at face value. Of course, there was the underlying hatred for his actions, the murder of thousands of innocents, but she could also lay that claim at the feet of the Ru'Edan Senate prior to the ceasefire that occurred long ago. On the other hand, humans had also acted in what some considered a predatory manner. *No one side is better or more in the right than another.*

With great effort, Meredith cleared her mind, letting go of the tension that had invaded her body. She lay still, enjoying the warmth and silence, releasing muscles that had tensed in painful knots along her arms, legs, and even shoulders. She savored the closeness, knowing it would only last until the alarm trilled.

"Meredith?" Chowd's voice, groggy with sleep, startled her slightly, and she turned to see his eyes open.

"Hey."

"Everything okay?" His hand moved to her shoulder, tracing lazy circles.

"Yeah, just thinking." She smiled, hoping he wouldn't see the shadow of dark thoughts in her eyes. The lights brightened a little, and the buzz of the alarm filled the air. She released the breath she had held onto, listening to the hiss as it escaped between her clenched teeth.

"Want to tell me what the problem is?" His eyes burned into the center of her head as if he could read her thoughts.

"It's nothing, really. Just nervous about the trip, I guess."

He frowned slightly. Meredith reached for the sheet, ready to slip out of the bed, but his hand gripped her wrist. "I thought lovers told the truth." His low and intense voice shocked her, and she realized the truth of his words.

"You're right. Of course you are." She turned, feeling vulnerable deep inside. "I hate that *he* made you distrusting. Constantly questioning and feeling like you need to keep your distance from everyone. It's wrong. Everything he did to you was so—" Her ire rose with each word, hands clasped before her as she looked at him, her own voice becoming more high-pitched. "— evil. And when we should be looking for him to shut him down, we're babysitting an ambassador."

Meredith winced and closed her eyes, not hiding her pain but fearful he would think less of her for the outburst and tone of her thoughts.

At the touch of his hand, the framing of her face, she opened her eyes. The softness in his gaze turned her insides warm and gooey. The absence of anger in his face gave her a measure of comfort, and she marveled at his ability to cast away his painful memories.

"The fact that you care enough to feel so much anger warms me, Meredith. Makes me feel alive, and even more importantly, makes me feel valued in a way I have never before experienced." He came closer, the soft whisper-touch of his lips on hers burning with an intensity.

Her body began to shake, her heart rate speeding up, but he pulled away and shared a soft smile. Her heart turned over, and she understood finally. *I love him. With all his issues, he's the one man I want to live with forever.*

A sense of wonder filled her, and she reached shaking fingers to hold his hand in place alongside her face. She nuzzled at the long fingers and turned to kiss them.

"We need to rise, Meredith." His fingers pulled away slightly before lightly touching her brow, feathering along the sides of her eye, and she nodded. He stopped her movements as she started to turn away. "But I need to tell you that I value you. Your independence. Your fiery defense of me. Your passion." He leaned in and warmed her with a quick kiss.

Chowd rose, his firm, taut body nude in the partial light, the planes and dips shadowed before her gaze, and she felt the now-familiar tug of arousal deep in her belly.

"Come on, sleepy. Time to get up." He grinned, and she pulled the sheet back, clambering out of the bed she now thought of as theirs.

She rooted around the pile of clothing on the small chair at the end of the bed. "I'm going to need to do some washing," she muttered, pulling on her last clean set of underwear, a wispy pink bra and matching panty set, before tugging on her uniform.

"I need to do some as well. After our shift, we can go down and put some in together if you would like," he murmured over her shoulder, and she had a mental vision of the two of them sorting colors and whites.

The thought of such a mundane task taking on an intimate slant had Meredith turning quickly to capture his mouth in a quick kiss.

"What was that for?"

"For being you, for giving me a mental picture of the two of us seeing to everyday, mundane tasks." She grabbed his hand, needing to anchor herself once more. "Now come on, I need a coffee and I'm starved."

Meredith hauled him into the office where the small tray he had set up the night before waited for them to break their fast. There they poured steaming hot coffee into mugs and snapped up small pastries.

"Meredith?"

She turned at the uncertainty in his voice.

"I know this sounds absurd, but I'd really like you to resume your combat training with some of my people. Something about this mission feels off, and I'd just feel safer if I was certain your skills were current. I know Duvall raised it, but we haven't followed through. That bothers me. More than it should. Please?"

Never before had it seemed so important to put anyone's mind to rest with the results of her training activities, but he mattered in so many ways. She, too, felt that level of anxiety, so it was easy to nod her assent. "Yes. I actually considered talking to you about that anyway, so it won't be any hardship."

He nodded, and some of the anxiety in his face bled away.

They drank quietly as she thought over his words, his disquiet mirroring her own. "I'll be free around thirteen hundred hours, if that suits? I want to run some final diagnostics on the decoding programs, then I need to meet with Duvall for lunch in his office."

He nodded. "I can make that work." He reached over and placed a quick kiss on her lips as he rose.

"Where are you going?"

"The ambassador wants to have a look at the plans of the base and hear what we're doing to ensure his safety. I'm meeting with him in Duvall's office first up." He smiled, but somehow the action missed his eyes.

"Take care then."

She watched as he turned and left her there.

✪ ✪ ✪ ✪ ✪

The drugs had finally arrived. Crick Sur Banden could dimly detect the voice of his second as he emerged from the foggy cloud his body seemed to rest in. Lifting up with the little strength he still had, he wrenched the drugs out of the hand of the medic, feeling the cool, slick surface of the pill in his palm. His hands shook almost uncontrollably as his body continued to purge itself of the last traces of the drugs.

I need this. I have waited so long. He didn't know or care if he spoke the words. He wasn't sure exactly how long he'd been in limbo. The days blurred into each other, while the hunger screamed at him for a hit of the chemicals that would return strength to his weakened and delirious body. He tore at the cords attached to him—the ones keeping him hydrated and nourished. The movement exhausted him momentarily, and he panted at the exertion.

It had been years since he had needed to make do without the drugs, and he didn't care to go through the experience again anytime soon. He grunted his joy at finally having the Xeradax here on board the ship, and he knew he would soon feel the relief that could only come from the capsule in his hands. The one that would make the endless pain leave his body.

Crick Sur Banden shoved the pill into his mouth as saliva ran down the side of one emaciated cheek. He knew his body had wasted in the days and perhaps weeks that had passed. He had heard the low conversations of the medics discussing his appearance and general health.

"My Lord, perhaps you should—" The short medic in the green suit tried to stop his automatic movement of pill to mouth, and his anger rose to new levels, warming him from the inside. He swatted at the hand, and the medic sprang back from his clutching fingers.

"You will not stop me." Since the first Xeradax all those years ago, he'd never had to survive without his drugs for long. All he could remember was how quickly he'd felt the relief. That, together with the speed of his renewed strength, made it essential. Yet, this time it took longer, and from experience, he knew the results wouldn't last as long. That alone had become a large factor in the need to have an ongoing supply on hand.

As his body calmed, his thoughts grew clear, and Crick congratulated himself. He welcomed the fast, though not instant, relief and the definition that returned to his sight as the fog lifted from his brain.

"My Lord..." The medic hovered, irritating him with fluttering hands and a concerned face.

"Shardup." Spittle flew into the air, and the medic looked horrified as a glob hit his face. The physician scurried quickly to clear the wet substance with the sleeve of his suit, while the muscles of Crick's body jerked with the effort of reaching and taking the drugs, but soon, he knew, he would follow through on his plan to rid himself of these idiots who surrounded him.

How dare they try to limit his Xeradax and drug him? He had to control the high-pitched squeal of laughter that fought to escape his mouth. Hadn't he single-handedly orchestrate the ongoing battle with the humans? Wasn't he the one who taught the warriors how to fight them off and created the alliances with the pirates of Phobos?

"How dare you look at me this way? You're nothing more than an insignificant creature." The angry litany slipped from his mouth, and the man blanched.

He wanted to reach out and grab the insect. To squeeze the life from his body slowly, watching as his round face purpled with oxygen loss.

With great care, Crick restrained himself, feeling the welcome relief from the pain and befuddlement that had filled his brain since they left the Alpha Star Colony as his endorphins levels rose. Crick Sur Banden breathed deeply for what felt like the first time in months, the recycled air filling his lungs as he rose from the small medical bay.

"How long?" he asked.

His second loomed. "Mere days, My Lord. Four days have passed."

He scowled. "Then we shall not waste another moment. We must plan the best course to save the campaign. I will not accept anything less."

When he caught sight of his second, a moment of concern filled him. It was clear he was nervous, the way he shadowed the door and cast uncertain looks to the corridor.

"Get me out of here. I need to know what is going on." His words, while slurred, still carried his intentions clear enough to have his second moving forward on silent feet.

The medic scurried away, slipping on the cold, tiled floor, and he felt a jolt of amusement as the surgeon fell hard to the floor with a crack. Crick's unsteady feet settled on the floor, and his second slipped a steadying hand under his arm. He wanted to brush it away, but his legs wobbled uncertainly beneath his weight, so he had to accept the assistance. *For now.*

"Your cabin?"

Crick shook his head. "My ward room."

He accepted the support as they proceeded out of the small bay and down the cramped corridor. Everything still undulated before his glazed eyes, but each minute he felt better as his body welcomed the chemical reaction from the minerals in the Xeradax.

Crick walked in silence as he thought over the information required to plan the next step in his scheme. He needed to know the number of men they had lost on the Colony as well as what firepower and ships were lost. How many pilots remained, and how had his allies responded to the loss of the colony world?

He waited until the door closed behind him before beginning his interrogation.

Anger grew once more in his chest at the memory of the loss of his concubine on the Alpha Star Colony. *How could this have happened? How could we be infiltrated, invaded, and beaten? To think a female was instrumental in the theft of my concubine! Inconceivable!* Raw hatred spewed from his very pores at that thought.

"I have received a report that your concubine is currently en route to the Earth Admiralty, and I've given orders that we must be apprised once she arrives. Would you like a full tactical report now or later, after a meal and changing?" The words sounded distant, and he resented the need to hear them from someone else.

"Bring me food and wine and deal with that ineffectual medic." He jerked his arms, his anger stealing the last of his composure. "I will take a report in an hour. I also want to know the status of my...son."

Chapter 7

"Captain? We're ready to exit hyperspace." Chowd waited on the bridge, the buckles of his safety belt holding him firmly to the seat as the engines whined. He watched as the bridge became a hive of activity. Preparations to drop out of hyperspace continued around him, and voices broadcast over the comm systems, giving the necessary warnings and requests to strap in.

The entire senior staff moved into position and the sound of straps being applied filled the air. He dragged in a deep breath. After the last attack on leaving the Alpha Star Colony, he knew every crewmember was aware of the danger that lay ahead.

"Take us out of hyperspace and prepare to scan." Duvall's tense voice rose over the noise of discussions and engine vibrations.

A whine split the air, discordant for a moment before it ceased. Chowd waited for the jolt, but the change took place seamlessly with Raven in charge of the engineering section of the *Elector*. He allowed himself a small moment of levity.

"It was never that easy with Corbin Jard," Duvall said. A trickle of laughter echoed before dying away.

The star trails disappeared, and for the first time in over a week, the stars once more became visible dots and flashes all around the ship.

Chowd's hands moved over the keyboard. "Initial scans show no problems. I'm about to conduct a secondary sweep. Comms, start broadcasting the instructions to any Ru'Edan ships in this sector."

During the last few days, Meredith had translated the required message they were to broadcast so that any local Ru'Edan ships would understand the *Elector* had embarked on a diplomatic mission. His gaze darted over the screen, pleased not to find any rogues at this point. He continued working the search strings he and Meredith had devised based on the information they'd received before departing from the Alpha Star Colony.

"Still nothing, Captain, but I would expect they are staying out of sight for the moment." His stomach knotted at the potential danger they could find now in the Border Worlds. The knowledge of the Phobos pirates' cloaking abilities concerned him immeasurably.

A breath on the back of his neck startled him. "What?"

"I just had a thought. Run a scan for ionic emissions. We know the cloaking can only affect the ship itself, not the shadows of where the ships have been. If we can use the trajectory, we may be able to determine by triangulation if and where any ships may be." Meredith's voice was soft, as if she were thinking aloud.

Her words made sense. He knew each of the scanners looked for visual clues and needed re-teaching to look for anomalies.

"Doing it now." His fingers flew over the keyboard, inputting the data and algorithms that would teach the program what to look for.

He grunted and told himself it was no wonder she rated in the genius category. The computer bleeped, requiring a command override. He entered his passcode, and it sounded once more.

"Duvall?" He turned to see his captain and friend look at him, tense in the pressure of the moment.

"What?" His voice sounded clipped above the murmuring of the bridge staff. Duvall prowled toward him.

"I need you to override a command to enable a new search dynamic." Chowd grinned as Duvall quirked an eyebrow in question.

"Tell me more before I activate the override." Duvall demanded an immediate answer, but Meredith stepped forward before Chowd could start to explain.

The shadows caused by the equipment flickered over her face as she scanned the screen. He watched as she maintained her pose, aware that it hid the true level of her anxiety from those around her. He had learned her body signals now, continually fascinated by the woman before him.

"Duvall, it's a theory I've been working on. When the computer is running scans, no matter how good the program is, it needs to be taught to look for certain telltale signs. In this instance, there are no indicators to look for anything other than a visual clue, so we're telling it to look for the ionic breadcrumbs a ship leaves behind." She answered swiftly, watching the screen, and Chowd felt a bubble of pride.

This is my woman, and by Eshra, she's amazing! Chowd ruthlessly cut off the thought, or at least attempted to. But now it was there, in his conscious mind. *What? Since when has she been mine?* The thought buffeted him, stripping away his hard-won confidence.

The concept of one person taking a risk on him made him yearn for something he had never experienced. But the thought lodged there, eating at his brain and leaving him with a hollow feeling inside his gut. *What if she did become mine but then leaves me?* The thoughts should have shattered his concentration, but his years of experience in dealing with situations that would leave others reeling bolstered him. Chowd called on that training as he pushed through the emotions threatening to hold him in an iron grip. Beads of sweat stung his upper lip as he finished the programming in uncharacteristic silence.

He gripped the metal edge of the console, seeking the reassurance of the cold metal while Duvall typed in his manual override command. He felt the grip and bite as the console cut into the flesh of his palms, not hard enough to draw blood, but enough to sting the nerves endings viciously as he searched for the strength to back away from the feelings and emotions he didn't want and couldn't afford.

"Chowd?" Duvall's voice broke through the fog.

"Captain, I'm ready to start the new search string." He knew that wasn't the answer that Duvall needed to hear. He heard the concern in his captain's voice, but he couldn't give anything more right now. He turned, cutting off the view, and started when a warm hand patted him gently on one shoulder.

"I'll leave you to your work."

He knew Duvall meant to give him time and space. Chowd also knew Duvall had concluded something had left him unsettled—some hint must be present on his face. He tore himself away from the troubling thoughts, working to bring his attention back to the console. The lives of everyone on the ship sat in his hands, and he had to do this. Get it right.

Chowd heard the command for the escort ships to be deployed. He breathed a sigh of relief, watching as the emissions from the small and maneuverable craft showed clearly on the screen. He would see the same for the cloaked vessels, but nothing was there. He released another breath in a hiss before he stood, turning to leave the bridge, and glanced back.

The puzzled look on Meredith's face hurt, but right now, the bubbling emotion grew tighter with each beat of his heart, and he had to escape. He glanced away from her stricken face, striding toward the door and off the bridge without looking back.

Meredith groaned and stretched slowly, once more sitting at the desk in the security area.

Her home away from home, she thought sourly as she struggled to focus on the screen. Her eyes burned, and her head ached. The muscles in her shoulders and back screamed in pain.

Something had happened on the bridge with Chowd. Something she couldn't pin down, but it had wrought a disastrous change in him. Meredith swiped a tired hand over her face before getting a look at the chrono. Nearly 1900 hours. She recalled the meeting in Duvall's office that she needed to attend. *Barsha! I should be there now!*

Meredith moved sluggishly out of the cramped area, willing her tired legs to move faster, and made her way through the doors to the long corridor. The clank and whir from engineering caught her attention, and she turned to see what was causing the noise from the room beyond. She stopped, instead catching sight of Raven and Jemma entwined in each other's arms, their bodies locked at hip and lip beyond the doorway.

A passionate clinch in progress. She turned away, feeling voyeuristic seeing them in the dark shadows of the half-open door, and moved on quickly, hoping they hadn't seen her watching.

She longed for a relationship with that one person who would accept her for herself. Meredith had come to terms with the reality that her scatterbrained nature impacted the more down-to-earth issues, such as cleaning and cooking, but she'd always considered her ability to decode just about anything and her ability to recreate system programs with ease as part of the trade-off for her failings. Her own personal balance of day and night. Good and bad.

Right now, though, that didn't seem like enough to outweigh her fears. She trudged along, lifting one weary foot after the other, and wondering where on the ship Chowd could have stashed himself.

"He'd better turn up to the meeting," she muttered. "Who?"

She jumped, startled by the voice behind her. "Chowd! Where have you been?" She knew she sounded ridiculously cross, but she had worried herself to a mass of anxieties since he had left the bridge. She hadn't seen or heard from him, and that lack of communication hurt her.

Cool it, Meredith! We've only had a week together. Subconsciously she knew they hadn't made any promises when they became lovers, and they'd only spent limited time together, but she'd thought they had some kind of deep connection. In her mind, it equated to much more than just super hot sex.

She wanted to grind her teeth in frustration. She wanted forever, but it looked like that wouldn't happen for them. A sharp stab of pain filled her. Meredith locked her knees and waited for it to pass.

"I had some things to do." His eyes slid away from her gaze, and emptiness settled in the pit of her belly.

He's cutting me off. The pain she felt at the thought of ending their relationship stole her breath before she pulled herself up straight. She needed to hold it together.

"Fine. Just so you know, I got a little further along with the messages and the plans." She threw the words over her shoulder as she whirled back toward the office door, but a soft hand resting on her arm stopped her.

"Meredith? I'm sorry. I didn't mean to worry you. I just...I just needed to work something out."

The uncertainty and the confusion in his voice made her close her eyes. The knowledge that he couldn't, for whatever reason, share his problems sat like a lump in her chest. *Is it that he doesn't trust me? Or is it something more? Why am I even worrying? Maybe I should go back to my own cabin or at least tell him he can sleep on the couch?* But the thoughts felt mean. No matter the pain, she wouldn't...she couldn't...treat him like that.

"I shouldn't have gotten upset with you. I'm sorry." She bit her lip, the sting of tooth on soft flesh reminding her to stay in the now.

"No. I should have contacted you. But I can't talk about it now. Please?"

She accepted that they couldn't get into the conversation they needed to have right now. Meredith lightly rubbed the hand still resting on her arm before she touched the palm screen, and the door slid open. Together they entered the office. Duvall, Mellissa, Grayson, and Elara sat waiting within the interior of the room. Meredith and Chowd sat down.

Duvall checked his chrono. "Do you know where Jemma and Raven are?"

Meredith blushed and avoided looking at her brother. It still embarrassed her to think of the hot kiss she had spied on her way there. "I think they were on their way when they got...ummm...sidetracked." She fumbled with her pocket as she mumbled the words past her stiff lips. She knew her glowing red skin gave away her discomfort.

Elara snorted. "More like lip-locked, you mean!" Her eyes twinkled in her scarred face— the marks on Elara's skin physical reminders of the torture she'd suffered at the hand of Crick

Sur Banden and his researchers.

Meredith stole a swift glance up, and she saw that Mellissa had to quietly cover a laugh with her hand. Meredith wished there was a hole in the floor to swallow her up. She wasn't quite sure how to react in these sorts of situations.

"I'm beginning to think this ship has become a floating dating service," groused Duvall. Meredith knew, though, that his words were in fun as he leaned back in his command chair. "We need to start. As we're entering the Border Worlds, we need our wits about us. Meredith?"

She smiled, finally finding level ground. Work, she not only understood but could also contain. She wasted no time pulling the small data card from her pocket and sliding it into the corresponding slot in front of her.

"I've started to make inroads on some of the code. We already know that they're aware Chowd is one of the crew, and they know he's the security chief. What we didn't know is that Crick Sur Banden planned on grabbing him at some point, once they re-established their earlier base on Rubicon VII. They have strategic bases in several sectors, including this—" Meredith pointed to a system on the holo-map she engaged. "—and this."

The door chimed, and Raven and Jemma entered together, hand in hand, a sheepish look on their faces. Their mouths were slightly swollen, and once more Meredith glanced away from them. The memory of the two lovers entwined around each other filled her with embarrassed heat.

"As I was saying, I've been scouring the plans we found on the Alpha Star Colony. I've also extrapolated that they continue to have a presence on Otega, but I'll come back to that later."

She stopped, looking around the table to see if anyone's face showed puzzlement at her words. The only one that did was Chowd's, which paled. She extended a hand and grabbed his under the table, wincing as he squeezed lightly.

"We also know Crick has an alliance with the Phobos pirates. I did note some information concerning them in my report, among many other factors. I have the location of their base, which we should relay back to the Admiralty, and as I also found a detailed layout of their base, I think it makes sense to send that through as well. Seems Crick only wanted them on his side while the going was good though. He plans to get rid of them once he has damaged the Earth Empire sufficiently to run a final incursion on Earth himself. It's all there in his coded tactical plan." She shoved the printed matter to Duvall who grunted.

"That's good to know, but do you have any information on the cloaking technology or their plans for the ruling Ru'Edan Senate?" Duvall asked.

"There's a lot more, but I've barely scratched the surface and have been running data matches pretty much without a break for the last week we've been in hyperspace. What you do need to know, though, the one biggest news flash...his log. It has a record of his rambling thoughts, and surprisingly, it's not coded or encrypted." Meredith rubbed her ear as she considered how best to explain her concerns. "It doesn't make an awful lot of sense. I mean, it's clear he never expected us to successfully infiltrate the colony base and capture it, but there's a rant, or several million, about you, Duvall, and about Chowd too. I also found his plans for the infiltrator we sent back to the Admiralty."

She gulped again as the remembered bile rose up.

"I have to say, I'm damned glad we got her out of there. His plan was to impregnate her and—" She glanced away, unable to air the revelations. "Well, it's all there. I've started a process of cross-matching the style of his later entries to earlier records that I found, but there seems to be a definite deterioration in his mental state. I'd like Elara to take a look, though, if possible. It would be handy to have a professional opinion of what I'm seeing."

Elara nodded slowly and added a little bit into the scrolling information on the screen with quick taps to the console before her. "I'd be quite interested to see them. While we're on that subject, Chowd, did you say you had heard he had a long-time addiction to Xeradax?"

"Yes. My contacts say it is long running, dating back to my escape."

For a moment, Meredith was sure she caught a glint of humor, but that quickly died away and she wondered if maybe she'd imagined it.

"Meredith, if you would transfer those files to my office desk screen," Elara requested. "I will ask that you remain available to me, though, in case there is something there that might help us work out his thought patterns."

"Of course, Elara. Now to Otega."

"I can fill you in there," Chowd said. "Otega is a planet in deep space, situated in the X'il quadrant. It's where he settled a base after he and the rogues first escaped. It's more of a planetoid, with a deep underground bunker. I have personal knowledge of it, Duvall, and will fill you in later."

Chowd's words sounded distant, and it occurred to her that this was probably where he grew up. The timeframe fit along with their knowledge of Crick's previous strongholds.

They settled into forming a plan, and for once she played an integral part, something she'd never before experienced, having always stayed sequestered on Aenna.

"Now," Duvall said, "we need to discuss the matter of the ambassador. Grayson has informed me that it could take us another few days to get through the Border Region and meet our escort. Elara, has Jemma been cleared for active duty?"

"Yes, as of this morning, I have signed her off to resume duty tomorrow." Elara smiled, and Jemma beamed exultantly.

"Thank God! Now I can be useful again." The words burst from the perfectly formed lips of the woman who had changed so much from the bad-tempered and demanding young woman Meredith had first met. Her status as a combat pilot attached to the *Elector* and a certified Ace clearly had made a change in her life. That, and her pairing with Raven, the engineer.

"Fine, then Grayson will roster you into the rotation flying wing for the *Elector* while we travel. Meredith will continue to search for the key to tracking these ships, but we all need to remain alert. We can't count on any help in this area of space."

Meredith got the impression that Duvall, while feeling the strain of his command, also relished the thrill of the hunt.

"Raven and Chowd? I'll need you to stay back for a few minutes to set up a security meeting. We'll reconvene when necessary. Dismissed."

She rose, not knowing what would happen once she left the room but hoping Duvall wouldn't get involved in her mixed-up relationship with Chowd. She already had enough on her plate with Chowd's hot and cold behavior and the task ahead of them.

✪ ✪ ✪ ✪ ✪

Meredith waited in the cabin, hoping Chowd would return soon. The tiny desk screen beeped as she continued tedious grunt work. "He can't be too far away, surely?"

He'd been brooding for the last few days, and it felt like she was balancing on a high-wire. All careful words and actions without the depth of emotion she'd started to rely on. She felt thin and stretched by the situation.

And Chowd? He'd been nearly silent.

Her head ached. It did that most days at the moment, and sleeping had become something she fought, not wanting to face the erotic fantasies her brain replayed nightly. "Ha! Erotic fantasies that are so far from my reality."

She knew each night he fought exhaustion. He'd work until late into the night, here in his office. He avoided sharing this bed with her. He averted his gaze and he didn't speak. That hurt most of all.

Last night, she'd worked until halfway through an algorithm when she must have dropped off, her body finally giving in. She'd woken this morning bent at an unnatural angle, her body twisted around the humming machine ready for the next layer of code. She'd cursed her dreams that left her body tense with arousal, nipples tight, and between her legs, her panties wet with hunger. It was the first night in nearly a week that she'd slept for more than four hours straight.

To make things worse, he hadn't joined her in the bed. Not once since that night. She knew of his confusion, though she didn't understand it. Meredith saw the longing in his eyes when he thought she wasn't looking, but the wall of ice between them kept growing, and she didn't know how to get through it. Truthfully, now she wasn't sure if she even wanted to. The burn in her eyes grew as moisture welled.

"I can't do this anymore," she said into the silence. "I can't stay with him any longer." Once said, she acknowledged the truth in the words. It hurt, shredding her deep inside where she knew she'd never recover.

Meredith stood up after making a split-second decision. In the bedroom, she grabbed the bag she'd brought to the cabin, then carefully scooped up her clothing and toiletries and stashed them within the confines of the leather. *No time like the present.*

It didn't seem fair to impose on him any longer, let alone continue the torture. Honestly, the situation just left her both hurting and angry. "I need to move back into my cabin." Her sight blurred, and she realized it was because of her tears. Meredith dashed away the wet tracks dribbling down her face with the back of her shaking fingers.

"What are you doing?"

The voice at the door startled her so that she dropped the lingerie to the bed. Her heart thudded wildly in her chest, and she cursed her bad timing. Why did he have to turn up now before she was done packing her things?

"I just...think I should go back..." Her words were thick as she kept her back turned to him. *Don't let him see.* Meredith wasn't sure though, if it was to spare him or herself the humiliation and pain.

One breath. Another. *Concentrate on blinking and clearing away the tears.* She furtively swiped the tears from her face. *Get yourself under control before you face him.*

"Meredith? Turn around, please. Tell me why you're leaving."

Could this pain grow any worse? He had no idea what he was doing to her. "Meredith?"

His voice was quiet but demanding, and stars save her, a sob ripped from her mouth, her chest heaving as the pressure released in the single eruption of sound. She covered her mouth with her shaking hand, hoping to hold the pain in, but it didn't work.

She sucked in a deep breath and held still, her eyes tightly shut. "I can't... I have to..." She didn't hear him move toward her. Shock zinged through her when his arms folded around her, steadying her, and she wanted to burrow in. She ached, needing his support, but unsure if it were really offered. Wring from him a declaration that he wouldn't do this to her, leave her in an emotional limbo.

She pushed against him as frustration mounted. Not ever again! Close her out of his thoughts? No! The voice inside her reminded her it was his actions. Not hers. He had closed the communication channels, avoided her, and pushed her away.

But her heart, battered and ripped to bleeding shreds, desperately needed the reassurance of him close to her. Her world shattered, leaving her stranded on an emotional sea while she searched for a way out.

"You can't leave. Please, Meredith. Don't leave me. Not now."

Meredith nearly missed his quietly spoken words in her

haze of misery. His hands, gentle on her, turned her to his chest before folding them around her. She inhaled the scent of him, the one she'd missed in the last few days. Felt the strength in his arms and the closeness she craved.

"I'm sorry. I didn't mean to hurt you. I just needed time to understand my feelings." He held her close. "I didn't know it would hurt you like this." His lips strayed close to the side of her face, and she felt the subtle whisper of his breath against her skin.

She shuddered as the feeling that had bloomed in her chest so large it threatened to choke her finally started to subside. "You pushed me away." The strangled words escaped like a painful accusation, and she felt him flinch.

"Yes, I did, and it was wrong. So wrong. I didn't know how to cope. I don't know how to do this without hurting you."

She willed her body to settle as he held her close to him. The heavy beating of his heart beneath her ear reassured her that he struggled just as much as she did.

"You don't just shut out someone unless you no longer want to be with them. You can't just ignore me and think it'll be fine. It won't be." She trembled but pushed out of his hold.

He took her hand and tugged her gently toward the bed. "It scares me. I feel myself falling deeper into this..." He waved his hand and looked so confused.

Meredith almost laughed. "This what?"

"I don't know. These emotions scare me. I've never experienced something like this." He sat down, and she followed, perched on the side of the bed. "But my reaction was wrong. Next time I do something like that, maybe you should just hit me over the head and make me see reason." His eyes pleaded with her for understanding.

The coldness that had settled around her heart began to melt, just a little. Not totally, but it left a chink unprotected. Meredith desperately wanted to believe his words.

She giggled, a watery hiccup sound. "Like that would do me any good."

"Meredith, I can't tell you enough how sorry I am. I don't know what to call this emotion inside me. Not yet." His eyes willed her to understand, and she nodded, understanding his need for time. "I just need to work it out. But I promise, from this point on, I will talk to you. As best I can. Just...just don't leave me?" His voice tapered off and his face shuttered.

He's truly scared. Love for this complicated and damaged man rushed up once more. Meredith inclined her head in acceptance. Maybe they still had a chance.

✪ ✪ ✪ ✪ ✪

Chowd waited at the table. The tactical meeting had gone well with everyone around the table offering workable solutions while Grayson chaired the meeting. Duvall and the ambassador had been absent as they communicated with the Ru'Edan ship and took the long-range transmissions from the mothership regarding the transportation of the ambassador to the small planet midway within the Ru'Edan Space.

Why is this taking so long? We've been here for weeks. Chowd curled his fist tightly, aware that this brinkmanship necessitated diplomatic handling. It wasn't his natural way of behaving.

He flexed a sore hand. He'd been burning off his frustration with long and involved training sessions. And nights shared with Meredith. He grinned at that. She was simply amazing.

"Chowd?" His commbadge squarked. "Yes?"

"Are there any developments?" His second was as tense as he was. In fact, all his men were tightly wound springs, but tempers were fraying as the frustration wore on the crew and the highly unstable atmosphere on the *Elector* came close to explosive.

"No. I'll update you after the meeting." He tapped his fingers on the tabletop. The meeting had already been deferred twice today. Hopefully it wouldn't be again.

Meredith sat down beside him and the peace she exuded swept over him, blanketing him and renewing his patience. He smiled and gripped her hands under the table, as had become their practice in the meetings.

Duvall strode into the room, his face tight, and the ambassador followed him, the door sliding quietly closed behind them. Clearly the negotiations had tanked. He released Meredith's hand, ready for anything.

"We've just received a message from the Ru'Edan mothership confirming that they will finalize the transfer of the ambassador to their ship. They stand by their refusal to allow the *Elector* any further into their space, so we'll need to send a small team with the ambassador to ensure his safety."

Chowd straightened in his chair, ready to object.

Duvall pinned him with a sharp glance. "After I'm done, Chowd. I've already made arrangements for the transfer. Jemma, you'll pilot the shuttle and I'll send Raven with you. He'll act as your engineer in this situation. Raven, you'll check the shuttle for bugs and anything... *inconvenient*." Duvall raised a hand before anyone could speak. "Not that I expect anything like that, but it's a necessary precaution. Chowd, handpick two of your men to accompany you and Meredith as guards."

When he glanced at Meredith, Chowd's gut froze.

"I'm sending you too, Meredith. While I would prefer you *here*, the Admiral did order that you be available to decode and translate, as required by the ambassador and his assistant. Chowd will ensure you are guarded at all times."

Duvall and Chowd's gazes met and he read the fear in his captain's eyes.

The ambassador looked away briefly, and a hint of moisture glossed his eyes. "Captain McCord, once more, I protest. There was an implied assurance given by the Admiralty to the Empire that I would remain aboard the *Elector* for the duration of the travel then return the same way. I want it placed on the record that I formally object." His voice betrayed his anger, the words steely and cold.

Chowd felt his fingers flex around the butt of his small laser pistol in an automatic response, and he released the hard, metallic surface as quickly as he had grasped it. While he doubted the ambassador posed any serious threat to Duvall, he would always protect his captain first.

The ambassador caught his action and blanched.

"Stop it," Meredith hissed at him, laying her hands on his. Chowd exhaled heavily but gave in to her demands.

"Chowd, explain to the ambassador my reasoning." Duvall's tight voice betrayed his frustration. It was clear Duvall was minding his manners, as he'd usually have exploded in a bubble of fury. It was obvious he hated every second of the restriction. *Maybe we'd all better watch ourselves for the next little while.*

"Ambassador, with all due respect, we are entering their planetary space, so they call the shots. In this case, we can offer a highly trained support team. Jemma is the best pilot we have. A certified Ace. Raven is our senior engineer, and can make sure it is as safe as we can make it. My men will be handpicked. Everyone is considered deadly in a range of combat types from hand-to-hand to extensive weaponry skills. Meredith can intercept and decode as needed, so we always know their movements." Chowd paused, waiting for the man to understand the lengths they were willing to take to protect him. "As we're also unsure of the fluency of the senators in our own language, it seems appropriate to have one of our own there, just in case her skills are required. She is also certified in high-level programming sequences, should the need arise. I am fluent in almost every dialect of Ru'Edan society, both high and low class."

Chowd stopped and looked meaningfully at the man before him.

"At no time will we allow you to be placed in jeopardy. Each and every one of us will give our all to protect you and ensure the treaty is negotiated successfully. In fact, we'll even take a hit if necessary to ensure your safety." He smiled at the ambassador, who paled at the last comment.

"What if we come under attack and someone is hurt?" The ambassador spat the words triumphantly at him. Chowd had prepared for this, knowing he meant if he was hurt.

"My men are all trained as field medics. They must pass stringent accreditation, and I can personally vouch for every man in my command."

The ambassador settled as every argument was countered.

Duvall indicated to Grayson, who took over. "We have approximately five hours to prepare the shuttle and have all of you aboard. I'm going to need you to run over it, Jemma, and ensure the pre-flight checks are completed ahead of time. It's being fueled as we speak. I suggest that you need to prepare for anything up to six or seven days. The *Elector* will enter into an orbit in the location of their choice within the hour. You will then travel to the coordinates we've received and rendezvous with them. From there, they will transport you to the satellite, where you, Ambassador, will be addressing the Senate. At all times, you will be guarded by our own people. Raven and Jemma will also continue to act as guards. The shuttle is to be placed at your service day and night."

The ambassador scowled at Grayson.

Chowd nodded at the list of precautions they would take. "Duvall, I believe that covers everything we need to know immediately."

Grayson and Duvall steepled their fingers on the tabletop, a signal Chowd knew meant the meeting had concluded.

"Then I believe this meeting is done. Be alert and aware. Anything at all that causes you concern, discuss it with Chowd. Meredith, you will remain with Chowd at all times." Duvall's voice was strained on the last words, and Chowd knew of his concern sending his sister into an unknown and potentially dangerous situation.

They both knew she was well trained and capable at her job, though there was some concern that she might not be capable of protecting herself, but the time had come to let her do what she did best in the field. His gut churned with worry. Until now, she'd remained mainly confined to a lab on Aenna. He would ensure her protection at all times.

They stood, and he grunted as her fingers twisted in his, and Chowd realized just how tightly he'd been squeezing them. He released them, and a muttered "Thanks" reached his ears.

Chowd smiled. *She's feisty, my Meredith. Now to make sure she comes home. In one piece.*

They left the office, making their way down the corridor at a quick clip. The clank of feet on the metallic planking filled the air, and they reached their cabin swiftly. His hand splayed over the palm reader as they reached the small office and lounge area, and she turned quickly to place her soft lips against his.

"Thank you." Meredith smiled at him, her eyes twinkling. "What for?"

"For not telling Duvall to keep me here." She cocked her head to one side, studying him. "Now, come on. We should pack and make sure everything we need is stowed aboard the ship."

He enjoyed the sight of her trim figure and firm, pert bottom as she headed to the dark cabin beyond.

Chapter 8

They buckled in. The clicks and clacks of tongues sliding home in the metal clasps filled the air. Chowd looked out into the bay, where Jemma manually checked everything outside the shuttle. This shuttle looked larger than the small craft she had flown on the Alpha Star Colony, which sat just beyond the tips of the shuttle's wings.

This shuttle was newer, its gray paint unmarked, unlike older shuttles the *Elector* had received from the *Star of Ishtar*, which wore their pockmarks and scratches as badges of honor.

The door slid open, and Duvall clambered in, which surprised him. "I just wanted to give something to Meredith," Duvall said as he made his way up to the seat before leaning across to reach his sister.

Chowd pushed back into his seat, allowing Duvall access.

"Stay safe." Duvall thrust something into her hands. He placed a quick kiss on her forehead before pulling back and piercing Chowd with his gaze. "I want her back in one piece." His voice sounded brusque, and Chowd nodded once, then Duvall pulled away and disappeared through the doorway.

A commotion at the door took his mind off what Duvall had handed over to Meredith. Jemma climbed in, making her way slowly to the front, followed by Raven. Just one seat remained empty in the passenger section of the shuttle. Chowd looked forward from his position at the back to the pilot's seat and spied the empty navigator and communications officers' chairs.

Jemma and Raven donned military issue headsets, but knowing Jemma, she would soon discard it, preferring to fly free of restrictions.

The ambassador hunched across the aisle, gazing out the window. He looked like a man alone and, from what Chowd could tell from his protective posture, frightened. Since the death of his PA, he'd hardly interacted with the personnel. Not that any of the crew had much common ground with him, but still, in the enclosed space of the *Elector*, and now traveling to some unknown planet on a ship full of potential threats, it was Chowd's responsibility to ensure that divide narrowed. The ambassador had to trust him and converse freely. They didn't need to be friends, but making a connection would help both sides feel comfortable communicating information.

"I like the idea of traveling like this." Meredith's voice, lazy in the silence, had him turning his head.

"Why?"

"Because it means I'm not just stuck in my small cubicle on Aenna. I love my work, don't get me wrong, but I don't want to be shut up like that forever." Her eyes closed as she smiled slightly.

The engines engaged and vibrated throughout the small cabin. Duvall had retreated from the hanger, and the shuttle whined as it rose off the plascrete and started its slow movement forward into the darkness beyond the *Elector*.

Chowd reclined into the padded seat, thinking over Meredith's words. He'd never really considered that she might not want to keep Aenna, or any safe place, as her base. Quiet voices echoed from the front of the ship. Most of the others assumed introspective poses. Some would watch as they traveled toward their mission. The air practically crackled with tension. But Meredith didn't twitch or seem to tighten any muscle, and for the first time he wondered if the steel spine she exhibited went deeper than the mask she showed the world.

Frustration at being unable to do anything clawed at him so he considered the roster of the ambassador's protection teams. They could work in three shifts, his shift splitting the focus between both Meredith and the ambassador. Eight hours on and sixteen off; it was the only workable solution he could come up with. Working alone was out of the question, particularly for the women, and he couldn't count on Meredith's skills. They'd improved but... He pinched the bridge of his nose as pressure welled. He knew Meredith was well trained, but still, he had qualms about taking her into a potentially dangerous situation. It felt...wrong...somehow.

Jemma and Raven had meshed together and became an effective team, and his two security officers had worked together for many years. Then he had himself and Meredith.

The engine of their shuttle had settled into a hum, and he glanced out the portal beside him. Two small fighters escorted them from the ship and would remain with them for the next hour before returning to the *Elector*. Then they would continue alone until the meeting point several hours away. Chowd released the tension in his shoulders, rolling them as the ship traveled through the inky blackness of space. The occasional blip of starlight filled the portal as they spun slightly, giving him a view of the *Elector* as they moved away.

He looked forward once more. He released a frustrated breath before unclipping his webbed safety belt.

"What are you doing?" Meredith asked, suspicious.

"I'm going to see if there is any sign of the ship we are supposed to rendezvous with." He stood and heard the snick of a belt.

"I'll come with you."

"No, stay in your seat. I'll only be a few minutes, and I promise to let you know once I have an idea." He lurched up the narrow path between the seats, reached the pilot's and co-pilot's seating, and squatted. "Any idea when we'll see the ship?"

"I have something on my radar on the heading they gave us but not enough information yet to make even an uninformed guess. I would imagine within an hour or two we should have enough information to relay back to the *Elector*." Jemma indicated the scanner on the surface in front of her. The scene outside was inky with flashes dotting here and there from the stars all around them. The reality of the vastness of space never ceased to inspire him.

"How is everyone else coping?" He could count on Raven to bring him back to the matter at hand.

"Fine. The ambassador's still very introspective and

quiet. I understand he is grieving, but he has a job to do. I just hope he's capable. At least his interest in Meredith has waned." Chowd added the last part under his breath.

"Yeah, well, maybe you better find out what's going on in his mind, so the rest of us know." Jemma's terse words made him smile. She always spoke her mind. Something he applauded, though he did have some concern at what she might say while on this mission.

"You know—" he started, but Raven shook his head in warning.

"What?" Jemma said. "To keep my mouth shut? Yeah, I can do that as much as I do my job. Just don't give me a reason to show them how damned good I am." Her cold words warred with the mutinous look on her face, and he swallowed his concerns.

"Jemma, you're a woman after my own heart." Chowd thought better of the time and place, and he laid a gentle hand on her shoulder, pleased when she laughed off his comment. Then he stood, made his way unsteadily back, and slipped into the seat beside the ambassador. "Sir?"

The older man turned toward him. "Yes?" He waited quietly, his faded eyes troubled and lost for an instant before turning flat. "How can I help?"

"Sir, I need to know your plans while we are in transit so I can make effective use of our team." He sat still, waiting as the ambassador gathered himself.

"What do you mean?"

Chowd felt a brief surge of pity for the man. That emotion swiftly disappeared, replaced by frustration at having to spell out what he needed to know. He controlled his temper.

"I need to know, are you planning on engaging with the Ru'Edan or keeping to your cabin or suite? That way I can finalize the roster as required and ensure your safety." He kept his words low and soft.

The lost look vanished for an instant, and he could see the canny man, the ambassador, he would expect to see under normal conditions.

"Without a personal assistant, it's difficult for me to undertake extra duties. Portia used to read through briefings and ensure I had the pertinent facts. She kept me on time and on track. Now...well, without her, I'll have to attempt to manage. Unless..." He brightened for an instant, casting a glance toward Meredith.

Chowd seethed at the thought of this man being any closer to her than necessary. Something about his attitude toward her continued to set off his inbuilt radar.

"Warrant Officer Gentry is within the team—" the ambassador started.

"No, I'm afraid she won't be available to you for that. She will continue monitoring communications and acting as my offsider. I will be your main guard during your hours of duty." He watched as the ambassador subsided against the padded seats with a heavy exhalation.

"Very well. Then I need to do some research." He turned his head away, and Chowd recognized dismissal when he saw it. He slipped from the seat and back across the aisle into the empty seat next to Meredith.

"So, did you find out what you needed to know?" Her eyes searched his face.

"Yeah. Now I can finish my plan." He pulled out his palm unit and waited for her to lean back and close her eyes before he started work, enjoying the feel of her body resting against his.

For just a moment, he stopped, knowing he would need to tell her soon about the potential threat his birthright could pose to the mission. For now, he took comfort in her closeness.

✪ ✪ ✪ ✪ ✪

Meredith dozed lightly, waking irregularly, welcoming Chowd's presence. At some point, she had a vague memory of shivering and his soothing words and touches. He must have covered her with a light material...something. *Is it a dream?* Maybe, she thought.

Now she woke fully, feeling heavy and unrefreshed with gritty eyes and a woolly head that interfered with clarity of thought. Travel naps never got any better. She stretched in the enclosed space, the material dropping to the ground with a barely discernible sound. She opened her eyes to see Chowd still working, the sleeves of his shirt rolled up and the tight sinews of his arms bared for her view.

"Where's your jacket?" Meredith looked around, noting for the first time that it lay pooled at her feet. "Chowd? You're going to get sick. Put it back on!" She hooked her fingers under the lightweight material and hefted it up before handing it over to him.

He turned and smiled. "You needed it more than me."

Meredith blushed and hoped her hair wasn't sticking up at all ends, as it usually did. She felt the heat spread over her face as she pushed hair back off her burning skin. "Where are we?" *He always puts me first.* She couldn't escape this truth.

"Well, you've been asleep for about two hours. The indications from Jemma and Raven show it should only be about another hour until we make visual contact with our rendezvous. Did you want to go freshen up?"

He spoke with a professionally remote tone, which had her looking up, a feeling of alarm sweeping through her. There was something he wasn't telling her. "What is it?"

"Nothing. I'd just feel happier if you were strapped back in sooner rather than later." He still evaded her question, averting his eyes. She couldn't find another description for his actions. He didn't want to share whatever it was that concerned him, but it was obviously important enough to bother him. She'd have to take that up with him at a later point.

He stood up to move aside for her. Meredith made her way to the sanitary unit at the back of the shuttle, closing the door and looking at herself in the small mirror. A tinge of pink still remained on her cheeks from her disjointed nap, and her hair sat in disarray, reminding her of a lover just leaving a passionate embrace. The thought made her smile, but the expression dropped from her face as a new thought rose in her mind. How would they handle their relationship aboard the Ru'Edan ship?

She shook her head and turned to make use of the ablution room. It truly wasn't the time or the place to consider physical intimacies, but she bit her lip as a frisson of arousal speared her.

She gripped the sink, waiting and willing it to pass, then she hurried through the personal tasks before slipping out the door.

As she returned to her seat, the thought rolled over in her mind. *Will he remain with me?* She knew Ru'Edanians had some interesting customs regarding living arrangements and gender roles, not that she had an extensive knowledge. How would this affect their relationship? Would he need to bunk elsewhere? Her internal tussle had to end. Maybe I'm just borrowing trouble, she reminded herself firmly, slipping back into the seat while Chowd waited.

Meredith shivered slightly as the buckles, cold in the shuttle's thin oxygen, clipped back together. Chowd reached across the space and covered her hand with his. She sucked in a deep breath, anticipating the mission ahead.

"It'll be okay. We'll get through this." His words were low, and in spite of his intentions, they didn't inspire confidence. Perhaps it was something in his eyes, or the way he said the words. Her knee jittered up as the tension zinged through her system. She held on to that hand like an anchor in a tossing sea. *That pretty much sums up the situation.*

His seat unit beeped, and he cast a quick look at the item, a frown marring his perfect face. "I'm needed up front, and you should probably come along too."

With a sigh, Meredith unclipped the buckles once again before he tugged on her hand as they made their way to the empty seats at the front of the shuttle.

"Glad you two are here. Okay, this is what we have. An incoming transmission from behind the moon. There's some interference there though. Can you clean that up, Meredith? Chowd, I need you to take Raven's place while he works the weapons. Not that we really have a lot, and I don't expect we'll need them, but we have to get through this, preferably in one piece. So it's better to be prepared."

Jemma's voice remained calm as she outlined the actions they would take in a worst-case scenario. Meredith knew Jemma had changed a lot since the bratty, young woman had boarded the *Elector* for the first time. Now she simply felt amazement at the woman who took control smoothly, making split-second decisions, which would save their lives if needed.

Meredith turned around, orienting herself to the console before placing her hands on the equipment to begin scanning and decoding the incoming transmission. Jemma could have done this herself, but Meredith knew that Jemma wanted to give her total attention to the role of pilot in case anything went wrong. The task itself was simple—clean up the transmission— yet she'd never felt the effects of the accuracy and speed of her work so keenly. A lump formed in her throat, and she felt the swift heartbeat under her skin as adrenalin started pumping into her veins.

A shaft of excitement sparked, and she smiled, knowing that what she did now was real. *This is what I'm meant to do.* The thought shocked her for just an instant before she found her equilibrium, and her fingers started moving over the desk screen with conviction.

"Jemma, I think we have a problem. From what I can tell, there is an intercept in place, with the order to forcibly board us." The words stuck in her throat as she rechecked her work, fingers now flying over the screen.

"Fuck! Are you sure?" Jemma spun her seat back to peer over her shoulder. "Of course you are. Okay, let's make sure everyone is buckled up. Raven, can you get everyone organized?"

Meredith took a moment to look over her shoulder, surprised to see the cold, hard look in Jemma's eyes. This

Jemma, the warrior woman, was one she'd never encountered before.

"Meredith, I need you to see if you can make your way through their jammers to find out what they are saying to each other, because I'd be damned surprised if there isn't another one out there. Can you manage that?" The violet eyes zeroed onto her face, and Meredith felt a smile forming. She quickly turned back to the screen.

"I can do better than that. I'm already seeking their secure bands and...hang on...there! I'm in." She turned back to look at Chowd. His face mirrored hers with a private smile of shared triumph.

"Damn. You're good, aren't you?" His voice rang with admiration, and she blushed. "Yeah, but it's no good being good at something if you can't use it in a practical application." She turned back to her screen. "Lots of my classmates were quick and efficient but unsuited to field work, which is the reason they continue to work for the Admiralty on station or planets. I was categorized as suitable for fieldwork, but because of my intelligence quotient was kept sequestered at the Admiralty. Each time I requested reassignment, they used the argument that I was too important to the Admiralty to be placed in a potential combat zone." The words trailed away to silence as Raven looked at her, amazed.

Ugh, too much information. Meredith rolled her eyes at herself before Raven rose and made his way between the rows of seating, requesting everyone prepare for any possible eventualities.

Meredith watched from the corner of her eye. The security officers betrayed nothing, their faces calm, but the ambassador blanched. She felt pity for the man who was now a fish out of proverbial water. This should have been a straightforward mission. Now they just had to survive long enough to finalize the treaty between the two species. She turned her mind back to the job at hand.

The flashing light on the screen alerted her as she shoved

the earpieces in, flicking on the comm system. "Incoming transmission," she muttered as she worked furiously to patch through a dual band system with the original Ru'Edan dialect and herself translating.

"This is the Ru'Edan ship *Fiemanskar*. Pull to and prepare to be boarded." The tinny words broadcast from behind the moon, interference making it harder to understand.

"Shit! No way. Preparing for evasive maneuvers." Jemma's voice chimed through the cold silence. "Tell them we carry the Earth Ambassador Vierghent, en route for the Ru'Edan mothership. Tell them we will not allow a boarding party."

Meredith nodded and sent the message in the native tongue of the Ru'Edan ruling class. She could hear muttering and a quick conversation, the guttural tones telling her which of the lesser dialects to try, but no matter how she recalibrated, she couldn't make out the discussion. So she placed a command to patch Chowd in.

"Chowd? Can you tell me what they're saying?" She imagined his eyes closing as he concentrated.

"No. It's a lesser dialect and one I don't know."

She exhaled heavily, knowing that put them at a distinct tactical disadvantage. She mentally filed away the knowledge of this new language for future investigation.

The whine of the engines grew as Jemma started talking again. "Tell them we're about to send a distress call, should they decide to push the issue. Tell them that we will also be taking this up directly with the senators on our arrival. See if we can't bluff our way through."

In the time Meredith spent preparing and sending the information, Jemma reprogrammed their heading for departure in case they needed to make a swift exit. The engines thrummed beneath their feet.

Meredith relayed the terse words and once more waited. Her leg started jiggling again, the up and down motion quick and tense.

"We'll wait for the mothership to arrive." Chowd's

answer left Meredith feeling shaky, and she still felt concern at their unprotected position.

Meredith shared the information and received a short nod from Jemma while Chowd looked coldly remote, one hand firmly resting on the laser pistol he wore.

"Raven? Check the scanners again and see if there is any sign of that goddamn mothership. I'd feel a whole heap better knowing it is on the way to give us some cover." Jemma's voice echoed in the enclosed cabin.

Meredith's stomach clenched for just a moment before she forced herself to relax. First fingers, then arms. Methodically, she worked on each section, aware, though, that she might need to work at any second.

"Here they come." Jemma chewed out the words, her gaze firmly on the ship ahead of them. They watched on the radar as the ship moved from its position hidden by the shadows of the moon, then ceased its trajectory. "Chowd? Start scanning that ship. We need to know exactly what they have. And keep an eye out for incoming. That mothership can't be too far away."

In the back of Meredith's mind, the sight of this ship—the fact it wasn't the one they were to meet—concerned her. They hadn't left, just stopped their motors. It was more than a little unnerving.

Meanwhile, Jemma maneuvered the ship to a more defensible position, cursing under her breath while Meredith continued listening on all channels. Some chatter here and there. She waited and watched.

After an interminable period, a large blip appeared on their scanners, heading in their direction.

"*Fiemanskar*? Stand down. Mothership *Elvmandar* here." A brief but garbled message acknowledged the direction. "Crew of the *Elector*? We apologize for the delay. We were held up briefly attending to an incident on one of our moon bases. However, we are here now. We will open the dock for your imminent arrival. Captain Vied'an out."

Meredith quickly translated the statement. Chowd

nodded quietly, though his face was shadowed.

"Fine then, we go in. Chowd? Prepare your security team, because they aren't getting on this shuttle. We'll keep Meredith up here."

Chowd rose as Raven's voice died away, moving along the corridor once more, squatting to talk to his team in quiet tones. They nodded and prepared their weapons before standing and moving to the back of the shuttle. Chowd moved in next to the ambassador, and a lightning quick exchange took place.

No further information was communicated through the comm though, and Meredith's skill as a translator was no longer required. At least, not at this point in the mission.

She breathed a silent sigh and kept an eye on the massive hull looming on the screen, almost from nowhere. Jemma moved the shuttle into position when she saw the opening and moved within the large gray walls. The Ru'Edan ships lined up in the bay as they entered, and Meredith wondered at the skill with which Jemma hovered the craft for just an instant before letting it land with a whisper-like kiss upon the floor.

They had arrived.

Chapter 9

Chowd positioned himself in front of his men and the ambassador as the door of the craft opened. Most of all, he made sure he remained in front of Meredith.

The atmosphere on the ship certainly felt warmer than the shuttle, and a gassy steam invaded the small shuttle as it stabilized the temperature. He kept one hand on his pistol as he waited.

A Ru'Edan official moved toward him, looking as cautious as he felt. Chowd and the official moved together, bowing once in the traditional manner, then the official extended his hand. "Jod Svan'Er, head of guardian services. Welcome aboard the *Elvmandar*."

"Chowd Sur Banden. Chief of security on the UEE *Elector*." He stopped and indicated first to Jemma. "Jemma Cardnew, our pilot. Raven Fraser, her partner. Meredith Gentry, attached to the *Elector* as translator. Ambassador Vierghent, and my security officers." His mouth tightened. *I refuse to make the positions of either Raven or Meredith clear at this time.* They were too important to the Empire, with Raven's knowledge of the *Elector* and Meredith's code-breaking skills. It would be unwise to provide too much information to anyone who didn't need to know.

Each person stepped out of the shuttle as Chowd named them, so they lined up along the obsidian-black floor. Some looked around in interest and not a little concern, others waiting in calm silence. He understood their tension, but they had a job to do.

His chest felt tight, and he expected someone—anyone— to come out and call him a traitor. To name his father and want to take him out for the crimes he had committed. He hadn't ever considered himself Ru'Edan, but neither did he consider himself human, although they might see it differently.

The man Chowd guessed was the captain, given his official decorations, moved forward. "Welcome, Ambassador, to our humble ship. I am Captain Vied'an. We will attempt to make your time aboard as comfortable as we can. We have arranged cabins as per the agreement for you and your personal entourage."

He gestured for the ambassador to move forward, and Chowd nodded to his people. They moved into position, flanking the man as directed before landing, their muscles and larger bodies notable among the fine-figured Ru'Edanians.

Chowd needed a level of freedom to look around and plan, so he had taken this unusual step of splitting the party up and moving closer to Jod Svan'Er. He hoped it wasn't a mistake. He trusted his people to know how to keep the ambassador safe.

The captain was tall for their kind at nearly six feet. Being of the high-class, his body had been better nurtured and he filled his ornate uniform, one he seemed to wear with great pride. His gray skin stretched over his sinewy frame, which was covered by a resplendent red-and-black-leathered jacket. As Chowd watched, the captain turned, and the ambassador followed him, walking quickly through an automatic doorway and out of sight, the two guards trailing him.

Chowd turned swiftly. "Jemma and Raven? I need you to supervise unloading and securing the shuttle. Meredith, come with me. I may need your skills." He nodded to Jod, knowing that he would need to follow him and find out exactly what security measures they had set in place and acquire any other intelligence he could glean.

Information was power, and his role required him to obtain as much as possible so he could ensure the safety of the people in his guardianship, and the ambassador particularly. He also refused to allow Meredith out of his sight. At least the rest of the crew stayed in pairs, and they'd remain so until he was assured of their safety.

Meredith moved close to him, and he battled the need to take her hand and offer the support he knew she needed but wouldn't ask for. He couldn't do that though. On the Ru'Edan homeworlds, and even their ships, the genders remained unequal, and he refused to put her in an even more precarious position than she was already in. No, he would play it by ear. For now, anyway.

"What provisions are there for cabins?" He kept his voice terse.

"We have allocated five as per our agreement," Jod Svan'Er answered, ushering them into a long, gray corridor. Their steps clanged on the floor, the lighting sufficient to see their way but no more.

Chowd nodded before saying, "We will only require four. Our teams are paired, and only the ambassador is currently unpaired."

The guardian stopped, looking at him with surprise. "Paired? As in...to stay together?" Chowd nodded, understanding they had reached a pivotal moment for his team. Chowd waited for the reaction from this Ru'Edan guardian, which could affect the balance of their mission.

"As in the women together, and the males similarly so?" Suspicion colored Jod's voice. "No. As in my pilot and her assistant are a pair, my two guards are paired, and I am

paired with this female."

"That might cause some issues. We do not allow that in our own ranks." His eyes narrowed. "Yet I had heard it was quite common for your males and females to cohabitate, and even to carry the same rank and position. That seems rather unwise, doesn't it?"

"Not at all," Chowd replied.

The guardian didn't speak again as he turned to walk quietly down the corridor, but Chowd sensed his unease.

"We are placed near the ambassador, I take it?"

The guardian nodded. "Yes, two cabins to one side and two to the other. We were instructed to do so, as the ambassador was bringing a full security detail and his assistant with him."

"His assistant is indisposed." No need to go into all the

details right now, in case they had something to do with it. He felt Meredith's unease but remained thankful for her silence at this time. *I will find an opportunity to take on her thoughts about the situation later.*

He breathed deeply, holding on to his emotions as they entered a large room. The overwhelming feeling of being trapped remained though.

"This is where the captain will hold a formal meal tonight. We have ensured that there are some of your local foodstuffs available as well."

Chowd looked around quickly. The room was sparse and gray with a single long table and hard seating fastened to the floor. The room looked just like the rest of the ship they had already seen—spartan.

They moved through the decks quickly, and Chowd memorized the layout of the ship, the security systems, and life-support pod locations. A prickle at the back of his neck continued to irk him, but he ignored it, knowing that he couldn't investigate the way he would on the *Elector*. His stomach churned while he filed away everything to reconsider later, leaving him unsatisfied, even while he continued the cursory inspection.

Ru'Edanian pilots, officers, and even conscripts passed by them, inspecting him closely, as if they knew his background, then they glanced at Meredith, their gazes shocked. A female clearly escorted by a male! He could read the horror and disbelief in their eyes before they quickly averted their faces. With each action he felt himself growing colder and more tightly wound as anger invaded his entire body.

Their steps echoed throughout the silence, and he heaved a great sigh of relief when they came to the final door.

"This is your cabin." The guardian indicated that they should both enter, and the door slid shut behind them, the palm pad glowing for just an instant as it locked. "If I may be so bold, it might be wise to keep personal behaviors to a minimum while here. The crew..." He stopped, obviously searching for the right words to complete his warning. "They do not have an easy understanding of...well, cross-gender relationships. They are not the norm on our homeworlds. We have very few female technicians, and they tend to remain in their sectors. It would be wise to ensure that the females remain with their male escort at all times. We do have some on board who adhere to the traditional view of women aboard being servicers only."

"Servicers?" Meredith's voice was high.

He remembered what the term meant, and pure, white-hot anger that any of the Ru'Edan males would treat Meredith like that zinged through his body. A primitive need to protect her raised its head as his muscles clenched, ready to defend.

"Servicers are female sexual companions. They are usually of the lower class and sterilized, as they are considered inappropriate or unsuitable breeders."

Chowd winced.

Meredith stepped forward, anger clear on her face. He grabbed Meredith's hand and squeezed. He hoped she understood that this wasn't the time for her to throw an anger fit about gender and sexual equality.

"We will, of course, adhere to your suggestion and pass the information along to the others," Chowd said. *Now I just want Jod to leave so I can settle Meredith down, pass along the information, and find out how the others fared with their work.*

Jod must have seen something in his face, since he bowed formally to them both then retreated from the cabin.

"Servicers? Sterilized sexual companions? What kind of animals are they?" she raged between clenched teeth as she stalked around the cabin.

"Meredith? You really shouldn't—" He stopped as she turned on him, her face thunderous.

"What shouldn't I say or do? That they're backward? That their culture demeans women in a way ours doesn't? That it's wrong to make them little more than sexual slaves?" Her eyes flashed.

He felt enchanted at the beauty of her heightened cheek color and the turbulence in her eyes. Then the importance of her words hit him. *In a way ours doesn't? Does that include me? Exclude me?* Even as the thoughts assailed him, he backed away. Now certainly wasn't the time.

He caught her hard against his body, bent, and whispered quietly in her ear, "Meredith, we don't know if they are listening to us at the moment. I need to check before we can talk freely."

Meredith nodded jerkily without another word.

Chowd pulled a small device from his pocket, tapped in a command, and waited. Two green lights flashed, then a red. He put a finger to his lips and walked to the wall, following it to a corner, turning and following the wall again. Nothing. The next wall showed no response either, yet the red light continued to glow.

A small unit sat on the desk, and when he approached it, the light glowed more deeply. There. He picked the item up to inspect it. Nothing that he could see. He breathed deeply, frustrated, looked at her, then held it up and dropped it. The unit fell apart, and the red indicator light on the device in his hand dimmed then spluttered once before finally winking out.

"Okay, the cabin should be safe, but never say anything until we get a chance to check the room out first."

"Fine. Is the sanitary unit safe, do you think?" Meredith's voice cut through the air, waspish with anger, as she turned, her movements jerky and more uncoordinated than he had ever seen.

Meredith stood in the sanitary unit, and like the rest of the ship, its decoration bordered on spartan. Creature comforts seemed to come second. Except of the sexual kind. She closed her eyes. Her outburst to Chowd was both childish and unfair. He wasn't truly Ru'Edan, but he was male and in striking distance. The knowledge of her behavior left a sour taste in her mouth, her head pounding and stomach churning.

Her fingers, white with the pressure of gripping the metal

bowl, stung. She looked up, grimacing further when she caught sight of his reflection in the mirror.

"Feel better now?" His soft voice warred with the concern in his eyes.

"Yeah. I shouldn't have reacted like that. Or taken it out on you. It was unfair and wrong of me." Meredith waited for his reaction.

A gentle hand touched her shoulder, and she nuzzled in, accepting the action. Her body loosened as the tension seeped from her tightly coiled muscles. She released her breath and turned toward him.

"I know you aren't like that. It just amazes me." For a fraction of a second, she floundered for the words to describe what she felt. "For centuries women on Earth have been the equal of men. It always seems wrong that other planets don't have that same outlook." She looked away briefly before turning her eyes to his. "More importantly, I know you wouldn't treat me, or any other woman, that way. That makes you so very special."

She leaned in close, fitting her lips against his, feeling his shuddering response and absorbing strength from him. Then she closed her eyes.

Light fingers traveled over her cheek, caressing for just an instant. "I know it's a culture shock for you. I couldn't tell you what to expect, because I don't have this kind of experience either. The way I grew up, with Crick...it was militaristic, but an unbalanced form of that. The women were essentially servicers. They had no role except to bear the children who would become the next generation of warriors, or servicers and staff. There was no tenderness or kindness. Not like I have experienced since I left," he whispered to her, and the warm touch of his breath made her knees wobble and her skin tingle.

Meredith opened her eyes to see him watching her intently.

"I don't want to be like that," he continued. "I want the softness I find with you. With the human way of life."

The words felt like a vow, and something deep and rich rippled through her system, filling her entire body with heat. "Chowd...I..." *Stars!* The words she needed to say were on the tip of her tongue, but she swallowed them instead. Now really wasn't the time.

He looked closely at her. "What?"

"I think we should get on and check on the others." She knew neither of them expected that response, but she couldn't, wouldn't say she loved him here. It would taint their relationship as furtive and dirty. The wrong words in the wrong place and at the wrong time could damage what grew between them. She had started mentally listing all the appropriate places and times when his voice interrupted.

"Yes, I know." His answer shocked her momentarily, her heart thudding in a deep, slow cadence before she realized he meant checking on the others. She castigated herself mentally for flights of fancy, but a seed of hurt lodged deep in her chest.

Meredith nodded, more because she knew he expected it. He stilled her when she made to move, his hand holding her, his gaze probing, as if for just an instant she had betrayed herself. She wondered if he somehow knew her thoughts before casting that idea aside. Of course he didn't.

After a moment, he stepped aside, and she followed him out of the sanitary unit and into the small cabin. For the first time she took a proper look. Her anger before hadn't allowed her to take in the surroundings of the gunmetal gray linoleum-looking floor and the matching gray of the walls. A small porthole gave her a view of the vast expanse of space, and long beds covered with thin, metallic blankets filled the room. She'd bet this was considered luxurious among the crew. Especially among the female techs.

"Was this like you experienced growing up?" she asked.

"No. This would have been extravagant. We stayed with our mothers for around the first ten years, then we were placed into a barracks-like structure. Rows of beds, three beds high. They would have fit around fifteen in here. Everything was communal. The only one who got anything different was my brother who died. But he was older and a pure blood."

Chowd shrugged.

"After we were placed in the barracks, we were forbidden contact with our mothers. Neither my mother or I allowed that to happen though. We would meet regularly in the kitchen. After my birth, something went wrong and she was no longer considered a breeder, so they relegated her to the kitchens. That meant it was easier for me to stay in contact. She listened and would share information." His eyes shuttered closed, and Meredith knew that part of the conversation was over for now.

"You know, she must have been very brave. I wish I'd met her. If she was anything like you are, I think I would have liked her a lot."

His eyes opened, and she saw the flash of pain deep within him. It hurt to see such misery, but he quickly turned away again.

"We need to get going," he said, his voice rough but controlled. With that, he moved to the door, and Meredith had no option but to follow him into the corridor.

Chapter 10

The ambassador sat on the edge of the bed in a room slightly larger than theirs. Meredith could tell from his grimace that he didn't think the appointment of the room was adequate to his needs or status. As with everything else she had noted since boarding the ship, creature comforts were few. There was a splash of color about this room though. Instead of the gunmetal gray everywhere, the room had obviously been newly refurbished, a streak of black now picking out the lintels above the sanitary unit door. The floor was carpeted, and there was even an image of some distant planet, complete with a pale sun and violet grasses, gracing the walls, though its importance was lost on her. A high-tech desk screen sat on a small desk in one corner, and the bed was slightly larger, though no more comfortably made up.

"Ambassador, I see they have placed two guards at your doorway." Chowd's voice was soft, as if coaxing a toddler in the middle of a tantrum, and she grinned inwardly. That was the best description of the ambassador currently.

"Yes, supposedly for my protection. However, I was assured I would have access to all areas of the ship and to its crew in an uninterrupted fashion so that I can get the average Ru'Edanians opinion, as well as that of the senators and officials. Which, clearly, I don't have." His voice betrayed his dismay and anger at being guarded by two species and stopped from going anywhere on the ship at will.

"Yes, but consider, that it is a mothership, with access to all sorts of classified information and technology. They will be very cautious about where you travel and who you will interact with. They want to ensure your safety and the completion of the treaty with the least amount of upheaval."

"It is still not within the terms of our agreement." His petulant voice filled the air before a knock sounded on the door, and a gruff voice called from beyond, "Two members of your crew. A Raven and a Jamma—"

Meredith depressed the door-open button, knowing that she had better be quick, and Jemma's voice filtered through. "It's pronounced *Jemma*, and—"

The door started to open, and Raven's voice filled the void. "Thank you."

Once the door opened fully, Meredith could clearly see Jemma, red-faced with flashing eyes, and Raven. He ushered her in and closed the door before finally rolling his eyes behind Jemma's back.

"Man! Chowd, it's a good thing you aren't like this lot. Otherwise I would've strangled you the minute we met." Jemma's voice filled the air with disgust as she flung herself against the wall, striking a devil-may-care pose.

A smile of indulgence played on Raven's lips. "Come on. He couldn't say your name right because he was struck by your beauty."

Meredith worked to contain a giggle, but it escaped. The strangled sound broke the tense atmosphere in the room, and others joined in, including Jemma. The ambassador lost the tense, white markings that had bracketed his mouth. The minute of companionship shattered the restraints of the team, and Meredith felt pleased that the coldness and sarcasm dissipated, even if it was only for a short time.

"Seriously, now that we're all here, we need to update our situation slightly." Chowd addressed the assembled crewmembers, looking at them one by one. "While it's disturbing, the chief guardian has made it clear Jemma and Meredith are not, on any occasion, to be left by themselves. The gender inequality could result in something more than just a mere situation of inconvenience. Secondly, I need to know exactly what you have seen and heard since boarding. Lastly, Ambassador, you need to be involved as your safety is paramount. We need to get you in and out with minimal danger."

All gazes zeroed in on Chowd, and Meredith had a

moment to watch the easy way he took command of the situation.

He continued. "I personally believe that Jod Svan'Er may, in time, become one of our strongest allies here, but it will require patience and care in how we deal with him in the short term." He paused, and Meredith remembered the way Jod's face had shown a flash of emotion, perhaps yearning, while watching the way the crew interacted with each other with an easy familiarity.

The *Elector*'s security team entered the room and joined them, then the members of the crew were silent. Meredith looked quickly at Jemma, who'd once more assumed her cross look. This was the Jemma they all remembered from their first meeting, and Meredith couldn't control the tiny smile that broke out. The Ru'Edanians didn't have a clue about what was coming their way!

Chowd waited for an instant before continuing, "Jemma and Raven, while you were securing the shuttle, did you hear anything that we need to know about?" Both shook their heads, and he looked at the security team. "Anything from you two?"

One stepped forward. "While we made our way here, there was a crewmember who called out, but they were quickly dealt with by...I guess a superior. I couldn't make out the words though."

Chowd looked to his partner.

The man quickly shook his head. "No, I didn't hear it either."

Chowd's brow furrowed, and she felt a flutter deep in her belly. "Okay. I need everyone to keep their ears open for whatever is said around you. If in doubt, check with Meredith or myself to seek a translation. We meet in an hour to attend the formal dinner. Meredith and myself, Jemma, and Raven will go change into formal uniforms now. Full dress blues with gloves are in order. Meredith and I will relieve you two when we're prepared."

The four of them headed to the door and stepped into the corridor. He stopped and held out a hand to Meredith as

Jemma and Raven disappeared into their cabin before turning to the Ru'Edan guards outside the door. "What are your orders concerning the ambassador?"

They looked alarmed for a moment at Chowd's question before one nodded to the other, their yellow eyes bright with apprehension. "We are to wait for the ambassador and the party. Then escort you to the formal dining zone. No one except the captain or the head guardian is to have access. And of course, your people."

Chowd nodded then turned back. "Let's go change." Without a word they walked away, and Meredith hid her surprise until safely within their cabin.

"You were rather abrupt just then."

"It is the way a member of the high-class talks to those of the lower classes. To do anything else would be inappropriate and invite an unwelcome level of interest in our affairs." He looked back at Meredith, and she saw a disconcerting distance in his eyes. "I know it seems confusing at times, a little like the caste system that those native of India continue to adhere to, but it's important that we follow these social rules while aboard. Promise me, Meredith, that you won't break that rule?"

She watched, perplexed, and waited for more, but it wasn't forthcoming, so she nodded in agreement before turning to grab her bag. "I'm going to wash and dress, then once we're both ready, we can head back to the ambassador's cabin." She snatched up the uniform and headed for the sanitary unit.

"Meredith?" The word was a plea, and she stopped, turning slowly.

"I understand and will try to do as you ask." She softened the words with a small smile before turning back to the unit and shutting the door.

Once inside the bathroom, Meredith engaged the shower, stripping quickly and stepping into the tiny cubicle while the issues they knew of spun around in her head. She sensed a well of distrust at the humans here on the ship, but surely it couldn't be as deeply ingrained as the others suggested. None of her work would have led her to that conclusion. Of course, she trusted what Chowd said, but she seriously doubted that there was as much danger as he alluded to. She ducked her head under the shower and let the thoughts wash away.

When the crewmembers were finally assembled inside the ambassador's cabin, Chowd opened the door and spoke to the guards waiting outside. Their sullen looks left him with a sense of uneasiness, but what else could he do? Jod Svan'Er would soon arrive, and they needed to hurry in order to be prepared.

Chowd instructed the guards to let him know as soon as the guardian arrived then ducked his head back into the cabin as he spied Jod coming around the corner. "It's time to go."

At his prodding, they stood as a group, all of the *Elector* crew and Meredith resplendent in their formal uniforms, white gloves gleaming under the bright lights, every one of them immaculately groomed and ready to show their pride in the Empire and their species. The ambassador wore his formal dress of red-and-white land suit, medals gleaming on his chest and across the sash.

Chowd felt a thrill that he was one of these few souls representing the *Elector*. They would certainly stand out from the drab colors of this ship and crew.

As one they formed up, flanking the ambassador as a guard of honor, more ceremonial than strategic. Chowd took the rear of the formation as they moved through the door, showing the precise movements which he knew were uncommon to the Ru'Edan. Jod nodded before taking the front, leading them down the cold, gray corridor toward the formal mess area he and Meredith had seen earlier.

As they entered, the senior crew and captain stood, the drab gray-and-black uniforms reflecting the utilitarian society.

The captain, the only one with a streak of red in his uniform, strode forward, bowing formally to the ambassador then to Chowd as the next highest-ranking official in the party. He acknowledged Raven next and stared for a moment at Jemma and Meredith. Chowd felt the tension rising once more in his chest, but the captain turned away without a sound, introducing his crewmembers one by one.

More than one rested hungry eyes on the two women, but no one dared approach them at the beginning of their meeting. One member of the crew, a junior comm officer, stepped toward Meredith and was reprimanded with a quick, single-word comment. He flushed and took a step back. The atmosphere settled into a cold and remote silence. Drinks circulated, but the crew of the *Elector* refused alcoholic beverages in favor of the more exotic juices on offer.

Chowd found himself standing on the sidelines with Jod Svan'Er. Raven watched the women close by, giving an impression of a sentinel, and Chowd nearly snorted at the implicit threat he posed.

"Is that supposed to be a warning to the crew?" Jod's question took Chowd by surprise. "No. I think it is an unconscious act of protecting his mate though."

"Probably wise. Most of these crewmembers have not had female interaction for several of your Earth months. I suppose the man next to them...Raven? He is as lethal as he looks?"

"He has been known to be. Of course, so have the women. Jemma in particular is cold in combat. She's not exactly someone I would want to cross."

Jod laughed, his eyes crinkling with mirth. "A female? Cold in combat? Now I am sure you tell me an untruth."

"No. She single-handedly took out many of Crick Sur Banden's own men in combat not so long ago." He continued to watch Jod's reaction, but all he betrayed at the moment was genuine surprise, taking another look at the women.

"Indeed? Well, I would be interested in seeing her in action at some point. But enough of that. I must inquire...how do you fare with being at odds with a member of your family? Surely Crick Sur Banden is some distant relation that causes you difficulties? After all, you carry the name Sur Banden, so that makes you a member of the house. Is that why you have aligned yourself with the humans?"

"Distant family member? I wish. No. He's my sire."

Jod reared back at this. "Sire? You're the son of Crick Sur Banden? Do not say that too loud. He should have assumed a seat on the Senate, but his actions made him an outcast." Chowd felt as if a blow had landed on him. "A member of the Senate? Surely not?" But it

made sense. Chowd remembered the sense of entitlement Crick had always exhibited. The power he wielded and how his men acquiesced to it. His access to intelligence and his level of education should have alerted Chowd to the high-born position of his father. He'd never dreamed that he should have taken a place on the Senate.

"Indeed. The whole family was called into disrepute and shamed publicly after he turned rogue. Furthermore, there are members of the crew from the family, and that will cause more issues for you and your team if it is known." Jod leaned forward now, making the point forcefully, and Chowd nodded. His stomach soured at the thought that he might have endangered someone with the knowledge of his unwanted kinship.

"I thank you for your assistance in this matter."

The captain's voice broke over the gathering after he stepped away from Jod. "Come, let us retire to the table and break our fast. Ambassador, would you take the top seat? The members of the crew each have an allocated position. I had our communications officer arrange for placement boards, so you will not have difficulties finding your assigned seating."

Chowd looked to the ambassador, who nodded, and they moved, seeking their names on the table. The women were seated between himself and Raven. The other two officers went further down the table, and he hoped they might collect valuable intelligence. Jemma started to seat herself, but he shook his head, and she stopped before nodding. The resident religious member of the crew undertook a lengthy series of ritualistic passes and mutterings over the table and those present before they could assume their seats, but finally the group was released from the confines of the rites.

From another room, plates came swiftly, carried by two small women. Neither said a word as they moved with speed, only stopping as they caught sight of the two women at the table. Meredith's murmured *thanks* drew a startled intake of breaths from those at the table and a stern look from the captain. Obviously her talent with their language did not include knowledge of their customs, Chowd thought humorlessly. He would need to run both the women through some of them to ensure they did not unintentionally insult anyone.

They returned with another couple of women, this time dragging pots from which they ladled a stew of some kind. While the smell wasn't terribly appetizing, it was obvious from the looks of the *Elvmandar*'s crewmembers that they thought it a delicacy.

"Rock hopper rat stew, Captain." The women bowed low and left the room.

An officer exclaimed excitedly over the dish, and Chowd's stomach dipped. Meredith made a noise, a cross between a gulp and a strangled, dry-retching sound, and Chowd laid a silent hand on her leg. Her fingers inched under the table to grip his in a tight hold.

"I can't eat this," she whispered.

Of course she would struggle with this, but to refuse would be considered an insult. "You must eat at least some. Come on, forget it is what they called it and swallow quickly."

He chanced a look and saw the pained expression on her face but cheered internally as she raised the spoon, full of stew, and lifted it to her mouth. The spoon disappeared and returned empty. He could see the tears glistening at the corner of her eyes as he lifted his spoon, also loaded with the gray vegetable and meat mass, and tasted. *Ugh!* The soggy mass had a flavor as bad as it looked, rancid and off to his taste buds. No wonder she looked green after the single spoonful.

His belly coiled in revulsion, and he had to work at keeping the contents in place. Chowd saw the members of the *Elvmandar*'s crew eat with appreciation, and he sighed, knowing that he would need to eat some more then make at least a positive comment. Not an easy thing when it tasted like pureed, regurgitated vomit, complete with a sour aftertaste. He filled another spoonful and lifted it to his mouth.

The grunts of approval filled the room, and he noted that the *Elector* crew and the ambassador at least each managed a spoonful or two.

"This is not to your taste?" Jod indicated the food with his left hand, his tone questioning. "It's not quite what we are used to." What else could he say?

The women returned, clearing the bowls from the table and replacing them with new plates. This time the tubers and avian-style meat looked at least semi-familiar. The *Elector* crew seemed to breathe a sigh of relief.

He took a bite, and although the taste was bland, it didn't have the sour aftertaste, and he and his crew ate hungrily. The members of the mothership moaned and groaned in appreciation of, he guessed, this new food and perhaps the taste and sensations. The desultory conversation among the groups died away.

Once more the women entered the room, and this time every plate was empty.

"You eat foods that taste like that all the time?" Jod's voice showed his amazement. "Well, no, that is a more basic meal. On our festival occasions the foods are somewhat different, ranging from aquatic life forms to fried or even wood-roasted items."

Jod's eyes grew larger and rounder in his face. "Indeed, then our foods must be quite unpalatable by your standards." His voice grew stiff, and Chowd knew he would need to tread carefully in his next answers, lest he alienate this potential ally.

"It is different, yes. But differences are not necessarily a bad thing. That's what makes us individuals." His diplomatic answer settled the Ru'Edan male sitting beside him.

The rest of the meal passed slowly. The assembled members made their way through the foods provided, but the conversation around the table petered away to nothing. Once the meal ended, the two crews stood.

Chowd indicated to the others that it was time to return to the cabins. Once outside the door of the ambassador's cabin, the two guards took up position, and Jemma and Raven entered their own, the door closing behind them. The locking palm pad turned red, and Chowd ushered Meredith into their cabin, setting the secure lock door.

✪ ✪ ✪ ✪ ✪

The morning chimes woke Meredith, her eyes gritty from lack of sleep that had finally come early in the morning. She stretched on the hard bed, and reached out, searching for a warm body. Finding nothing but open air, she rolled, grabbing the edge of the bed as she moved over. She fell to the floor with an audible thud.

"Oww!" She rubbed at her side, the sting radiating.

"Are you okay?" Chowd's voice came from the sanitary unit, but as much as she wanted to respond, the wind had been knocked out of her.

Meredith lay on the floor, gasping for air as the sound of movement came closer. "What happened?" Chowd's face appeared in front of hers.

"I rolled and fell out of the bed," she whispered, and he helped her to move back into a sitting position. "Gee, those beds aren't very wide, are they?" Meredith brushed her hair away from her eyes in time to see a gentle smile.

"No, not really." Chowd lifted her up only to sit down on the bed with her in his arms. "I didn't want to wake you, but now that you're up, let me say good morning." His lips gently met hers, the silent mating leaving her feeling warm and full and slightly aroused.

She framed his face and gazed into his eyes. "I prefer to wake up that way." Once again, she shortened the distance between them and laid her lips to his. They opened and the kiss deepened. She moaned and leaned closer, needing more than this kiss, her body straining against the hands that kept her still.

He laughed, the sound husky as he pulled away. "Come on, sleepyhead. If you feel all right, you should get dressed. We are on duty in an hour and we still have some things to attend to."

She sighed. Meredith rose out of his arms with regret, knowing he was correct. "I'd better grab some clothes and shower."

Chowd snickered, pointing to a pile already waiting on his bed. "I thought it would be easier for you."

She rolled her eyes. "You don't need to wait on me hand and foot." "I like to. It makes me feel connected to you. Now go on, hurry up."

He gently pushed her toward the sanitary unit, and she accepted the hurry-along with a smile before shutting the door behind her and quickly stripping down. She moved with speed, stepping under the shower and running the water as she soaped. When she had finished, Meredith toweled, dressed, and tamed her hair before emerging into the cabin where he waited.

Once he caught sight of her, he smiled and tugged her close. She sighed heavily, wishing they had more time.

"Tonight." With the heated word, he led her toward the ambassador's cabin. The guardians remained outside, and Chowd knocked on the door, which opened slowly. The ambassador stood with a copy of something in his hands.

"Good morning, Chowd. Warrant Officer Gentry, I am pleased to see you looking so well this morning." The ambassador smiled.

"Thank you, Ambassador." Chowd wandered over to Jemma and Raven and started a rapid-fire handover before they left the cabin. Chowd turned back to the Ambassador. "You had an uneventful night, I've just been informed. I also understood from last night that you hoped to head for the bridge this morning?"

The ambassador smiled enigmatically and shrugged.

Chowd cocked his head to the side. "I've made arrangements for Jod Svan'Er to meet us and show us the way. If you are ready, of course?"

The ambassador nodded. His eyes slid back to Meredith time and time again and there in the depths of his gaze she read something that didn't feel right. Inwardly, she shrugged. There wasn't anything she could do about that right now.

Once more, they made their way into the long, gray corridor, and by now Jod had joined them. Chowd turned back and smiled, and she grinned at him. He resumed his movements at the front as they kept going.

A thudding sound caught her attention. She stopped, wondering at its origin, and turned back just as something covered her mouth. She attempted to shout, but all that escaped was a muffled "Oof."

Meredith moved her feet, attempting to kick out, but strong and rough arms lifted her. She struggled against them, but the material covering her mouth must have contained a soporific agent. The longer she struggled, the weaker she felt, her consciousness fading to gray.

She fought against the tide that washed over her senses, felt her heart rate increase with the pumping of adrenaline, but her body started to turn heavy and clumsy and then she finally succumbed to the darkness.

✪ ✪ ✪ ✪ ✪

Chowd turned around to ask Meredith a question only to find no one behind him. He stopped. "Wait."

He strode quickly back in the direction they had traveled, but he could detect no sign of Meredith. A cold knot of fear lodged low in his belly.

"Jod!" he bellowed, watching as the light of recognition dawned in the Ru'Edan's eyes. "*Destata*! I know nothing about this!" He lifted a comm unit to his lips and gave a rapid-fire set of directions. Jod's face was drawn with anger while rage pumped through Chowd's body. "We need to start by retracing our steps, go back to where we last saw her."

Chowd didn't wait though, already giving commands via his comm for the off-duty guards from the *Elector* to join them. He felt torn. His orders were to guard the ambassador, but Meredith's danger felt more urgent. His unit bleeped again, this time Raven demanding to know what had happened.

"Meredith is missing. She was behind me, but there's no sign of her now." Chowd worked to keep the anguish from his voice. On a ship like this, they would have difficulty locating her.

Images of the things he had seen before and during his time with the Admiralty assailed him. Memories of Jemma shot at the hands of his father's warriors and bleeding. Memories of Mellissa under the sonic cutter—when Duvall had saved her on Earth. The eviscerated females damaged and abused under Crick Sur Banden. He wanted to double over at the pain these memories brought him. The knowledge that he might never see Meredith again burned, yet if he didn't find her quickly, she could sustain emotional damage resulting in her never wanting him again. The memory of the women who had been held by his father after he had used them filled him with horror.

"Do you need me to come help with the search?" Raven asked.

"No. You need to ensure Jemma is safe. Until we know who or what is involved we cannot leave any member of our crew unsupervised." It hurt to say the words when he wanted to demand that everyone look for Meredith. Duty warred with his personal feelings, overwhelming him for just an instant, and he had to close his eyes.

He stopped, clearing his mind before opening his eyes at

the sound of footsteps moving quickly down the hall. He saw his men and felt relief that he could now search for Meredith, leaving the ambassador in their hands.

"Get the ambassador to the bridge. Remain with him at all times. The guardians will show you the way." His voice was brittle, and he looked at Jod, who nodded immediately.

"Come. We can go back and start where you last saw her." Jod moved swiftly, but Chowd kept pace.

"It was here. I looked around and she was there." He dropped to the ground, seeking something, anything. "Do you have surveillance?"

"Not in this area, but we do have motion scanners that we can check." He lifted his hand and gave the order, waiting just an instant before an answer returned from an unseen crewmember. "There was a range of people moving through this area in the last ten minutes or so. They have a record of us, then quickly after at least another two. A little further down, where the next scan was conducted, our group was five instead of six, so that means they probably used this exit point." Jod pointed to a hidden access way. He pulled open a hidden door and stepped within.

The gloom of the passage almost overwhelmed Chowd at first, but he could see Jod in the darkness fumbling in his pockets. Chowd reached into his utility belt, found a small light, and turned it on. It illuminated the corridor just enough to see the ground and walls.

He bent, seeing a scuff mark on the floor. "This is new. It could be from Meredith." Anger burned white-hot once more in his chest.

"Let's see if it goes any further." Jod no doubt meant to make him feel more settled with his calm words, but the lead weight in Chowd's throat was growing as each minute passed.

They kept moving, the rustle of uniforms and the distant bangs and clanks filling the air. "Where does this lead?"

"It veers in a few metros, the left leading to the lower-class conscript cabins and the right taking us to engineering. If she's there, it will be harder for us to investigate." For the first time Chowd could hear real concern in Jod's voice.

The access way had started to narrow when Chowd saw a piece of material caught on the rough surface of the walls. "What's that?" He touched a trembling finger to the material. The soft, light gray fabric he had seen her wearing. "Stars. She was here." He flicked the light up. "Who has access to these tunnels?"

"Most of the engineering crew, the cleaners. Lower-class members with employment on our level," Jod said thoughtfully. "Let me have my men cross-check who is currently stationed where. That will give us at least a cross section to work with." Once more Jod lifted his comm unit and began speaking.

Chowd couldn't wait quietly though, so he began prowling around the area, looking for scuff marks and other clues. His stomach churned, and his heart pounded. He sent a prayer to any and all deities that she would be found safe.

Chapter 11

Meredith felt the pounding in her head and the ache of abused muscles, particularly her arms. She opened her eyes to a dingy darkness. Machinery and pipes a couple of meters from where she'd been propped up suggested that her location was somewhere deep in the bowels of the ship. The smell of burning oils and the greasiness of the floor confirmed that thought.

Engines moaned and groaned loudly, and she knew that yelling over the cacophony would be pointless. She glanced around the area, relieved to see that no one else was stashed there with her for her to worry about. Getting herself out would be enough right now.

The thud in her head beat in time with the rattles around her. That would hide the sound of her escape, she thought, but also the sound of her approaching captor. Something she knew might mean death, or possibly even worse.

Meredith pulled on the bonds around her wrists, testing the material. It felt hardy and strong but rough, and it scraped against her already abraded skin. How long could have passed? She didn't feel much more thirsty or hungry than before, so it couldn't have been long.

She grunted, pulling again but feeling no give in the textile. Panic rose, threatening to choke her, until her training kicked in. She needed to defeat the panic if she hoped to escape from this makeshift prison.

"Come on, Meredith. You're bright and resourceful. Clever. If anyone can get out of here alive and in one piece, it's you." She said the words aloud, hunting for positive affirmation in the sound of them.

Whoever had taken her had not tied the material well. She craned her neck, looking at the knots. She crooked a finger, trying to get enough purchase to push it through the woven textile. Finding a loose thread, she tugged as firmly as she could manage. It moved a little, and she tried again.

Meredith shimmied upward, hunting for a better angle or even something to catch the material on, without success. She tugged once more, and by the third time, the muscles in her hand spasmed painfully. Again and again she worked until she finally got the first knot undone. She angled to look up and around before looking back down. Only another three knots to go before she could get her hands free, then she could begin to release her legs. With a heartfelt sigh, she went back to work, stopping every now and again to glance around.

Sweat trickled down the side of her face, and the passing of time sat in the forefront of her consciousness. From time to time a bubble of panic would escape, nearly overwhelming her, and she would talk herself back down. "Come on, Meredith. You nearly have the knots undone, then you can release your legs and get out of this stinking hole."

Once more the panic subsided, and she would begin again, but each tug took longer and felt harder. Meredith's hand hurt viciously, and she expected it would be swollen once she escaped. With a sigh, she concentrated on pulling the remaining knot. Her hand protested as the bones and muscles wrenched again.

She couldn't contain the small cry of pain, tears running down her face, but the final knot unraveled. Her hands dropped to the floor with a thud. She looked about nervously. Still no one there, but she knew that wouldn't last forever. For the first time, she realized she had to pee.

Time's getting away. The longer I'm here, the greater chance of discovery and recapture.

Scooching forward with bent knees, she could finally extend her arms enough to work at the knots at her ankles, making short work of the bad ties. Her breath came in jerky pants as she pushed herself to her wobbly knees. She ran her tongue over her dry lips, catching a taste of sweaty salt on them, and grimaced. Her legs unsteady as she rose to stand, she quickly surveyed the area around her.

Her wrists stung, and when she looked down she saw that they were raw and red, and blood was trickling down her sleeve. But right then she had no time to do anything except try to get out. She moved forward clumsily, seeing a brighter light ahead.

Bang! She accidently hit one of the pipes with her palm, wincing as yet another shaft of pain echoed through her body. She pulled her hand to her mouth, attempting to stifle the sound of her cry as she slipped behind a large pipe. Her chest bellowed in fear but no one came to investigate the noise.

Chowd will be looking for you. Worrying. Don't be a baby. Go find him, then you can fall apart. The words offered her a little bit of encouragement as she moved forward again, this time more slowly, taking note of her surroundings. She reached the lighted corridor, the brightness stinging her sore eyes.

Up and down she gazed, but no one was in sight. Meredith had slipped around the corner, making her way along the gray corridor, when she heard shuffling footsteps. Her heart rate sped up again, and she frantically searched for somewhere to hide. *There!* A small alcove. She slipped in and got as low as she could.

Meredith turned. A drawn, gray face loomed above her. Fetid breath assaulted her as rough hands grabbed her.

"Nooooo!" She twisted and turned away as the hands grabbed her hair and yanked. "You are mine. I found you." He slurred the basic words. "You belong to me now."

"I belong to nobody. Now get your hands off me, you disgusting creature." Even as she screamed at him, he started to haul her backward.

Her mind scrabbled for a way to save herself, and the pain started again. She arched, swiping at him, grabbing his arm, digging in her fingernails, feeling them tear the flesh beneath. He roared, throwing her roughly against the dingy, gray wall opposite the tiny aperture she had tried hiding in.

Meredith scrambled to her feet and watched as he started

his ungainly run toward her, ignoring the latest aches in her body. Aware that she really only had one opportunity to escape and that it had to work, Meredith waited, time slipping slowly as she widened her stance.

He reached her, and she moved, tripping him with a well-aimed leg. The pain splintered through her body, but he fell heavily to the floor. Once she had him down, she aimed a kick directly at his genitals. He curled into a fetal position, retching as his body twitched. A stench filled the air, and her stomach heaved.

The sound of running feet caught her attention. *I won't allow anyone to take me again.* Once again she prepared to fight, but a familiar face rounded the corner. *Chowd.* She stood straight and tall, waiting for him to come toward her.

His face, a mask of anger and misery that showed some relief overlaid with wariness once he saw her. "Meredith? Are you all right?" He stopped several steps away as if waiting cautiously to see her reaction.

"Yeah. I'm a little battered and sore, but in one piece." The bravado in her system dissipated, replaced with a bone-deep exhaustion. "Chowd? Get me out of here."

The trembling began, growing stronger and more violent as she waited, and she thanked whatever deity there was when he moved toward her in silence and gathered her into his arms.

Chowd muttered and paced. The mothership had taken three days to travel from the rendezvous point to the station where the ambassador would conclude the final talks with the members of the Ru'Edan ruling Senate. Three very long days filled with anger, despair, and hope in alternating bursts.

After retrieving Meredith, who'd effectively saved herself, the captain, Jod Svan'Er, and the senior officers had shown amazing empathy toward both Meredith and Jemma, allowing Meredith to rest in the cabin under the joint guard of Jemma and Raven when Chowd left her.

He knew the offending Ru'Edan would face punishment, more than likely a flogging at the very least. The Ru'Edan usually considered women as chattel, and under normal circumstances there would have been no action taken. In this instance, Meredith, as a member of a crew currently undertaking diplomatic relations with the Ru'Edan, caused a muddying of the waters. They would likely never know exactly what happened to the kidnapper.

Chowd understood that Meredith felt the difficulties of the cloistered environs and sympathized with her, yet against her wishes, he had given the order for Raven to remain on guard with the two women while he and his two men took over the primary security detail of the ambassador. Meredith still jumped at the slightest sound, something he couldn't blame her for. She tried to reassure him that she felt better, but he could see the shadows in her eyes from time to time.

Right now, the entire crew from the *Elector* waited on the bridge as they approached the station. Chowd chanced a look at Meredith, the strain still evident around her lips, and he sidled over, letting his fingers brush against hers before tangling. She sent him a thankful look and closed her fingers more tightly around his.

"I never thought we would see this day, let alone be part of the actual ambassadorial detail." Her quiet words made him smile. Even in this midst of coming to grips with what had nearly happened, she still found wonder and happiness in her work. It humbled him that this wonderful woman had chosen to share herself with him.

"You deserve to be here. The work you have done with the Admiralty meant they would need your skills for this momentous event."

She wrinkled her nose. They both turned back to view the gaily lit station, growing larger while ships moved around it in a dance, darting here and there. Glancing at her again, he noticed the faint bruising on her skin, and once more he fought down the sensation of fury that scalded him inside.

"So once we get there, what should we expect?" she asked.

For a moment, he didn't answer. What was there to say? He could only be honest with her. "I don't know, Meredith. I imagine that we'll meet the senators, find our apartments, then conduct a meeting with the ambassador." Since they hadn't managed a team meeting after Meredith had freed herself from her abductor, this meeting would be way overdue.

"Okay. Are we likely to meet with...the same attitudes again?"

His heart plummeted at the quiet words. Truly, he didn't know for sure, but he could guess that the patriarchal society wouldn't have evolved that much, unless the high-class circles demanded it. "I don't know, but we'll take steps to ensure it doesn't happen again. I have also been informed that Jod Svan'Er will remain with us, along with some of his most loyal guards."

Chowd knew Meredith remained leery of Jod Svan'Er, but in the last few days, he'd personally handpicked guards for the women to augment their stretched security resources.

"Okay. I guess we'll have to wait until we dock. I packed up all our things, so they are ready for when we transfer."

"Excellent. Thank you, Meredith."

He wondered if she would ask what would happen to her assailant. She'd circumvented any discussion regarding the incident, which worried him. She surely needed to know what happened in order to move on. If Elara had been there, he would have sought her advice, but they were thousands of miles away and out of radio contact.

Meredith turned away from him, looking toward the front screen, her fingers still entwined in his as they drew closer to the station. Lights winked and glittered against the inky blackness, the bridge of the ship almost silent. It was easy to lose oneself in the fantasy of the silence of space.

One of the young comm officers who'd exclaimed over

the rat stew made his way over. "If you please, the captain asks you to prepare yourself for docking maneuvers." He indicated to the banks of seats, and with a silent nod he returned to his own perch.

Meredith engaged the safety harness, then Chowd adjusted his own. The feel of the thrusters setting them into the required trajectory and the metallic thuds as the tugs attached safety lines to the mothership before pulling them to their allocated berth captured his attention. The ship bumped against the station, a slight kiss of metal to the dock as voices, muted and unhurried, reported the status of the ship. Clamps attached, and finally the captain stood.

"Ambassador, crew? Welcome to the Dors'Mar satellite station. Guardian Svan'Er will see to your transfer. I shall remain here and, once the discussions are concluded, will convey you back to your own ship." He bowed formally, and the ambassador returned the obeisance.

Jod stood and walked over to them, indicating with a languid hand for them to follow. "I've arranged for my security teams to bring your items. We can transfer immediately onto the station. The security service is on standby, ready for you."

They entered the corridor, making their way down its length toward the back of the ship. About halfway along, they turned to the left and walked a little further. A large metal door separated them from the airlock, and even as they approached, a whizzing sound filled the air as oxygen filtered into the small area. The light above the door glowed a steady red before changing to green. The door clanked and rattled, and Jod turned the wheel, muscles straining beneath his uniform as he worked to open the hatch.

The door opened with a groan, and they stepped through. A wall of gray-and-blue-suited security guards invited them to step through a small arch and proceeded to check them for combustibles. Chowd knew this was standard procedure and waited patiently as they all proceeded through individually.

One guard took Chowd by surprise though. It was scary

in some ways and more than a little intimidating to come face to face with a man who looked like his father. Chowd swallowed reflexively and took a step forward.

"My Lord? I have important information for you. We believe that the members of the crew of the *Elector* have rendezvoused with the Ru'Edan and that they are due to meet with the ruling Senate."

Crick turned his head to look at his second-in-command. "Indeed?" The situation had become precarious of late. Losing the Alpha Star Colony base and many of his rogues had hurt. But if he had to go down, he'd be taking out the *Elector* and her crew.

"Your...your son is one of the members meeting with them."

Crick started at the news. "My son and heir? That traitorous bastard!"

Anger welled, white hot and burning. He tried to clench his fist, but his hand refused to cooperate. Lately, the functions of his body didn't work so well. He knew it was a conspiracy and that the medics had something to do with this.

He waited for his body to calm. His eyes closed. Since removing himself from the medical facility on the shuttle, his second had become somewhat...cautious around him.

"Where are they currently located?" His words slurred, and his fingers scrabbled around on the desk for his Xeradax, but found nothing. His heartbeat sped up. "Where is my Xeradax?"

He turned his head slowly, seeking the small, black pills the medics had created on his orders. The small Ru'Edan male stepped forward, hesitation clear in every step, and the brittle edge of Crick Sur Banden's temper snapped.

"What are you doing? Get away!"

The male looked at him. "I can see your Xeradax and was

going to pass it to you." The quiet answer soothed him slightly, for the first time he took a good long look at the male. His eyes glittered when he thought Crick wasn't looking.

Was the man after his position? Everyone wanted his place. The little voice in his head reminded him of all the times when his second had taken it upon himself to do things without orders. He had allowed the man to act as his go-between with the medics. Was that why he couldn't control his body? *That's it!*

The thought bloomed in his mind as he pushed himself out of the mobility chair he had started using since leaving the medical facility. On the suggestion of this Ru'Edan male! Of course! It all made sense now. Make him seem weak and ineffectual.

Something must have shown on his face, though, as the male backed away. "My Lord?" The fright in his face filled Crick with satisfaction. *I know how to deal with traitors!* He slumped back to the chair heavily. He raised his fingers once more, finding the small laser pistol he kept on himself at all times. Under the table, his hands shook as he aimed the pistol then pressed the trigger. The male went down.

"What?" his second cried as Crick pushed himself upward, his body burning with the need for his drugs as he accepted the truth of the betrayal.

"I know you betrayed me. How long have you been going behind my back?"

The man pushed away, scooching on the metallic floor. His shaking fingers covered the hole in his chest, the blood pumping onto the floor. "My Lord! I haven't—"

"Don't lie to me! I know you have," he screamed, shaking with intensity as he watched the eyes of his foe round with shock and horror.

"No! No, My Lord! I have been loyal! I have..." The voice weakened as the horror of what was to come must have finally occurred to the male.

"Silence!" Crick Sur Banden advanced, unsteady but

nevertheless determined to finish what he'd begun. Elation roared as he raised the muzzle of the pistol once more. "Traitors deserve only death and dishonor!"

"My Lord! I didn't—" The whine of the laser split the air and cut off the words in mid-cry. The light faded from the male's eyes.

Feet pounded somewhere close by, but he only dimly heard them as he turned away, once more seeking his Xeradax with shaking hands. He stuffed them into his mouth then gripped the goblet and raised it. Drips escaped and cascaded down his shirt, but he ignored them.

"Remove the remains of the traitor." He didn't turn at the sound of the shuffling feet and dragging. Why should he? He could deal with having one more traitor removed from his immediate location.

"My Lord?" Yet another of his rogues had entered the room.

"What do you want?" His nerves had begun settling as the warmth of the Xeradax filled him with strength.

"We need to know what heading you wish to settle on."

He turned slowly and saw the evident fear in the rogue's eyes. "Bring me the charts and our current status of intelligence. Make sure Fu Xander attends me as well."

Fu had proven himself so far. He was also high-class. Educated enough to make decisions. *I can trust him. For now anyway.*

Crick made his way back to his desk, sitting down in the padded chair. His gaze settled on the pool of blood on the floor, and he depressed the commbutton on his desk. "Get someone in here to clean up this mess!"

Then he settled in to wait once more.

This time their allocated room was much bigger, more

comfortably arranged and furnished, Meredith thought, sitting down on the edge of the bed. The bed alone had room for two, unlike the one on the ship they had just disembarked from, and she smiled as wicked and lustful thoughts came to her.

"Hot time on the old space station tonight," she muttered. The words echoed, and she snickered.

Overall, she found the station more inviting, and the staff appeared more forward thinking, to her mind. Since arriving, she had seen more women gathering around, not holding senior positions, but at least not just dead-end drudges. They looked happier, not downtrodden or cowed, and that heartened her somewhat.

She smiled. "Chowd? Did you see the women in the hallway?"

He grunted absently, and she knew he hadn't heard her. Meredith looked a little closer before standing and wandering over to him. He stood, looking out of the large, reinforced window into the vast, inky blackness of space. The introspective mask that he had donned many times before when lost in thought met her eyes.

"Chowd? Is something wrong?" His manner had become more distracted since their arrival. Her feet stopped mere inches from him, his eyes devoid of happiness and hope.

"What?"

For the first time she saw something in the depths of his eyes that she would never have expected from him. Fear. *What could he possibly have to fear here on the station?* Well, obviously except an attack by rogues, but the level of security clearance looked almost too extreme, so it seemed an unlikely explanation for his distraction. Unless he was hiding something else. The thoughts tumbled wildly through her mind.

"Chowd? What's wrong?"

"I can't..." He struggled for words.

A sense of helplessness assailed her. *What more could keep us apart now?* A silent cry came from the very depths of her soul. He stepped away, and the loss of his body heat chilled her.

"Chowd? I can't help if you don't tell me what it is."

Meredith took one step then another. The look in his eyes left her with a cold, oily sensation deep in the bottom of her stomach. Concern warred with the sure knowledge that she couldn't do anything until he told her his thoughts.

A split-second decision saw her wrapping her arms around him, feeling him tense before releasing the muscles. The warmth of his body reassured her for an instant.

His arms slid around her in response, and she released the breath she hadn't realized she'd held, feeling her chest expand once again as the whisper of his exhalation ruffled her hair.

"I could have sworn for a minute that was him. At the gate when we entered."

She understood immediately. She too had seen the resemblance. It must have hit him much harder than her, and she castigated herself for missing that connection.

Quick on the tail of that realization came another. If they knew he was Crick Sur Banden's son, then they might threaten him. A primitive emotion flowed through her. Chowd was a good man. Unlike his father, he made a stand, and against all odds became someone the crew could look up to.

"Did he say something to you?" she asked.

The seed of her suspicion grew with his slow response. "What? Oh. No." But when she moved out of his arms, he evaded her eyes.

"Chowd? What did he say?"

"Nothing. He said nothing. Now let's just... Let's just change the subject."

She wouldn't let it drop knowing that something had already happened. Something that made him doubt who and what he had become. Yet their relationship had already undergone so many false starts and tests in their short time together that she felt it best to drop the issue for now.

"Fine. What are we supposed to be doing now?"

Chowd had started pacing, something he only did in the

depths of agitation. It bothered her that whatever concerned him or had occurred, he still felt unable to share it with her. The thought hurt, but she accepted that it wasn't about her.

"I need to arrange the security detail, find out the schedule of meetings and meals. However, I can't do that until Jod comes back with the timetable." He moved back to the window, and Meredith had to hold back a sigh as he once more looked sightlessly out of it.

The silence stretched as she watched him. The feeling of helplessness didn't sit well, but at this point she couldn't do anything else. Maybe she could talk to Jemma, but as quickly as that thought came, she discarded it. With Chowd in charge of the mission, it seemed wrong to discuss him with another member of the team. Right now, she wished for either Mellissa or even Elara so she could seek their advice. A slow friendship had formed between herself and Jemma, but she still felt wary of asking a lot just yet. While she thought she sat, her head dropped back to the arm of her conformable seat.

"Meredith?" His voice intruded on her thoughts. "Yeah?"

"Promise me...whatever happens, you will stay safe?"

The question had her head snapping back up, her eyes seeking his. She hated the distance she could see in them. Doubt, so deep and cold, settled in her chest, along with an unhealthy dose of despair. What did he think would happen? The fear gripped her chest like an iron vise, squeezing her breath from her lungs, choking her.

"I will if you will." What else could she say? *Yes?* She knew that was the answer he wanted, but what was the point of promising to stay safe if he couldn't or wouldn't do the same?

"Meredith...please. Promise me you'll stay safe."

"I'll try. But you need to as well. I..." She stopped and cleared her throat, starting again. "I can't...I can't go back without you." The words *I love you* lodged in her throat.

He nodded, but the action didn't make her feel any better. "I'm going to go see where Jod is. I need to talk to him." He turned abruptly and left her sitting on the seat, the emptiness crushing her spirit as hot, salty tears began to fall.

Chapter 12

Chowd paced as the anxiety ate at him. He understood Meredith's confusion; hell, she had every right to be blazingly angry at his attitude. However, right at this very moment, he felt fear that someone would recognize him. If they worked out his identity... He'd seen the look the security officer flashed his way. A slow burn of anger started once more in his gut. He hadn't asked for the dubious honor of his birth, but each time he turned around it hit him in the face.

He wanted to scream, throw something, anything to relieve the pressure, but he couldn't. No, in all honesty, he'd known that at some point this millstone around his neck would come back to drag him to the depths of hell. He closed his burning eyes. For one brief time, though, he had known physical closeness with another human, and that warmed him.

Meredith shouldn't have to deal with this mess. He turned away from the thoughts, cutting them off, and yet the pain didn't go away. It burned through him. None of it was his fault, yet he would have to deal with the ramifications and possibly— probably—hurt her. Something he never planned on doing when they got involved.

Footsteps echoed down the hall, and he looked around to see Jod Svan'Er striding toward him. "You're ready to begin then?"

Chowd nodded in silence as Jod indicated the direction they needed to take toward the meeting chamber. Neither man felt the need for talk, and Chowd relaxed. He absorbed a steady stream of information regarding corridor layouts and doorway placements. Here he could see a security vid feed, there a palm pad. Well-armed guards stood at attention at locations along the walkways and corridors.

"They are well trained?" Chowd asked.

"Each of the guards located here have been specially

chosen. Their backgrounds are thoroughly investigated. Many are members from the ruling houses, lesser sons of lesser sons. They are trained from a young age, and we test their psychological status as well to ensure that they are compatible with the roles," Jod answered.

That gave Chowd pause. "And your position?" He stopped, for the first time wondering who Jod was the son of.

"My father is the high senator. Esrau Svan'Er." He gave a half-smile before bowing.

"So, how does that affect your position?" The idea of a son of the most senior senator guarding them intrigued him. He wanted to know more, a desire he had brushed aside his whole life, yet it drove him to understand his roots.

"I was placed with the Guardian Guild at around ten cycles. As a lesser son, it was a way I could bring honor to my house." Jod paused and shrugged. "I had to have some form of employment and training. I was educated, fed, housed, and trained. In time, I will probably become the head of the Senate guard or some other security posting, depending if my father lives that long. We tend to promote within families."

Chowd considered this information. "What about those from outside the families? What chance of advancement is there for them?" The thought that the decisions of his father affected the entire family disturbed Chowd.

"There is little room. From time to time, somebody will rise up, but that doesn't happen very often. They need to be capable of something extraordinary as a healer, craftsman, or other such skills. If you're thinking about the members of your family, while they would not be removed from their positions, and many are almost hereditary positions, the lack of a Sur Banden taking the seat in the Senate means that there is no one to advocate for them, unless by marriage or by strategic alliance."

Chowd waited quietly for just a moment. "What about other things? Justice and so on?" For some reason, he felt an urgency to understand just how far the ramifications of his father's action had rippled.

"Justice is meted out by the head of the house. Given that there was no member who could rightly claim that position, there were...altercations. A distant cousin has taken over the position as head. However, as he is not of the main line, he was refused the right to take the seat on the Senate. Anyway, his position is precarious, and he rules, some might say, using might rather than knowledge." Jod shrugged. "He is harsh in handing out sentences, but generally all members abide by his rulings."

Chowd got the uncomfortable feeling that Jod was scrutinizing his reactions. "Should I...

How would it be received if I..." The words stuck in his throat. He didn't want the position of head...did he?

His confusion angered him deeply. He wasn't usually given to this level of indecision. He probably owed the members of the house something, but what? He could state his case, but that would probably cause trouble in itself. He growled deep in his throat as he considered the options open to him.

"Should you meet with him? I don't know." Jod cocked his head to one side. "It depends on what you intend to do now that you have this information. There are members of the household here. One in particular is of the main line. I am sure he would be willing to meet without letting anyone else know your intentions or thoughts."

"Let me think about it." But even as he replied, he reminded himself that time grew short. If he wanted to meet with them, he would need to arrange it soon.

Jod nodded in silence, and they moved on.

The food came in, the metallic tray carried by the serving women. Lately, Crick Sur Banden had taken to muting the light, but the women complained they couldn't see, and this had resulted in more than one accident involving spilled food.

Their eyes darted hither and thither, avoiding his questing

gaze, their movements jerky as if expecting something to burst up and smite them, which it very well could if they angered him further. He smiled, baring razor-sharp teeth, and watched as the women quaked in front of him.

He derived great entertainment from their reactions and nearly laughed out loud.

He felt good when they displayed their fear for him. These cows were only here for his comfort, after all. The thought buoyed him, making him feel masculine and more than a little aroused.

"You!" he bellowed, and all the women in the room paled, their gazes flicking to him nervously.

Which one would he command this time? The one by the door would do. She was young and reasonably fresh.

"Come here!"

She looked around, and his frustration rose. He had commanded, and they must do his bidding.

"I said get over here!"

Realization dawned, clear in the way she stopped still then bowed deeply before she slowly moved forward. His need had grown for days, and a female companion would satisfy his urges. He smiled. She looked comely enough, at the moment anyway.

"My Lord?" she whispered nervously, her eyes wide and skin pale, her body shaking before him.

She sweated profusely, the salty tang filling the air and souring his stomach. Fury spiked in his veins, the carnal need evaporating as rage took its place. He wavered then upended the tray of food to the floor with a clatter. Food wouldn't stop the pitch of his belly now.

"Get out!" He jerked his body upright, and all the women moved faster than he would have given them credit for, reaching the door and disappearing from view. Even the young one he'd commanded had left, and his body relaxed once the taint in the air was removed. The need that had rocketed through his system had fled like water down a fast-running drain.

"Whores. They're all whores." The sound of his words in the air pleased him.

The crew of his ship, nothing more than frightened Yock rabbits, bowed and scraped to him. He'd replaced his second-in-command with another youngster. But this one he would have to watch.

His head ached viciously again. He needed more Xeradax. Depressing the commbutton exhausted him, but he waited for the voice to answer. "My Lord?"

"Bring me medication." He flicked off the unit.

If they refused, he would repay them. He had plenty more to choose from. The chimes of the door rang, irritating him. "Who is it?"

"Ve'Jar, My Lord. I come with news."

The firm voice captured his attention. News? What news could he have? Perhaps this news was the capture or at least knowledge of the location of the *Elector*. That would be the perfect piece of intelligence. Once he destroyed it, then he could consider sending the Phobos pirates to destroy the Admiralty on Aenna. Of course, he had to ensure that the Phobos pirates, stinking creatures that they were, understood the need to wait until he could attend the destruction.

His alliance with the Phobos pirates had become rather tiring of late. They demanded more of him. More resources, more funding, more men. The knowledge that he would soon dissolve their agreement gave him a small measure of relief.

As soon as I have fortified my troops enough to mount an attack on Earth, then I will dissolve the agreement. I'm not ready yet, but soon I will have the resources I need. He rubbed his hands with glee at the thought of those humans finally reduced to nothing more than the refuse of their solar system. "Come."

"My Lord, I have news that the Phobos pirates tried an attack on the *Elector*. It was unsuccessful."

"*Destata*! What did they do that for? I authorized no such attack!" Anger coursed through his system once more.

The Phobos pirates had started exceeding the terms of the

agreement, and for a moment his mind weighed up the necessity of keeping them on side. He only needed them to defeat the Admiralty, then he would give the order for their destruction. The thought didn't calm him though. His thoughts splintered. *Xeradax. I need my Xeradax. Where is it?*

"Is there still a contingent of rogues near Phobos III?" He would need to teach them a lesson. His mind see-sawed now between competing issues, his hand sliding into pockets, searching for the pills that would clear his mind. Surely he had some left?

"Yes." His new second stood silent while he waited for orders, and once more Crick was filled with wariness for this newly promoted rogue.

"Order an attack. Take no prisoners. We'll teach them a lesson about following my orders."

His rogue bowed and left the room as the medic scurried in. He tore the small, black capsules from his hands and swallowed them, waiting for the relief he craved.

The meal tasted much better than that on the mothership. This time, at least Meredith could work out what she ate. The pieces of meat and vegetables were marginally identifiable, and she enjoyed the traditional music that filled the air.

The senators had also welcomed the crew and ambassador, more so than she had experienced aboard the ship. The women, seated further down, kept sending her glances. No doubt they wondered why she sat with the official party. Meredith made a mental note to talk to them.

In the meantime she listened to the conversation that flowed around her. Each of the senators had surprised her with their ability to talk in the basic human language.

"Of course, there are some houses that are not represented. Chiefly among those absent is the house of Sur Banden."

Chowd's line of questioning had baffled her up until this point of the conversation. *So now I understand why he asked about the hereditary status of the houses.* On his return from the inspection of the meeting chamber, he'd seemed aloof and distant, at least until he had taken her in his arms and kissed her. Then those worries had been forgotten.

Meredith tugged on the collar of her formal uniform as the heat of the memory bloomed, and she looked over toward him. His face was more drawn than usual, the fine features and high cheekbones accented with hollows, his eyes shadowed, and for the first time, the term 'haunted' came to mind.

The meal ended, and the ambassador and senators headed into the comfortable room beyond. She was surprised when, on inquiring if he required her translation skills, the ambassador had declined.

What else could she do? One look at Chowd showed him deep in conversation with Jod again. The fact that the two had become almost inseparable started to grate, but it was, after all, a mission.

She made her way over to the women who gathered at the other end of the room. "Greetings."

The one she picked as their leader, based on her bright clothing and ornate hair arrangement, bowed low and murmured, "Greetings."

"Forgive me, but you seem to have a position of authority." The woman inclined her head, and Meredith smiled. "The Earth Empire and its allied planets encourage women to take positions of authority. I understand that is not the case for you."

One of the women hissed slightly, and Meredith looked around.

"That is not appropriate conversation." The younger woman looked nervous, and for an instant, Meredith wondered if her thoughtless remark would stop the conversation before it started, but the older woman laid a soft hand on the younger one's arm.

"Be calm," she said, then turned her attention back to

Meredith. "While we are here on the station, we do have a wider amount of freedom. Many of our men—" She glanced meaningfully toward the room beyond. "—are more forward thinking than their predecessors. They understand that we feel a great sense of fulfillment when we have the freedom to do things and make decisions for ourselves. They are very...liberated." She smiled softly, and Meredith felt encouraged at this.

Some men, but not all. The unspoken words weren't lost on her.

"Hush, Veshnartu. We should not be discussing this," the younger woman implored. "No. If we want change, we must ask for help to affect it. Our men are open to these suggestions. I want to see our women have opportunities to be something more than a drudge." The woman, Veshnartu, turned back to Meredith. "You understand, don't you? I cannot see you being subservient to a man, no matter who he is." She smiled broadly. "And he is such a man." Her eyes glinted with amusement.

"Indeed, it's true. I am the senior cryptologist."

The women's confused expression betrayed their ignorance of the term. "Err, I decode messages and languages."

The younger woman squinted at her. "You have learned other languages?"

"Yes, I can read and write eight languages. That includes the basic language of your homeworlds. As well as that, I can also work most cryptological programs, meaning I am versed in the use of programming systems to decode languages that I cannot read or write."

The younger woman's eyes grew large.

Veshnartu smiled. "If only I had the chances you have as a younger woman, I too would have traveled the stars. But I cannot complain. I have a man who chose me to be his mate, I have carried five children and seen my sons grow up to become important men. Although I feel Jod will surpass the others in opportunities."

The information startled Meredith and she couldn't control the involuntary question. "Jod Svan'Er?"

The woman smiled slightly. "Yes. His older brother is destined to take the place of his father, and my other son will become a priest in the temples. My daughters have the opportunities to become mates to other Senate hopefuls. I worry more about their future, yet they are in a better position than most." Veshnartu sat down heavily. "Our women have few rights. My mate is working to change that within our house and those who owe us, but it will take a long time for them to find a way to make such changes. Meanwhile, the women of our houses are abducted to be little more than servicers."

"Perhaps once the treaty is finalized, there may be a way to send your daughters to us for training so they can enjoy a future as productive members of your society." Meredith snapped her mouth shut. *Barsha! I have spoken beyond my authority.* Yet she felt deeply that this was the future for the daughters of these women.

Veshnartu nodded. "That may be something we can consider. I will think on it." Then she smiled. "What house is your man from? He is a Ru'Edan? Hybrid?"

Meredith felt her hackles rise. "He is not a hybrid. He is a being with thoughts and feelings."

For the first time the knowledge assailed her of what he must have been through countless times. The thoughtless whispers and comments angered her, the same ones which must have wounded and stung him his entire life. The thought made her chest ache.

Veshnartu raised a hand. "I meant no disrespect. His name is Chowd, I understand? But what house? The only Ru'Edan I know of that would have that name is Sur Banden..." The words came slowly. "Is he? Is he a son of the house Sur Banden?"

Meredith turned to him, seeking help. It wasn't for her to tell. But they would know soon.

The back of Chowd's neck prickled. He turned, searching for the threat, only to see Meredith, her face tight, and the knot of tension he carried since arriving became even more pronounced, if that was possible.

"Excuse me," he muttered to Jod before stepping toward Meredith. Her eyes beseeched him, yet he could discern no apparent reason. "Meredith?"

She gripped his fingers wordlessly, telling him of her worry.

"Are you of the house of Sur Banden?" the older woman Meredith had been talking to asked, and he turned to assess her. Perhaps in her fourth or fifth decade, the woman was obviously of the high-class. Gray-green eyes, laser sharp, watched his movements. He felt no malice in her searching gaze. "Are you?"

"Yes, ma'am. I am."

"Of what rank?" Here lay the question he had hoped to dodge, but this woman likely held the rank of mate to a high senator, and he couldn't ignore her question.

"Immediate son and heir."

The women hissed their anger in reaction to his bald statement.

"Yet you travel with the humans? Actively work with them in the hunt for your father?" By now all talk had ceased in the room, and he felt the awareness of gazes burning him. "I do and would again. My mother was a human he took to service his needs. She bore a son. Neither of us chose our fate." He waited quietly for someone to denounce him.

"Then you would hold the seat on the Senate? Will you accept it and the position of the head of the house?"

Her words shocked him momentarily, and the tug at his hand as Meredith pulled away surprised him. The confusion ate at him from the inside out, as if a vat of acid exploded in his belly. This question had remained a constant companion since their arrival, and even when he slept there was no escaping it. Right now, he still had no answer, and looked helplessly at the woman.

"It is your fate to head your house, to lead them through these trying times. It is in disarray, women promised without acceptance to those unworthy to build alliances that should never stand," one of the other women said harshly, and he wanted to turn away from her, but responsibility was something he understood only too well. This one weighted him down against his will though.

"I don't know, yet." His hoarse words fell into the silence, and the woman turned away, dashing tears from her pale face.

He felt her keen pain, but he had to make the right decision for him and the house. He also had his oath to the Admiralty to consider, and he couldn't ask Meredith to stay with him. That thought alone sent another shaft of pain through his chest.

Suddenly the doors to the Senate chamber opened and the ambassador and senators re-entered the room, initially oblivious to the charged atmosphere. However, they quickly realized that something had happened, and all eyes settled back on Chowd.

The high senator stepped forward. "What has occurred?"

Jod pointed to Chowd. "We have the heir to the house of Sur Banden in our midst. Crick Sur Banden is the sire of Chowd Sur Banden, the chief of security for the *Elector*, My Lord." Jod bowed low, and the senators and ambassador fixed stares on Chowd, some filled with hate, others understanding, but all of them with surprise.

Chowd wanted to sink into the floor, or at least slink away. But that had never been his way, so instead he bowed low to the senators. "Indeed it is true, My Lord Senators."

The high senator, Esrau Svan'Er, looked at him, his pale, grayish-yellow eyes narrowed. "Really? You are the son of Crick Sur Banden?" The senator moved forward, and Meredith tried to step in front of Chowd, but he stayed her with a firm hand.

"No, Meredith. This had to come at some point."

"Chowd. This isn't your problem."

He knew she feared him choosing the Ru'Edan way, that it would take priority over his oath to the Admiralty. It would also mean the end of any hope for a future together, and as much as he wanted to shy away from that knowledge, the time had come to make a choice between responsibility for his house or for his humanity. He couldn't have both. He had to choose one or the other.

"My Lord Senator, if I might intercede on behalf of Chowd." The ambassador's words filled the silence.

"Indeed, Ambassador, I feel that we should sleep on this and return to this discussion in the morning. At the moment we are not fresh enough of mind to make decisions. Chowd Sur Banden, your presence will be required in the Senate chamber in the morn." With that implicit dismissal, the senators and their partners bowed low and retired from the room.

Chowd opened his mouth to explain the situation to the ambassador, but the ambassador held up a hand. "Not now. It's late, and we need our rest. I suggest we retire and discuss this in the morning when we are also fresh."

Chowd felt dissatisfaction at the situation. He turned toward Meredith to find her lips compressed, white strain lines evident. Her eyes glinted with the pain he knew the situation brought her.

"I guess we'd better head back to our cabin then." She too headed for the door as he watched.

Chowd woke slowly, thoughts of the night before battering him. Once they had arrived back at their cabin, Meredith had turned her back, grabbing nightclothes from the pile on the small shelf, and headed in silence to the sanitary unit. He waited patiently, but when she finally returned she climbed into the bed and turned her back. He understood her fears that he would leave to take his place in Ru'Edan society as Crick Sur Banden's heir, but right now he didn't have an answer to give her. *I should have told her.*

He couldn't blame her. He could barely live with himself

at the moment as he alternated between doing what felt right for others and doing the right thing for himself, and Meredith. He pushed out of the bed, heading for the sanitary unit and shutting the door. The face in the mirror looked haunted.

"You are going to have to make a choice." His statement hung in the air, a tacit acknowledgement of not just his needs but everyone else's as well.

He opened his bathing bag and reached for the denta-tab he kept handy and wiped his face. Once these small tasks were completed, he opened the door, checking to see Meredith in the same position, before stripping down and pulling on a clean uniform.

He acknowledged he'd chosen the coward's way out, but right now, he didn't want to see the withdrawal in her face. He looked back at her before swooping in to lay a kiss on her brow, careful to keep it light and not wake her. She murmured and shifted before a soft snuffle told him she had settled back in.

He opened the door and headed into the corridor. Once Chowd checked his wrist chrono and ascertained the hour, he headed to the ambassador's cabin, nodding at the two guards on night duty.

"Anything interesting?" he asked.

They shook their heads, and he depressed the call button. The disembodied voice came through the intercom. "Yes?"

"It's Chowd Sur Banden, Ambassador. Are you ready?" He hoped that there would be no waiting. He wanted to get this meeting over and done with as swiftly as possible.

"Yes. I'm coming now." The door slid open in silence, and the ambassador stepped out into the corridor. "Lead the way, Commander Sur Banden."

He bowed, and they started off, the guards taking their position at the rear as they moved down the corridors and through the checkpoints to the meeting areas. Here the senators waited, many sporting frowns. Together with the ambassador, he stopped just inside the doorway.

"Chowd Sur Banden, we thank you for attending.

Come, we will move into the discussion chamber. Ambassador Vierghent, we would appreciate your attendance as well," Esrau Svan'Er spoke gravely before indicating the next room.

They formed their ceremonial line and trooped in, the ambassador and Chowd taking the rear positions as they crossed the threshold. The chamber itself was comfortably furnished. A large, semi-circular table sat in the middle of the room, and high-backed chairs sat at intervals, all dark woods with blue textile coverings, which he soon discovered were actually fur pads.

He took a seat, nervous flutterings in his belly assailing him. He longed for a drink of water. The senators took their seats, whispering among themselves and checking desk screens. "Chowd Sur Banden, we have asked you here to discuss the situation that has arisen. For our records, please state your name, sire, and current designation."

"Chowd Sturat Sur Banden. My sire is Crick Sur Banden, fugitive, rogue, and head of the house of Sur Banden. My current designation is commander. Chief of security aboard the Earth Empire vessel *Elector*." His voice remained steady.

Esrau Svan'Er nodded before continuing. "What is the current status of your fealty?" *Barsha!* There was only one answer he could give. "My fealty is to the Earth Empire."

He took a deep, expanding breath, attempting to clear his mind. He had no idea where this would lead.

"Will you assume the mantle of head of the house of Sur Banden?" another senator asked, and many watched, waiting for the answer to the question.

"I don't know," he answered as truthfully as he could.

"What? How can you not know? What mischief is this?" A younger senator pushed back from the table in anger, and the ambassador raised his hand calmly.

"Senators, I would imagine Commander Sur Banden does not know the status of the house. He was unaware of the situation until the last few days. Isn't that right?" The ambassador looked meaningfully at him, but he didn't need coaching.

"I was unaware of this. I had long ago given my pledge

to the Empire. Any changes to that will require thought. I can't and won't change my allegiance without considering the implications fully. You would expect that of those who have sworn themselves for the Ru'Edan worlds, and I can only do the same for the Empire." He did not need this right now. Anger at the situation burned, but he wrestled with his warring emotions, reminding himself to remain calm.

He watched as Esrau nodded. *Surely they will accept that for now?*

"Under the circumstances, then, I feel it is important to share with you certain information that has come to our attention in the last few galactic days." Esrau raised a hand as some of his fellow Ru'Edan began to protest. "No. As Crick Sur Banden is his sire, it is his right to know this."

Esrau extended his long, slim hands to the holo sequence actualizer on the table in front of him. Images, hazy at first, formed into a planet. One Chowd had not seen in many years. Not since his flight from Otega.

"We have become aware that Crick Sur Banden is running and is probably in poor condition. After the battle on the Alpha Star Colony—" Esrau stopped and nodded deeply, acknowledging the part the *Elector* had played in the situation, before continuing. "He and the few rogues that were with him escaped in a shuttle. All of which you already know. What you do not know is that our spy within his camp has informed us they are headed for Otega. To his base there. They made a stop on a merchant planet, one that has no political ties to either ourselves or the Empire. At the time of the loss of the Alpha Star Colony, he suffered other losses. Losses that he may not yet be aware of, if our intelligence is correct, but that we understand will cause him some discomfort. Some females and rogues he held by force escaped from the planet. Among them, we know of one other hybrid." Esrau stopped and looked hard at Chowd.

Another like me? Before any reply could form in Chowd's confused mind, Esrau continued.

"Like you, this one is also a child of Crick Sur Banden.

Of course, as with yourself, the daughter was born of a human mother. We believe that he was holding on to her in order to create an alliance. At this stage, we do not know who with, though it wouldn't surprise me if it were the Phobos pirates."

Chowd stood slowly, his mind whirling around the ramifications as he paced behind his seat, fingers spearing through his hair. This news shouldn't surprise him, yet he found the knowledge both unexpected and worrisome. *Another hybrid like me? One Crick will sell to the highest bidder?* Anger churned in his gut at the thought of another creature bought and sold for Crick Sur Banden's ugly purposes. A half-sister, bred to use to curry favor. He turned back to look at the senators, concentrating on taking the information and filing it for later consideration and investigation.

"What else?" His voice sounded strangled and tight as anger bubbled, but he controlled himself.

"We know that the injuries he sustained when you escaped have been causing him to become unstable. He is addicted to Xeradax."

Chowd nodded. He too had learned that. He still had contacts within the base, but none of them had shared the other information. He wondered about that briefly before shoving the questions aside.

"And?" He looked at the senator, waiting for whatever else he had to share.

"You do not seem surprised by this news. Tell me, Commander, have you an informant within the base?" the younger senator called out, and Chowd turned, fixing him with a stare he hoped would quiet his outbursts. In response, the senator scrunched down in his seat.

"Will you accept the position of the head of the house and renounce your fealty to the Empire?" Esrau waited for his answer.

Ahh, how I wish I could avoid this boggy ground. He opened his mouth to reply, but the ambassador beat him to it. "Senator, I must protest—"

Esrau raised a hand. "In all fairness, Ambassador, I need the commander to answer." His eyes turned cold while rapid-fire thoughts tumbled around in Chowd's mind.

I can only give one answer. "Senator, I will not renounce my fealty to the Empire." He expected an angry outburst, yet Esrau simply smiled.

"Thank you, Commander. I think we are concluded for now. However, you must realize that this opens a can of worms. One that must be addressed. Either you accept the role you should, by birthright, assume, or step aside. In this case, I need you to be sure. On that basis, I believe you should have time to reconsider." He spread his hands. "You are excused."

Chowd took a step back, glancing at the ambassador, who looked as confused as he felt. Yet even now, some of the sting in the air began to dissipate.

"What will... What will happen to the house if I don't accept?"

"In this instance, it was necessary for an heir come forward. They need to renounce it before we could mandate a new head. There is one here. He is... He thinks as we do. But we will require you to formally denounce your position, should you choose to take that path. Take some time and think it over, because once you make a decision, it's final." Esrau smiled, and Chowd felt the heavy chain of responsibility.

"I'm ready now." Chowd thrust forward his chin, but Esrau shook his head. "Later. You must reconsider the choices and opportunities that come with it."

Chowd nodded and backed out of the room, the door closing in front of him. He walked over to a chair and sat with a thud. What in *Eshra*'s name has just occurred?

His comm bleeped, and he lifted the device. "Yes?"

"Chowd? Where are you?" Meredith's voice filled the air, and for the first time since leaving the cabin, he smiled.

"Outside the meeting chamber. Why?"

"Because something's happened, and I think you need to come and see." Her voice was strained, and he felt a moment of panic. He had left her alone. What if something had happened to her? *Barsha!* How could he face Duvall if Meredith was hurt? How could he live with himself?

"Meredith—" A buzzing noise emanated from his communicator. He shook it. "Meredith? Are you there?" All sorts of visions filled his mind, but there was only one thing he knew for certain—he had to get to Meredith. *Now.*

Chapter 13

"I can't..." Meredith looked at the blackened shell of the ambassador's room. Someone had obviously expected to find him there. Not even she'd known of his absence this early. Something had exploded with a bang, catching her attention and creating a mess of the ambassador's suite. The smell of burned textiles filled her nose, and she grimaced. Eyes running, she coughed and took a step back from the smoky doorway.

She'd tried to finish telling Chowd what had occurred and that she was unharmed, but her communicator had failed right when she'd needed it most. Her stomach churned when she thought about how he might get the wrong impression that something had happened to her, but there wasn't much else she could do right now. He'd be there momentarily.

Raven stood in the doorway with Jemma. "Whatever it was, there is very little evidence for us to collect. The sooner we get back to the *Elector* and away from these Ru'Edanians, the better," he added under his breath, and she smiled, knowing he hadn't wanted anyone to hear.

"Chowd will be here soon, and he'll know what to do," Meredith said.

For the first time since this mission began, she allowed her misgivings to take form in her mind. She was unsure of her ability to hold her own in the face of the repeated attacks on them. After all, she'd done nothing but cause more problems than she solved.

Jod Svan'Er had deployed guards to seal off both ends of the corridor, so the sound of thudding footsteps captured her attention. *Maybe it's Chowd.* She turned, her hair swinging free.

"What in *Eshra*'s name happened here?" His voice cut through the air, and she slumped a little, feeling reassured by his presence. He didn't look in her direction and that cut her to the core. She twisted her fingers together as she watched.

"Some sort of incendiary device. I can't find a starter of any description, so I think it must have been quite rudimentary." Raven grimaced. "Jod Svan'Er has called for an investigative team from the guardian unit. He says they should be here soon."

Chowd grunted and moved into the room. He crouched beside the remains of the device on the floor and began talking quietly to Jod. Jod's hands moved as he said something very low, and they rose together, checking something against the wall before nodding and going their separate ways.

"I'm taking Meredith to our cabin for debriefing. Raven, take Jemma and wait outside the chamber for the ambassador."

He gripped Meredith by the arm and propelled her forward without another word. Once within the cabin, he flung his arms around her. "*Barsha*! I was so worried when I received your hail. If anything had happened..." He crushed her more firmly against his body. "Chowd—"

"No. Don't."

The distress in his voice concerned her, but she remained still in his arms, waiting. He'd cut her dead, but his reaction now... it confused her further. She accepted the embrace, returning it in equal measure as the silence stretched, broken only by his ragged breathing in her ear.

At length, he loosened his grip. "Meredith, we need to talk."

Her heartbeat stopped, and her knees trembled. No woman ever wanted to hear those words. She'd never categorized herself as a coward. Her expectations of this relationship had always been short.

"Perhaps we had better sit down."

She moved to the bed, lowering herself to the soft surface. She would accept his decision with grace and dignity, she thought, all the while knowing that she lied to herself.

"So? You want to tell me it's over?" She kept her words blunt as she waited for him to agree.

"What? No!" He sounded affronted, and for the first

time she chanced a look at him. On his face she saw such a look of shock that she almost laughed. But the distance between them, and the ups and downs of their relationship in the last few weeks had reinforced their differences. That he could exist without her in his life. *Could I be wrong?* Her traitorous heart whispered *What if?* while her head told her to act sensibly and accept reality.

"Chowd. Just spit the words out. I can't continue like this." To her horror, her voice broke as emotions roiled inside her. She turned away, but his hands reached out, pulling her back, gentle yet unrelenting.

"No. Meredith, you have it all wrong."

She dragged in a ragged breath. "Then what?" Her eyes burned, her chest so tight she felt sure suffocation would soon follow.

"For the first time since I realized who and what I am, the way forward is clear to me."

He stopped, and she wanted to scream as the silence continued.

"What? What then? What do you want from me?" The words escaped, and *Eshra* help her, she couldn't call them back.

"What do I want? I want forever. With you. Meredith, I'm not exactly the best you could do, but no one will love you like I do. When you called me over the comm, I swear, I envisioned everything that could possibly happen. Then Jod let me know that no one had been hurt." He ducked his head. When he lifted it again, his eyes shone. "I had to stop and compose myself before I got here. The guards must wonder what's wrong with me. Stars alone know, I don't act like this." He punctuated each of the last words with a hard fist to his chest.

She opened her mouth to reply, but nothing came out. Instead, she looked at him mute and lost.

"*Barsha*! Meredith, put me out of my misery. Tell me you will accept me, forever. Commune with me?"

She sat back as shock ricocheted through her. *It can't be this easy. This simple. Could it?* His quiet request hung in the air between them. "What happened beforehand, Chowd?"

He winced, and she swallowed the lump that returned to her throat.

"They asked me to take my father's position as head of the house. To accept a seat in the Senate. They asked me to renounce my loyalty to the Empire and make an oath of fealty to the Ru'Edan Senate. I couldn't. Then when you called, it was clear to me. You...you are where my loyalty lies. First and foremost. Then to the Empire. They took me in when I had no one else. When there was nowhere else. But you accepted me for who and what I really am."

Her eyes stung. "Are you sure? You could have your choice of any of their women. Status. Everything." I need to be sure, her heart cried.

"You. Only you, Meredith."

She cast about, considering her answer, unable to frame the words he needed to hear. "Say yes, Meredith. Three letters is all it will take."

"Ye... Yes." The word was a croak but the look on his face, the exultation, told her it was the correct answer.

He leaned in, and for the first time since they boarded the mothership, she felt the frisson of arousal his touch invoked burn brightly. "Now, let me love you the way I need to."

Slowly, he pushed her back to the bed, unmade beneath her. His tender kiss, so soft and gentle, filled her body with heat, with need, and her lips parted to accept his tongue.

"Stars, Meredith. What you do to me." His quiet words echoed in the cabin as his long fingers quested for the fastener of her uniform before pushing the material aside gently. He removed her bra as she strained against him.

Meredith wriggled her hands free, returning the favor, savoring the touch of sinewy muscles. Each kiss became a vow and every touch a promise. "Chowd!" Her whisper broke as his lips trailed down her throat, nipping and sucking alternately. She shivered in reaction to his lovemaking.

Movements became urgent as they fought against the

bonds before they finally lay entwined and naked, skin against burning skin. Meredith hissed in reaction, the pleasure spearing through her body.

She raced her greedy fingers up and down his back, gripping his backside, as his fingers plucked at her sensitive nipples. She keened with need, and he growled deep in his throat.

She pushed at him, and he raised his head. "What?" The word was little more than a grunt. His cheeks were flushed and the glitter of desire shimmered in his eyes.

"This." One quick, hard push and she had him on his back.

His eyes were wide as she straddled him, seating herself against his erection. Hot. So damned hot. This time he gripped her hips, understanding dawning as she slowly, so achingly slowly, lowered herself down, showing she was ready. She was more than ready for his intimate invasion. He entered, and the slickness of her need made it easy. She whimpered at the feeling as his hands moved again to her breasts.

"Meredith! How I love you."

She moved, and he did too. Meredith closed her eyes, her heart hammering in her chest in tune to the sensual web they wove together, each thrust winding her tighter.

"I need you, Chowd."

Faster they moved against each other, searching for the place only lovers can experience, and finally she exploded, holding still as her body rippled in the act of climax. His fierce cry filled her with exultation, and she smiled as her body slumped against his.

The cool air chilled her damp skin. He tugged the covers over them, his arms holding her firm against his body. Forever was within her grasp.

Chapter 14

Crick Sur Banden made his way around the cabin, each fumbling step surer than the last as his mind finally started to clear. They had landed on Otega just this morning, and he had staggered to his suite. His new second had tried to offer him support, but he knew now what they wanted. *They want to control me.*

His commander on Otega entered, looking grave and concerned. What could be of greater concern than his current situation? His mind cleared, and he knew what the medics had done. The way they scurried off after the landing told him they knew that once his mind cleared, he would need to exact retribution for drugging him against his will. But before he made them pay, he would enjoy himself.

"My Lord. I have information of great consternation to impart." His voice wobbled slightly, intriguing Crick. Perhaps more had happened than he thought.

"Then report."

"Lord, after news of the Alpha Star Colony was received, several of our more...uncooperative assistants shared the information and absconded in one of the shuttles. They took your daughter, her mother, and a few other slaves with him. Together with the scientists you held here." He bowed low, and the news hit Crick Sur Banden like a physical blow.

"How could this have happened?" He grasped the back of the table, needing the support. How could things go so wrong now? The answer firmed in his mind. He needed to get his heir, Chowd, to come back to the fold and take his rightful position. He needed to destroy his enemies. Duvall McCord and the *Elector* stood in the way. And every human had to die. Then it would be as it should be.

He had no more time. Now, more than ever, he needed the Phobos pirates to think that he was prepared to give them a connection to form an alliance with his rogues. Of course the girl was nothing more than a pawn and her loss a minor irritation. Once he had dealt with the pirates, he would have used her again. For as long as she had trading value, he would have made use of her.

His lip curled, and he ran a tongue over his ragged teeth. *Think.* He needed to think.

"Bring the strategists here in four hours. The time for waiting is past. But before you do that, exterminate every one of the medics who traveled aboard the shuttle." He waited for a second before adding, "Oh, and I shall require my second to attend the meeting, Nexus has a new job." He smiled as the commander blanched.

For the first time, the noose he had evaded for so many years felt like it was tightening around his neck. Someone on the shuttle had shared the news of the Alpha Star Colony, causing this latest mess. He would find them, and they would suffer an excruciating punishment.

He found his way to his seat and hunkered down, the carafe of Arturian wine awaiting him. He poured a goblet, lifting it to his lips and drinking deeply. The Xeradax he had taken had warmed his body once more, and he relaxed fully, letting the goblet rest on the table beside his seat—the one he thought of as his throne.

He had suspicions his new second had informed on him, and now he had all the proof he needed. The knowledge ate away at him, but finally the end of this particular game loomed. Crick rubbed his hands together as he began to consider the viable steps he could take to destroy the Earth Empire.

Meredith slept while Chowd drowsed in the bed. He smiled. The lovemaking had been so much sweeter than at any other point in their relationship.

Thoughts of the political mess he had caused rose in his mind, and he gulped, knowing he would need to talk to Meredith, explain his position and the choices he was about to declare. It was the only fair and right thing to do. He couldn't ask her to commit to him without knowing everything. And she deserved to know before he declared his intentions to everyone else.

He would also need to let the ambassador and the Senate know of his final decision. How they would react...well, that was anyone's guess. He flung an arm over his eyes. He shouldn't have taken this personal time with Meredith, but it had seemed somehow imperative that he show her just how much she meant to him.

She murmured and turned. "Chowd? What's wrong?" Her husky question turned his insides soft once more.

"We need to talk."

"That's what started this." The amusement in her voice made him laugh. "Well, I don't know about that, but this is serious, Meredith. I have a problem."

Admitting that didn't exactly come easily. "As I told you, I've been asked to take a position on the Senate, but I can't. It's not right. My allegiance is to the Empire, but firstly, to you. So I need to tell them, make a final declaration, as such. I'm going to refuse the position as head of the house. I don't know what the ramifications will be. But I gave my allegiance to the Admiralty, and now I'm giving it to you as well. You, Meredith, are the single most important reason. Not my uncle, not my connections or friendships. You."

She sighed and wriggled in closer against him, her fingers rubbing over his chest in circles. "I think I already knew this. But you have given me the most tremendous gift." She kissed him lightly. "So now we plan. The ambassador will state your case if need be. Plus, I doubt any of us will leave unless you're with us. Me? Well, that goes without saying. Raven and Jemma certainly won't, and I'd be willing to bet that your security team wouldn't either. We'll get through this. Together."

He closed his eyes for just an instant, hoping he could

make her words come true, but wishing and hoping wouldn't be enough, so he carefully disentangled himself. "I need to go discuss this with him and the Senate." He pushed himself away, picking up his clothes, and she sprang up after him.

"Not without me, you aren't." She hurriedly pulled on her clothes, covering her beautiful flesh and straightening her hair with rapid motions of her fingers. "Throw me a denta-tab, would you?" Meredith called as she headed with a determined stride toward the door. She caught the tiny packet he tossed in her direction. "Come on, slow poke!" Her eyes glittered with mirth, and he smiled, even in the midst of his concern.

The door slid open, and they moved down the long corridor, first checking the ambassador's cabin. It was empty so they continued, hand in hand, stepping through the security measures until they reached the dining area. As they reached it the ambassador stepped out of the room, his guards closely behind him.

"Ah, Chowd! I need to talk to you." His words sounded serious, yet Chowd detected a spring in his step.

"Ambassador, I was just coming to give you and the senators my final answer." Instead of acknowledging those words though, the ambassador gripped him under one elbow. For a man employed in a sedentary position, the grip was tight. "Son, let's talk." Chowd cast a glance at Meredith, who looked confused.

"No, no. Warrant Officer Gentry should wait here."

"No way. I'm coming with you." He felt the tug of her hand, and with a small shrug, the ambassador led them toward the Senate chamber.

"Quickly, tell me your decision, Commander. What will it be?"

Chowd looked at the ambassador, his face pale and drawn in the partial light. "After due consideration, I can't give up my position with the *Elector*. My allegiance is to the Empire." He said the words simply, and the ambassador's face split with a large grin. His blue eyes, clouded just seconds before, now cleared.

"Yes, that is indeed a wise choice. Will you tell me why?"

Chowd shook his head. "Ambassador, it would take so long, and some of it isn't just with my needs in mind."

The ambassador nodded. "Yes. Well, if it's best done, it's best done soonest. Come on, we need to let the senators know your decision."

They trailed the older man into the chamber. The ambassador smiled. Chowd held Meredith's shaking hand firmly in his, and the shivers betrayed her nerves. They waited, standing just inside the chamber.

"Senators, I believe the commander has made his decision. Commander?" Ambassador Vierghent inclined his head, and Chowd had to swallow a lump in his throat.

His mouth dried as he stepped forward, and Chowd wished he had some cold water as he let go of Meredith's hand. "Senators, after much consideration, I must decline to take up the position as the head of the house. My allegiance has been to the Earth Empire. They have given me position, training, and a life. While I am aware of the honor this position will bestow, I cannot in all conscience accept it." Chowd steeled himself for the reaction, only to feel surprise when Esrau started to clap.

"You have chosen well. There would have been reservations on our part should you have accepted so easily. However, you do still owe your house a debt of allegiance as well."

Chowd opened his mouth but was stayed once more by the hand of the senator. "I understand you cannot take on the position, yet should we enter into this final agreement with the ambassador, both sides will need good people. For our part, and I speak for the entire Senate, we would humbly request that Chowd Sturat Sur Banden of the house of Sur Banden should act as emissary to your homeworlds, Ambassador."

"I am sure that can easily be arranged, Senator. I am authorized to make certain arrangements, and I believe that falls within those guidelines."

"Then, Ambassador, Commander Sur Banden, and Warrant Office Gentry." There were some surprised looks at her inclusion, and the question in the senator's voice echoed their wonderment at a female in this chamber. "We have reached an agreement."

The entire Senate stood and bowed low. For the first time since arriving, Chowd breathed deeply, the shackles falling away. He returned the bow as servants came, parchment in hand with the agreement terms, before all members of the Senate made their mark, followed by the ambassador.

"I would ask that you take Jod Svan'Er with you on your next mission, and some of our guards as well. We have already opened discussions with your Admiralty to ensure that this takes place. We propose a joint strike force to once and for all deal with the scourge of Crick Sur Banden. I believe it was one of his men who was behind the destruction of your cabin here, Ambassador, but I must wait for a final report from the guardians." The senator's face tightened, and Chowd felt sorry for any human or Ru'Edan who dared cross such a powerful, composed, and intelligent leader.

"I will also put this to the Admiralty, Senator. Now, with your permission, since we have concluded our negotiations, we will make arrangements to leave in the morning. If your men could liaise with Commander Sur Banden to make this happen, we can deal with any issues that may arise, swiftly." They bowed low before the guards showed them out with great ceremony.

✪ ✪ ✪ ✪ ✪

Meredith folded their items and stowed them into travel sacks while she waited for Chowd to return. So much had happened in the last few weeks. Peace with the Ru'Edan was on its way, and most of all, of importance to her personally, she and Chowd had finally come to an agreement about their relationship.

She'd experienced shock and pleasure to see how well the senators had accepted his decision, and she suspected she hadn't been the only one. Then the reality of the situation had descended. They'd never really expected him to accept the role. Perhaps they had wanted a way of testing his loyalty. To see if he really would change sides.

The door slipped open, and Chowd stood there, a broad smile on his face. Jod Svan'Er waited behind him, face averted as Chowd stepped forward, reaching for her. Meredith reveled in the zing of awareness as his strong fingers framed her face in a way that made her stomach flip-flop. The touch of his lips on hers ignited the fire within, and she wanted more. The brief interlude came to a quick end as he pulled away, his eyes shining, truly happy in a way she had only glimpsed during their lovemaking.

Chowd grasped the bags from her, hefting them over his shoulder. "Come on, let's get on board and start the journey home."

Home. The *Elector* felt more like home than her parents' house had for a long time. Not that she didn't love her parents, stars knew she adored them, but the time for making her own way had long since passed. Up until now, though, she hadn't had a home of her own. Instead she had existed in her suite on Aenna and had never bothered getting an apartment on Earth, preferring instead to return to her parents. No, she had no single place that felt like home to her, at least not like the cabin she shared with Chowd on the *Elector*.

"Yeah, let's go home." The words filled her with warmth and a longing for her own bed. Sure, she was aware of the grave danger ahead. Who knew how long it would take for them to complete their next mission, or when they would be safe from Crick Sur Banden? But she promised herself to make the most of every minute they had together.

Meredith glanced over her shoulder, taking one final look at the room where her life had finally come into focus before turning toward the corridor and her future. With Chowd.

They moved down the hall, the sound of footsteps absorbed by the floor coverings with Jod Svan'Er, head of the guardians, trailing in their wake. She'd caught sight of the broad smile on his face. If she didn't know better, she would say he relished the opportunity opening before him too.

They entered the customs area where they'd first boarded the station, voices calling to them, and she looked around to see most of the team members wearing smiles like hers. The transfer took place, and crewmembers accepted the designations of their previous cabins. They remained just as uncomfortable and spartan as she remembered, but the spirits were high, even among their newer Ru'Edan comrades. Jod informed them that he had handpicked the Ru'Edan members of the crew based on their ability to accept new situations, and their skills had gone over very well with the *Elector* contingent.

Each day traveling back to the *Elector* they spent working with the new team members, teaching them about the functions of the ship, translating directives, and forming connections while training in various combat skills. The training needed to turn them into a cohesive unit. Finally the ship halted within hailing range of the *Elector*. Chowd hailed Duvall, and they waited in the quiet on the bridge for the *Elector* to answer. The screen cleared, and then Duvall's face, wreathed with a smile, filled the viewing screen.

"*Barsha*! It's great to see you all back. When do you make the transfer?" His eyes twinkled.

"Soon. Did you receive a directive from Admiralty?" Chowd kept his query brief and to the point.

"Yeah. Bring 'em aboard."

Chowd nodded to the waiting *Elector* crew. Meredith released the arms of her seat, feeling the sting as the blood rushed back into her fingers. Her nerves had quivered and shook while she waited for the official response to the agreement that would form a unified task force between the Ru'Edan and the Empire.

"Right then," Chowd said. "We'll head directly to the

shuttle. A second shuttle will travel with us to carry the new crewmembers. I have split both teams into two to make the transfer as easy as possible. We plan to launch in around half an hour."

"Fine. I'll meet you in the cargo bay within the hour. McCord out." With that the feed dissolved.

The ambassador unstrapped himself from the safety harness, as did the rest of the crew, and stood before moving toward the captain.

"We thank you for your hospitality and hope that the goddess bestows safe travels and a cycle of goodwill upon you." The Ru'Edan ritual words of farewell were met with deep bows and similar sentiments. Then the ambassador left the bridge, and the crew traipsed behind him.

The team chattered as they boarded the shuttle. The trip from the mothership back to the *Elector* felt like it was made in near record time, probably because the spirits of the *Elector*'s crew were high.

Once they'd disembarked, the second shuttle disgorged its passengers. Chowd's men hurried down the stairs of the second shuttle as the Ru'Edan guardians wandered more slowly into unfamiliar territory.

Duvall waited with a smile on his face. "Ambassador, good to have you back here. We intend to rendezvous with the *Star of Ishtar* as quickly as possible then continue on toward our next mission."

The ambassador merely grunted, his behavior once more cool toward the crew. He now avoided Meredith completely. While on one level, Chowd felt pleased that she would be spared his amorous attention, the dismissal of her and her skills sat poorly with Chowd. He felt the professional slight keenly and wondered for an instant if there had been a more politically appropriate way to deal with the situation, but he pushed the thoughts aside. It was too late to change it now.

Duvall turned to him. "I'm glad to see everyone back in one piece. First introduce me to your new team members, then we'll set up a debriefing." His voice was calm, but his eyes narrowed on the shadows of the bruises still on Meredith's face. "And we'll talk later," he told his sister.

"Captain? I have some things to deliver to the security suite. So if you'll excuse me..." With a quick turn, Meredith left the hangar.

"Captain Duvall, this is Guardian Jod Svan'Er. He'll remain with us until we have completed our mission to hunt down and neutralize Crick Sur Banden and his rogues."

Jod strode forward, hand extended in a human gesture of goodwill. "Captain McCord, over the years, we've heard about you and your team. It is indeed an honor to make your acquaintance."

Duvall looked at him, and Chowd considered just how enigmatic the man truly was as he smiled and shook the hand of the Ru'Edan. Duvall countered Jod's comments with a dry, "Well, I don't know about that."

Mellissa stepped forward to take over. "Guardian Svan'Er, allow me to conduct you and your men to your cabins. I have arranged for members of our crew to help you find your way around. I do hope the accommodations will fit your needs appropriately."

Jod looked back with a smile before gesturing to his people, who followed Mellissa from the hangar.

"Fill me in on what happened quickly, before there are any interruptions, Chowd. Don't leave anything out."

Chowd accepted Duvall's cold words, quickly running through everything that happened, not sparing details when describing Meredith's abduction and escape, the offer of a place on the Senate, and the failed attempt on the ambassador's life. He also described the conditions of food and accommodation aboard the mothership, and together they laughed, making their way toward Chowd's cabin.

"I think we need at least an hour to sort ourselves out, along with a quick handover from my security staff, then I can meet with you?"

Duvall nodded. "That works. My office. I'll alert the senior crew and…What did you say his name was? Jude?"

"Jod. He's the son of the high senator, so it wouldn't hurt to get him used to our way of doing things."

"Yeah, I'll beep him and get Jemma and Raven to show him to my office. One hour." With that Duvall strode away, and Chowd entered the cabin, dropping his small bag to the floor as he moved toward his desk.

He was in the middle of taking a video report from his second when the door opened, revealing Meredith, travel bag slung over her shoulder. He could only watch from the corner of his eye as she looked at him in silence then to the floor where his bag lay. He grimaced as she collected it with a smile and carried it to the bedroom.

His second hurried through the last stages of his report; not that much had occurred, but the stocktaking of the armaments, munitions, and catching up of paperwork, which always seemed to get pushed aside for later. Chowd had requested its completion while they guarded the ambassador and Ah Run had attended to the task. Chowd smiled at the harassed quality in his second's voice as the screen turned black. He rose and headed to the bedroom, stripping as he went, and entered the sanitary unit.

The water turned off, the sound of the final drips that never seemed to go away filling the air as he entered the small room just as Meredith left the shower cabinet. "I would have left the water running, but you looked busy and I didn't want to bother you."

"You didn't. I'll just be a minute. When you're dressed maybe you could arrange a coffee for us before we attend the meeting?"

She moved into the cabin, the slight flare of her hips tapering down to softly rounded buttocks drawing his eyes as he fought to concentrate.

"You know we could always forgo the coffee and see what we have time for instead." Her cheeky grin flashed over one shoulder, and he discarded the idea of a shower for something far more satisfying.

The expanded senior crew entered the office. Meredith watched the newer members find seats at the table as Duvall entered, a frown marring his face. Meredith knew something big was coming.

The young ensign who usually delivered foodstuffs stood there, dispensing coffee, tea, and water to the gathered crew. Once everyone was served, Duvall waved him away, and he left the room, the door of the office sliding closed behind him.

"Door, lock with override only by me or senior crew."

This is new. Her stomach dipped as Chowd gripped her hand beneath the table.

"The Admiral wishes to address us." He pressed a button, and a holographic transmission rose above the table.

The Admiral cleared his throat, his face tense. "Before I begin, I would like to extend a welcome to the Ru'Edan members who are joining us in the taskforce. This is indeed an occasion I never thought to see in my lifetime."

He paused for what seemed like forever, and Meredith squirmed in her chair, waiting for the news of their mission. While she had a vague outline, the detail would make clearer exactly what was required of the *Elector* and her crew.

"I have received a communiqué from the Ru'Edan Senate. Their information shows that Crick Sur Banden has made for Otega, a planet in the Pavo-Indus supercluster. We know that for many years he used that as his permanent command base, with a range of other haunts that he frequents. However, after an attempt on his life, he abandoned it."

The Admiral spoke slowly and with deliberation, and a cold feeling of pre-sentiment flickered through Meredith.

"All reports point to his return. It could be that he has munitions and rogues, or he could be running. Indications make us believe he has returned to Otega as he's been weakened to the point that his power base is questionable now. From what we have been able to glean through our contacts, there has been an attempt at a coup, which was spectacularly unsuccessful."

He scratched his head, and looked gravely at the crew gathered around the table. "We know that his mental state is fragile at best, resulting in manic and paranoid episodes, likely related to his addiction to the chemical, Xeradax. We are aware that he has executed members of his medical teams and his immediate second. Intelligence we have received from our Ru'Edan friends also tells us that many of the scientists and others he has forcibly held made their escape some time back and he's taken that information badly. Given that we believe his mental condition is highly unstable and that there is a move afoot to mutiny against him, we, the Ru'Edan Senate and the Admiralty, feel that this is the best time to mount an assault. To be clear, all and any force necessary is acceptable, including the use of deadly force."

Meredith gulped, realizing the importance of this mission.

"Therefore, your orders are to make your way forthwith to the supercluster, find, and once and for all neutralize the threat of Crick Sur Banden. I've instructed Captain McCord to make arrangements for all non-essential staff and, of course, the ambassador to immediately transfer to the *Star of Ishtar*. The *Ishtar* should be within range to make the personnel transfer within the next twelve hours. The *Elector* will take on a small squadron of six fighters to bolster your current numbers. Warrant Officer Gentry, you are to remain aboard the *Elector* and offer any and all assistance required."

He looked them in the eye and she saw the sorrow and regret. Meredith's stomach curdled.

"Ladies and gentlemen, I take this opportunity to wish

you all the best. This is singly the most dangerous mission you will undertake for the Empire. As such, please ensure that any documentation of succession is complete and undertake the transfer of personal effects to the *Star of Ishtar*. The fate of the alliance between our worlds is in your hands now. Good luck. Elphin out."

By the end of the transmission, Meredith's mouth felt dry, and she reached for the glass of water in front of her, noting that her hand shook slightly.

"Are you okay?" Chowd had leaned in, his eyes concerned.

"Honestly? I don't know. I'm scared silly." What else was there to say? She wished she could cry or scream, but she felt cold. Strangely detached from the realities that loomed.

"I have made arrangements for papers to be brought in," Duvall stated. "At this time, given the gravity of the mission we are about to embark on, I would ask that you prepare any final messages and wills, so that in the event we are unsuccessful, they may be sent to families. I will ensure that these are transferred to the *Star of Ishtar* for circulation as appropriate, should there be a loss to the *Elector*." The words echoed through the room.

The young ensign returned, bearing paper and pens in the tradition of the Admiralty, ensuring that the families would have a tangible last communication with family members lost in battle. His eyes were red-rimmed as he laid the items before the members of the crew, and Meredith knew he had already prepared for what was about to come. He placed extra sheets in the middle of the table and withdrew once more.

She glanced around the table where the crewmembers were either bent over the parchment or leaning back, eyes closed, as if lost in thought.

"I don't..." She looked at Chowd.

His face was grave as he returned her look. "Write from the heart, my love." Taking a deep breath, Meredith picked up her pen.

Dear Mum and Dad, I hope you never read this letter...

The mood on the ship had dropped to its lowest. The crew scurried here and there, removing their personal effects and transferring desk screens and readers. Others checked the life capsules, making sure they had adequate oxygen, armaments, munitions, and life-sustaining supplies. Engineering staff checked the hibernatory settings of the pods, ensuring that each was adequately provisioned, and double-checked for oxygen and remote location sensors.

There wasn't an inch of the *Elector* that went uninspected. Duvall walked the halls and ordered anything suspect to either be repaired or replaced.

On the night before departure, Meredith lay quietly in the bed. "Chowd, what are our chances?"

He rolled to his back and exhaled with a hiss. "I don't know. The one thing I do wish is that you weren't here."

She bit her lip and frowned. "I'd rather you weren't either. But when we joined the Admiralty we knew chances were that we'd see action at some point."

"I just... I want you safe, Meredith. If only we'd had more time." She laughed. "Well, I did try before."

He sighed at her arch comment. "Yes. You did." He gathered her close and they slept until morning, wound around each other.

The following day was the same. No one stood still. Even the kitchen staff kept busy, preparing meals and placing them in the feeder chutes for those remaining on board. No one knew how long the mission would take, but the atmosphere told Chowd that everyone shared the knowledge that this was a life-or-death mission.

He checked and rechecked rosters and the results of the inventory check, redeploying his crew, making decisions on which *Elector* crewmembers would stay and who would transfer to the *Ishtar*. Duvall and Grayson had requested he attended to those matters while they dealt with other aspects of the mission.

The whole time he worked he wished he could ask Meredith to leave. That decision wasn't his to make though.

Meredith sat in the security office, checking and rechecking every transmission she could find, looking for holes and loops in the little they knew. *So damned little.* He racked his brains, making notations on the pad beside him. The memories of nearly twenty years ago were probably faulty, he admitted silently, but it might give them some edge, so he continued making small notes.

Once the *Ishtar* came within hailing distance, Duvall called the entire crew together in the cargo bay. Red-eyed members of the crew assembled in the hangar. Jemma suited up, ready to fly the shuttle back and forth. Duvall stepped forward to address the crew, and a cold hush fell over the area. Everyone, including the new Ru'Edan crew, stood waiting in silence.

"We have assembled for one final time. You are all aware of the gravity of our mission. Those who stay behind have been chosen for specific skill sets. Those who will transfer to the *Star of Ishtar* leave, not because they have nothing to offer, but because this mission needs you to continue on a different path. As a crew, we have come together, taken a new and untried craft, and set a standard much higher than any other ship in the Admiralty has ever before achieved."

He paused, and every member of the crew watched him, waiting for him to continue. "The Admiralty has since launched other craft like her, but no other will be the *Elector*.

Whether we live or die, no other crew will be like our *Elector*. And no other crew can do me as proud as those of you standing before me. You made the *Elector* what she is today. If this is to be goodbye, then do so not with long faces, but the light of battle in your eye. For we are the *Elector*."

Harsh cries of battle filled the air as everyone accepted the words spoken by their captain. Duvall gave a single salute, then turned away and walked swiftly through the door and beyond sight, and the hush once more descended.

Many were overcome, wiping away tears as Grayson

stepped forward, his words ringing through the air. "You have all been assigned to a role, be it reporting to the various commanders on the *Star of Ishtar* or here. Wear your uniform and your *Elector* badge with pride. Remember, you represent all who've taken shelter within her. Everyone wants to be one of us, but few will ever achieve that. Safe travels and farewell to those leaving. Dismissed."

For just an instant longer, they waited before the tide of movement began. Jemma clambered up into her shuttle, and crewmembers assigned to the first run swiftly entered the holds on the small shuttles that arrived to redeploy the crew. Then the doors clacked shut, the cargo bay door opened, and the shuttles rose, heading for the *Star of Ishtar*.

Chowd remained there, watching the movement as the doors shut once more and the plasglass of the secure shielding opened with a whoosh. Great metallic cargo boxes were filled and stacked, ready for the return of the shuttles. From time to time, the klaxon wailed, and they moved within the safe zone again as people came and went in the small crafts that arrived and left with monotonous regularity. Those who would swell the ranks of his security crew came first, and he met them, sending them with his second to attend meetings and find their designated cabins.

Medics arrived as well, along with the captain of the *Star of Ishtar*, for a final face-to-face briefing with Duvall, the gravity of the visit clear in his quick look and long sigh before he disappeared into the corridor with Grayson. The extra combat pilots arrived together with their ships, seasoned pilots with the best crafts to offer support to the *Elector* in what they hoped would be the final battle of the war.

The long days of preparation continued with a level of organization that belied the rush, while people moved like ants across the plascrete of the bay until finally the *Elector* settled into a waiting silence.

The final shuttle landed, and Jemma quickly stowed everything away. The extra combat jets hung from the roof of the cargo bay, fuelled and ready to go. Chowd took one last opportunity to walk around the hanger, checking and rechecking the security settings.

"Secure the hanger bay." He threw the command over his shoulder as he exited. There was nothing more he could do there.

Chapter 15

Rage coursed through Crick Sur Banden's system, making him burn. So they'd once more been infiltrated. Even days after learning this fact, he still couldn't dismiss the anger that rose in his gut. The death of the medics had made a proportion of his rogues so much less compliant, and he feared that this could somehow stop him from achieving the result he knew would allow him to reign supreme.

How could this happen? The words had become an almost constant refrain in his mind, stopping him from sleeping. Is this all I can look forward to, he wondered as the weariness dragged at him.

His most loyal rogues now stayed with him all the time. They alone offered him protection, yet even among them, he could sense discontent. They need a victory. Something to offer them a break from the waiting and watching.

Warriors could not, and should not, have to wait for battle. Soon, though, his body would recover, and he would lead them to the mightiest victory they had ever celebrated. *But that's a lie, isn't it?* The Xeradax now only gave him nominal relief. His body tensed and released, spasming constantly as his mind dimmed then refocused.

The only remaining medic searched for alternatives, though he hadn't missed the look in his eye. The Xeradax was failing, and he needed another option quickly.

He knew his periods of lucidity grew shorter, and he feared what would happen soon. One of the rogues would take the final step and ascend to the coveted position his only remaining son and heir should assume. Not that he showed any signs of being worthy, but at this time, Crick had no further options. *I need my son.* He would have to find some way to make Chowd come on his own if force didn't work.

Steps moving quickly caught his attention. "What's the

latest?"

One of the rogues scurried over to report. The small unit in his hand beeped furiously. "Sir, there is movement afoot. The treaty between Earth and Ru'Edan has been finalized. We believe they will now send a joint strike force after you." He looked fearfully toward Crick.

"Nonsense. They don't have the resources yet, nor a team sufficiently cohesive." He brushed the report off. After all, years of war had weakened everyone and caused so much dissent, it couldn't have come to an accord so quickly. And a joint strike force? No, that was just another rumor.

I have weakened them with my constant incursions. Besides, he told himself, they don't know about Otega. He stopped for a moment. *Do they?*

"What about my spies in the Admiralty?" The question came out thick and slurred, but he pierced the rogue with a cold look, one that would have had them running in the past, but he still retained enough power that the rogue paled.

"Nothing. My Lord...I believe they have been compromised."

The rogue's quiet voice had Crick working hard to hear, and the Ru'Edan shook, his hands convulsively moving with fright as the pupils of his eyes dilated and his nostrils flared. The scent of sweat filled the air, acrid and biting.

Compromised? Well, I have spies surrounding the senators too. "The spies on station?" The rogue gulped. "My Lord...we have heard nothing...for days. I believe they have also been compromised."

He scurried backward as Crick rose. Unsteady though he was, he still moved with purpose. The rogue slipped backward to the ground in his attempt to escape. Crick bared his teeth. Anger lent him speed and sureness of step.

Fools! Always surrounded by fools!

He reached for the laser he now perpetually kept holstered on himself. His finger itched, and even as he fought against the urge, it rose in his hands, and the whine once more split the air.

Fzzt!

His second came running, the sound of pounding footsteps loud in the sudden silence. "My Lord..." The words died away as he spied the rogue writhing in his death throes upon the floor, a stench filling the air.

"Fools, I am surrounded by fools and ingrates," he muttered. "What? What news do you bring me now?"

His second swallowed heavily, and Crick's eyes were drawn to his neck. The constriction of muscles suddenly seemed of great importance.

"Nothing, My Lord. I came when I heard the sound. However, is there anything you require?"

The words came out thinly, as if trying to escape an obstruction, and Crick began to laugh at the idea of a blockage in the rogue's throat. Maybe that was something he could try on the humans. For an instant his thoughts splintered, whirling away, but the question was repeated, and his need redoubled, gripping him tight.

"Xeradax! Bring me more Xeradax!" He stumbled back to his seat, the pain in his limbs suddenly overcoming his mind as he lifted the goblet of wine to his mouth. He felt the liquid spilling over his hand. "We must begin preparations to invade Aenna..." he mumbled as once more his head slumped backward and his eyes closed.

Chowd ached. He stretched the muscles of his shoulders again, looking for relief in the meeting that had droned on for hours.

"We believe that Crick Sur Banden has an extensive underground tunnel system. Chowd has drawn as much as he remembers of it, but the problem is, we really don't know what fortifications he has." Duvall's voice, strained and tired, filled the air.

They all shared a level of exhaustion in the lead-up to the mission, averaging eighteen to twenty hour days, returning to their cabins to sleep then back at their posts after forcing the nutritional supplements and foods that tasted like sandpaper down their throats.

"One thing we do know, though, is he has new fortifications in place since I got away," Chowd said. "The information has come from a number of sources, Duvall. We need to find a way of jamming them first before we consider anything else. So far we've managed to find a way to do so on the small installations he has placed, but there are others, much bigger. That's before we get into the whole deal of how to cope with the underground tunnels when we do reach the planet. He has Phobos pirates constantly circulating. Given the situations when we have met them previously, we can be assured he has other surprises as well. To be honest, the thing we need right now is downtime for the entire crew."

"Chowd, we're all tired, but we need to formulate plans to deal with every aspect of the mission. We can't go until we know what we can expect to face." Duvall's words were firm, and Chowd took a look at his friend's face. Shadowed eyes and a five o'clock shadow shouted of his exhaustion. He knew the same look could be found mirrored on his face.

Beside him, Meredith drooped in her chair. They'd been at this for hours, checking all the information they had on file about Otega, collecting and sharing the information they had gleaned from the Ru'Edan. That included details of the capture of the insurgents who'd attempted to kill the ambassador on the station.

Elara stood. "You know, as the SurgiTech, I'm going to overrule all of you. We've been in this meeting now for over eight hours. None of us can continue to work at this pace without adequate downtime, as Chowd has pointed out. So I'm ordering this meeting closed." She looked sternly at Duvall, who had opened his mouth only to close it again with a tired nod. "With all due respect, Captain, none of us are functioning at our best.

We need rest. *You* need rest. A minimum of four hours, but my preference is eight. Time to sleep and eat.”

Duvall nodded as they stood, ready to leave. Meredith swayed slightly, and Chowd put out a hand to steady her.

“Chowd, can you stay for a minute.” Duvall’s words weren’t a question, he knew, and he looked into Meredith’s owlish eyes. She slowly blinked then nodded as if she understood and made her way out the door with the others.

Once the door shut, Chowd turned. “What?”

“I know you’re concerned. We all are. I’m also aware of the amount of pressure you are feeling right now.” Chowd opened his mouth, but Duvall held up a hand. “Listen, you of all of us have no love for Otega, but we have to get it together. If we don’t, many more will die.”

Chowd closed his eyes. His friend had hit his fears smack in the center. His memories, the things he’d tried to forget. But remembering the scene he’d left behind hurt. He had so much to lose this time. Last time he’d lost his mother. He didn’t want to lose his family, his friends, and more importantly, the woman he loved.

“I asked her.”

“I know.” Duvall paused with a heavy sigh. “She told Mellissa. That makes you my brother, although in every way that counts you already were. Let’s get through this so we have something to celebrate afterward. Now I’m ordering you to rest. Make sure Meredith does too. If you don’t, she won’t either, and I need both of you ready to go in the morning.” Duvall turned away before muttering, “And for *Eshra*’s sake, if your shoulders hurt in the morning, go see Elara.” Duvall moved toward his desk in tacit dismissal.

“Are you going to tell on me?” For a moment they resumed their customary banter. “Yeah, I might at that.” Duvall sat behind his desk, logging back in.

“Go to bed, Duvall. I’m heading for mine.” “Not yet, I still have a few things to do.”

“I’ll beep Elara if you don’t take her advice.” He smiled

for the first time since the situation had evolved, knowing his words sounded childish.

Duvall looked at him, shock clear on his face, then he too smiled, which became a laugh. "Yeah. You're right. Let's get some shut-eye."

Duvall rose, and Chowd left the room without looking back. He wandered slowly down the corridor, the ship settling in for the night in silence, and he found that comforting. Meredith would wait for him, but he needed the brief time alone. He needed time to sort through his emotions as they twisted through him.

His last view of Otega had been in the screens of the ship as he'd run away. The day his mother had died. Now he would return and do everything in his power to save the Empire. His mind told him he couldn't even save his mother. "Dammit, I was little more than a child at the time."

He'd return as an adult. It didn't make the sting any easier to bear though. He had carried the loss of his mother for so long like a stone around his neck, and now he had to cast it off. He didn't know if he could do that as easily as he wanted to. Chowd sighed.

The door stood in front of him, and he needed Meredith. Not just the feel of her body, but her soothing presence too.

The door slid open, and there she sat. "I've been waiting for you." Simple really. As if she'd read his mind.

In the morning he would talk to her, but right now, he needed to sleep with her in his arms.

Morning arrived, just like it did every day on the *Elector*. Soft chimes wakened him as the lighting automatically switched on, but today would be unlike any other. They should reach Otega today. He really needed to talk to Meredith. Those two facts converged in his mind.

She rolled, stretching slightly, her beautiful eyes searching his face. "Good morning. I can see your mind is already turning over." The amusement in her voice faded away as she watched him. "You're worried. Tell me what concerns you." She would always face life head-on, his Meredith.

"Otega. I'm thinking about the last time I was there. The day my mother died. She got me out, gave up her life." He gazed sightlessly at the wall, reliving the horror he felt. But he had to get the words out. He felt a burning need to explain to her so she understood his fears. He didn't know why, but it seemed of great importance.

She waited in silence as he drew ragged breaths. Her small fingers linked with his as his chest expanded, and he let go.

"She knew the time was coming when I would be conscripted, essentially. Once my brother died, there was no option, and we already had bags packed and hidden. She'd trained me, prepared me for our escape, even plotted a course. She was the one who ensured I learned how to pilot the shuttle. I always had suspicions of what she did to arrange it, but I never asked. Not then."

His heart beat like a drum in his chest, and pushing the words out hurt, as if pushing them past a lump in his throat.

"We got word that morning that he, my half-brother, had been killed in combat. " The memories came fast, cycling through his mind. "She all but dragged me to the cargo bay, but they shot her down just as we were heading up the ramp. They shot her like an animal. She made me go. I didn't want to, didn't really understand at the time, but she did. It was the chance she gave me, that meant I could..."

He looked into her eyes, unable to continue. His eyes burned with a mixture of remembered emotions and fury. He hadn't ever allowed himself to feel the grief, not properly, since that day.

"She died in the hanger. I engaged the thrusters, and that's how he got the injuries. That's why he relies on the Xeradax.

I don't even know what they did with her. I never found out what happened to her body, how they disposed of it. I don't even know if there was anything much left to deal with after..." A river of hot tears ran down his face, and he turned away.

She placed a soft finger under his chin. "You did exactly what you had to do. She wanted you to get away. To survive. You did that, and now you can avenge her. Chowd? Don't ever turn away from me. I could handle most things, but not that." She leaned forward and laid a chaste kiss on his lips, all the while enfolding him in her arms.

She waited quietly, not saying a word, just holding him, giving him the strength he needed to face the herculean task ahead of all of them.

After he'd settled, she loosened her grip. He looked at the wall for just a minute longer. "I've never told anyone everything."

Her smile was sad. "You needed to talk about it. Having it bottled up for years made it so much harder. We can talk again about your mother when all this is over."

"I'd like that." He cast Meredith a quick, grateful look as he rose, his body and mind more refreshed than it had felt in a long time.

He pulled on the clothes he had laid out the night before as she tugged on her own flight suit.

"When this is done, I want us to arrange a communing ceremony. With your family and my uncle present." His voice echoed in the silence.

"I'd like to do that too." She smiled softly, and he felt the warmth of her love once again filling up the empty places inside him.

They left the cabin together, walking in the direction of the mess area to grab a quick bite before heading to Duvall's office.

The mess hall was full of Ru'Edan fighter pilots and what remained of the crew. With nowhere to sit, they grabbed their trays and headed straight for Duvall's office. The door slid open to reveal Grayson and Duvall making last-minute adjustments to their flight path. They would have backed out, but Duvall motioned for them to come forward.

"We have just intercepted this." He held out a communication log, which was clearly from Crick Sur Banden It was full of invectives. Each answer and question from the Phobos pirates grew shorter and more curt after Crick instructed them not to openly engage the *Elector*. "Meredith, does it look like anything you have seen from Crick Sur Banden before?"

She gripped the printed sheet in both hands, scanning through the text. "This is along the lines of some communications I have seen from him, though this looks more...I don't know... uh, almost paranoid. Chowd?"

He quickly read the log. "It's the Xeradax. It affects the user's brain in the long term, and it fits with the information we've previously received that he is showing paranoid tendencies. It looks like his deterioration is more rapid than I expected at this point." He stopped for a minute. "Where did you get this?"

"From a friendly passing Phobos pirate." Duvall's dry words took him aback. "The words *friendly* and *Phobos* don't usually go together."

Duvall's face split into a grin. "This one was. He's headed as far and as fast away from Otega as he can. The other interesting piece of intelligence he passed on is that there is major dissent in the Phobos ranks."

Chowd looked at Grayson. "Indeed? How is there dissent?"

Grayson grinned. "Apparently the head of the Phobos pirates had been promised a wife to cement the treaty between the two factions of Phobons and Ru'Edanian rogues. She isn't forthcoming. To make it even more interesting, he also stated that Crick is, in his opinion, no longer capable of leading the rogues."

A wife? Could that be his half-sister? He brushed it aside for thinking over later and digested the information Grayson and Duvall shared.

The chimes on the door rang once again and the rest of the senior crew trooped in, looking rested. They stood upright, clearly determined to make the mission a success. He wondered what they would make of the latest development.

Duvall moved to the end of the table, watching them all with a small smile. "Let's get started. We have some very welcome news, if it is indeed true. Grayson?"

"We have received information that tells us the Phobos pirates might not be committed to Crick and his plans. In fact, we think that they are abandoning him. We've already heard whispers of mutiny within the rogues. All of this could..." Grayson stopped, allowing the words to sink in before resuming. "We think this could make Crick just a little bit easier to defeat. It doesn't mean simple, but perhaps this is the divine assistance we've needed for a long time."

No one made a sound, and Chowd waited as they absorbed the facts Grayson had shared. He did detect a lightening of their moods, and as they leaned forward their eyes glinted a little brighter.

Grayson slipped another image up on the screen, and a video ran, showing small craft leaving the surface of Otega. "We've already heard from one stating that he feels Crick may be more than just a little paranoid. If that is the case, then we might be able to use that as leverage. He also suggested that there is a similar situation on the ground. If the rogues are truly in disarray, and we attack quickly, I feel we have a strong chance of success."

Duvall nodded. "I need to send some combat pilots, or one anyway, in to scout the area. We need someone who can get in and out quickly. I need a volunteer who can drop a relay device that will bounce transmissions back to us without being seen. Jemma? Are you up to that task?"

"Yeah, I can manage that. I'm guessing you want me to take one of their spooks down and pretend I'm one of them?" Jemma's fingers flew over her small palm unit. Her lips pursed as she checked something on her screen before glancing up. "Once that relay is in place, we'll be able to hear and see what's going on, making it easier to utilize our pilots to maximum efficiency. That works for me."

"We need to strike hard and fast." Duvall rammed home his last statement with a clenched fist banging on the tabletop.

Last night the crew had been unable to find the energy to begin, but with this new information and sleep, they were once more the cohesive unit Chowd remembered.

The others had flipped open their hand units and began making notations, calling out points to consider in the plan. Chowd's spirit rose, and the weight in his chest lifted again. This crew, the *Elector*'s family, would finish this. They were ready for whatever eventuated.

"Just let me check this bit of code on the booster." Meredith pinged the booster one last time, ensuring it worked optimally and nodded. "Yeah, that should be good."

Jemma climbed into the cockpit of the small spook as Raven fitted the booster into the missile bay. A feeling of excitement and trepidation hung in the air. People moved with purpose as they made preparations to take shelter behind one of the moons some fifty-thousand kilometers from Otega.

Jemma would need to make a slow and circuitous entry, drop the relay booster onto the lunar-like landscape, then slingshot around the planet, using a convoluted trajectory to get away. Meredith knew the maneuver would be tricky, as did Raven and Jemma herself.

The alarm wailed its mournful warning, and they moved into the safe zone, the glass sliding shut between them and the decompressing shuttle bay. They watched as the small ship powered up, Raven holding his breath beside her, and she detected stress lines fanning around his mouth. The shuttle rose and exited the bay, into the blackness of space.

"She'll be fine. If anyone can achieve this, it's Jemma."

Raven nodded stiffly but said nothing, his gaze following the trail of her burners before she executed a sharp turn and was beyond their sight.

Meredith rubbed his arm. "When you're ready, join us for a coffee in my office."

He gave a curt nod without a word and she left the area, heading for the security suite. She could do nothing more there.

For herself, there was great uncertainty. This could all go horribly wrong, and her gut churned almost continuously. She had gotten what she wanted, to see the action, but deep down she acknowledged her fear at being quite this close.

She hooked up the listening equipment in her seat, watching the blip of Jemma's stolen ship move slowly toward their projected location. She swallowed, waiting for anything that could go wrong.

Meredith continued working on the information they had, though in all honesty, it felt unnecessary at this point. But the coffee and actions kept her mind employed while she waited. If she didn't have something to do, she'd go mad. No one had ever told her about the long, anxious hours of waiting before this kind of mission.

They'd counted on Jemma's part of the mission taking maybe an hour or so, and that time had nearly elapsed. Meredith looked forward to seeing Jemma return safely to the *Elector*.

"How's it going?" Chowd's words had her jumping with fright. Her intense concentration meant she hadn't heard him move in behind her. Meredith dropped her head back to lie against him, savoring the heat of his body.

"Won't be long, and we should see her drop the relay beacon. Once that's in place, then we'll get a more accurate idea of what is happening." Even as she murmured, Meredith could see the effective deployment of the relay.

"How soon can you bring it online?"

"Once it lands, it will open the casing shell, releasing the relay dish. Thank heavens Raven was able to manufacture this so quickly."

Chowd's body tensed behind her. "What are the chances of it not working?" Fingers kneaded at her knotted shoulder muscles, and she groaned slightly as they released under his touch.

"Around five percent."

A blip appeared on the screen beside her, and she waited. Another blip appeared, then another.

"It's working." Her hands flew over the keyboard, tapping in the command to activate the program that would allow the data to start flowing to her screen.

"I'll inform Duvall immediately." But he didn't move. Instead he continued to rub her shoulders and watch the screen.

"Go on. I'll let you know if anything happens."

Chowd gave her shoulders a final squeeze before he left.

Once more she waited alone, the air cool in the empty security offices. Meredith looked for ways to extrapolate as much as possible from the jumble of information flowing through the system. Voice messages streamed around her, though it wasn't her job to scan them. No, the comm officer would deal with that. But she listened as she worked, looking for something that would tell her what was going on inside the bunker on Otega.

She tweaked and the squark of a voice transmission filled the air. It was hard to hear over the static, and she tapped into the system, adjusting the levels until she could clearly hear the words.

"I don't care that the one you had is gone. That was the agreement." The tense words came through the comm link, and she stopped. She didn't recognize the voice, but it angrily demanded an answer.

"Our lord does not answer to you," a haughty voice returned, and she nearly giggled, but she managed to restrain herself. *I really don't need vids with this lot to listen in on.*

"So you have no intention of completing our agreement. Get Crick Sur Banden for me, or this alliance is concluded."

"Oh my!" The import of what she listened to hit her.

There was more than just dissent in the ranks, and here she had the proof they sought. She touched a trembling hand to the commbutton. "Duvall? Are you listening to what I am?"

"Meredith? What are you talking about? We haven't got past the jumble of voices yet. What can you hear?" Duvall demanded.

"Hang on and I'll patch it in through your personal comm." Once more she tapped into the systems. "Okay. You should be able to hear them in a minute. The Phobons have just demanded something that is gone. I'm thinking it's the girl we've heard about. The Ru'Edans are saying Crick doesn't have to answer though, and that wasn't taken very well. Just hang on."

Another voice came across the line. One she knew. Crick Sur Banden. "How dare you demand my presence."

"We had a deal, Crick, the girl for the alliance. Get her for me, or it's done. We all know you cannot hold anything now, anyway," the pirate taunted, and Crick Sur Banden's harsh breathing filled the air.

"I don't need you now. My rogues don't need you to bolster their ranks. We number in the thousands and can defeat anyone."

Meredith could hear the false bravado clearly in the wobble of his words. *Barsha!* He didn't believe what he was saying.

"Then our alliance is at an end."

The communication ended abruptly, and she sat there, stunned. "Duvall? Did you hear that?"

"Yeah. Get up to the bridge right now."

She stood, taking only a second to grab her personal unit and stuffing it into a pocket before taking off at a run. Crew got out of her way as she ran, her chest heaving with the exertion.

Meredith reached the bridge in record time. Duvall was in conversation with Chowd and Grayson, and she moved forward. "Started without me?"

"Something like that. Jemma is due back soon. But

judging by the exodus I'm seeing from Otega—" He indicated toward the screen, where blips of ships departed from the planet. "—we need to attack sooner rather than later. He's going to be off-balance with the Phobos departure. His men will be questioning his leadership." Duvall stalked around, spearing his fingers through his hair while he spoke. Nervous excitement rippled through her belly.

"I can see if I can tap into my source. See what's going on down there. I don't normally do this directly, but I think in the situation, we don't have time to use the more roundabout fashion." Chowd pulled a small, portable device from his pocket, one that she'd never seen before. He tapped in a message and waited.

The comm officer hurried toward them. "We have an incoming message from Pilot Cardnew."

Chowd turned. "Put her on speaker."

"Can you hear me?" Jemma's voice filled the air.

"Yeah. What's going on?" Duvall demanded as he watched the radar feed.

"There are ships going everywhere. All Phobos pirates, but they're heading away from the planet. Duvall, what the hell is happening down there?"

"There's been a major event. Do you think you can break away and take a different route?"

"Already doing that. I should to be there in about an hour or two. Have a hot coffee waiting for me. I suspect I'm going to need it." The fierce words made them laugh.

The communication between the small Phobos craft and the *Elector* faded away. "I want to know as soon as she lands. Prepare for a meeting in thirty. My office." Duvall turned away, and Meredith knew they had been dismissed.

Chapter 16

"**C**howd has received an answer from the surface. The rogues are in mutiny, the Phobos pirates have pulled out, and Crick is holed up currently with his closest allies. I think, though, that rather than an assault on the planet, we would be better coaxing him out." Duvall strode around the table.

Chowd's body was tight, every muscle locked down as his mind absorbed the plans they'd laid. Soon. Then he would avenge his mother and the many thousands who'd died at his father's hand. With the thoughts came the grip of tension.

Everyone at the table and those standing behind nodded, each and every one of them committed to whatever it took to rid the universe of Crick Sur Banden.

"In his current state, I think he'd be more open to this kind of ruse, but still, it needs to be executed carefully. We need to take the *Elector* in closer to the surface. I know of an area of dead space, somewhere outside of the trajectory of weapons fire, where we can hold him off. One of my contacts discovered it some time back." Chowd stood and pointed to a section on the surface. "We have to be exact in our piloting, but it's something they wouldn't expect us to be aware of. I'm not sure they are even aware of it, it was only discovered by accident by my contact down there." He jabbed a finger at the map, showing a clear patch, free of asteroids and space junk. "If we stand off here, making sure our Raptors are behind these moons here and here, we can use the *Elector* itself as bait. They'll bring everything they have to bear and we'll be under heavy fire. Any pilots he has left will pour into the breach." He closed his eyes, and let the final point coalesce in his mind.

Duvall countered, "We should also formulate an alternate plan, one in preparation that he won't take the bait. He's a wily opponent. I wouldn't be surprised, even in his least lucid moment, that he doesn't sniff a trap."

Meredith tensed beside him, and he gripped her shoulder. Chowed spoke quietly but with determination. "In that instance, I will take a small crew down to the surface while you continue to engage with the rogues."

"I'm not so happy about that, but I do agree," Duvall said. "We need to get to Crick and neutralize him. Based on the information we've gathered, it's clear that if we remove the head, then the rest of the body will follow. My only wish is that I could join you."

Chowd smiled at how his old friend still wished to command every landing team they sent away.

"Everyone needs to be armed, so when this meeting breaks, Chowd and the security officers will need to see you down in the firearm hold. Everyone dons flak jackets as well as breathing apparatus. If we fail, we might be on our own in a life capsule." Duvall's words were terse.

"If it's going to happen, it should be sooner rather than later. We don't want to give them time to regroup," Grayson said thoughtfully. "I'll also give the command for every non-essential power system to be turned off. We can re-route the power to our shields, guns, and thrusters.

That will increase our ability to react."

"When do we expect backup?" Jod's voice broke through the subdued conversations as orders were relayed to subordinates in low tones.

"In the next twenty-four to forty-eight hours. None of us expected this break or that we'd be engaging so soon." Duvall shook his head. "We can't rely on them helping at this point."

"If we can generate a message once we're about to take position, one that doesn't sound staged, I think we could entice him out. Get him on one of the shuttles." Meredith spoke quietly, and Chowd knew she didn't want him leading the charge on Otega. She continued to look for any way possible to make that a non-event. He laid a hand over her trembling fingers. They tensed then relaxed.

"Okay. I want to be in position in the next hour. Make all

arrangements, then ping me to let me know your preparations are in place. Meredith? Continue to monitor every system. I want to know if he so much as sniffs our plan in the air." Duvall looked directly at Meredith, and she nodded.

A mixture of emotions, elation that it would soon be done and fear that they could fail, ran through Chowd. He took a long look at everyone around the table, memorizing their faces, the determination, and in more than one, a tinge of expectation and apprehension. Then he stood. "Captain, before we go, I want to say it has been an honor to serve with you, and I truly hope that isn't the last time I get to say that."

A ripple of laughter broke out around the room.

One by one, they filed out, until it was just Chowd, Mellissa, Duvall, and Meredith.

"Duvall..."

Duvall stopped Chowd's words with a raised hand. "I know. When this is over, though, you'd better be planning a damn good ceremony."

Chowd nodded before reaching for Meredith's fingers. They left the room, and he tugged her along the corridor to his cabin. "Chowd, what are you doing? We don't have—"

His kissed her. Once wasn't enough. She tasted ripe and sweet, and he savored her. For an instant, his muscles tightened, and he pulled her close to his body.

"I need you to stay out of the way. No jumping in and trying to save the day. Promise me, Meredith."

"I promise. But you stay safe too. No heroics. I have a plan for the rest of our lives. And that's going to be a long time. Together." Her voice sounded ragged with intense emotions, and it pained him that she felt such fear. But not once did she ask him to walk away.

"Wear the jacket and make sure you have your pistol on you at all times." He pressed a last, hard kiss against her lips before he turned. He found it the hardest move he'd ever made and the fire in his chest seared him. But he had to get to the firearms hold and start arming everyone. She could look after herself, but the physical wrench felt like he had left a part of himself behind.

He took an unsteady breath and started walking.

The *Elector* took up position in clear sight of Crick's base while Meredith sat by the monitors. She had several of the security and comm teams help her haul the basic machinery and find an empty data port to plug into on the bridge. That way they could shut down security and turn off the life-support systems.

Mellissa waited in sick bay with Elara and the medics, the transmission system turned on so that they could shut down most of the ship. Jemma lead the charge from the small, stolen Phobos craft.

"Everyone is in position here, Captain. We await your signal." Jemma checked in last. Raven had his team re-routing everything they could into the shields and thrusters. Life support in the non-essential areas had been disengaged.

Chowd and his men had suited up, prowling the halls using their EVA suits. The bridge remained silent as Grayson brought the *Elector* into position.

"Comms, initiate transmission sequence now," Duvall said. The sound of his voice arguing with Chowd filled the air, just as they'd agreed, broadcasting for the universe to hear. "I am not going to let you leave. Dammit, Chowd, you gave your allegiance to the humans and the Empire."

"Duvall McCord, I never promised to do anything. I'm going back to my father. I will lead the rogues eventually. It's my destiny."

The rapid pulse of Meredith's heart echoed in her ears. Surely everyone else could hear it too? Now they were entering the final phase of their plan, her mind focused on the task before her. If the situation went exactly as planned, the ruse should flush Crick Sur Banden out. She winced, though, at the grade-school script. It was the best they could come up with between the preparations.

"Transmission is now completed, Captain." She waited for the reaction. How long until he took the bait? Hopefully Crick would act quickly.

"Captain? We're being hailed," the young comm officer called out, and everyone turned to Duvall.

"Patch the two of us in. No video though." She held still, barely breathing.

"So, my son is finally come home. Release him and I will spare you, Captain McCord." Duvall raised a hand, and the empty life capsule ejected.

"You are a fool if you think we would be taken in by an empty capsule!" The voice was slurred and angry.

So far so good as Crick Sur Banden reacted as they expected. Her fingers curled into the palm of her hand, cutting into the flesh. She kept her eyes on the equipment before her.

Crick launched a volley of missiles, but Chowd was right. There was indeed a dead space, one Crick was unaware of, and they detonated without making any contact.

She silently thanked Chowd's contacts on the planet for that little piece of intelligence before looking to the monitor ahead. The first of the ships they expected erupted from their hiding places. The two small combat craft they had kept by the *Elector* met them. More ships launched, and the fighting began.

The two small craft dodged and wove, avoiding damage. One of the rogue ships strafed the front of the *Elector*, but the laser guns dealt with it quickly, a flare lighting the darkness before fizzling away.

So far the *Elector* had only taken minimal damage. The channels started buzzing, and

Meredith listened in to the sea of voices. Instructions to the ships filled the headset she had put on.

"Duvall! I think he's about to launch the whole damn lot!" Her stomach curdled as she called out.

He whipped around. "Everything?" His eyes glittered in

the red light.

"Yeah, his own shuttle is being readied, and they've entered lockdown." Her fingers tapped quickly on the screen. "I'm bringing up everything we know about it. *Barsha*!" She gulped but kept reading. "It's supposed to have sub-atomic missiles," she whispered.

"Keep listening, Mer. We need to know everything."

"One of their attack ships has launched. They are bringing missiles online," the comm officer called, and they braced for the wave of impact.

With an audible bang, the *Elector* shuddered. Another missile made contact and the ship yawed again.

"Firing!" one of the tactical officers called, and they cheered as the first ship disappeared in a cloud of light and parts spinning out into the inky blackness.

"Another!" The incursions came thick and fast.

The *Elector* used its thrust, moving quickly, looking to avoid the ground-to-space weapons. Every now and again, one exploded close by, the ship enduring another shuddering wave.

The combat pilots now emerged from their hiding place, joining the firefight. Meredith could see the sparks and explosions on the screen, watching the dance of death play out before her eyes.

"Shields are falling to thirty percent. Our stern is also down to fifteen." Grayson's voice was almost lost in the hubbub.

"Is there any way you can increase it?" But even as her brother spoke, Grayson shook his head.

Yet another missile hit, and she pitched to the floor, feeling the jar and aches before looking around, then grappled to pull herself upright. Duvall remained in his chair, face grim as he clutched the arms of his command seat. One of the lights flickered and went out, yet mechanics waiting on the bridge for such eventualities had already started working, scrambling to refit it to the ceiling.

An ensign flung from his seat, one arm now hanging limp, whimpered, and with the limb obviously broken, he was transmitted to sick bay immediately. Someone else took his place, and they kept going. The scent of sweat and fried electrics filled the air, the noise horrific as everyone called out status updates.

More than one member of the crew died, hit by debris, their bodies moved to the side of the bridge, and others took their seats. Conduits sparked while cords hung from the roof of the seriously damaged bridge. *How can we possibly prevail?* Looking around, she seriously doubted the *Elector* would survive.

The thoughts assailed her, yet when she looked at her flickering console, she knew that for all the damage they had sustained, they'd made headway. That's when she saw the blip of the tiny shuttle heading in their direction. "Duvall. The shuttle is closing on us."

He turned his grim face toward her. "Let him come."

Another crash, and the ship shuddered wildly. The klaxon stopped wailing now, and an eerie silence descended. This time the feeling in the doomed ship changed as screens flickered and died along with lights. Everyone on the bridge hushed, and all eyes turned to Grayson.

"They've hit our steering and thruster units. Both are beyond repair. The damage to our matrix is also irreversible." His words froze her stomach.

"Sir, the damage to the stern is over all the decks. We have a section of hull plating missing on the cargo bay too." The officer called out a litany of damage, and her fingers curled in reaction to the fear eating at her belly.

"Raven?" Duvall's voice was thin, and for the first time he leaned forward, his eyes closed.

"The matrix is compromised. I'm giving the order to abandon engineering. But first I'm flooding the corridors with oxygen so everyone can get to the life pods." Raven's tired voice over the comm betrayed the battle he had fought and lost deep in the bowels of the ship.

"Elara? What's your report?"

"I have a range of injuries here. Three fatal, five are critical and with no hope of recovery. Another five I can make partially mobile."

"Get as many of them as you can to life pods and strap them. Then get yourself and your people settled into others. I have a plan." He turned away, his face graven in the green emergency lighting. "Jod, I need you to help Elara with her patients then leave with them."

"I would—" Jod's voice filled the air, but Meredith could see the determination on her brother's face. He had an idea.

Duvall cut him off. "Go help her. She can't do it alone, and they may need a male there for protection."

She saw the pain in Duvall's expression. The *Elector* had entered her death throes. That explained why Duvall wanted the patients in SurgiTech moved, but not what he planned to do.

With slow movements, Duvall reached for the comm. "All crew, prepare to abandon ship."

They were dead in space, what more could they do?

The *Elector* hung in space before Crick's shuttle, lights flickering along its hull, and the gaping section of emptiness filled him with joy. His whole body ached, but finally his son was ready to return. Of course, that could be another ploy, but Crick Sur Banden no longer cared. The *Elector* lay within his grasp, and that meant Duvall McCord too. He would kill that creature yet.

"My Lord? Our pilots have hit their steering and thruster units."

He smiled. "Good. Keep going. I want all shields gone. There must be no way they can escape. None at all." His hand cramped once more. He finally accepted that his body was failing and that he would not survive, but he could make one last statement. *If I have to die, I will take as many as I can with me.*

Dragging his body to the ship, he knew the pilot and crew had realized the extent of his infirmity and that their leader would soon be gone. Up until now, he'd managed to control the pain, allowing him to ignore the truth, but the Xeradax could do no more for him. Crick's mind cleared as his organs started to shut down. The pain racked him, urging him to finish his task quickly, before it was too late. Time melted away, and he had to make preparations. Crick knew he had to name a successor soon.

"My Lord? What would you have us do?"

"Do? We will board the vessel. Kill Duvall McCord and take the women. Capture my son. Then blow the *Elector* out of existence." He stopped. "Board her once all the shields are gone. I will come with you. I want to see the final seconds as Duvall McCord realizes he has lost and that I have won."

A spasm wound its way through his body. He gripped the nearest surface while his rogue watched. "My Lord, what can I do for you?"

For a moment, a brief flash of something filled him. Something that felt warm. He brushed the thought aside. Now he could not spare any emotion, not even softness. "Nothing. Make sure the preparations are in hand. Go now." He waved a hand.

The mobility chair sat nearby, and he eased himself down into it. The leather squeaked as it moved to make room for his body. His wasted legs ached, and he rubbed them. He could feel the scarring on his flesh, now more evident than ever to his touch. His thin skin, stretching over bones and wasted sinews, offered no resistance. Over the years, what had remained of muscle had wasted away until only the scarring from the blast from the thrusters could be seen.

His eyes closed. Failure wasn't an option. Not now. All that remained now were the few rogues. Everyone else had either deserted him or died along the way. He felt no sense of loss at the many who died or those who continued to do so. They had served their purpose to give their all for him. The final burst of anger had resulted in the loss of the Phobos pirates, long before he'd planned to dispense with them.

His refusal to accept their ultimatum had destroyed the fragile alliance that he had needed. But he couldn't find the energy to regret it. No. They were little more than usurpers anyway. They'd used him as effectively as he'd used them.

Crick began to drowse, and his body swayed. He caught himself as his head slipped forward toward his chest. In the last few days since the drug had failed, his medic, the only one to survive the murderous vengeance, had found a temporary alternative. With effort, he slipped a hand into his pocket, drawing out the Strontal powder tube. Mixed with a goblet of wine, it cleared his mind enough to continue the fight while giving his body a boost of adrenalin. He pulled the stopper from the small glass vial and emptied it into his wine. His body might fail, but he wouldn't let his mind. Not yet.

I have one last task to complete. One last vengeance to exact.

"I want to board the *Elector*. Tell your fighter pilots to ensure she is both unarmed as well as unable to run or shield. Then assemble the men in preparation to board. The time has come to destroy those on the *Elector*."

He pushed out of the seat, watching the viewer on the wall. Yes, the *Elector* was his, and he felt a wave of joy. He would finally have his revenge. He might not see the downfall of the Earth Empire, but he would put the rogues into a position of power to finish the job.

Duvall gave the order. "All crew, abandon ship. Self-destruct sequence alpha." Chowd closed his eyes. "Chowd, get to the bridge."

Chowd turned, the vacuum slowly receding as they pumped oxygen through the halls. The lights in the corridor now alternated between bright white and red, and he saw the members of the crew clambering into the tubes, heard the hiss as they opened and the crunch as they locked down, each pod big enough for one person only. Thankfully, they had more than enough.

Each capsule carried enough oxygen for three days under normal circumstances or could sustain life in a hibernatory fashion for up to three weeks. Long enough for the beacons they'd fitted over the last few days to send a distress signal. It would allow for the person on board to be retrieved. Duvall had not yet given the order for the pods to eject, and Chowd frowned.

He searched for Meredith, but he couldn't see her. His heart beat fast even though he knew her brother never endanger her. *Would he?*

He reached the bridge. Meredith sat hunched over a console, and for a moment his heart felt frozen, but she moved and the cold sensation fizzled away. She worked fast, fingers flying over the keypad as she shut down systems, scrambling what she couldn't copy.

"Meredith?"

She didn't turn around though, just waved to acknowledge that she'd heard him. Duvall stood behind her, and she sucked in a deep breath. "What? What's going on?"

On the bridge there now remained just four. Duvall, Meredith, Grayson, and himself. Duvall's gaze was steady. "We think we can lure him. There's a secure zone in the security section. We're going to lead him there, unless we can take him out beforehand. It's closer to the only hatch he can use to board, so it should be easy enough."

Chowd thought over the plan. He didn't like it, but it was as good as any. "Okay, who's going to be the lure?"

Duvall smiled, and Chowd's stomach soured.

"We know he'll come for Duvall," Meredith explained. "But I have an idea. The self-actualized holograms? We're going to relay it through the ship. So what he sees and thinks is Duvall really isn't. He and I are going to wait inside the secure zone."

Chowd's heart stopped at her words. "No. You're going to get off the *Elector*—" Meredith waved a hand, stopping him. "Someone has to close the doors and set the

sequences to lock and make sure he can't trip any overrides. I can do it faster and more efficiently than any of you. You and Grayson need to keep the zone clear so I can do my part." Meredith lifted her head as she finished talking.

My Meredith will be in the secure zone? The final line of defense? No way!

He opened his mouth to protest again, and Duvall shook his head. "No. She's the only one of us who can change any of the programming at that level and with any speed. We've enabled the silent self-destruct sequence. We only have about eighteen minutes, so every second counts." He turned back to Meredith. "Done?"

She pushed the console to one side and grabbed a tiny handscreen. She tapped a command in and bit her lip. "Come on. Just one more." Her fingers completed a final sequence of tapping, a frown on her face. "Yeah, let's finish this now." She flipped the lid shut and slid the unit into her pocket.

She made to stand, and Chowd grabbed her, pulling her close, his eyes closing as he inhaled. His fears crested. What if they never... He needed to tell her one last time, in case they never had the opportunity again. "Stay safe, because...I love you." Then he opened his eyes and looked at her.

"I love you too." She touched his face, swiping a finger over the moisture beneath his eyes. "See you on the other side." Meredith drew back, winked, and she slapped a small personal communicator on his arm. "So I can hear you."

He noted the others wore similar devices as well before taking a last glance at her as she scurried behind Duvall and out of sight.

"Right, ready now?" Grayson looked at him, the amusement in his eyes strained. "Yeah, let's get out of here." Chowd didn't look back at the bridge as they left, just gave the lockdown command, and the doors jammed shut behind him. "Why did you do that?" Grayson asked as they moved quickly.

"We need to channel them to the security zone and ensure there is nowhere else for them to go. I'm about to lock down the cabins and mess as well as SurgiTech."

He gave a moment's thought to those critically injured who remained on board. They could do nothing more for them, he knew, but it still felt wrong. Yet this was war, and they had no safe way to move them to another vessel. He, too, had seen the failing life support systems, the dropping oxygen levels, and with the matrix compromised, they couldn't salvage the *Elector*.

"When will you give the order for the pods?" Chowd asked.

"As soon as we have Crick on board," Grayson muttered as they moved swiftly. Once they had finished locking down the ship as much as they could, they moved into position behind the security offices. The small alcoves now doubled as hiding spots for those left on the *Elector* as the boarding party tackled the airlock.

"Pods away." Grayson hissed the command into the communicator, and the sound of the disengaging pods filled the air.

Chowd hoped that Crick only had a small landing party and watched with barely controlled breaths as the hatch flew open. The rogues entered stealthily, guns ready, moving side to side as they scanned for any danger. Crick himself moved with them, leaning heavily on a mobility stick. For the first time in many years, Chowd saw Crick Sur Banden, wizened and doubled over, moving slowly as if each step pained him. The holographic vision of Duvall disappeared around a corner while Crick watched, his face scrunched as if the pain was about to overcome him.

Chowd breathed shallowly, his eyes watchful as three... four...no, five rogues traveled with him. They formed into two groups of three, Crick and two taking the front while three stood guard on the rear.

The back three never saw the attack coming. Grayson and Chowd moved fast and in perfect unison, gripping the nearest guards, each overpowering them with a quick movement. The third spied Grayson much too late, as his arms wound around his neck and gave a sudden jerk. Chowd checked the others on the floor. He nodded quickly, silently informing Grayson that they were indeed dead.

They dragged the bodies into the alcoves, not wanting anyone from the shuttle to find them and raise the alarm. Then they moved swiftly on silent feet once more. They had left their shoes behind in the alcoves in order to avoid a betraying rattle or clank. They caught sight at the door of the holograph disappearing into the secure room. The two guards moved in first.

Barsha! He tapped the comm. "Guards are entering. Crick outside." His stomach clenched. He could take Crick, but that would alert the guards. He wasn't prepared to risk that. Meredith waited in the secured room, and he felt helpless. *She'll have to protect herself.*

A quiet whisper caught Meredith's attention. "Guards are entering. Crick outside."

From her position by the door, she waved her arms at Duvall. "We have a problem. Crick is sending his guards in first. We need to do something."

Duvall nodded silently. He pointed to the corner, out of sight, then made a shooing motion.

She felt a brief flash of irritation at his actions. *I'm his little sister, but I actually know how to defend myself.* Meredith rolled her eyes, moved back, and gripped her laser. Her hands were slippery with sweat, and she had to work on controlling her breathing.

Bent down behind one of the empty consoles, Duvall

watched, his face tense as he eyed the door. The guards entered, looking here and there, moving forward slowly.

She waited. *Just a little closer.* Then they were in. She hurled herself from her hidey-hole just as Duvall sprang up.

The whine of a laser split the silence, and for just an instant, she looked away. Hands grabbed her hard, and she cried out. From the corner of her eye, she could see Duvall bobbing down behind the console again. The *fzzt* of the laser fire only dimly entered her consciousness as she grappled with the angry warrior who tried to control her.

Meredith kicked backward, her feet missing anything useful, and she moved and bobbed, the fingers pulling on the cloth of her uniform. She reached a hand up and sank her nails in.

When in doubt, fight like a girl.

She grimaced for an instant, but the movement beneath her hand drew her attention. She sank her teeth into the grasping hand. While the rogue cried out in pain, she whipped up her laser and fired at point-blank range. The rogue slumped to the floor, and she moved back. The smell of burning flesh made her feel sick. *My first kill.*

The thought should have left her a little hysterical, but she stopped, turning to see that Duvall finally had his assailant on the ground and stood watching her.

"What was that? You bit him and used your nails? After being trained in a range of combat maneuvers?" His harsh words made her smile as she rubbed her shoulder. She knew he was just running on the adrenalin.

"Any port in a storm? Anyway, it worked. Now let's get this sucker and get out of here before it's too late," she whispered to him, then moved to the door. "Remember what to do?"

Her brother grimaced before moving forward and calling out, "You want me, Crick?"

Chowd watched from behind the wall. "You want me, Crick?" Duvall asked.

Chowd breathed a sigh of relief at hearing his voice. Thank heavens...they had survived the guards.

Crick moved into the room. Chowd refused to think of him as his father. No familial connection existed between them, just the need to get rid of this one Ru'Edan who had terrorized and brought nothing but death to so many. He watched as the wizened Ru'Edan entered the room, knowing that Duvall and Meredith would have already sealed it from the other side, then Grayson pushed the corridor door shut, engaging the lockdown.

"Done here," Grayson rasped into the communicator.

"Same here." Meredith's breathless voice, although it sounded strained, filled him with exultation.

"What are you doing?" Crick Sur Banden turned slowly, moved in the direction of the sealed door, and placed both hands flat against the plasglass viewing window inside it.

Chowd nodded to Grayson, who disappeared around the corner.

"What had to be done. You can't be allowed to continue your reign of terror. This is the end. You lose, we win." Chowd stepped backward.

"You're my heir. This can all be yours."

Chowd turned away as Crick yelled at him. He didn't need or want what was offered and deep inside, he felt sadness and guilt that he needed to take this final step.

Regret ballooned, knowing that the only relationship with this man would have had to include more death and destruction, something he abhorred. Guilt filled him that Crick felt no remorse for his actions.

"No. I don't want what you're offering." He refused to give Crick anything more of himself and moved swiftly away from the door that held the screaming figure.

The others waited for him just around the corner. "They have a shuttle. We can either choose that or a life capsule. I vote the shuttle." Duvall looked closely at him, and Chowd nodded.

Together the four entered the shuttle. Only the pilot remained on board, and once he saw the four of them, he rose, lifting both hands in a sign of surrender and moving from the controls.

Grayson closed the airlock. Speed now important, Chowd moved into the pilot's seat.

Duvall took responsibility for the prisoner, securing him, and Meredith moved toward the communications unit.

"Chowd, we're down to two minutes. We have to get out of here now, or it will be too late." She moved quickly, opening her personal palm screen. On it he could see the image of Crick moving slowly, looking for an exit. His stomach clenched.

Grayson crawled into the copilot's seat as Chowd maneuvered away from the *Elector*, hitting the thrusters.

Duvall looked at his ship then looked away, pain and loss clear in his eyes. "She was the best."

For all of them, it had been so much more than a ship.

"Do you want me to turn on the countdown for the self-destruct? I found my way into the schematics and patched myself in so we could make a video of the death of Crick." She cast sorrowful and apologetic eyes at Chowd, and he understood. They needed proof, not for them, but for the dissenters and disbelievers.

"Yeah. I want him to know," Duvall muttered, and her fingers moved again. "Self-destruct in sixty seconds." The words were melodious, and Crick looked shocked on the tiny viewscreen in Meredith's hands

"What have you done?" he screamed before he slumped. "It wasn't meant to end like this!"

The countdown continued, and time slowed for Chowd. Self-destruct in ten seconds...nine...eight...seven...six...five...four...

A sound of pain filled the cabin of the small shuttle. Life capsules littered his view, and he slowed to avoid a collision.

He clicked on the stern viewing screen. Three...two...one...

Lights filtered along the edges of the *Elector*, the feed finally breaking down to static. The ship ripped itself apart. They watched, stunned, as the bird that had carried them safely finally died.

"I'd better patch into Jemma's ship, I think." Meredith's voice was thick with tears as she worked in silence, opening the communicator to the frequency Jemma would use.

"No!" The cry of Jemma's pain-filled voice filled the cabin, an emotion they all shared for different reasons.

"Jemma, it's okay. We got away. All of us." Meredith sniffled as she shared the news. "But the *Elector*'s gone. We are heading for Otega. Duvall will prepare a report to send to the Admiralty once we land and clean up any further resistance."

She glanced at Duvall who took the communicator. "Head on down now."

Epilogue

They reclined in the mess hall on the *Star of Ishtar*, waiting for the shuttle to return them to the Admiralty base on Aenna. The entire crew of the *Elector* had been treated like heroes, yet none of them wanted that tag. They'd done their job, protecting the Empire from Crick Sur Banden.

Chowd watched as the team members finally moved forward. In the three weeks since they had liberated the base on Otega, Meredith had often held his hand, walking with him when they finally found out what had become of the remains of his mother. Instead of dealing with the dead, the Ru'Edan had dumped the bodies of those who had met similar fates on one of the moon installations, so they hadn't decayed. But nothing had remained of his mother. One of the female cooks, his informant, told him that little more than ash had remained after the thrusters had caught both her and Crick that day. They'd then disposed her remains. Chowd had accepted Meredith's embrace dry eyed.

On Otega, they found the evidence they needed to prove their actions were the only option. Videos of the experiments chilled them as they watched men, women, and children tortured. He wouldn't ever forget those images anytime soon.

"So what's next, I wonder?" Elara stood, hefting her small bag of possessions, returned after they arrived on the *Ishtar*. "It seems weird coming back to Aenna on this old bird." She patted the seat affectionately as an officer called their names and indicated it was their turn to make the short journey to the base.

As one group, the nine, including Jod, headed toward the shuttle bay. Only Meredith had never served upon this ship, yet somehow, the gravity of the occasion had enveloped her too.

They waited quietly then were ushered into the captain's private shuttle to make the transfer, each sitting in silence. Once the ship had spun away, Chowd refused to look back.

Now, with peace assured, he could look forward to seeing his uncle, and his communion with the woman he loved. Of course, pockets of resistance remained, but finally a respite from war had been achieved. Life really couldn't get better.

"I wonder where they'll send us now that it's all over?" Meredith voiced what the others thought, and several nodded wearily. The small shuttle entered the hangar where most of them had assembled so long ago before they first stepped onto the *Elector*.

This time, their arrival was minus the ship. The massed workers stopped moving as they stepped down onto the plascrete. A ragged cheer rose, and he felt himself flushing, wanting to be anywhere but there. He wasn't a hero. Far from it.

"Let's get out of here."

As if Duvall's words had cast a magical spell, they moved, heading quickly toward the reception desk. Entering what they had previously considered a quiet and plush area, Chowd felt amazement at the scene before him.

A harried-looking blonde woman took in their arrival, a smile on her face. "The Admiral is waiting for you. Please come this way."

They moved down the carpeted corridor, the wooden doors replaced with one of brushed metal, and unlike their previous visits before the battle for the Alpha Star Colony, a code unit waited.

Chowd looked to the woman as she opened the cover of the unit. "Why has this changed?" He indicated to the door and keypad.

She glanced at him. "There was an attack on the Admiral."

"The Admiral?"

"He's fine. It was dealt with quickly." The woman keyed in a combination, and they entered the wood-furnished waiting area.

The woman the *Elector* had rescued from the Alpha Star Colony—he racked his brains...Kera—waited inside. As they entered, she stood and extended her hand.

"Welcome. Gustav will be pleased to see you. Please take a seat." She indicated the chairs against the wall and returned to the desk, hailing the Admiral.

The door slid open, and a smiling Gustav Elphin stood before them. He looked curiously happier than Chowd had ever seen him.

"Chowd, Duvall, Grayson. I've never been happier to see a crew than I am to see you all well. Come into my office. Kera, join us?"

Chowd wondered at this development. His uncle had called the security officer by name. The door slid shut behind them, and the Admiral took a seat, Kera Aarens standing behind the chair, one proprietary hand resting on his shoulder while she grinned.

His uncle glanced at the man who stood out behind them.

"Jod Svan'Er," the Ru'Edan introduced himself, bowing formally.

"Right, Duvall. Let's get the business out of the way first. I have your report, and I am pleased to have such comprehensive detail. I'm authorized to inform you that each of you is either receiving a promotion or being increased in grade. Now, where do I start?" He opened the file in front of him. "Duvall, for your service, you are being transferred to the Admiralty, where you will take command of my flagship, the *Star of Ishtar*. Mellissa, your transfer is also effective immediately. We won't ask that you be separated given what you've both already given up."

Chowd could see the surprise on Duvall's face, though he considered it a well-deserved promotion.

His uncle continued, "Congratulations, Flag Captain McCord. Grayson, for exceptional service, you're also being awarded with your own command. The *Star of Morning* will be here in the next few days. You will assume your position there. Elara, you will of course be transferred as Chief SurgiTech. She's an older ship, but worthy of you both."

Elara and Grayson embraced quickly. He was pleased for them. Grayson had always acted as second to Duvall for as long as he had known them. Now he'd be his own man.

"Chowd. For you, we have had a special request from the Senate. With your gift of languages and your ability to move between the two worlds, the Admiralty would like to offer you a position as the roving ambassador. There's much work to be done, and the Senate has also promoted Jod Svan'Er and has requested that you work together. Is that agreeable to you?"

"What? Me? But...I'm..." *How do I tell someone, especially my uncle, that I could never and would never have expected such an honored position?* "I...er...can I have a moment?" He turned to Meredith. "Well?"

"If you want it, go for it." Her words lacked hesitancy, and just the feel of her hand in his told him that she would stand beside him whatever decision he made.

He looked back to this uncle. "Not without Meredith. Where I go, she goes too." He said the words clearly, making sure his uncle understood.

"I'm sure that can be arranged. Though I have to say, it's unfair of you to take my best cryptologist away. So I take it that's a yes?"

He nodded, his heart full to bursting.

"Jemma Cardnew and Raven Fraser. The new ambassador is going to need a pilot and his own engineer to keep his personal craft in order. That is to be your new posting." He turned back to Meredith. "So, Meredith?" She met the question in his tone with her smile, and Chowd wanted to laugh out loud. "It seems I should welcome you to the family. Before we go any further, though, I too have an announcement. Kera and I will be communing."

Shock filtered through Chowd's system until he saw the rightness of the two together. He smiled as his uncle continued.

"Maybe we should make it a double celebration?" the Admiral suggested. Meredith looked at Chowd. What could he say? "That sounds about right." Laughter broke out around the room as congratulations flowed.

Once the room became silent again, Gustav smiled.

"Then we need to get the ladies into organizing themselves. I have arranged it for tomorrow, and I guess you are going to want your family to attend?"

Meredith nodded furiously, dashing away tears. "Leave it to me."

They stood, the voices loud and celebratory. Chowd took a look at the faces before him. His family. Every one of them made up his family. Surely life couldn't get much sweeter.

The Star of Eternity

Chapter One

od Svan'Er looked out the shuttle window pondering the new intelligence he'd received. Jod slid his hands through his hair, betraying his frustration. The missing Sur Banden—Olivia—had been tracked to a small planet in the Cypher quadrant. Months of searching—he'd checked on the chrono-graph and at least eighteen had passed—had turned up nothing. At least not until now.

"She'll be wary when we arrive," Jemma, their pilot warned. Amazingly to him, this *female* had become one of his closest friends. In his culture women were kept separate. They were less: Little more than brood mares for the Ru'Edan males of Crick Sur Banden's rogues.

As he stared out the window beside his seat, Jod questioned everything he'd known before. The flash of stars as they hurtled closer to their destination captured his attention. He'd never travelled so far away before—an opportunity that hadn't arisen previously.

The peace that had been so hard won now allowed freedoms they could have only imagined in the past. The knowledge that everything had changed filled him with both concern and trepidation.

"That's why you and Raven, Chowd and Meredith are important to the overall plan. I need to make contact and somehow get her to accept what I'm saying is truth. We must retrieve her before the Remnant find her."

The Remnant—the last vestiges of Crick Sur Banden's rebel force—were also on Olivia's tail, and had been ever since she'd escaped from the moon installation. After the battle where the Elector and the newly formed coalition of Ru'Edan and humans finally found and destroyed Crick Sur Banden, the Rogues had scattered throughout the universe. Some, who saw an opportunity to advance their opportunities, planned and plotted how they could fill the vacuum and gain the power for themselves.

The click of a door behind him had Jod turning. Chowd, the Ambassador for the allied planets entered the cockpit and smiled. The thud of him dropping into the comfortable seat beside Jod was loud in the sudden silence.

"You're sure this lead is legitimate?"

Jod was amazed that Chowd sounded so strained. But to be honest, searching for Olivia Sur Banden had been hard on the entire crew.

Since the destruction of the Elector, the tight crew of her warriors, Duvall and Mellissa, Grayson, Elara, Chowd and Meredith, Raven and Jemma had included him in their intimate circle. They'd made him one of their own. The close-knit relationship was nothing he'd ever experienced.

Even the Admiral and his partner, Kera, had accepted him. A Ru'Edan Warrior as one of theirs made an incongruous partnership.

That they could put aside the past, turning away from the memories of war humbled and surprise him.

Many of his peers still struggled with the reality.

"I'm unable to be one hundred percent sure, Chowd. However, it feels like the best lead we've had in months," Jod muttered.

Chowd sighed heavily, the deep tones echoing as he demonstrated frustration. "We nearly had her before on Jerilus IV, but she disappeared before we could get to her. Almost as if someone tipped her off."

"Perhaps she just has an excellent sense of self-preservation," Jod muttered.

Chowd just grunted.

"Chowd, we'll find her. The universe is large, but we've got scouts looking for Olivia." Jod sincerely hoped it would work like that, but nothing could be taken for granted.

"The question is, will we find her before they do? The last place she was seen concerned me." Chowd sounded defeated, and Jod detested the unusual lack of self-confidence his friend exhibited.

But then, Chowd's search for his sister had taken its toll on everyone.

"Jod? There's an incoming coded message. I'm sending it through to your office." Jemma's voice broke through the sudden silence and he rose.

"On my way."

Before he left the cockpit, he smiled at the half human half Ru'Edan man who inhaled deeply. "We'll find her, Chowd. I've a feeling this is the opportunity we've been looking for."

✪ ✪ ✪ ✪ ✪

Olivia breathed heavily willing the pain away, as her damaged and bloodied coveralls fell to the deck with a clank. *I honestly didn't need this.*

She clamped her hand against her side, hoping to stem the blood that seeped slowly. A bar fight wasn't her idea of a good time, but she'd been caught up in the thrown punches. This whole planet was a god-forsaken dustbowl in her mind, yet her ship was in need of emergency repairs, her credits running low and her need for employment pushed her to interact with others.

The bar, she'd been reliably informed, was the place to seek work. All had been going well until a disagreement over some wager. "Dammit. If only the drunk had kept his mouth shut."

He hadn't of course, and that was where it all went wrong.

Then someone turned their gaze on her and commented on the grey tinge to her skin and her yellow eyes. At least she had not used her real name, because that would have engendered far more interest than she'd needed.

"If they'd known who I was, someone would have reported back and I'd be in a worse situation."

Safely within the shuttle, she reached into the small

ablution cabinet, stripped off her stained clothing and examined the wound in her side. Some combatant had tried to stick her with a sharp knife. It was the metal clip at her side which saved her from a more extensive injury. At least he'd only managed a shallow glance along her flesh, searing her flesh like a hot iron.

The medical kit contained an antibacterial spray that she applied liberally, ignoring the flash of pain it brought with it. "Don't know what that lot were carrying," she groused before spraying the flesh adhesive.

The container emptied rapidly; once again reminding her of the precarious state of her finances and she sighed. "Yet another thing to restock, when I have enough credits."

Olivia dragged on clean coveralls from the tiny cupboard and shuffled toward the makeshift bed she'd cobbled together long months ago. The ship was on lock down, ensuring no one would enter while she slept. A small comfort when mercenaries hunted her.

Some were Crick Sur Banden's men. Sure she'd be available to kill or, if not that, at least offer sexual relief or 'comfort' to their men. And of course the power that being his daughter represented.

She snickered at that thought. "He barely acknowledged me in life, except as a commodity, so I don't know why they think I'd be useful after his death."

It was easier to focus on the sexual commodity that she represented. Most of the girls she'd grown up with had become 'comfort women'—little more than pleasure tools for the Ru'Edan males of *his* army.

She'd only been saved from that fate because he'd thought her a tradable commodity. The thought rose, unbidden and much as she wished it away, it stood out like a stark truth. *He'd* been most insistent that she would be more useful as a virgin sacrifice to help him forge an alliance.

Memories assailed her, and she locked them down quickly, before they could beat her into submission. She'd become quite adept at that over the years. Even as she reached the narrow couch that she'd converted into her bunk, the light of the communicator flared.

"Vivian! I've found employment for you. There's a farm that requires laborers in the district, gathering the sheaves. It's only for a couple of weeks, but the credits are good."

Olivia swallowed. This was the break she needed. "Yes. When am I required?"

"Tomorrow." The voice filtered, scratchy and loud in the cabin, then she sighed. The work had to take precedence over her discomfort.

Her mind whirled at a million cycles—she'd need painkillers to dull the savage ache in her side, but she'd do what was needed. Just as she always had.

"Send me the details as soon as you can and let them know I'll be there." The light winked off, the active communication faded from the console and she huffed out a breath.

"It's a start." Whether it would allow her to repair the shuttle, restock her dwindling supplies and refuel was yet to be seen. But it would help to resupply her dwindling credit balance.

On that thought she gingerly lay down and closed her eyes. The pounding behind her abated a little, and the hiss that escaped from between tightly clenched lips echoed in the empty shuttle.

Focus. The cool of the air, the silence and the feeling of security she'd come to associate with the night hours filtered through her brain and she relaxed before finally dropping into a deep sleep.

Jod paced back and forth waiting for Jemma to finalize the flight plan to the planet below. Ever since receiving the transmission a sense of urgency beat at him.

Why, he didn't know. But every second that passed placed Olivia Sur Banden in greater danger. She'd been noted in a tavern, just before a wild fracas had erupted, then she'd disappeared again, but not before she'd been injured. "She should be under lock and key." The communication he'd received tipped him off, alerting him to another rebel in the area also seeking the daughter of Crick Sur Banden.

Women held such little importance in Ru'Edan society, yet they'd decided, Olivia, was the key to rallying support to build their army. As the only surviving child, not affiliated to the Allied Planets, she represented continuity, even from beyond the grave. It couldn't be allowed to happen.

"Jod, can you please come to the bridge, I've finished the calculations needed and we should be able to enter the atmosphere in the next hour. I've sought an expedited entry slot for us and I think I've pinpointed her location." Jemma's voice wafted from the small unit in his hand.

Excitement zinged through his stomach, wild fluttering that fizzed through nerve endings, and he pressed the button to speak. "Acknowledged. On my way," he answered, then he tugged away from the desk and moved to the bridge of the vessel, long strides eating up the decking.

Jemma spun her chair and looked up as the door whooshed closed behind him, the smile on her face surprising him, as it always did. "We've got a slot and I'm about to call the diplomatic party to the bridge. I'm sending the details to your handheld now before I set up the entry." Jemma's hands flew over the screen as she completed her tasks and he settled into what had become his chair. Then she sat back in her seat, adjusted her headset so the mouthpiece was before her lips. "Alerting all to preparation for entry sequence. All appropriate personnel please proceed to the bridge immediately for briefing." Jemma clicked off the comm.

Jod began running through the files and calculations she'd flicked to his communication unit. Trajectories, possible entry sequences and landing sites were detailed. "Thorough as always, Jemma."

She grinned, her violet eyes twinkling in her small pixie

shaped face. "Nothing but the best for the twin Ambassadors."

He frowned at her words. "I'm only a security officer." He still struggled with the change in status.

Jemma snickered. "So was Chowd beforehand. You really need to learn to relax more. I know you're Ru'Edan but your outlook has loosened since you've been with us. Maybe you need to find a mate and settle down."

Her words surprised him. Had he really changed that much? Were the amendments to his outlook enough for him to be considered *humanized*?

He wasn't sure he was ready for that, just as he was still coming to terms with his new role. The sense of disquiet which plagued him for days ricocheted, his mind a dark-well of confusion. Something he was totally unprepared for.

Instead of analyzing, he frowned over the information. "How long will descent take?"

"Give or take, an hour. I'm not rushing though because our parking slot won't be open for a while. Besides, with the changes of gravity and so on, the slower I make our descent, the easier it will be on everyone on board. I can actualize our gravity slowly, or at least until we are almost ready to land. Then I plan to segue our systems to the natural gravity. It'll allow our bodies time to acclimate to the locale."

"You've never done that before." He pinned her with his gaze, sure there was more to her plans than she was sharing. He didn't like being left in the dark on important tactical decisions.

Jemma shrugged. "Usually the gravity is plus or minus up to twenty or thirty percent. This time, its closer to three times, so we'll really feel it. Our bodies will be pulled down, meaning we'll be unable to function at our normal levels."

Nodding at her words, he calculated and considered everything she said as the others in the immediate crew trooped in. Jod waited as the snick of belts clicking into place filled the air, until he was sure the plans Jemma had suggested were efficient.

Clearing his throat, he held up his communicator. "Jemma

has completed her planning for entry to the planet, including time to acclimate to the changed gravitational environment." All gazes settled on his face and he looked down, forwarding the plans to their pre-organized comm unit group. "Details should be on your communicators now."

He noticed, as he had in the past, the way Meredith slid her hand onto Chowd's knee, but also saw how she bit her lip.

"Will you be changing the gravity throughout the ship?" Meredith spoke with a waver in her voice and he frowned, glancing at Jemma.

Their pilot pinked and he wondered at her reaction as she shook her head. He opened his mouth, but Jemma held up a hand, stopping him. "Ah, no. I will need to seal off the bridge and command center, including the senior officers cabins and mess. I'll send most of the crew to lower situations before we begin the final descent."

"Jemma?" He couldn't stop the words of concern.

"Don't worry, Jod. I've a good reason why I won't be leaving the ship." There was excitement and something close to longing in her voice.

He searched her face. "Why?"

"Well," and Jemma looked at those assembled on the bridge, her smile settling on her life partner, Raven. "I'm pregnant."

Ah. Now he understood, the effects of the gravitational pull could become harmful in a developing fetus and the gestating female.

"Well, I guess that means I should stay here too," Meredith whispered.

Jod whipped around and stared at Meredith, surprised that Chowd would have allowed his mate to procreate while they sought Olivia Sur Banden and potentially placed themselves at risk.

Before he could question the men, Chowd smiled. "As we have no medic with obstetric training aboard, I agree, the women shouldn't leave the ship. In this instance, you and I have sufficient skills to complete the mission, should all go to plan."

Jod was totally confused.

Ru'Edan men didn't fuss over their partners. The females were usually sent away until after the arrival of the young so as not to inconvenience the male, who usually took a bedmate during this time. In his experience, the women only returned to their mates after the offspring were presented to the Goddess at the shrines.

But he'd seen the way the humans preened over the growth of the younglings within their partners. The pride with which they made such an announcement and for the first time, he wanted to ask how it felt. But that was a human reaction. Not one in line with his Ru'Edan heritage. Instead of enquiring about the emotions, he shrugged.

Maybe he'd investigate the oddities of their behavior later.

"Everyone needs to be strapped in now, because we're about to attempt entry." Jemma spoke tersely as she toggled the comm switch. "All hands strap in now."

Jod tugged the straps more securely over his shoulders, feeling them pull tight as they increased velocity. Since the first time he'd watched Jemma—a pilot of exceptional skill—he'd come to appreciate her abilities behind the console. Yet again she didn't disappoint.

Each movement was calculated meticulously before the craft made its way through the layers of atmosphere ensuring their landing was smooth.

She flew for at least forty minutes, then stabilized their position, the ground before them visible on the screen.

The terrain was flat and brown mainly, bisected every now and again with rugged canyons and some hillocks. In the distance he made out the port and city, the grey-silver of agricultural structures jutting up against the dun brown of the township's squat buildings.

"Gentlemen, it's time you decamped to the small shuttle bay. Meredith and I will remain here and once I know you're safely strapped in, I'll initiate the lockdown and gravity stabilization. "

The men around him rose, and with a long look at his Life Partner, Chowd led them out and along the corridor to the rear stairs. They moved swiftly, feet clanking on the metal grating that made up the stairwell. At the bottom he slid his hand over the palm reader and the door opened smoothly beneath his touch.

They entered the bay, Chowd re-engaging the safety locks and they hurried to the seating zone beyond a plas-glass screen.

Once assured everyone was buckled in, Jod touched his comm. badge. "Ready and secured in the Cargo Bay, Captain." Chowd and Raven met his gaze and each nodded.

"Fine. Initiation will begin on my mark." Long seconds passed then Jemma spoke again. "Mark."

The floor beneath them rattled louder than he'd ever experienced and he couldn't help looking to Raven.

"It's normal. The bay doesn't have the same level of dampeners and insulation we usually experience in the cockpit. You'll get used to it, if you have to do this again."

The pull of gravity made itself known by slow degrees. The sensation of weight dragging at him grew harder to ignore. He felt the shuttle flying as the vibrations turned from noticeable to urgent. A final transmission from Jemma interrupted his concentration of the physical changes he was experiencing.

"We're landing now. Prepare. Once I've touched down, I'll force the main bay doors to open, so you can leave. When you're ready to rejoin the ship, let me know via the external communication point."

With that they experienced a heavy thud, jostling, then the whine of the engines slowed before finally dying away. "I don't wish to do that again," he muttered.

Chowd rose, his belt undone already. "It's not the most comfortable way to travel. So let's go find Olivia and get out of here."

Jod tore at his restraints and only dimly heard them thud to the floor.

Olivia woke, her computer pinging loud and clear, half rising from her pallet. "Ugh, that time already?"

She felt rotten, with aching body and head. "I should stay here." She slumped back against the bed but the need to sort out her problems was rapidly becoming most urgent.

The provisions she'd laid in several planets back were running low. Her belly ached and Olivia sighed. "I'd better eat before heading out." She grabbed a nutrition pack and shoved it into the heat-unit, waiting for the ding before tugging the door open and devouring the meal. It wasn't much but it calmed the gnawing of her belly.

Quickly Olivia tugged on a small backpack she'd left at the base of the bed, thrust inside another nutrition pack and a tube of water. *Best to be prepared.*

With quick movements she attended to the needs of her body, then slung the pack over her shoulder and hurried to the door, casting a final glance in the direction of the chrono on the wall.

Down the ramp she hurried, ignoring the undulation beneath her feet. Dawn was breaking as she engaged the locks on the shuttle, and though still dim, she could gaze around. A collection of shuttles lay abandoned in various states of disrepair gathered on the old landing way. She shuddered imagining the rodents who'd taken up residence in this abandoned area, but while the situation here wasn't secure, she didn't have the credits for that, it was free. Besides which, it also meant no one would note her coming and going or enquire about her coloring. With Crick's men searching for her, this was an advantage.

"At least I can lock my shuttle." She spoke quickly as she hurried toward the meet point she'd arranged the previous evening. Olivia had taken great pains to reinforce the plating on the hull, to increase the security settings on the shuttle and to fit other, less legal means of locking down her ship.

As she emerged from the dark surrounds of the abandoned ships, and trudged to the older hanger she noted that others waited. She hadn't realized until now, that the shuttles dotting the edge of the old landing pad were inhabited.

She took stock of the mixture of men and women, most dressed in the ragged remains of uniforms yet she took great pains to look disinterested. If she'd learned nothing else, it was being nosy was dangerous. Besides, she didn't want too many asking questions and they came when you asked your own.

A lumbering ground transport rattled toward them, the engine clanging unhappily as it kicked up dust. Olivia turned away, covering her nose and mouth. *The soil has to contain contaminants*, her mind helpfully supplied. After all, this had been one of the hotly contested mining planets before falling on hard times and taking on the guise of agriculture.

It had seen heavy bombardments by both Ru'Edan and humans before the cease-fire had ended the stalemate.

Around her others coughed and wheezed, while the vehicle came to a grinding halt.

A large man, bloated and florid stepped down and called names. Eventually he called, "Vivian?" It took a second for Olivia's brain to remember that was the name she'd given. She raised her hand and was rewarded with a grunt.

He herded them to the transport and as she reached the front he stopped her. "Here." He shoved a sack at her and indicated a seat at the front of the transport and she climbed aboard, all the time concerned that she'd have to face this day after day, at least until the harvest was completed.

They drove in silence and Olivia carefully contemplated the distance, noted the arroyo they traversed until the craft came to a shuddering halt at the edge of a marginal field.

"Collect as many sheaves as you can. You're paid by the weight," barked the man as he waved them out into the desert like conditions.

Olivia didn't wait. Time and effort was money and she was far too low on both to stand on ceremony. Scampering to the field, she chose a row and began picking. The sheaves had clearly been harvested some time back, given their shrunken appearance. Each time she bent, the ache at her side and the pound of her head increased.

Heat undulated in waves, gusts of dusty winds flew up and the heat increased. A whistle blew, shrill in the silence and she took a moment, drinking deeply from the water bottle she'd brought with her and swallowing a pain tablet, hoping it would ease the agony that held her in its grip. Then with another shrill sound the work began again.

The heat from the three suns beat down incessantly. Olivia fished around in the backpack and found a cap, donned it and kept working. When they stopped for a midday break, she gladly relieved herself and noted the black that dotted her clothes and hands, sticking to the sweaty patches of the coverall she wore.

"You're new to this, aren't you?" A crusty old matron sidled up to her and scanned Olivia.

"Yes. Why?" She hated the weakness she heard in her voice.

"You're working fast, but moving slow. After you've been doing this awhile you'll get used to the routine. Most of us don't straighten fully until the sack is full and the supervisor empties it."

Olivia bit her lip and scanned the woman. She wasn't as old as she first appeared, but she was bent over from constant agricultural tasks. Her face weathered and hands gnarled from years of constant labor made her look much older than was clearly her age in cycles. "How long have you been doing this?" She took a bite of the dry food rations she'd packed, while the woman smiled at her.

"A long time. At least ten cycles. It's hard, but pays well. Puts food on the table for my younglings. You'll get used to it."

Olivia had to fight to control the shudder of distaste that rippled through her. *Years of this? Of constant drudgery?* "I'm not planning on staying here too long."

The woman gazed more deeply into her eyes. "Ru'Edan. Not used to this kind of manual labor, are you?" She gave a cackle and pushed up off the stone she'd perched on and headed toward the knot of laborers at the far side of the meal area.

Silently, Olivia castigated herself. Too much chatter equal to many questions and that led to mistakes: People finding out who she was. The whole plan of setting down on this planet was to earn credits, repair her ship and get out of here, she reminded herself. Not to make friends or earn anyone's respect.

The woman's words stayed with her as they resumed their task. If she'd already picked up Olivia's Ru'Edan heritage, then so could anyone. A female half Ru'Edan working an agricultural field, one who'd only lately arrived would be a giveaway if her whereabouts became widely known. The threat that one of the remaining Rebels would find her, use her, left her queasy.

Olivia settled into the task, banishing the dangerous thoughts. Right now, there wasn't much she could do. Her ship needed work before she could get out of here. The sooner she amassed enough credits, the sooner she could leave this benighted planet.

By the end of the day, she was spent. Her body a mass of aches and pains and once she made it to her ship, she was ready to collapse onto the bed. But food and cleaning had to come first. She wouldn't allow herself to become like the other laborers. So she hurried through her tasks, set the alarm, ate a simple meal and relaxed. The shower, brief though it had been, helped to re-hydrate her parched skin as much as the water she consumed.

Finally replete, clean and medicated she crawled onto the bed and slept, until the suns rose again.

The airfield wasn't quite empty, but apart from some old possibly abandoned craft, there was only a mixture of old hulks. Nothing spoke of habitation. No one loitered and Jod sighed. "This is the third airfield and we've struck out at all of them."

Chowd shadowed his eyes and glanced into the distance. "If she's found some kind of employment, we won't know just yet. She'll only return at the end of the day. It's an agri-planet so they'll be keeping harvest timetables."

Jod gave a grunt. "How many more airfields on our list of possible sites?" It was the same conversation he'd had with Chowd at other fields over the last two days of their search.

"Twelve, not including passenger and paid parking. I doubt she'd choose that, based on previous information, though." Chowd looked at him thoughtfully. "We can try another, but I believe it will be early morning or night when we'll find her."

Jod swore under his breath. After all this time, he wanted the hunt done. The woman was more slippery than a fengore eel. The only thing in their favor was that she'd been seen at one of the bars. In fact, they knew she'd sustained an injury in a bar fight after seeking a position, on the pretext she needed to repair her ship. If that was true...

"What do you think are the chances that the story she spun the barman was factual?"

Chowd sucked in a deep breath, and once more gazed out to the horizon. "Raven is following up with any mechanical agents, but I'd say the chances are good, otherwise why stop here? It doesn't make sense that she'd tell an untruth in those circumstances. He got the impression she was down on her luck, so he felt sorry for her and asked around."

"I understand that, but until now, she's been exceptionally careful. Never staying in one place for more than a lunar passage. She's chosen out of the way places to land. It doesn't make sense to me." Jod rubbed at his brow thinking over the known facts.

"I don't think we're going to find anything here to change what we've found so far. Let's move on." Chowd clapped his shoulder then peeled off and headed in the direction of their transport. They'd requisitioned a set of all terrain ground bikes before their mission, and the vehicles had proven time and again to be an efficient means of getting around on the many moon installations and planets they'd visited looking for the last Sur Banden offspring.

Jod donned his helmet and straddled the large black beast as Chowd did the same.

"There's one more airfield in this quadrant. Let's check it out before heading back to the ship." Chowd sent him the co-ordinates before tapping his ignition. The bike rose slightly and leapt forward under his direction then tore over the ground, eating up the distance as they hurtled toward the final stop of the day.

It took over an hour before they came to a screeching halt at the side of an ancient airfield. Older craft sat there, some obviously in varying states of decay. They stopped the engines and clambered down. Jod removed his helmet. "I'm not sure there's anything much here, either."

Chowd shrugged. "Doesn't hurt to look around though, does it?"

Jod didn't have an opportunity to agree as the other man strode off.

With a sigh, Jod headed in the other direction, toward a lean-to. He'd reached the wooden side, his hands brushing over the rough edges when the sight of a newer craft caught his eye.

He squinted, sure his mind was playing tricks under the beating suns. But it remained there, even after he blinked. This time, he accepted what his brain was telling him. A Phobos Mark VI was sitting in the center of a small group of rusting hulks. Hidden from sight.

Or at least the pilot had attempted to hide it.

Hand on the small laser pistol adorning his hip Jod moved carefully in the direction of the ship. Past the first hulk he stilled and examined the sandy ground. Footprints. One set of small, boot-shod feet had shuffled the dusty surface. He followed the path, seeking where they'd ended. The newest set, deeper and more pronounced heading to the lean-to and to the tracks of a vehicle.

He pressed the communicator. "Chowd? I've found a possible. Head to the old building and I'll meet you."

Olivia ached, though not quite as badly as the day before. Clearly the tablets were keeping things at bay.

The ancient laborers transport pulled to a stop, a cloud of dust rising up and she coughed. *I need to get off this dustbowl soon, before I develop some kind of lung virus.* She clambered from the machine—her backpack weighed down with the credit chips for the last seven-day payment. She'd count them back on her ship. At least now she was close to the payment for the repairs, if what the contractor had told her was included in her packet was correct.

Head down, watching the shuffle of her feet she headed for the hiding spot where she'd left her shuttle. The dust kicked up in the darkening evening as she rounded the old shuttles and came to a dead stop.

Footprints.

Two pairs.

Not hers.

She sucked in an unsteady breath. They'd found her. Her stomach congealed.

Adrenaline surged as she snapped up her head and scanned the area. Nothing. That didn't mean they weren't hiding somewhere. Automatically she settled her hand on her belt, seeking the tiny laser pistol she'd secreted on herself.

Silence and speed were of the essence.

All she needed was time to reach the shuttle. If she could just get in, she'd activate the shield before deciding her next step. That would buy her time.

Olivia padded around the shuttle hulk, remaining in the

shadows and cursing the fact she hadn't had her mind on what she was doing.

If she could just make it to the center of the next one, she could rush to her shuttle, while remotely unlocking to decrease the time she'd waste fumbling to get in. She fingered the tiny disc-like item in her pocket.

Timing is everything.

She crept closer, slowly, eyes scanning here and there, looking for signs of movement. Past the first craft and across to the next. She sucked in a deep breath, gathered herself—

"Olivia Sur Banden!"

Her body stilled, a hang over from the conditioning of her childhood, and a puff of dirt filled the air. Every muscle stretched taut as she waited for either the burn of a laser shot or the stun of a long distance hypo-dart.

Neither came and she barely breathed, her glance settled straight ahead.

"Olivia Sur Banden. I'm here to help"

From the other side of her craft a man appeared and she turned from the waist up. He was tall, shorthaired and his yellow eyes betrayed his heritage.

Ru'Edan!

Is he one of the Rebels? What could he want with me, or is that the most stupid question ever?

Her heart stuttered. "What do you want?"

As an opening it sucked she knew, but Olivia gritted her teeth, tightened her grip on her pistol and waited. To get to the craft, she'd have to go through him. Where one rebel existed there'd have to be another. They never travelled alone.

"My name is Jod Svan'Er. I'm here to protect you."

Olivia snorted. Protect her? Likely story. "What are you after? I've got no munitions. I'm not interested in my father's machinations and whatever you're selling…I'm not wanting to know." Her voice wavered, betraying her nerves and she wanted to curse.

"Nothing. I just want to help you." He emerged further

from the shadows, hand pushed out in the attitude of peace.

Her heart skittered. "Why?"

"Because you left when you could have stayed and that puts you in even greater danger. I'm also here because your brother Chowd is concerned about you."

Olivia frowned. *Chowd. My brother?*

She had vague recollections of a boy, gangly and thin. Older than her, and kept with the other males. He'd never fit in with her father's warriors. Instead of embracing the privations, lifestyle and perks that could have come his way, he'd remained closer to his mother. Olivia remembered when he'd escaped her father's wrath. Hell, she thought she still carried the odd scar from her beating after that. He'd hunted down several of the offspring. It all made sense now! Not that any of the others had survived. She nearly hadn't, either.

"Where is he, then?"

"I'm here Olivia." Another man emerged. Tall, yes. Muscular and dark haired so different from the coloring she remembered of the boy. His eye colour and skin tone were different to her memory as well, in fact they were closer to the colour of a human.

A trick!

She feinted to the left, sure now that this was a set up. She needed to escape. One of the other shuttles was prepared. The value of preparation had been learned early in her youth. Pounding footsteps echoed behind her. She swung away rounding another decayed body, then sped up. The shuttle ahead, carefully disguised was all she needed, if only she could reach it before they caught her.

One pounding step.

Another.

Head jarring.

She reached out, almost to the handhold when a heavy grip caught her, pulled her back.

She spun, puffs of dust flying up. "You aren't taking me!" Olivia fisted her hand and thrust, he dodged, his grip tangling in her ship suit.

A kick, badly aimed was avoided. "Olivia, dammit! Listen to me. I'm not here to hurt you."

"I've heard that before!" She twisted and turned, pulling at him.

"Chowd, hypo. We'll get her secured then show her the info we have."

Her gaze narrowed as the man who claimed to be Chowd moved up to her left. Her hands were manacled by the grip of the man who called himself Jod, legs apart avoiding hers. As *Chowd* advanced a final opportunity arose. She couldn't grab him, or kick but she had one last trick up her sleeve.

He dragged the hypo from his pocket, came closer and as he made to inject her, she bared her teeth. He was quick. Far too quick and the hypo connected with her arm before her teeth connected with flesh.

The warm sensation and heaviness pounded through her, as her blood pulsed within her veins.

"No…" The moan was groggy and slow. "Don't... Don't drug me."

She fought the lethargy pulling at her senses. Felt the droop of her eyelids, and sensations of weightlessness. She slumped as a black cloud descended.

Chapter Two

"**D**ammit, she fought like she expected us to kill her." Jod glanced at the tranked woman in his arms and to her shuttle. She didn't weigh a lot, and her skin was tanned to a deep berry brown and yet there were patches of red, abrasions on her hands.

"She lived with the women. Saw how they were used and abused. If I were her, I'd be wary of anyone's plans for me as well." Chowd shook his head as they stomped to the shuttle. "Check her pockets for some kind of remote. These babies have all kinds of fail safes we don't want to trigger."

Jod shifted her in his arms, trying to ignore her many curves as he fished in her pocket. He found the tiny unit and pulled it out. The grey box was covered in runes. At least he'd been educated enough that he knew what each meant. One was a self-destruct and he wondered, not for the first time on this mission, how many uneducated died from pressing the wrong button.

He depressed the button marked enter and they shuffled back as the gangway dropped. They hurried into the shuttle and he relocked it behind them.

Intruders would be a problem. Best to be safe.

Jod looked about, taking in the tiny internal dimensions, the small couch she'd turned into a bed. "Chowd, check the sanitary unit and see if you can find something to clean her up. Then we'll need food when she wakes."

For a moment Jod stared at the woman where he'd draped her on the bed.

Her slight frame was deceptive, he thought. She fought like a tigress protecting her cubs. Her hair, dusty and flecked with violet grass was long and wavy. Dark. Black maybe. In the half-light he'd caught the shimmer of gold in her eyes. That tiny indicator betrayed her partial Ru'Edan heritage.

"You should secure her." Chowd returned with a damp cloth but waited a step or two away.

Jod sighed before reaching into his pocket and removing the tiny set of sonic cuffs he carried. "It doesn't seem right."

"No. But until we can prove we're not here to hurt her, and particularly in these close quarters, she's a danger to herself and us." Chowd dropped into one of the seats against the opposite side of the wall with an *oomph*.

Jod flicked the restraints on where they hummed into life, and the bare metal supports of the seat were perfect for his needs. He stepped back and looked down. "How long do you think the hypo will work?"

"That I don't know. Look, I'm going to head back to our ship. I'll take my bike and we can stash yours in the cargo bay here. Can you fly this to our location?" Chowd glanced about. "I mean, it isn't old, but looking from the outside..."

Jod nodded. "I know. She's in rough condition. Let me check the schematics before you leave in case there are any unknown factors." He shifted away and headed for the pilots chair.

The lights flashed quickly enough and he ran a diagnostic. "Seems she's low on fuel, and there's a problem with the enviro systems. Other than that, I can lay in a course to the shuttle. Let's load the bike then you can get out of here."

He tossed the tiny remote to Chowd and depressed the door override, before tromping down the gangway. At the bottom Jod scanned the area, then trotted over to where they'd stashed the bikes. The cargo bay opened and he thrust the hover vehicle inside the compartment.

"Fine. I'll see you soon. Any problems, hail me." Chowd turned away and jogged to his bike and Jod watched it rise before he zoomed away.

One last scan assured Jod that no-one was around and watching. Finally satisfied, he stepped onto the gangplank and inside.

Her head ached, her body felt stiff and... *I'm restrained.* Olivia thrust her way through the layers of consciousness. "Where am I?" When she opened her eyes, she knew exactly where she was: The cabin of her shuttle.

"*Barsha*!" The curse word erupted as she fought against the bindings at her wrists, the zinging sensation informing her that they'd used sonic restraints.

Footsteps echoed and she spun enough to see a pair of legs in her vision. Glancing up showed her a man, long and lean, she ignored the clamoring of her body to gaze on his face. "You!"

"Yes. We need to talk." The man who called himself Jod squatted in front of her. "I want to undo the restraints, but I need you to settle down first. There's Rebels hunting you and I'm here as part of a diplomatic mission from the Ru'Edan Senate."

She snorted. "The Ru'Edan Senate? Yeah, I've heard of them. They wouldn't send someone after me unless it was to kill me. Since you haven't done that, clearly you're from the Rebels and need me to further your plans, right?" Fury dripped from her voice.

"No, Olivia. I really am from the Senate. Chowd—"

She thrashed, violent jerks that didn't do any good. "That wasn't my brother. He looks like him, but the eyes and skin—"

"DNA therapy. He undertook it after he escaped and his uncle, Admiral Elphin, helped him to join the Alliance Fleet. He's now an ambassador." Jod's words sounded so believable. So *rational*. That made these males even more dangerous.

"No. Who are you really and what do you want?" Maybe she could trade her way out of this. She'd been in sticky situations before.

"We need to get this shuttle in the air, make contact with the others, then I'll explain further."

Get it in the air. She gulped. The enviro barely worked with only one on board. Two was suicidal at best. She bit her lip.

He obviously hadn't run a detailed diagnostic, otherwise he'd know that. She opened her lips, but he waved a hand.

"I know about the enviro issue. Once we get to my craft, I've got an engineer on standby waiting to attend to the issue. Or we can just load this into their cargo bay."

Now Olivia screeched, tugging against her restraints. "No! You can't do this. *Please.*" The rational, detached part of her brain told her there was nothing she could do. That pleading wouldn't help. Panic set in a black greasy bubble filling her chest, shoving any form of rationality aside.

She hadn't come this far and run for so long only to be caught like this!

"Easy, Olivia. I don't want to hurt you."

For a second as she caught sight of his gaze, she was sure there was sympathy in the depths, but that flash disappeared.

"That's what they all say, until they get what they want." The waspish tones did little to control the bitterness in her voice. If she were honest, she didn't want to control it.

He grunted against her. "I'm not like them. We aren't wanting you for gain or pleasure. Our role is to help you."

"Right. I've heard that so many times in my life. You think you're the only one who's claimed wanting to help me?" She squirmed again, sure she'd dislocate her shoulders, but willing to do whatever it took to secure her freedom.

"We know about Crick and his men, but he's dead, Olivia. Now we just want to help you."

She laughed at that. She'd heard the reports of his death and seen the carnage of the bombing of the moon installation. He possibly was dead, and good riddance, but in her mind there was still a seed of doubt. Crick had managed to dodge the authorities with that line before. Made them think he was no more well before her birth. It wouldn't be a surprise if he'd done it again.

"I was there, Olivia. I saw how he died. I was involved in the action."

She stilled, every muscle tense as she watched the tic at the corner of his mouth.

"Liar."

"No. My friends on the shuttle, they can show you the transmission. The *Elector* was destroyed and Crick with it."

If that were true, then maybe there was a chance. The seed of hope took root, started to bloom. She squashed it. "No. He sent you and your people, like the ones who've tried to capture me before." She shook her head. "You can't fool me."

His sigh was laced with frustration. "Then I'll have to show you, but until then, you remain restrained."

He marched away, footsteps echoing before settling himself in the pilots seat. Quick and precise hand movements set the shuttle to humming. He'd engaged the drives and she hadn't even noticed, before their heated exchange.

The rumble grew, pulsing beneath her.

She felt the push as they lifted from the ground. Vibrations filled the air as he nosed it forward, view screens open to admit the sunlight.

He knew his way around the shuttle, she admitted, watching as best she could, fastened to the couch. She craned and glanced down her body, but even though she fought against the insidious warmth that filled her at the sight of him, the casual way he accepted control that called to her on a primal level. Not that she'd tell him that, of course. Last thing she needed was an inconvenient emotional tie to her captor.

Jod felt the odd vibration as an ache in his inner ear as they rose high into the air. He shook his head trying to settle the dull throb but it continued. He frowned and checked the screen. Everything *looked* okay. Clearly it wasn't. Was there an imbalance with the crystal drive?

It dosen't feel right, his instincts whispered. "Computer, diagnostic run."

Beep. Beep. *"All systems, optimal."*

Now he knew something wasn't right. He'd already ascertained there was an enviro issue. It should have picked that up.

Figuring it best to contact the others, Jod reached into his pocket, pulling out the personal communicator. Depressing the button, he heard only static. "Hello? Chowd? Jemma?"

No answer. *Interference?* No time to consider, he told himself.

He checked his altimeter and the compass. It flashed once then spun in crazy circles a fast whirring blur. "*What the...*"

"What's wrong?" The voice echoed from behind him.

His adrenaline spiked as he ran his hands over the command keys. "Nothing." He sounded unruffled, which was just as well, because the pressure was building in his chest. Panic.

He glanced out the viewfinder, looking for a landmark he remembered. Nothing—just the dry dustbowl that seemed to stretch forever.

Clang! Something banged, and it was an ominous reminder that he was flying a damaged shuttle. A small red light lit up on the console. "Barsha!"

"Uh, what's wrong?" He heard the tones of concern and ignored it, hunting for the reason the light suddenly dimmed in the cabin.

The whine of the engines changed, the pitch suddenly higher and more piercing.

Another red light lit up, then another. Dammit. They needed to get down. Now!

He started the descent sequence when everything stopped. The lights disappeared, the sound stopped.

For a miniscule stretch of time, the shuttle hung there, in the air, as if he'd brought it safely down to the ground. He knew better.

"No!" He heard the squeal and damned himself for not clicking on her safety belt. No time to get to her though. She'd have to take her chances.

"Brace yourself."

The shuttle tipped, nosing forward and he hurried to fasten his own belt then gripped the seat arms as the ground rose to meet them, the shuttle now tumbling.

Spinning.

Hurtling.

Crash!

This time when she attempted to open her eyes, agony bloomed. Shoulders felt like they'd been wrenched out of their sockets, fire streaked down her arms. Tears squeezed between her tightly closed eyes.

"Ooohhh." The low wail was from her.

"Stay still, Olivia. I'm trying to get to you."

Things crushed down on her, weights pushing on her chest and legs. Stings and aches. She wiggled her toes and a shaft of agony spiraled up to her groin. Wiggled her fingers even as she fought the darkness at the edges of her vision.

"I hurt." The words were more than a moan—they were a gasp of pain. She shifted her backside, trying to relieve the pressure, but the squirm didn't move her. The space around her was dark, confined, and hysteria lurked at the edges of her mind. "Where am I?"

"The shuttle crashed and I'm trying to get you out." *Jod.* She knew that voice.

Why? Where from? Unable to pinpoint the reason, she closed her eyes and tried to focus on her breathing. Short choppy pants were all she could manage.

Rustle. Bang. Crash! Olivia opened her eyes and gazed upward.

"Beis vand har!" He swore. Each invective he chewed out was newer and more inventive than the last. Many she'd never heard before.

"Just get me out of here. Soon." A glimmer of light peeked through the items covering her.

"Nearly there, Olivia."

She heard grunts and sounds of activity, before finally the last item squeezing her down to the couch was pulled away.

"How bad are you hurt?"

She blinked at the suddenly stunning light, taking stock of her body. "I don't know: My shoulders, and arms. There's pain in my chest, but it feels more like a broken rib. My legs. I think I've broken one."

He swore again. "Let me get you unhooked first." He did, then gingerly tested her shoulders, pressure and pain blooming through her body. "I need your medical kit, if it survived. Stay where you are."

She laughed through gritted teeth at that suggestion, the sound thin and pain ridden. "I'm not planning on going anywhere." Olivia squeezed her eyes shut again and focused on breathing. In. Out.

He returned and she could hear the beep beep of the diag unit.

"Okay, you've sprained your shoulders. Three broken ribs which we can deal with quickly and yes, a broken leg." He ran the tool up and down her body, grunting. "Bruises and some cuts. No time for those right now. We need to find a way to contact the others and get them to come pick us up."

"Didn't you try before? Where's your communicator?"

He set to work, placing the bone regen on her leg and chest. "It got broken in the crash. I don't think the compass was working before the impact, so I have no idea where we are."

"Ahh." She understood. Their situation right now was precarious. They didn't know where they were. Food and water were low and she was injured. "How badly damaged is the shuttle?"

"Total loss. The chassis is compromised. The outer skin of the craft is torn and twisted. The viewport smashed."

"We're in trouble then." Olivia bit her lip and

contemplated the situation—from bad to worse. She'd have to rely on Jod now, no matter what she thought or how scary it was. Without him, she wouldn't survive. In her experience, the wild life in these environs were tough and brutal. She already knew the heat meant it was necessary to focus on hydration.

Two options came to mind. "You could leave me here and go find the others."

He shook his head. "No. Then you'd be a sitting duck and I know there are rebels looking for you."

"But staying here isn't an option either."

"No. I've been thinking about that. I need to check the cargo bay. If my bike survived..."

She narrowed her gaze. "If the shuttle didn't, then chances are—"

"Slim. Yes. But if it's intact or even only slightly damaged, I can load you on it. Wheel our way to shelter while we consider the situation."

The theory sounded good but... "Which direction?"

He huffed. "Yeah, that's part of the weakness in my plan."

"We could stay here." Not a great option, but it was something. They had shelter, such as it was. Access to the water and food for now...

"And hope the others come find us? I've a sneaking suspicion we are well off course. It could take days. Meanwhile we're sitting ducks. Only my laser pistol and yours—"

"No. That's not entirely correct." She grinned as the analgesic kicked in and Jod quirked a brow. "I have a small cache of weapons. Under the second pilots console, there's a couple more laser pistols, a rapid-fire sniper rifle and..."

His eyes narrowed and he leaned in. "And?" His breath feathered her face, making her insides jump and dance.

"A ground to air assault weapon."

"Certainly well prepared, aren't you?" The amusement in his voice had her smiling.

"I wasn't going to be unprepared. I knew where they kept the armaments. I'd already made a copy of the keycodes. When the attack on the base came... I took my chance. I knew what he had planned for me and there was no way I was going to be used as a pawn."

"No. That's why we came. To help you." He swore again. "Except I didn't do a very good job, did I?"

She shrugged, causing a burn to streak through her shoulders and she hissed. "It was already broken. I had a close shave before I headed for here. They nearly caught me. And if you remember, I did try to warn you."

The buzz of the regen filled the air. *"Initial treatment complete."* Jod released the straps and slid the unit into his pocket.

"Yeah. You did try, but I didn't listen. Okay, let's get you a little more settled." With care he tugged her into a sitting position, lowered her arms, the muscle relaxant he'd administered to Olivia was in full force. "We need to plan a way out of this mess."

✪ ✪ ✪ ✪ ✪

It was full dark by the time he collected the necessities for his plan. One thing you could count on when a planet had multiple suns, it wouldn't be dark for long.

The backpack swung against him, bumping him heavily on the back. Jod had located the dry foods Olivia stashed in the shuttle. Filled water bottles and grabbed what ammunition and weapons he could carry. His bike was damaged beyond repair. Instead he'd fashioned a sleigh using the shuttle door, chains and the bedding she'd been using then loaded it with firewood and the varied items he'd stockpiled.

Their location, if he could believe what he'd seen during the reconnaissance before they'd found Olivia, indicated the presence of caves within several clicks. If they could reach them before the first sun rose, they could shelter. They were defensible too, making it a logical choice. The intelligence he'd gained warned them there was little time between them and the rebels hunting her.

"If you pull me on a sleigh, and they come across the shuttle, they'll know the direction we took."

"Perhaps, but Olivia, I have a plan. It involves you brushing away the evidence of my footprints. You can do that from the sleigh."

She shook her head at him. "You're mad."

"But resourceful."

Olivia laughed at that, the rumble deep and sensuous. Darkly erotic.

His body reacted again, tightening in an unfamiliar way as he remembered the exchange. Blood surged and he shifted, surprised at the way his body acted to her proximity.

No other woman ever made him feel like this. Strong. Resourceful.

It wasn't the way of a Ru'Edan male to be drawn to a female. They were chosen, and at his station, it was the necessity of an alliance that usually decided who he'd pair with. He ruthlessly shoved those thoughts aside.

Jod cleared his throat and strode toward the remains of the shuttle.

"Ready?"

"Yeah. Can you help me?" She was stranded in the middle of chaos, a large pipe in her hand.

"What's that for?" He indicated to the metal she gripped.

"A cane." She waved it around, weaving unsteadily then gave a strangled gasp as she started to wobble and quickly lowered the metal. "A weapon. At least I won't be totally reliant on you. Especially when I have to..." She stopped and colored a little.

He understood: When she needed to relieve herself. "Of course."

Jod strode up to her, scooped her up and Olivia sighed. "What's wrong?"

"I don't want to rely on someone. This feels so much like I've given in."

He laughed and she batted at him with her free hand. "What's that supposed to mean?"

"I can't see you ever giving up Olivia. You're resourceful and quick. Eighteen months evading the rebels is no mean feat."

"Ha! You found me."

"With a lot of help, your shuttle was damaged and—"

"Just get me on that damned sleigh," she muttered.

Walking with her, aware and wiggling in his arms was harder than before, when she'd been unconscious. Now the curves of her body swayed as she remained upright. The mounds of her breasts and the rigid tips of her nipples rubbed against him. His body continued to react, muscles he tried to ignore throbbed with arousal.

When he had her settled in the travois he grabbed up the rope and started off, heading for the darker shadows in the distance.

Chapter Three

They reached the valley by the break of dawn. The first sun rising above the horizon while heat filtered through the air like a ripple, sapping their energy.

Jod placed a hand on her shoulder and she leaned into his support. She'd insisted some distance back that she'd walk once they were past the soft silty ground but the sweat trickling between her breasts and the ache in her leg left her wondering about that decision. "If we follow this arroyo, we might find a cavern big enough to hide the litter and ourselves."

Olivia slumped down to the sled and sighed, then licked her dry salty lips.

In the hours they'd travelled she'd refused to use the precious water, figuring he was the one who would dehydrate fastest.

She looked out, back in the direction they'd come. The blackened hulk of the craft still smoking on the horizon. "I still can't believe you burned my shuttle."

He sighed. They'd discussed this several times since he'd torched it. "It wasn't salvageable. And we need them to take a look and decide no one survived. It ensures we have a chance to get away and back to my ship."

Cupping one hand over the brow of her eye she surveyed the flat distance. "You never said how you know the rebels are chasing me."

Jod shrugged. "My people talk to other people. There's chatter. In the bars."

For the first time she felt a wave of fear. "It makes no sense why they want me. It's not like I'm anything special."

"You're Crick Sur Banden's daughter. That's all they need to know." Frustration laced Jod's words and she shrugged. She couldn't change that.

"Anyway, when your people see the shuttle, they'll think

we're dead too. Then we're stuck here."

"They're not green, Olivia. They'll check the craft, if only to ensure my body is returned to my father. Trust me on that." He'd intimated that his father wouldn't be impressed, but when she tried to find out why, he'd dodged the question.

Scanning the area again, Olivia's gaze settled on a darker impression. "There." She pointed one finger in the direction of the shuttle. Whatever it was, it moved quickly. "What's that?"

Jod visually followed where she indicated. "Stay here." He hefted the small pistol and collected a hand full of rocks. His quick moves ratcheting her anxiety so that the greasy knot inside her almost filled her chest.

She pushed off the bed he'd made with a twisted panel as he dropped the rope and headed off.

"Be careful." She couldn't say why it was important to say the words, but they were. After all she'd been through— all the times her subconscious had prompted her to move, and mostly her instincts about situations were right about looming danger—this was no time to question it.

At the edge of the cavern he hefted the rocks. She waited, sure something big and dangerous would emerge.

One breath.

Another.

A third.

He threw again. The wait resumed. Her pipe cane shifted slightly in the rocky ground as she leaned heavily on it. He glanced in her direction. "Looks clear. I'm going in."

He disappeared down the mouth and she licked her lips again, suddenly frightened of being left alone out here. *Without him.*

Funny, that kind of loneliness and concern had never occurred before meeting him. She pushed the thought to the very back of her brain. That was a concept to consider another time.

Jod re-emerged, dusting webs and dust from his shoulders and hair. "It's good. Pull the litter over if you can and then get yourself in here. We'll need the bedding, because the ground is hard. There's also a spring so you can finally drink."

She swallowed, knowing he'd understood her reluctance and feeling, if not embarrassed, then wary of the amount of awareness he had of her thought patterns. "Sure."

Olivia hobbled back to the sled, grabbed up the rope and tugged. It was heavier than she'd thought and she wondered how he'd coped in the heat with it, her weight and the grip of the sand. Plus the bouncing over rocky ground.

He met her half way. "Get in there and find a spot. We won't be able to warm any food up because fire will give us away, but at least we can defend ourselves, refresh and rest." She started down the hole as a whine filled the air.

"Barsha, it's a newer craft. Fast." His mutter was joined by a gentle shove and she hobbled faster at his, "move."

She moved as quickly as she could, watching as Jod jerked the sleigh inside. They'd just made it when a small, highly maneuverable craft skimmed overhead. "Out of sight."

"Did they see us?" She crouched against the wall, noting the shadow of the craft zooming overhead.

His finger against his lip, he waited, eyes rolled to an upward position. Fraught seconds passed. "I don't think so, but we'll exercise caution."

Olivia waited, pressed against the wall, the pipe behind her in case it reflected and gave them away. The ship made several passes while Jod indicated she should remain still and silent. He did the same.

It felt like hours, the slow advance of time, and she breathed lightly, well aware that any sound might be picked up by sensitive scanning equipment.

The shuttle turned then hurried back toward the wreck where it hovered and she deduced they were likely scanning for life forms. "At least the rock is too dense for them to check these caves," Olivia whispered.

Jod simply grunted.

A good five to ten minutes passed and she bit her lip fearing they might decide to look closer.

Suddenly the ship rose, turned on its tail and left.

The sound died away and she released the breath she'd held. "That was close. You're sure it wasn't...?"

"No." Jod sounded adamant. "They'll come soon. Those were rebels. I've seen those ships before. It's a Phobos craft. They're well made and highly maneuverable."

He helped her to rise with a gentle pull then indicated that she should enter the cavern further, where she noted several large rocks. They were big enough to act as seats and Olivia gratefully settled onto one. "That was as close as I've come yet." She looked up, capturing his gaze. "I'm still not sure about you, Jod, but at the moment I'm counting you as one of the good guys." Olivia scrubbed her hands over gritty eyes. "My biggest concern is to find somewhere safe to attend to toileting, washing my face, getting a drink and sleeping for the moment though."

He gave a bark of a laugh. "Stay here and I'll see what lies beyond that opening." He nodded in the direction of an opening. "Call me if you hear another craft."

Jod pushed past her, long legs brushing against hers and she swallowed heavily, the punch of electricity surprising her. She couldn't remember ever feeling that before.

When he returned he motioned her to follow, trusty pipe in hand. A little further back there was a smaller cavern, with sand for the ground. "This should do."

She nodded and waited for him to leave then went about the process of attending her needs.

By the time Olivia returned to the larger cavern she was aching again, her leg a morass of pain and she leaned heavily on her support, sweat dotting her upper lip.

"Come on. Sit down and I'll check your leg again. We might need the bone regen on for the day."

She wasn't at all surprised when he scowled over the diagnostic results. "You've done too much."

A giggle escaped, brought on by the results of the crash, their close shave with whoever and the stress. "Well, it wasn't like there was much choice, was there? Now, I don't know about you, but I really would welcome something to drink and I'll grab a nutrient pack out for each of us."

They both reached at the same time for the pack, heads colliding. "Ouch!"

"Oomph."

Their hands tangled as they reached for each other. "Sorry, I didn't mean—"

"Olivia—"

Stillness.

Her heart thudding like a madly beating drum. Him. The whisper of his breath.

Warmth. Excitement.

No one feeling or emotion adequately described how she felt.

Arousal. He leaned in. Closer.

Their lips touched, tasted. Quested. *Devoured.*

She slept. He brooded and watched. Since the kiss he'd been in a state of discomfort, well aware that what he was experiencing was out of the ordinary for a Ru'Edan male. Women, mates even, were chosen by their sires. The connections were all about alliances and breeding, but never about feelings and emotions. Not for the likes of him, anyway.

Right now, the mass of seething passion confused him further. What the hell did he do?

He was Ru'Edan. Not human.

He wanted what Chowd and Meredith, Raven and Jemma had though. He'd had eighteen months to learn and study them. Eighteen months that had opened his eyes and broadened his horizons.

A sound echoed and he stood, made his way to the entrance and watched, hidden in the shadows.

A craft approached. Slowly. Lumbering over the cavern

where they hid.

It wasn't theirs either.

Two craft in a short period of time increased his concern. Was this Ru'Edan? Was it the rebels double-checking? It wasn't Raven and Jemma.

This time, it hovered, and he was sure they were testing the wreck again.

She crept up beside him, rested her hand on his shoulder. "They haven't found us. It looks like the one that was at the plantation where I was working."

Jod twisted round. "You're sure?"

"Well, if I could see the identification number, then yes I'd be able to tell you categorically. Other than that, I'm guessing."

The rattle grew as the shuttle moved on.

He spun, facing her front on. "What id number did you have?"

"Oh *A78-FGL-1490Z*. Standard Gold Dream Shuttle. Older model. Maybe a '54 or '55."

He stared at her. "You can identify shuttles to that level of detail?"

She shrugged. "I was kept out of the kitchens and away from the men. It kind of limited the use I could be to *him*, so I was kept in the communications rooms. That's how I knew what was going on at the end. Plus, I needed to know the varied models of shuttles and years, so I could double check whether they were friendly or not. I was interested, so I made sure to learn as much as I could. I managed to get someone to give me lessons on shuttle piloting, and the rest is history."

He gaped at her.

"Don't look so surprised. My mother was human, and she'd been a top-level communications officer before Crick took her as a hostage. He rather liked it when the women he subjugated were capable, well trained and that their loss to the Admiralty weakened the Alliance. I think it made him feel it increased his prestige too."

Not for the first time, he wondered how his Sire and his mother would see this woman. Would they consider her a threat to the Ru'Edan way of life? Would they welcome her?

Jod decided to take a chance. "My mother... She was surprised by Chowd's Life Partner, Meredith, when they were on station together and the human way of life. My mother is more, forward thinking than a lot of Ru'Edan women. She believes that there should be equal status for both sexes."

Olivia smiled, the tension he'd noticed on her face in the fine white lines melted away. "I think I'd like meeting her. The Ru'Edan could learn from the humans. And the humans could learn from the Ru'Edan too. I spent some time learning about the Ru'Edan homeworld and the family structures. Crick bastardized it, but it seems to me that the families are strong and support each other."

"They do." Every layer that peeled away from this woman, showed him she was resilient. He decided that was a trait he enjoyed in a female. He shoved the next thought from his mind before it could form.

"Come on, let's drink, then work out what we're going to do next."

She followed him back to the cavern, took up the position on the stone where she'd perched earlier.

"Jod, you said Chowd underwent Gene Therapy. Why?"

He looked at her, surprised by the question. "The way I understand it, he wanted to do something tangible, but the color of his skin and eyes were a total giveaway. His uncle, the Admiral, suggested that by undertaking the therapy, he might be able to fit in better. Make him more human. I think it took a while even with that though, before he was accepted." He grasped two cups and passed one to her along with a nutrient bar.

"But, if the humans wish to accept the Ru'Edan, then that means the hybrids too." Her voice softened, but it also contained a wobble of fear.

He crouched before her. "That was before the formal peace agreement. Now there are younglings and the acceptance grows. Back then, it wasn't a regular thing."

She turned away. "What about the others from the moon?"

He sighed. "To be honest only a few survived. Crick must have given the order to exterminate the hybrids before the final attack on the *Elector*. Those that survived suffered horrific injuries. It was the Ru'Edan woman who they protected, and even that is a strange decision in many ways."

She shook her head. "So much destruction, because he thought his way was the only one. So what happened after that?"

"Let's talk about that another time. Food and water first, I think."

They settled in and ate in silence. Olivia focusing on what Jod had shared, and more importantly what he hadn't. Questions rose and she banished them, a yawn escaping and she wriggled down searching for a spot comfortable enough to nap.

Chapter Four

Olivia took up her post, watching as Jod slept. It was light, just as she remembered the Ru'Edan rogues had done. As the hours passed he'd become increasingly more withdrawn and worried.

A low rumble sounded and she peered out. Within a moment, Jod was awake, up and ready with pistol in hand. "Pull back, Olivia, so they don't see you."

She glanced at him, but followed his instructions wordlessly.

He watched, his yellow gaze narrowed, lips pursed.

"Barsha!" Jod scrambled up, pulling himself past the rocky entrance.

"Who is it?" She had a fair idea. This must be his crew, but the shuttle itself was a large craft. "Is that one of the new Warrior class transport shuttles?"

"Yes. It's smaller than the Stealth ships, but just as maneuverable and well armed."

"Wow." She meant it. The Stealth class ships had been whispered of. Duvall McCord, one of Crick's worst enemies had captained one. The Elector had been there right at the end and he'd noted its presence as she'd made her getaway from the moon installation.

Olivia followed Jod beyond the mouth of the cave and watched its trajectory.

"If only I had a flare." Jod shadowed his eyes as he watched the slow descent to the ground.

"Well, we don't. There wasn't one on my ship, otherwise, I'd have brought it with the weapons." She tapped her fingers against her lips. "But there are other ways to catch their attention."

He turned, and she felt his gaze settle on her like a palpable thing. "What?"

"Go grab the small burner off the sleigh and some of the bedding."

Now he grinned. "I like the way you think."

She shrugged. "Just makes sense to me."

Then he was gone, while she maintained her watch. The shuttle was the only ship that had actually landed, allowing for inspection of the remains and she bitterly wished there was a pair of long-seeing optics that they'd brought with them.

Jod returned quickly, the small burner, bedding and a bag she'd seen slung over his back in his hands. He thrust the items at her then settled on the ground to open his bag.

Olivia grabbed the material and twined the bedding around her pole. She didn't need it now or at least hoped she wouldn't. After a full day with the bone regen, so long as she didn't have to run a marathon, or escape a murderous creature, she should be fine to walk. She would just need to baby her leg for another couple of days.

Once her first task was completed, she glanced in Jod's direction, seeing the tiny binoculars he'd retrieved from the pack. "We think far too much alike. I was just wishing for a pair."

The laugh he gave rattled her insides. Deep. Rich. Dammit, *masculine.* Bits of her body warmed and swelled and she could barely contain the damnably inconvenient arousal that had assailed her ever since Jod turned up.

"Help me get this going." She struggled with the burner and the look he slanted at her questioned the sudden shortness of tone.

How the hell am I supposed to deal with this? The refrain kept looping in her mind: Men only used women. They didn't forge a commitment, or at least not Ru'Edan males. *It's ridiculous to even contemplate, so get your mind on the task!*

Olivia bumped into the burner and it crashed to the ground, sparks flying everywhere. "Barsha!"

Carefully, she adjusted it upright and glanced up to see Jod shake his head.

"Here, let me." With a deft movement, he had the burner flaring and took the bedding wrapped pipe and held it over the open flame.

It caught with a whoosh and he held it up, waving it to and fro with one hand, binoculars in the other. With his attention focused on the craft, Olivia took a moment, breathed deeply and attempted to clear the fog that settled in her brain.

A hum and rattle split the air and Olivia glanced at Jod, unable to contain the grin as excitement raced along nerve endings in her body.

Jod whooped, dropped the binoculars and thrust the pipe to the ground. "They've seen us."

Reaching down, he took Olivia's hand and pulled her up, and wound his arms around her. "They've seen us and are on the way."

The tighter he hugged her, the more of his body came in direct contact with hers. She sucked in a deep breath, and noted how her breasts rose and rubbed against his chest.

Catching sight of the yellow flare in his eyes surprised Olivia, her gaze narrowing at the depth and heat. He muttered a word then swooped, settling his mouth on hers in a soul-stealing kiss. His tongue moved into the dark cavern of her mouth, sending licking flames of fire through her body. His hands settled, somewhere down near her backside, the movement slow and deliberate, before cupping her closer.

His arousal, hard and demanding pushed against her belly.

Hers hollowed in response and warmed.

Olivia gripped his shoulders, seeking the support of him. The sinews of his shoulders, hard and corded demanded she caress the strength she'd found there.

Stars, she couldn't stop even if she wanted to. Instead, Olivia welcomed his demands and returned them with her own. She would have given him everything if the sudden increase in the whine of a ship hadn't interrupted.

Stepping back, wobbling a little at the loss of contact

between them, Olivia sucked in a deep breath and glanced to the ground, refusing to look at Jod. Her lips were swollen, body heated five ways to dinner and the gnawing emptiness in her belly alarmed her. Maybe there was something wrong with her and it wasn't arousal? Olivia wasn't sure if that thought made her feel any better. Perhaps there was a healer aboard who'd be able to reassure her that it was the stress and fright of the last months affecting her like this. That idea had her biting her lip with confusion until Jod cleared his throat.

"They're here." He sounded steady, comfortable with whatever the emotional *thing* that just passed between them might be.

She seethed, suddenly filled with rancor at his ability to throw off the affects of their heated interaction. "I can tell that."

The craft settled beyond them, on the other side of the dry riverbed, kicking up clouds of dust and Olivia coughed, closed her eyes and covered her mouth and nose. Air whooshed around her, while her hair streamed like long thin ribbons. A sensation of heat flowed over her and she moved slightly beyond the draft.

The whine dropped and she opened her eyes wide. The sheer size of this shuttle amazed her. "It doesn't have trouble leaving the atmosphere?"

Her experience of being with shuttles was limited to smaller craft, yet given the dimensions, surely there would need to be immense gravitation issues to contend with? This planet, with the increased gravitational forces plus that would require serious thrust, and the atmosphere wouldn't likely release it easily.

"No. Our pilot, Jemma, is exceptionally talented. She wouldn't have put down if she didn't think it capable to safely takeoff."

Hmm. A female pilot. Something more to consider. Crick would never have allowed it, and neither would the Ru'Edan in her experience, yet here was Jod, clearly a high-ranking male aboard a ship with a female in charge.

Two of the shuttle's passengers clambered down the

gangway. Both males.

"Raven! Chowd! Glad you finally arrived."

Jod walked over and clapped the two men on the shoulder and she watched this unfamiliar behavior. Ru'Edan males didn't traditionally touch each other either and Jod's status as an enigma, in her mind, grew to larger proportions.

"Come over and meet Raven, Olivia. He's our engineer and the one who was going to look at your shuttle."

No sign of any women, Olivia frowned. "Where are they?"

Jod screwed his face up, clearly unsure what she was asking. "Who?"

"The women. You said there was a female pilot."

"Ah, there is. She's onboard because..." His weary glance had her shaking her head.

"Never mind." Olivia shunted the question to the back of her mind. *I'll investigate after I'm on board. For now, I'd best meet these men.* She'd already met one and he didn't rank high in her estimation after encouraging Jod to secure her in the shuttle. The one that now lay some distance away in ruins.

Jod knew the instant Chowd came into sight that she would tighten up even more than she had. The kiss, as wonderful and hot as it had been, tested her a bit too much. It had been ill advised but by the stars, it had been amazing. She'd responded for a minute or two and he'd felt the way her body heated beneath his touch. She became pliant in his arms, pushing in as if nothing was too much.

He might be a virgin, but he was no innocent when it came to women. He'd seen men rutting. Yet, if he was asked, he'd say what they'd shared was more than the easing of a sexual ache.

"When you didn't turn up, we started to worry. Raven

went out and reconnoitered. The news of a shuttle crash, a burning mess in the desert left us concerned. Of course, as a result the airfield was on shut down, meaning we couldn't get out here sooner. Then Jemma wasn't in any fit state to fly this morning so it was necessary to wait until her nausea passed."

"It's probably best you did, Chowd. There were two fly-pasts. One I'm sure was a rebel. The other, Olivia thinks was the farmer from where she'd been working."

Chowd glanced at Olivia, keeping his distance and possibly remembering the way she'd tried to escape them. "Good to see you're both okay though."

Raven shook his head. "The ship was a total write-off. There wasn't one panel or item left aboard worth salvaging."

Jod shrugged, aware that after he'd torched the ship everything would have been damaged. "I'd thought maybe my bike after the crash, but after I checked I realised it too was beyond repair. Having said that, it's not a bad idea to leave everything as it is. Make them think there was a total loss. Right down to the personnel."

"Jod, you don't think they'll check for a body?" Raven rubbed his hands over his chin and Jod shook his head.

"No. They're rebels. Not trained for that kind of retrieval operation. They'd likely be lesser status drones looking to use Olivia so they can assume the mantle of leader."

Olivia stood quietly watching the proceedings before walking to the side of the shuttle and inspecting it. "Where's the pilot?"

"Inside the craft. She's unable to enter the atmosphere due to medical issues." Olivia turned, looked in his direction and quirked a brow. Jod watched the byplay with an interested grin.

He stared at Raven, weighing up the situation. Unlike most of the Ru'Edan slaves, she'd been unafraid to go toe-to-toe with the burly engineer. He could intervene, but also knew she faced no harm so let it be. She would need to find her own balance in their world.

"Medical Issues? Is that a euphemism for—"

Raven took a step forward, crowding Olivia and Jod's smile died away as he tensed, unsure for the first time as to how the Engineer would respond to her question about his mate. "No. It means that medically it would be unwise for her at this time." Raven spoke harshly, his features tight.

Jod's long dormant protective instincts rose. "She's used to Crick's way of doing things. Remember that."

It stopped the man in his tracks. Raven frowned clearly unhappy with his reminder. "Yeah. Maybe." The irate man stalked off back into the ship.

Chowd indicated to Olivia. "She's not likely to attack us, is she?"

"No. Just let me get the stuff from the cave, then we'll join you aboard the ship."

He waved to catch Olivia's eye and indicated his intention to enter the cave and she followed him down. "We should gather up the weapons and ammunition and anything else you intend keeping."

Olivia stood her ground, her gaze narrowed. "Am I going to be safe? Or will there be something medically wrong with me too, at the next port?"

He coughed, a vision of her rounded and heavily pregnant rising in his mind. "Oh Olivia." He gasped as the image in his mind ground into his brain. "She's breeding. They're concerned about her ability to maintain in the higher gravity."

Olivia colored and bit her lip. Jod found her reaction endearing and grinned as she brushed aside an errant strand of hair. "Well, I really should have asked what the medical condition was."

She bent and collected the items, shoving them into the backpack, but his mind continued to turn over the idea of Olivia and him...

Get your mind on the mission, Jod.

When she turned and thrust the bag at him, he managed to recollect himself slightly.

"I'll follow you." He scooped up his backpack with his free arm and made his way back to the ship. She led the way and at the gangplank he stopped, as he'd seen Raven and Chowd do many times while she glanced at him.

Her glance told him she was confused. "You go first."

She stared. "Why?"

"Because that's what they do in the Alliance."

On a sigh, Olivia boarded the shuttle.

✪ ✪ ✪ ✪ ✪

Together they approached the bridge and she felt the clang of the door closing once the gangplank had retracted. Not a word passed between the four of them as Raven, Chowd, Jod and herself made their way down the long corridor toward the cockpit.

The shuttle reminded her of the few she'd traveled on previously. Grey with exposed riveting, metal grating for the floor and large thick security doors.

Even as they swung open, Olivia felt the change in atmospheric conditions. "What happened?"

"They're stabilizing the internal gravity of the ship." Jod placed a light hand on her shoulder and she accepted the tiny caress that followed, letting it soothe her ragged nerves.

"Oh." Surprised filled Olivia. She'd heard that such actions were possible once in space, yet here they were informing her they'd managed to harness that ability on terra. "That's a fairly new advancement in technology, isn't it?"

"Jemma and Raven have been working on it for some time. This ship is the first to have implemented it, yes." Chowd spoke quietly and it took Olivia a moment to remember this was her half-brother and an Alliance Ambassador.

Now she turned and really looked at the wiry warrior before her. "Jod says you were on the *Elector*."

Chowd smiled. "I was with Duvall, Raven and Grayson."

"But not Jod?" Olivia needed to understand how he'd come to be part of this highly trained group of warriors.

"Only at the end. Jod was sent to us for the strike on the moon base. He'd been the head of security for Esrau Svan'Er of the Ru'Edan Senate."

Now Olivia gulped. No wonder he'd joined the crew. He too was an enforcer, feared by the Rogues.

"Then I'm in good hands, I believe." She spoke quietly, and embraced the small amount of comfort the notion brought her.

The group reached the door to the cockpit and it slid open. One woman, slender with short dark hair smiled and waved them in before making her way to Chowd and embracing him.

Olivia watched, entranced at the gesture. She'd never seen an action like that before between a male and a female. Except of course, the one she'd just been part of, her brain chimed in.

The other male, Raven, headed to the pilot, brushed a hand over her shoulder and took up the secondary pilot position beside her.

Jod cleared his throat. "Olivia, this is Meredith and Jemma."

She took a moment, orienting herself. Meredith was the one who now held Chowd's hand and Jemma—the one who was breeding, she reminded herself—was the pilot. In Olivia's experience *breeding* meant banishment to the kitchens until the offspring was delivered. That's what females were for, according to Crick and his rogues. But Jemma seemed totally unconcerned.

Olivia bit her lip. "You both have positions of authority on the ship?"

Meredith laughed. "Yes we do. I'm a Warrant Officer with a particular specialization in languages. Jemma is a certified Ace."

Olivia frowned. "But who chose those roles for you? Why aren't you breeding also?"

Meredith frowned. "Breeding?" She glanced to Chowd

who sighed.

"Pregnant, Meredith."

"Oh!" Now the short-haired woman gave a small nod. "I am pregnant, uh, breeding."

"Then why aren't you confined to the kitchens?" Olivia's confusion grew. Two breeding women and neither giving up their roles seemed inconceivable.

"Human women choose their own vocations. Your mother would have before Crick abducted her." Meredith spoke quietly and clearly, obviously understanding the difficulty Olivia was having reconciling what she knew of human women and the Ru'Edan way of life.

"I don't remember. Once we were old enough, we were usually separated from our mothers. I had some interaction but not a lot. I'd been lucky to have the opportunity to learn how to fly a shuttle, but that was because Crick felt it would make me a more interesting commodity when he traded me for an alliance."

Meredith blanched a little, but honesty seemed the best option with the situation Olivia faced. She shrugged.

Jod took her hand. "Come and sit down. We'll need to be strapped in to leave. That's what we're doing, isn't it Jemma?"

"Yeah. I don't fancy spending any more time here cooped up. Let's head back to the Admiralty." The woman in the pilots seat swung around and Olivia almost gasped once she noted the violet shade of her eyes. She'd never before seen such amazing eyes.

"Let me assist you." Jod reached across and started tugging on the straps as Olivia sat in the spot Jod indicated for her, next to him. She noticed that Chowd and Meredith sat together, hands tightly twined.

I wonder what it would feel like to have such a level of emotional ties to a male. Unable to help herself, she reached out to Jod and clasped his hand. It felt good. Right. Comforting.

Soaking it up for a moment more, she stored the emotions away, before letting go and closing her eyes. She wanted to store these memories away because she couldn't believe that such a deeply intimate connection lay in her future.

"All crew, strap in and prepare for ascent." Jemma's voice echoed through the communications systems and Olivia's eyes flicked open, searching for and finding the pocket sized human piloting the craft.

"You can learn to do this, should that be your wish." Jod spoke close to her ear. The whisper of his breath did that crazy mad thing to her system again: Made her stomach wobble.

"I... I'd like that." Olivia looked away.

This wasn't like her. She was resourceful. Strong. Didn't need a male to tell her how to live her life. *Get your act together, Olivia. He's turning you into some kind of addled mush!*

The truth was, he wasn't turning her into mush. She was doing it to herself with these secret longings and hungers.

Maybe if I act on them, they'll go away? It wasn't much of a plan, but given her lack of knowledge of these kinds of emotions—she'd never discussed anything like this with her mother—she didn't have anything else to go on. And the lack of empirical evidence had her wondering. She could ask these females, and they might tell her. Perhaps.

Or she could wait, and undertake a broader study.

To wait or not right now was immaterial. Jod was going to be hanging around for some time. Each time he touched her made it harder to consider why touching him and more wasn't such a great idea.

The vibrations of the shuttle increased, while the shields on the viewport flamed in oranges and reds, before glowing blue then white.

It was truly amazing what science had allowed humans and Ru'Edan to survive. The beauty was elemental, similar to her hunger to survive.

The ship could withstand immense external pressures. Could she?

With a sigh, she settled back against the seat, closed her eyes and let the wash of tiredness drag her away to nothingness.

Chapter Five

"**J**od, she's going to need to see a Surgi-Tech when we get to Admiralty, the Admiral is going to need to meet with her. And it's going to be overwhelming if she doesn't make any attempt to integrate. This is a small crew, so staying sequestered in her cabin isn't going to help much."

Chowd outlined his concerns with the way Olivia was determined to keep to herself. She'd accessed the widely available historical files for humans—they'd kept tabs on that— but had hardly emerged, except for meals, before closing herself off again.

"I am aware of your concerns. Yet if I direct her, then she won't be able to express her free will. That was part of the brief from Elphin for once we'd ascertained if she was friendly toward the Alliance and Ru'Edan coalition."

Concern had gnawed at Jod since they'd left the planet. Jemma had plotted the most direct course, understanding the need to get Olivia into a safe space before anyone realized she hadn't died in the crash.

"I would also appreciate the opportunity to discuss Crick with her. I feel she is unsure of my presence." Chowd spoke uncertain, the merest quaver evident in his voice. Jod understood his fears. Thus far, she'd avoided any further personal encounters with her brother.

Jod found the situation to be quite unsatisfactory. On one hand, he didn't want any kind of personal entanglement with this female. He was a high-ranking Ru'Edan male and supposed to take a Life Partner from a similarly ranked female, sired by a senior male from another house. That's how it was done in his society. On the other hand, there was the intriguing but inexplicable need to get closer. He shied away from the emotional hunger and possessive need that reminded him of Chowd and Meredith.

Jemma and Raven were also close, but they didn't seem to be stymied by the whole hybrid human situation. "How do you manage?" The question blurted out before he could contain it.

"Manage what?" Chowd looked up from the screen, where he was browsing incoming intelligence.

"With Meredith. I mean, you're a hybrid and she human. How does that work?"

Chowd sat back in his seat, steepled his fingers and peered at him. "Why do you ask?"

Frustration ate at Jod. He knew Chowd had picked up on his interest in Olivia. "She's hybrid. What affect does that have on a partnership? Does it cause friction?"

Chowd gave him a steely look. "You're interested in Olivia, but want my advice on how to proceed?"

"No. What I want to know is what were the ramifications for you, personally and how you overcame it. Her house—did they approve of your partnership?" Jod sighed. "I honestly am confused, Chowd. It's a constant state of frustration for me. I see you and Meredith and the commitment between you. It's been educational for me and expanded my horizons. I think I'm becoming more like a human than Ru'Edan sometimes and have found the human way of taking Life Partners more..." he fished around for a word that adequately described what he'd learned. "It seems more fulfilling."

Chowd nodded. "It is. Deeper." He leaned over the desk. "My advice is to be honest with yourself and her. She's going to have a lot of unconventional ideas. Most likely, she'll probably shy away from emotional entanglements. That's why, to my mind, she's shut herself away. To protect herself because it's the best way to cope emotionally."

Everything Chowd said made sense. Yet if she kept her distance, how would he go forward with any form of relationship?

"Meredith and I have called a welcome aboard meal in the Ready Room with the senior staff. Use that as your first opportunity. Tonight. 1800 hours."

Jod rubbed a hand over his eyes. "How?"

"Escort her from her cabin. Take the opportunity of being alone to simply talk. Be her friend."

Friendship was a new concept to Jod. It meant companionship, freedom to talk. He could manage that. "Fine. Issue the invitation and let her know I'll escort her."

On that, he rose and left Chowd's office, pondering the evening ahead. He'd wear his formal Ru'Edanian uniform, he decided before heading for his own office. He had reports to write for the Senate. They may be a coalition, but his political masters still required their data.

✪ ✪ ✪ ✪ ✪

Olivia scrolled through the information she'd been able to access. Human mating rituals, dating and courting seemed positively alien to her.

They danced and sang, ate and simply were around each other. Then came the more serious aspects: Kissing and other intimacies. She knew about the rutting of Ru'Edan males.

"That's all well and good, but what about Ru'Edan rituals?"

"*Searching...*" The melodious tones of the computer took her by surprise. She'd been merely musing, having avoided the concept over the last few days.

A small window appeared in the corner of her screen. "*Your presence is required for a meal in the Ready Room with senior members of the crew. You will be escorted from your cabin at 1800 hours.*"

"If Jod is there, I should be safe from the rest of the crew. After all, he won't open himself up to that kind of behavior while they are all there." The seed of satisfaction was overlaid by a hint of disappointment. Jod had made no attempt to make contact since she'd been shown to her quarters. Other crew had initially acted as escorts, showing her to the main dining mess and anywhere else she needed to be.

Olivia supposed she should be grateful they treated her like the rest of the crew, down to making the simple grey shipsuit available to her. Her fingers hovered over the keys, knowing they required her to respond to the invitation. *'I look forward to it. O'*

"Search completed. Display results on screen?" She jumped at the computer's voice filling the air.

"Display." She hovered her finger over the rollerball, aware there were few results. The first one simply detailed the political associations of individual houses through the taking of Life Partners. "Bloodless," she murmured.

The next was a humans guide to the process of Life Partnering: Negotiations, contracts and a sample filing of intent. The only female involvement in the contract was the procession to the male's abode. That level of disregard for the women left her cold. Nowhere in the negotiations and treaties was passion, need or the woman considered. No connection existed between the female and male prior to the short ceremony of introduction.

The sparse information didn't settle her nerves.

"Enough!" She shoved away from the computer. *My life is worth more than my value to some damned house!*

It was time to consider what she had to do for herself and ensure her freedom. How she would be able to go forward? "I'm not going to blithely go off to the Sur Banden house and wait for them to use me as a pawn. I've already escaped that outcome once." She chewed her nails and shook her head.

"Computer, show me the options available within the Admiralty to Ru'Edan females."

"Unable to compute."

Scalding anger at herself and the restrictions placed on her bubbled below the surface. "Why?"

The computer remained silent, as if unable to understand her question. With a groan of sudden anger, Olivia threw herself on the narrow bed, mentally taking stock of possible options.

Hand-to-hand combat wasn't her strong point. What

little ability she'd acquired would likely improve with training, but right now that future career didn't rate highly. What she did know was informal and dirty.

She'd received some training in communications, particularly traffic control with shuttle movements. Mainly air to ground control she amended.

Piloting. Not quite at the level of Jemma, she knew, but smaller terrestrial craft or inter-system shuttles.

She could attach herself to the Alliance. It seemed there might be more opportunities given they had females in a range of ranking positions. And Chowd. "My brother." She gave a moue of discomfort. There was another situation that would require some kind of resolution. But not yet. She wasn't ready to address that issue.

"I'll broach my opportunities with Jod this evening."

She wasn't sure she trusted him overmuch, but he might be able to suggest a plan for entry into the Alliance. Possibly even the academy.

Olivia lay back and closed her eyes.

✪ ✪ ✪ ✪ ✪

At 1800, Jod waited outside Olivia's cabin. *Friends. Discussion. Enjoyment.* They were his aim for the night. Not powerful, mind-blowing kisses.

He knocked. Firm and controlled, then tweaked his uniform, ensuring it was sitting per Senate regulations.

The palm-screen at her door changed from red to green then the slider opened and she stepped out.

The grey of her suit did little for her skin tone, yet she'd never looked better. The slightly gaunt look she'd carried was replaced with a gentle roundness. Her eyes shone bright and her lush hair, caught up at the back of her head, displayed the planes of her face perfectly. "Ready to go?"

For an instant he considered holding out his hand as he'd

seen Chowd do, then dismissed the idea. "This way."

She followed him down the corridor. "It's a bigger ship than I thought."

"Yes. She carries a full compliment of thirty-six, plus myself, Chowd as Ambassador for the Alliance and Meredith as his primary staff. Have you seen the whole ship yet?"

"Uh, no. Just the medical facility and mess."

He frowned. "Why did you go to the medical facility?"

He heard her sigh. "Chowd was insistent that my leg and ribs be checked. I'm not sure it was enough for him, but it seems you don't have a Surgi-Tech aboard."

"No. Even with the size of this shuttle, its still far too compact for a full surgi-tech suite. " He indicated the stairs and followed her up. They stopped at a reinforced door and he placed his hand to the reader. The light changed from red to green as it slid wide.

She waited and he sighed. "You are supposed to go first."

"Oh." She stepped into the room.

Olivia had to confess to being more than a little lost. Jod hadn't made a single move that could be considered out of the ordinary. He'd been polite. Friendly. When they'd arrived he'd ensured she was comfortable then gravitated toward Raven, while she stood there, conversing with Jemma.

"It's a most deceiving craft."

Jemma, the small compact pilot, grinned at her. "Isn't it? She's a total cracker and it's a compliment to be able to pilot it for Chowd and Jod. I think they had this ship because she was the first of her class, and Admiralty wanted to send a message that the F.A.P.—"

"F.A.P?" Olivia screwed up her nose, not totally sure what that was.

"Oh, the Federation of Alliance Planets. I'm lazy and just

call it FAP."

"Ah. So the F.A.P. sent a message by..."

"The coalition is so new, and the fighting bitter. Not that I saw any of the previous actions."

Olivia frowned. "Why not?"

"Oh, I forgot you wouldn't know. When Crick, your father—" Jemma grimaced. "Sorry. I can talk about something else if it makes you uncomfortable."

Olivia shook her head. "No. He was a biological figure but I have no emotional attachment to him."

"Ah, right." Jemma cleared her throat. "So you know that he travelled back in time, and that's where I came from. Duvall and Meredith knew what my future would be if I stayed, so with some quick thinking, they brought me to the future—as in now—and that's how I ended up here. It's been almost three years."

Olivia considered the pilot's words. Crick had been committed to changing not just the life of now, but had even attempted to change the past. He'd been so arrogant. A familiar wave of revulsion rushed through her body, heat licking at every nerve ending.

"Are you okay?" Jemma peered at her.

"Yes. I was just unaware that he'd undertaken such an action, but am unsurprised. But you were telling me about the F.A.P. and this craft."

"Sure. So, even with the ceasefire years ago, there was so much bad blood between the Ru'Edan and humans. When the treaty was signed, the F.A.P. decided to make a statement and offer Jod and Chowd a joint Ambassadorial mission to find you. But the F.A.P. went one better and made this ship, hot off the dock, available for use."

"Oh." It surprised her to realise they felt she was important enough to act in such a way and told Jemma so.

"Well, there was concern that the remaining rebels would see you as a point to rally around. The only remaining offspring of Crick Sur Banden, apart from Chowd, who'd already shown he was firmly in the camp of the Alliance and of course, partnered with a human."

"That's what the symbols on your wrist mean, isn't it?"

Jemma held up her wrist so Olivia could see the three tiny teardrops. "Yeah. Raven and I were joined aboard the Elector."

Olivia bent down and inspected them. "The Ru'Edan don't do anything like that. The woman is handed over, like a piece of furniture."

"So I'd heard. But things are changing. Jod's sisters are being sent to Admiralty, so they can learn skills that would be valuable to the coalition. Things are changing rapidly for the Ru'Edan. Jod says it's for the better."

Olivia chanced a look at him. "He's very human, for a Ru'Edan."

Jemma laughed. "He is. Not as much as Chowd, but he's learning."

Raven came over then and Olivia slipped away, considering Jemma's words. He was changing. What exactly did that mean?

The clinking of glasses captured everyone's attention then and Olivia waited as Jod made his way back to her.

"Please take your places," announced Chowd and Jod directed her to a seat before he settled himself beside her. The table was laid in shining ceramics and silver utensils. She stared at them. "What do I do with these?" Uncertainty rippled through her belly, making it quiver.

"I'll help you. It was like that for me when I first joined the *Elector*. I'm getting used to it now."

Jod grabbed the snowy white cloth and draped it over her leg, then did the same with his own as a crewmember came around, ladling out soup. Her stomach gurgled at the smell. She looked at Jod and he grinned. "Trust me, it'll taste good."

Meals on Ortega had been at best bland, the Ru'Edan preferring stodgy curdled masses they called food. This bore no resemblance.

The scent wafting up had her mouth watering. Jod picked

up an implement and she followed his lead, scooping the liquid up and to her mouth. The first taste was heaven. The tang settled on her tongue, surprising her. She tried another taste and almost closed her eyes so she could enjoy the subtle flavors more.

The food in the mess had been a surprise but this was a revelation. Textures and flavors she'd never known fed some portion of her soul she'd been unaware existed.

She ate in silence, speeding through the bowl until there was nothing left, then raised her head to catch sight of Meredith smiling at her.

Jod placed his spoon in the empty dish and once again, she followed his actions. "I've never tasted anything like that."

"I hadn't either, until the treaty negotiations. I don't think I could go back to Ru'Edan foods after this."

"Why do you dismiss your heritage, Jod? You're Ru'Edan, yet you are more human in choice. You say you prefer their food, act more like them and even seem to dress like them. What is it about humans you feel is an improvement on your ways?"

Jod smiled. "It's not any one thing, but a range of beliefs that allow for equality. Ru'Edan society is structured and strict. Women are owned and genders segregated. But for all that, there is no opportunity within my society to be more than I am. The coalition has allowed me to experience and learn in a way that would have been forever denied me. I can be more than I was. It satisfied a certain hunger that I have. One that would have eventually starved me. I am drawn deeper with every action and choice I make. However, I make them consciously."

A beep echoed and Chowd and Jod both stood. "Excuse us." Jod's spoke quietly and she watched as the two males moved to a corner of the dining room.

Jemma left her chair and headed for the console where she conversed animatedly with the two males. Chowd shook his head while Jod's lips thinned, white creases forming as muscles tensed at the side of his mouth. The conversation continued for another minute or two before Jemma curled her finger to Raven and he stood, excusing himself to join her, then they spun and left the room.

Jod returned to Olivia, his gaze hooded. "We have a problem. We need to go directly to the cockpit." He blinked and his face changed, taking on a drawn look while his yellow eyes glinted with fury.

"What's wrong?" She stood, the white material fluttering to the floor, forgotten.

"We were followed and they've hailed us. Come on." He reached for and grabbed her hand and together they hurried out of the room and joined the rest of the assembled party along the corridor. At the entry to the cockpit, two guards, armed with tactical rifles had taken up position.

"They've come for me, haven't they?"

Now when Jod looked at her, she could only see determination. "They won't get you. They'll have to go through me first."

The intensity in his voice left Olivia shivering.

Jod settled her into the seat, ensuring she was strapped in before marching over to Chowd. "Have we managed to gather any support yet?" Jod's eyes settled on the blip on the radar, searching for some form of assistance.

"No." Chowd seethed, face drawn tight and Jod understood. Everyone on the ship, including Chowd's partner, Meredith, was under threat. As was his unborn child.

"They won't get the women."

Chowd gave a tight nod. "We need weapons, though."

Together they walked to Raven who wordlessly handed them laser-sighted rifles. "If they board, shoot to kill. Pass along the command and have the security officer distribute armaments." Raven grunted and turned away.

"Arm the women, too." Hearing himself issue the

command surprised Jod. Raven nodded agreeing with his terse suggestion. Then the tall engineer handed him a smaller, compact pistol, the same as Chowd's. He toggled the console and gave the command while Chowd and Jod waited.

Once that was complete, Raven headed to Jemma.

Jod watched as he placed it in Jemma's hand.

A hail split through the air. "Star of Eternity. You carry one of ours. Release her to us, or prepare to be boarded."

Jemma punched the communicator, so she could answer. "Over my fucking dead body. This is a diplomatic ship and any act towards us will be considered aggressive."

"Release Olivia Sur Banden to us, her rightful people and we'll allow you to continue on your mission." The words floated over the comm system and Jod felt the jitters of fury gathering. His muscles clenched tightly as Jemma clicked the unit again.

"We will not negotiate. Olivia Sur Banden is a member of the coalition. There will be no surrendering of a member of the F.A.P."

Jod's stomach knotted. They'd prepared and practiced for this. She may not have sworn fealty to the Federation or Coalition, but it was the stand the Admiralty had insisted upon and the Senate had agreed fully.

He settled into the seat beside Olivia and cinched the straps tight. "We should secure ourselves. Raven?"

The tall man settled into the seat beside the pilot while Chowd issued a ship-wide command.

In the fraught seconds that past, Jod rubbed his brow and scanned the communications system in front of him. "Jemma, do you see any signs of assistance?"

Jemma would have the best idea, but even as she swiveled in her seat he caught the signs of stark terror in the paleness of her skin. "We've received verbal verification of ships in the area. They're changing course to assist but they won't be here in time."

"Who are they?"

"The *Star of Morning* and the *Star of Ishtar.* They have

changed course and should be here within about fifteen minutes. I'm just not sure we can hang on until they arrive."

"Jemma! Their ion ports are hot." Raven's voice contained anger and concern. "We need to raise the shields now." Jemma turned back, her hands flying over the keys.

A wavering wall of white slid over the viewport, before settling to an opaque skin, shimmering against starlight.

Three small Phobos craft disgorged from the shuttle cruiser before them, spinning in tight circles, as if passing time until ordered to attack.

Another swarm joined them and the ice-forming crystals in Jod's veins chilled him.

Suddenly the combatants zoomed forward, bright shots of lightning arcing over the *Star of Eternity.*

Tremors rocked the ship slightly as Jemma hissed. "Increasing engine speed to maximum. Maybe we can outrun them."

While the increase in speed would help, the *Star* wasn't built to run. It wasn't equipped with heavy armor-plating either. It was meant for peace, not war.

The blast of an ion cannon from the cruiser surprised him and he felt the tug of the webbing against his body, sucking the breath as his skin stung. The ship shuddered under the sudden intrusion. Alarms blared, lights flashed to red in the cockpit.

"Dammit! That dropped our shields to seventy-three percent." Jemma's angry tones barked over the noise.

"Recalibrating shields now." Raven glanced to Jemma and Jod watched their movements, aware that right now, there was nothing he could do. He wasn't the security chief on this ship. Frustration at his position of simple onlooker gnawed at Jod. Chowd was nominally the Commander of this craft and Jod had no authority. As much as he itched to assist he had to sit back and wait like everyone else. His fingers curled into a fist.

"Time 'til assistance?" Chowd called his query.

Raven answered with, "ten minutes but closing fast."

He clenched the seat, and felt a touch, Olivia's hand

burrowing into his grip. "I don't want to go back." She whispered the words and that's all it took for him to give in and accept that he was irretrievably committed to this woman. No more questioning his motives.

"I won't let that happen, Olivia. We'll survive." He wanted to say more, but now wasn't the time or place.

Another, stronger blast hit, the ship rocking under the force of the strike.

"I need someone to arm the torpedoes. We can't survive another attack like that." Chowd called his orders.

"I'll do it." Jod unbuckled his belt and pushed to the weapons station. He threw himself into the seat and grappled with the webbed straps one handed until the click sounded that he was secured. He began the sequence, setting in the command that took the torpedoes from cargo to armament in preparation. Another strike hit the ship and now she listed starboard; just slightly, but enough to reinforce how desperate their situation was.

"Shields fifteen percent. Get those weapons hot and ready to fire, Jod!" Chowd yelled instructions, "Jemma, how much longer?"

"Five minutes and closing. They've got the rebels in their sights and need another minute or two before they can fire!" she replied.

The weapons armed, Jod turned. "Chowd. We're hot. Fire?"

His gaze met Chowd's. "At. Will."

Jod depressed buttons one and two, unsure that the systems hadn't been damaged. They were sluggish and he breathed out, waiting. If they were compromised, he'd killed everyone on board. If they worked, it might save them.

He watched the radar, saw two of the highly maneuverable Phobos shuttles intercept the missiles. For a moment, the flash of light through the viewport blinded him.

"*Beis vand har*!" He struggled to make out the symbols on the keyboard in front of him when a whoop sounded. "They've fired again."

Simultaneously, Jemma called, "They're here!"

The resounding applause from the crew raised their spirits. Jod turned in his seat, seeking Olivia's gaze while Jemma released her straps and shoved away from her console.

"Wait!" The roar was drowned out as a rogue detonation sounded, a surprise Jemma clearly didn't expect. He watched in horror as the young pilot lost her footing, arms wheeling for something to hold and flew through the air. Raven bellowed her name as everyone stilled.

The sound of her body hitting the deck with a horrifying *thunk*, silenced them. Then everything was quiet again.

Olivia released her restraints, her eyes on the woman lying at her feet. She knelt before anyone else got there. "Someone grab me the diagnostic device."

It was thrust into her hands, and she ran the wand over the unconscious woman. Silence reigned as the familiar *beep beep* pulsed from the device.

"Jemma?" Raven's voice was the only sound.

"She's not sustained any serious injuries, but we need to get her to the medical unit.

"The... The child?" He sounded almost broken and without a word, Olivia recalibrated the device, searching for the heartbeat. It fluttered as expected in early pregnancy.

"How far along is she?"

"About fifteen weeks," he answered.

"So just past first trimester. It should be okay. There's a steady beat, but she needs a surgi-tech and appropriate equipment to be sure. I need someone to assist me getting her to sickbay."

She glanced up, Raven looked torn. "Jod?"

"Yes." He stood and carefully gathered the unconscious woman in his arms.

"I'll do everything I can, Raven to make sure she gets the best possible care." Olivia touched his arm then followed Jod from the room.

They moved rapidly, crews working repairs shifted out of their way, eyes glued to the injured pilot. At the medical room, the door shifted open and the personnel moving swiftly glared at her. "Life threatening?"

"No."

"Then over there." The first crewmember indicated to a bed and went back to dealing with the injured personnel they'd been attending. Jod laid her down on the small bed, and together they strapped her in for safety.

"I'll stay with her, Jod. You'll be needed on the bridge, won't you?"

"Yeah. Look, stay safe." He turned as if to go, then spun back and gripped her hard. Pulled her against his chest and kissed her. Hard. Quick. Then he tugged away and left.

She wanted to consider his actions, but right now, she had a task, one she'd promised to give her full attention to. A child, a human child, fragile and new depended on her.

She ran the diag wand over again, confirming the fetus seemed to have suffered no ill effects, then tugged the blanket over the woman. She'd return to consciousness soon, Olivia was sure, but she'd make her as comfortable as she could.

It was only minutes until Jemma's eyes fluttered weakly then opened. "Raven?" She spoke in a thready whisper, before she slid urgent hands over her abdomen. "The baby?"

"Raven should be here soon. We're waiting for the *Star of Ishtar* and *Star of Morning* to make a secure connection to the ship. They tell me a surgi-tech will make their way over here, to check on you. But you have to rest. It's best for you and your offspring."

The tension that coiled in Jemma's body seemed to drain away and Olivia took that as a good thing. She'd seen miscarriages in the past, though most of them had been the result of beatings, she'd hate to see this brave and passionate woman face such an emotional upheaval.

It wasn't much after that the clangs echoed through the ship as the other, much larger vessels locked together.

The crewmember who had been short with them as they'd entered sickbay must have stabilized his patient as he headed in her direction. "She's fine. Regained consciousness and—"

"You would know because..." He frowned and loomed over her.

Olivia seethed at the tone, but answered, "I've had experience in triage and some obstetric environments."

"Obstetric?" His blue eyes turned cold.

"Yes. She's pregnant and I checked with the diagnostic device. Everything seems to be as it should be."

Olivia was shaking her head, handing over the device when another woman, her face lined with faint pink and white scars entered. "Where's Jemma?"

"Here." Olivia waved and Jemma's eyes opened.

"Elara. Thank heavens you're here." The feebleness in Jemma's tone concerned Olivia, but she banked her worries. Elara—the surgi-tech judging by the medi-scanner clipped to her belt and the symbol on her shoulder—would do what she could.

"Chowd contacted me. Let me through the privacy screen and I'll get a look at you." Olivia remained where she was until she knew who the woman was.

Now Olivia stepped back, knowing the woman would do what was required for Jemma and the child. Perhaps she should leave, she thought, so after dragging the curtains back around the bed, after opening it enough to admit Elara, she made to leave, but Jemma's voice stopped her. "Please stay, Olivia."

She spun, uncertain what to do or say, but crept to the corner, out of the way.

Elara pulled out a far more advanced diagnostic unit, and swung it over Jemma. "You should have stayed in your restraints. It wasn't the wisest choice," gentle reproof colored Elara's words.

"I know. But I didn't see the last whatever it was."

"No. Obviously not. Now, what do we have here?" Elara glanced sharply at Jemma who slid her hand over her belly.

"I'm pregnant, Elara."

Olivia heard the intake of breath from the scarred woman.

"Let me recalibrate the scanner and check that Junior is alright." She fiddled with knobs, touched a button, hummed then pressed another. "Okay, let's see..." She swung the wand over Jemma's belly and smiled at the *whoosh, whoosh, whoosh* sound. "Junior looks okay, but you have to rest. Eat better and take care of yourself."

The concept of a supportive environment wasn't totally alien to Olivia. The women on Otega had banded together, particularly the humans, who'd been imprisoned by the Rogues. Birth and death had been closely observed, but that the males would be involved—emotionally entangled in the day-to-day lives of their partners—was beyond alien. The concept surprised and enticed in equal measure.

A commotion intruded from beyond the curtain, which was roughly thrust aside by a meaty hand.

Raven strode in, his face taut with worry. "Jemma?"

Elara and Olivia stepped back, allowing the harried partner access.

"Fine, Raven. She's good and so's the babe." A swift look to Olivia, engaged her attention. "Come on, let's leave them be. Raven? When you're ready, find me in the mess and I'll explain her prognosis."

Olivia followed Elara from the cubicle, and the woman turned and held out a hand. "Hi, now let's get formally introduced. I'm Elara. Medic from the *Star of Morning*."

"Uh, I'm Olivia." Flustered she returned the greeting.

"So you're Chowd's sister. Welcome to the Alliance. I'm so pleased to finally meet you."

Chapter Six

Jod found them in the mess, Olivia nursing a mug while Elara chattered away. The bonding of females amused him. Men had war and discipline to build those bonds. Women, it seemed had family and chatter.

He stopped at the doorway and simply observed. Olivia was uncomfortable, her posture stiff. Unresponsive. He considered what he knew about her life with the Ru'Edan.

The conditions they'd discovered on the moon installation of Otega were primitive. The death and destruction close to total annihilation of the human population.

"She's coping better than I would have expected."

Jod hadn't heard Chowd step up to him, yet right now, he was the only one who could answer his questions with any understanding of the tug-of-war he was trying to overcome.

"I feel confused, Chowd. She's... How do I cope with these emotions?" He turned to his peer, unsure of himself as never before.

"You embrace them. It's not easy and Olivia will need time. She's half human and yet, half Ru'Edan. She grew up in an environment that didn't allow for families. Passion was simply the aegis of the male, the women there subjugated and used."

Jod cocked his head. "You overcame your early training fast.

Chowd barked a short laugh. "Only because Meredith showed me how, and my mother." A shadow, the first he'd seen in a long time, passed over Chowd's face. He'd heard whispers of the death of his mother, the courage she'd shown to ensure her son escaped. He claimed Meredith showed him how, but he'd already been exposed to those emotions.

Chowd was Ru'Edan, though; or at least half. He'd been raised among the Rogues and seen the casual way they'd used and abused women.

Jod thought over his own upbringing with the House he'd been raised in. As soon as his father had been named Senator, he'd shipped his family to the satellite installation. In hindsight, Jod understood how different his upbringing was from most of his peers. His mother had encouraged more interaction with herself and his female siblings, and his father had allowed it. Had even basked in it.

"I want things I don't understand." The words were murmured to himself as much as Chowd.

"Then you need to do something about it. Don't let her get away." Then Chowd stepped beyond, into the mess leaving him there, propped against the wall, considering the words of wisdom.

He took a deep breath and followed the other man into the room, grabbed a hot beverage and pushed into the seat beside Olivia. She glanced at him, surprise making her eyes shine.

"I came to see how Jemma was getting on and that you weren't being swamped."

Olivia colored—a flush settling on her cheeks.

"I'm fine."

He'd flustered her. Not something he would have expected. He gazed at Elara, who watched in silence. "Jemma?"

"Fine. The baby too. She needs rest and relaxation. I've requested she be transferred to my ship, so I can make sure she actually does that. Grayson informed me that the *Ishtar* and *Morning* will act as escort until the *Eternity* reaches Aenna."

Jod relaxed. With the two ships handily close by, he'd have no concerns about Olivia's safety. At least not in the physical sense. It was more his ability to reign in the inconvenient urges.

"What happened to the ship that targeted us?" Olivia placed her hand on his arm and he hissed, desperately aware of her. Trying hard to fight the urge to kiss her, touch her and do far more satisfying things with her.

"It pulled back as the ships joined us. Moved fast."

"Hmm. Could I take a look at the logs? I'd like to know who it was, if possible." Olivia spoke quietly and he frowned.

"I'm not sure. I'd need to talk to Chowd." Jod sipped on his drink and waited.

"Alright then." She looked at him, nervous and distracted.

Elara drained her cup and set it down as she pushed up from the table. "I need to go check my patient and as Raven hasn't yet come to me, I think I should find him and make sure he lets Jemma rest."

Jod let her go, his concentration fully on Olivia. "You looked quite uncomfortable talking with Elara." He couldn't think of anything else to say.

"She was asking about what happened on the bridge. So I told her." The ruddy glow of her cheeks drained to a paler tone.

"What's wrong?" He reached out, clasped her hand as she shoved out of her seat, awkward movements, jerky; alerting him that she was laboring under an intense emotion.

"I need... I need to get out of here." The urgent way she spoke had him moving, making way for her. She walked, a quick step to the doorway and down the corridor. It ran almost the length of the ship, with large viewing ports dotting the side. At the final port, Olivia stopped. Hands gripping the molding. "It's my fault. Jemma and the baby got injured. I should have run faster."

She breathed heavily, the rise and fall of her chest betrayed the depth of her turmoil.

He didn't know how to help her. Wasn't sure if there was anything he could say or do. So he wrapped his arms around her waist and pulled her close.

The muscles of her body relaxed, and she sagged against him. It took all his will power to remain silent, his body locked in the torment of sudden and insatiable hunger.

"I tried so hard, Jod. I didn't want to be found and I thought I'd succeeded. Then *you* found me. I reconciled myself to being alone. But I'm here and I... I'm so *lonely*."

Stark emotion rippled from her, like radiating starlight. "It's okay. They won't get to you again."

She settled in his embrace with a groan. "You can't

promise me that. No one can. The thing is, they don't want me for me. They want me for who I represent. That's all I've ever been. I want more, Jod. I want to be myself and..." She tugged, trying to pull away, but now she was here, he refused to let her go. Needing, like never before to support and soothe.

To have.

To keep.

To love.

A crewmember pushed past them and she sighed. "There's no peace anywhere here in the public areas, is there?" She sounded vaguely slurred and he sighed, having caught the glint of moisture in her eyes.

"Let me take you to your cabin."

"Yes, maybe I should rest." Her shoulders slumped.

Jod wasn't sure that resting would soothe his ragged mental state. Urgency pounded through him, but he ignored it, pushed away its carnality and stepped away. She watched, eyes hooded as he held out a hand, and she took it. The feel of her palm against his had nerves jumping.

In silence they made their way to the cabin door, and she pressed her hand to the reader. When the slider moved open they stepped within. "Door close."

Olivia turned, her eyes widened with surprise as he stepped closer. He leaned in, giving her time to refuse the contact, before his lips touched hers.

Her hands rose and came to rest on his shoulder, holding him close as she tentatively opened her mouth. He groaned, touching the tip of his tongue to hers, while losing himself in the darkly sensual taste of her.

Jod slid his hands around her waist, clasping her to him as he wallowed in the feel of her, curves and dips pressing against his hungry body.

His turned rock hard as she deepened the kiss, rubbing the length of her tongue against his, rocking her hips slightly.

Tugging his mouth away, he breathed hard before kissing the side of her wide lips. He traced his way along her jaw line, finding her pulse beating wildly at the junction of her neck and shoulder.

She hissed. "Oh, Jod."

It wasn't nearly enough for the raging hunger that beat at him, demanding he continue. He slid hard fingers down to her butt, kneading and pressing in an alternate rhythm.

Skin. He needed to touch her skin.

Blindly, he reached out, fumbling in the material, seeking the zip and button that fastened her flight suit.

Olivia found his, tearing at the closures until she reached the shirt beneath his outer covering.

"I want to touch you."

The vibration of her words echoed in his nerve endings. They quivered as he finally tugged the material away, leaving him amazed at the luscious skin he uncovered. Her breasts were hidden by a utilitarian bra of white, that could have been the finest lace creation for all he cared.

He slid the straps down, eager to touch every inch of her skin. The straps sagged but caught on her suit where it lay open, caught up at her elbows. "Let me."

He slowed the pace, aware of the thrumming of his blood and the lust that drove him mercilessly. The first time shouldn't be a race, he tried to tell himself as he completed the unbuttoning of her suit.

She watched him, eyes wide with surprise. "I want you Olivia. I won't force you, but if I stay, I will have you. All of you." He continued divesting her of clothing, waiting for the dismissal.

"Stay with me, Jod. I want you and I want this."

He released the pent up breath ballooning in his chest, and unsnapped the belt at her waist so the suit fell to the floor.

Underwear and pooling material didn't detract from her beauty.

His hand shook as he reached out, slid a fingertip over the edge of the bra cup. She hissed and her belly quivering against his.

Olivia reached up and behind to unsnap the fastener. The scrap of cloth that had covered and held her breasts floated to the ground.

He gazed on the bounty she'd revealed. Tiny, perfect pink nipples were stark against the grey tone of her skin.

With one hand he cupped a breast, firmed it, so it plumped in the palm of his hand. He slid his thumb over the peaked nipple and she hissed again, bucking slightly.

The need to taste her overrode thought and he leaned in, mouth closing over the firm flesh.

The moan that filled the air tightened every inch of his body. He pushed and shoved at his own clothes, dragging them down as he feasted on her. Wet dragging kisses were met with the steely grip of her fingers on his skull, pulling him closer to her, demanding more.

Hunger raged.

Jod pulled away and snatched her against him, knowing his cock, spike hard rammed into the softness of her belly. "Come with me."

They both toed out of their boots, left them in the tangle of clothes as he dragged her to the bed.

In the back of his mind, the academic knowledge of intercourse flared, then was swiftly lost in the need to hold and brand.

Flesh to flesh, the hard nubs of her nipples grazed the skin of his chest, chasing away coherent thought.

Pleasure pain exploded deep in his nerves and he had to stop, suck in a breath, or else he wouldn't last.

His first time. Hers. It had to be right.

"So perfect." He barely recognized the deep rumble that emerged from his chest.

Jod skimmed his fingers along the edge of her panties before he hooked them under the elastic, dragged the material down the long line of her legs then threw them over his shoulder.

The kiss, furnace hot urged him on. Lip-to-lip and tongue-to-tongue he felt and tasted her groans, letting them feed the well of lava boiling in his belly. Pressure was building and he wouldn't last long. For a moment, he closed his eyes, sucking in a gulping breath and forcing sanity to re-establish itself. *Slow down.*

He slid a hand down over her abdomen, before pushing the swollen lips of her labia apart.

Wet and hot.

Perfect.

He slid a finger into her, her body parting for him. The pulsing of muscles was too much and he pulled out, back.

Gripping her shoulders as she spread her legs further. He positioned himself at her entrance.

"Olivia?"

"Yes Jod. I'm ready." And she was. He read the knowledge in the brightness of her eyes, the damp sheen of her skin and the rhythmic gripping of her fingers. They told him everything he needed to know. She was ready. *For him.*

His cock nudged her entrance, the tip slid just a little way inside and she sucked in a deep breath, her breasts rising and falling as her eyes closed. "More." Her gentle demand finished him and he plunged deep.

When Jod thrust within her body, Olivia almost screamed. It took every ounce of her will to contain the split second of intense pain. She'd been told about it, but had forgotten. She squeezed her eyes shut, but the moisture gathering behind her lids eked out.

He stilled. "Olivia?"

She held still. They'd told her that was the best way of dealing with it.

"I've hurt you." His groan indicated just how much he felt responsible, but she'd wanted it as much as he had.

"It'll pass. The women in the kitchens said the first

time was always painful." She bit her lip though as he moved, preparing to disengage. She gripped his hands. "No. Stay."

He did, but the urgency of their lovemaking tamped down somewhat.

She waited: inhaling and exhaling. Concentrating on clearing her mind until finally the sting dulled.

"I should go." Sorrow, deep and overwhelming resounded in his words.

"Don't go. Please. It's getting better." She glanced at him, saw the dark frown on his face.

"You don't need to make me feel better, Olivia." Once more he moved, but this time, a tingle of pleasure radiated.

"Oh, my..." A sigh escaped and his gaze narrowed. "I told you. They said it would pass." She moved, testing with a small thrust of her hips and felt another frisson of electricity skittering along nerve endings. Her breasts grazed his hairless chest and she hissed, as the urgent hunger rose again. "Please Jod. Don't go."

She undulated now, openly embracing the lust that washed over her.

He gave in, groaning and thrusting lightly. He was swelling again and she grinned as she gave in to the pleasure mounting in her body.

This time, the dance was slower, the two moving in time, letting the ratcheting desire grow between them.

They caressed and kissed, fingers roaming as they learned the feel of each other's flesh. Seeking spots to increase the fervor of their movements.

Desire crested, their thrusts frenzied, in and out. Pumping while her heart rate galloped. "Jod!"

The explosion that crashed through her stole her breath and thoughts as she stiffened, holding onto him. Lost in the whirlwind of sensation.

When she opened her eyes, he was staring at her. "I've never..."

She grinned, feeling silly and giddy in equal measure.

"Me either."

Olivia slumped to the bed and he followed her down, bodies still joined. "Thank you."

His arms burrowed beneath her, holding her close. "Sleep now." When she woke, he was gone.

Chapter Seven

Jod paced, unsure of the protocols involved in such a situation as his. Should he have stayed? Would she have welcomed that?

The communicator squawked. "Jod here."

"We need you both in the Ready Room. Ten minutes." Chowd's voice was strained, as if laboring under some kind of immense stress. Jod huffed out a sigh. His inner worries and procrastination had been cut off at the knees.

He raked his fingers through his hair, then breathed deeply and left his cabin.

She'd been asleep when he'd left her and the door light still glowed green. He knocked.

"Enter."

The door slid open and he quirked an eyebrow at the sight of her standing by the desk screen. "You left."

"I didn't know what to do. It seemed best. But more important than that, why was the door unlocked?"

Olivia shrugged looking pale and hugging herself tightly. "It's what I'm used to."

He bit back the curse word that threatened to erupt. "In future, lock it."

She nodded silently and his stomach roiled at her immediate capitulation.

He sighed and marched over to her, reached out and clasped one of her hands. "Chowd needs us in the Ready Room."

A spark of interest lit her gaze. "Why?"

"I don't know. Let's go find out, shall we?"

He led her out, waited as she engaged the locks then together they walked, neither speaking.

Jod now realized leaving had been a misstep. He should have stayed and... But what would he have done? She obviously didn't need comforting. The whole situation went from bad to undecipherable in two-point-three seconds. With so little understanding of females, he was lost negotiating the emotional landscape. This was unfamiliar territory to him. It didn't help that he had no prior familial knowledge to call upon either. He could ask Chowd...

"Olivia, I..." She glanced in his direction as they reached the door.

"Later. We'll talk about our issues…later. Once we find out what Chowd needs from us."

She marched ahead and for a moment, he couldn't think past the gentle sway of her hips. He snorted, shook his head and followed her in.

Chowd, Duvall and Grayson waited in silence. The holo-communicator perched on the table before them.

First one, then another form appeared before him. Esrau Svan-Er and Admiral Elphin, their outlines flickering with blue and white lights.

Never a good sign, he told himself. He led Olivia to a seat then perched beside her, waiting.

The hiss of the door sliding shut echoed in the silence.

"Door lock. No admittance without my authorization." Chowd ordered and turned in their direction. "We have orders from the joint administration." He gestured to the two figures waiting.

"Greetings Olivia Sur Banden." He heard his father's formal tones, then the Admirals', "So you're Chowd's sister. Good to have you aboard."

His stomach curdled.

"The joint administration is concerned that even when you arrive at Aenna, there are enough Rogues still on the loose, that they will attempt to capture you. Use you, as you are aware, as a final thrust to reinvigorate their cause. "

The Admiral cleared his throat and steepled his fingers. "It's like this, Olivia. The joint administration has been working hard, securing support from within our individual governments to clear out the remnants of Crick's forces. But until now, we've only been able to pick them off as we find them. There's been no real systematic plan. But with you..." He broke off and frowned. "Senator Svan'Er?"

"Crick Sur Banden was a rallying cry for a long time of the disaffected. Houses were nearly destroyed as warriors disaffected by your culture deserted them. The Rogues were always vicious, but over time their lack of moral indicators allowed them to perpetrate acts so vile. Until then, we'd relied on our strict cultural values to halt the all but the most depraved."

His father, Esrau Svan'Er, sucked in a deep breath and Jod felt a spurt of concern. They wouldn't have gone to all this trouble to simply welcome her. No, something else was afoot.

The Admiral raised a hand. "After Otega, we hoped there would be no single factor strong enough to bring the remnants back together. We were unaware of Olivia at that time. He kept her existence hidden from most of his warriors. Yet once they knew, she became the one thing they believed that would rally their troops. I'm sorry Olivia, but we must ask you to oblige both our governments. We need bait and you're the only one with enough pull."

Her hands shook and he held tight, controlling any outward sign of the fury that coursed in his veins. "Senator and Admiral, with all respect, Olivia is a civilian. You're asking her to..."

"Ambassador Svan'Er, I understand the situation is unusual, however, we see no other way of containing the ongoing threat. We must, once and for all destroy the small bands, otherwise there can be no peace for humans and Ru'Edan." The Admiral's words were damning.

"I... What would I need to do, Senator? Admiral?" Olivia's unsteady voice filled the sudden silence.

"Olivia, don't do this." He pulled her seat around so she gazed into his eyes. Instead of fear though, he read resolve and something far deeper. Hope.

"I have to do this Jod. If this one act can help bring peace, then every danger is worthwhile." She pulled her hand away, lifted it and cupped his cheek. "I want peace as much as the next person. Only then can I start to live my life." The words were soft, like a promise and they pummeled him.

He watched as she swung back, giving her attention to the holographic men. "So, what exactly do I need to do?"

"We need to arrange a set up. Have you leave the safety of the shuttle. Act as if you're running away. Your shuttle was damaged, but our techs think they've come up with something that will be fast enough to make them think you're on the run."

Jod cleared his throat. "She doesn't go alone. I'll go with her. As her guard."

His father searched his face then he gave a short nod. "I would agree to that."

"You've my agreement too." Elphin's words died away as Duvall tapped out a sequence, lighting desk screens within the table.

"The best techs of both races have been working on a prototype of a speed shuttle; small, maneuverable and highly armored. There's no time for trials, but we have all the componentry available aboard the *Star of Morning*. My—Our people can have this ready within days."

"I have a Ru'Edan cruiser on standby. We can have them change course to intercept within the hour with the necessary componentry that you require. It will also reinforce the scenario that your are running away." Senator Svan'Er spoke quietly, his eyes never leaving Jod's face and, even across the distance of space, he was sure his father read his emotional attachment to the woman.

"Then we'll leave you to make arrangements. Duvall and Grayson, expect a coded transmission within the next few hours. Elphin out."

He needed to speak and looked in the direction of where he'd seen his father. But without a word, only a pale imitation of a smile, the light of the holo-emitter winked out and Jod sat, staring into space.

Olivia made a sound, a hiccup and sob combined as she

rose to leave. He followed but at the door his name was called by Chowd. He turned.

"My sister. You'll protect her?" The harsh planes of Chowd's face stood out under the bright lighting.

"With my life."

Jod turned and followed the retreating footsteps of Olivia down the corridor.

Olivia walked, blind with anger and fear, toward the stairs. She didn't want to be in the middle of the Ru'Edan and human plotting. Jod called her name and she turned, suddenly blinded by tears. "I don't want this, Jod. I want a life where I can find someone who needs me. Wants only me, not some idea of universal domination."

He enfolded her in his arms. "I want you Olivia. I'm so lost in you, that I don't want you to do this either." His lips brushed her hair and she sagged against him.

"I... I'm in love with you Jod. But you left me this morning and I'm confused. Why? Why did you leave me, yet insist on being with me on the shuttle when I go?"

She suddenly needed to know. The desperation clawed at her gut.

Her body tightened with fear and hope intertwining in her heart, her stomach a mass of butterflies ready to take wing and the shadow of a headache forming.

"I left because I didn't know what else to do. I didn't want you to think I was taking you and your freedoms away. I want you to be free enough that if you wish it, you'll stay with me."

It certainly wasn't a confession of love, yet knowing the Ru'Edan way it was a deep and heartfelt confession of emotional confusion. If that were all she had right now, she'd take it and be thankful.

"I need a coffee and time to think." Olivia held out her hand and he took it. She knew that time now would be in short supply. Once the techs did their thing, and the Ru'Edan crew docked, there would be planning sessions. Then they'd have to transfer to another ship and there'd be no time to be quiet and calm. The atmosphere would be tense for the duration of their so-called escape.

"I'm glad you'll be with me." The words were less than a whisper. He probably didn't hear her, but she needed to say them.

Jod surprised her, though, spinning her around so she faced him and he kissed her: A hard passionate embrace that stole her thoughts.

When he let her go, they were both breathing hard. "Well..."

Jod smiled. "That's just a promise."

Chapter Eight

Four days—long and fraught days, with nights holding Olivia in his arms. Loving her. Now they'd settled into the retrofitted shuttle and the door clanged shut.

Olivia's nerves had thinned in the last twenty-four hours as the final details of the set up were planned. She'd snarled and grunted at people and he'd smiled at her, soothing her ragged emotions as best he could.

They'd decided to head in the direction of one of the mining planets, Omega Nine, after receiving tactical advice from both the Alliance and Senate. It was their job to lead the rogues to them, enter the atmosphere and appear to be heading for an abandoned installation.

A squadron was already heading in that direction, four battle cruisers waited beyond the heliopause, screened by a moon cluster. Her total agreement and assistance of the Coalition would shaft the message home to those remaining rebels that she was neither compliant, nor willing to aid them.

Olivia depressed the switch for the internal communication center and slouched back in her seat. They both knew after this last transmission, everything would be on full silence between them and their supporters.

"Preparing for launch. Going to silent running." The last press was slow and she breathed out. "That's it. Now there's no more communicating with them."

The bay doors opened and the shuttle vibrated before she punched it out into the blackness beyond. The gravitational forces shunted them back in their seats and she clutched the small stick, they'd all agreed she should pilot it on manual for the first hour or so. "Computer, engage the map on viewscreen."

The starfield they were navigating superimposed over their view of the darkness. "Show detailed trajectory, fuel usage and engage audible alarms."

Jod glanced at the weapons console, aware that at least three small fighters would be sent after them. They'd discussed everything from how long after launch through to the break off sequence in the planning and strategy meetings.

"Initiating sweeps." His fingers moved over the screen, seeking any watchers. They were out there, but finding them would be part of their scheme.

A ping, solitary and hidden within the shadows of asteroids, echoed. "Watcher at three kodeks."

"Initial fighter launch, three following." He glanced at the screen, checking the timing of her words.

"Three minutes. Believable, particularly based on their pilot rotations."

She punched the booster, the initial pull of takeoff having eased. "How long till break off?"

Jod shrugged. "They were planning on ten, but that depends on how this shuttle handles. We can't be too fast or too determined in our initial plotting, otherwise that could tip them off that we planned this."

So they watched, flew and his fingers cramped, his gaze locked to the screen. Searching for threats.

At the fifteen-minute mark the small fighters that followed them broke off. "There's our last support craft gone." Her voice wobbled and he reached out, touching her hand.

"No. It's just our last visible support. So long as we're aware and alert we'll make it through this."

He hoped he spoke right, because anything else was unacceptable. If they were caught, there'd be no reason to keep him alive. He was the son of a Senator, but not high enough in the hierarchy to make any difference. They needed Olivia though and they'd pass her off to whoever they thought was the strongest of their warriors.

Time passed slowly. War, he mused, was simply small bites of frenetic action and long periods of waiting. This was a final skirmish in his mind.

He refused to contemplate failure. It hurt too much.

"Jod, if this goes badly. I need you to do something for me. Don't let them get me." Her quiet words fractured his heart, the one he was coming to understand a little better.

"Don't ask that of me, Olivia. I couldn't—"

The face she turned to him now was stark white, despair etched deeply. "Please. I mean, I hope it doesn't come to that, but promise me now. I can't go back to that. Not after you."

"I won't let them take you, Olivia. I'd die before that happened." She opened her mouth, and he thought she was about to argue, but he shook his head, ready to embrace the passion and promise that lured him deeper into her web. "You mean too much for me to make the promise you want."

"But you don't love me, Jod. You can't say the words." Tears trickled down her face.

"I didn't know until now exactly what love is, Olivia. Like you, I grew up among the Ru'Edan. Until meeting Chowd and the others, I had little knowledge of these emotions." He rose and lurched over to her, needing to tell her what he'd come to recognize. "I do love you. I didn't understand it until now."

Olivia's hair flew like a curtain around her face and she shook her head. "No. You're just saying it because..."

"Dammit Olivia. I don't say things to make anyone feel better. If I say the words, then I mean them. Believe me, saying 'I love you' doesn't come lightly."

He released a pent up breath as she stared at him, mouth open.

"You mean it?"

He gave a slow but decisive nod. "Yes. I mean it."

She scrubbed at her eyes then turned back to the console. "I'm not usually so emotional."

He laughed. "Neither am I."

Four hours of manual flight sapped her energy, yet the

knowledge and zing of his emotions buoyed her. He loved her. She wanted him to say the words again, but this was the most dangerous part of the route they'd planned and she really needed to get control of herself. Entering hyperspace meant slowing, entering the slipstream and hoping no one blasted them out of the traffic lane they'd chosen. Splitting her concentration could result in their death.

The *Star of Morning* and *Star of Ishtar* were on their tail and waiting for them to catch up, would show their hand. Instead, they'd all decided to use different entry points, as if the ships were looking for ways to cage her in.

"I need the exact sequence for entry, Jod."

He ran the calculations and for the first time since she'd met him, she watched as he worked, creating the data-file she'd import into the nav systems.

She couldn't help the tiny chortle. "You're pretty good at this stuff."

He shrugged. "I was trained in Ru'Edan navy from my eighth year. Served as navigation and helm support until I was trained for guardian duties."

"Yet, Chowd was nominally in charge of the Warrior. Why?"

He grinned. "I was placed on there to act as a go between when Chowd was elevated to Ambassador. His wife, Meredith is a specialist in languages but sometimes only a Ru'Edan can negotiate with other Ru'Edan, particularly when Meredith is female."

Olivia frowned at that, but understood. There was a long way to go before females had equal status in Ru'Edan culture.

"Anyway, it was decided that if I were also an Ambassador, I'd have more sway. But that didn't happen until several months into our mission. By then the crew were used to Chowd's leadership and I wanted to learn more about humans and humanity." He shrugged. "It was that simple."

"But when this is over, what then?" She gnawed at her lip, aware after that her words could be considered an ultimatum.

"I want to make a difference Olivia. I mean, there is much work to do, but the political world doesn't interest me. My brother will eventually rise to the position of Senator. It's not my path. But there are things I can do, stands I can take that will improve the opportunities and lives of my people. I need to find a path where we can, *together*, make the lives of the hybrid better."

She seized on his words. "Why the hybrid?"

"Because that's what you are. I want you to be accepted for the woman you are. You're an exceptional pilot, a strong woman and a fierce warrior. I've seen all these qualities first hand. It's not acceptable to me that you don't have the rights and status of your equals."

"But I'm not really Ru'Edan. I'm not really human. For all that, I don't want to be forever tagged as a hybrid like some kind of second class citizen." The words were full of passion and she needed to settle herself before continuing. Focusing on his declaration of *them,* she said, "You're an amazing man Jod."

With a shake of her head she ended any further conversation. She had more than enough to consider. So she waited until he sent the string of information then entered the data into the system, tapping her foot as she waited for it to resolve in the nav banks.

It took an immense amount of effort to shunt the conversation to the back of her mind. So much to consider and yet now wasn't the time or place.

With a heavy sigh, Olivia inspected the packet of information that Duvall had thrust at her before boarding the shuttle.

She sifted through the papers, arrested by one written in Meredith's hand.

Olivia,

I have wanted to talk with you, but things have been fraught as you know. Chowd deeply regrets that he never knew of your existence. If he had, he would have moved heaven and earth to get you on that shuttle when he left.

The guilt makes him seem remote so he's kept his distance. That's made talking with you difficult, especially on a personal level.

Having said that, when this mission is complete, I hope you will allow me to get to know you better.

Jod is new to our group, yet he's one of us. That makes you one of us too.

I've asked Duvall to include this, as a tangible reminder that we support you.

Both of you.

Stay safe and come back.

I want to know my sister better.

Meredith

Olivia ran her finger over the last line. Sister. Not sibling. Not hybrid. Jod's words replayed in her mind as a ping echoed throughout the cabin.

"There's the indicator. Fasten up, we're about to enter the slipstream."

With careful movements she guided the shuttle into the trajectory and entered hyper drive.

Jod spent the next few days talking with Olivia. Learning about her. It amazed him that she enjoyed hand cooking. "It's one of the few things the rogues seemed to prefer about human life!"

He chuckled, remembering his first experience of human fare. "On the station, when the crew of the Elector were there with the Ambassador, we had a formal meal. I remember watching their faces as we served up the usual slop. Their people had instructed ours on one of their basic dishes. I'd never tasted real food until then. The flavors and succulence of the food made me want more." Even now the memory made him smile. "The other Ru'Edan were stunned. It made them realize that there were facets of humanity that would enhance our lives."

She touched his face, sitting next to him in the bed they'd claimed. "The rogues preferred the human women to cook, the Ru'Edan were pretty awful at it to be honest." She grinned. "My mother was a cook. Crick had found her on a small mining asteroid when they'd destroyed the installation; he needed a concubine. Chowd's mother was only one of many, yet the others found a quicker way out of their situation. They either died—their own choice—or were unable to conceive after time with Crick. A few more got rid of the pregnancies before anyone found out. We all knew, but no one discussed those things."

He waited as she lifted her pained gaze to him.

She bit her lip, and pushed the food on her plate around as she remembered her formative years. "For many, it was the easiest way out and those unable to conceive were either disposed of or put to work in other areas of the base."

He touched her hand, a soft gentle gesture. "But your mother didn't get rid of you."

Olivia shook her head. "No. Her father was a holy man. Believed in the sanctity of life and so did she. It must have been dreadful for her though, hoping for a daughter and fearing a son. Then she had me. He had me taken to a separate area on Otega, schooled in Ru'Edan ways, but I had too much outside influence from the human women. No way to contain it, I suppose, which must have irked him a lot. It was only as I got older that I worked out who my mother was. I had to come up with reasons to be in the kitchens and she'd tell me as much as possible without alerting the guards."

He ached for her. *Such a loveless upbringing.* Of course, it was no different from the way many Ru'Edan offspring were raised and not for the first time, he reflected he'd had a gentler and kinder upbringing.

Jod tugged her close. "You won't go back to that."

He tangled his hands in her hair, pulling her down with

him as he leaned back to the pillows.

Then he kissed her. A soft brush of lip, like the caress of a butterfly. He'd give her softness now. He'd found out that dragging out the pleasure made her sigh and moan and left them both feeling relaxed in the aftermath.

Jod moved over her, sliding his hands over her breasts, rubbing his thumbs over the rosy tips before moving in to suckle.

"Jod!" She writhed beneath his touch, fingers greedy and reaching for more.

Skimming his mouth over her belly, he skittered away, glorying in the way the muscles tensed beneath the homage he paid.

Following his instincts, Jod traced the path lower, until he found her core, then set his mouth over her.

"Oh Stars!"

Olivia bucked, tangling her hands in the sheets, heels digging into the mattress. Her musky taste and scent overrode his rational senses, urging him on.

Then Olivia stilled, body taut as she came, her shriek music to his ears and he drew away, licking the taste of her from his lips and tongue.

Her body quivered as he placed one hand against her belly.

Olivia opened her eyes, sheened with tears. "But you didn't..."

"Not yet. My turn comes now."

Her eyes widened, as he seated himself between her legs.

"Olivia?" He waited for her to show him that she was ready, his body tense with concern until she wound her legs around his waist. He sighed as she pulled him against her body then impaled herself on his rigid cock.

He slid in, all the way to the hilt then stilled.

Olivia sighed quietly. "I love you Jod."

His heart filled, nearly bursting with emotion. "I love you too, Olivia. I love you so deeply that I don't know all the ways to show you." His eyes slid shut, allowing him to savor the moment on multiple levels. The sensuality of the here and now dragged him deeper under her spell.

He rocked, enjoying the slickness of her flesh. The way she welcomed him deep within herself. Each move: a long slow glide. He flexed his hips, each time a little faster and harder.

Heat and light built behind his closed eyes as she gasped out his name again. The climax built fast, his movements more urgent and hungry.

It crashed down on him, his chest seizing, his body hard as stone, then the release shattered his senses.

✪ ✪ ✪ ✪ ✪

In the aftermath, Olivia lay there, threading her fingers through his hair; the silky darkness had grown somewhat since they'd met. He'd loosened in personality too. His character now subtle to her and what she'd taken as harsh and abrasive was merely a front used to keep people at bay.

The depth of his soul was humbling.

He'd fallen asleep in her embrace. Ru'Edan males never did that, from what she knew. They took their pleasure and left the female. Instead of demanding what was his, he ensured her needs came first. Cared for her.

"Why? What makes you so different?" She kept her words quiet, not seeking an answer from him and hoping he'd remain asleep a while longer so she could think.

He'd spoken little about his upbringing. She knew his sire was Senator Esrau Svan'Er. He had sisters and a brother, but the day-to-day mundanity… The things that made him— she hesitated to use the word, even in the depths of her mind— human—continued to elude her.

The buzz of an alarm caught her attention and she shook Jod, needing him to get off her.

"Huh? What?"

"An alarm. I need to see what it is." She moved the

instant he rolled away, grabbing up the loose robe and donning it as she hurried to the console. Her gaze roamed over the screen. "Dammit. We've been increasing speed in slip-stream and the exit is ten minutes ahead. I can't slow the engines here." She ran a quick diagnostic, realizing that it would put the *Ishtar* and *Morning* about two hours behind them. She'd need to create some kind of diversion to allow them to catch up.

She bit her lip as Jod placed a hand on her shoulder. "What caused this?" His soft-spoken words sent her body quivering in response to the play of his breath over her skin. It took seconds for her mind to clear and consider his query.

"The engines work on a multiplying velocity platform. So as we increase speed, there is a flow on effect. I expected to have another two to three hours grace period, having slowed down the engines before entering the stream but I've somehow messed up the calculations." She swiped an unsteady hand over her brow, needing to stave off the defeat that wound through her. They'd come so far and one tiny mistake might put everything and everyone she cared about in jeopardy.

The thing was, what *had* she missed? She gnawed on her lip as she reached for the book pad she'd used to work out her speeds.

Jod must have read the despair that surrounded her like a cloak, because he gathered her close, gently pushing her head to his shoulder. "We'll sort it out Olivia. Let's dress then we can deal with the problem."

She pulled her hand away from the unit and gave a convulsive nod, checked the time—seven minutes— and pulled away. "We need to be quick."

They were. Returning to the cockpit and settling into the pilots seat in under five, she scooped up her device and began to run the calculations again. She was well aware there was nothing more to do until they reached the exit.

Jod joined her a moment later, clipping a beverage container into its holder. "You should eat now, because we'll likely be busy once we're back out in real space."

Olivia allowed herself a moment to look at him, this man she loved. "You're right, but I can't face food just yet. I need to check this before its too late. There might be something I can do."

With that, she turned her attention to the pad.

Chapter Nine

Jod watched Olivia like a hawk as they exited the slip-stream. Since the moment she'd realized they were too far ahead, she'd been grim. Determined to accept all the consequences of this mistake on her shoulders.

He'd alleviate it if he could, but she was a pilot and he wasn't. Sure he knew nav systems and could fly an ordinary shuttle with a small crew, but her ability to calculate trajectories and speed vectors was well above his knowledge.

He gave a sigh as the engine sounds changed with a clunk. "Real Space."

"Yeah. Have you—"

"Run a bogey check? On that now." His gaze returned to the screen, fingers tapping in slow progression over the keys as he checked for ion signatures, traces of fuel types and even the ripple of cloaked ships. So far, nothing. All good news to his way of thinking.

"Anything?" He heard the hopefulness in her voice and nearly grinned.

"Nothing yet, Olivia. Maybe we can find somewhere, take a more round about route to our location. Give the other ships time to..."

She was shaking her head. "You know, as well as I do, that won't work, Jod. But thank you."

"For what?" He was genuinely surprised at her answer.

"I looked at the maps with Chowd, Duvall and Grayson while you worked with Raven on the tech. We all agreed this was the safest and most believable option. We couldn't take a roundabout route, because the chances of interception increased too much for all our liking."

He frowned. "What if we slow down, just a little?"

She bit her lip and he reached out for her free hand, the one that wasn't entering data into her console.

"We can't afford to wash off more than two percent of speed." She nodded. "That might give us another twenty minutes or so." She tapped the information into her pad. "It's not enough, but a start."

He watched as she pulled her hand away, and began to enter the correction into the system.

Jod needed to touch her but with too many conflicting needs he retreated within himself. Focused on the task at hand and set up another check, his blood running cold as a tiny blip appeared. "Olivia? We have something on the radar."

"What?" Her tone was strangled as she spun the seat to look at his screen.

"It's off the starboard side. One hour to intercept and counting."

The slow beat of his heart sped up. This could be anything, the identity of the ship cloaked.

"Could it be Phobos Pirates? A Rogue shuttle?" She couldn't control the waver in her voice and the knowledge of her terror whipped him.

He glanced in her direction. "I don't know, Olivia. That will become evident as they get closer but..."

She grunted and rubbed a hand over her belly. "Okay, we have time up our sleeve with the engines. Let's hope its friendly though."

He turned away and ran diagnostic on the shielding, looking for ways to increase its capacity. The weapons systems were ready, having all ready been checked thoroughly.

The waiting, prior to the engagement always seemed so long.

The muscles in his body tensed and he relaxed them one by one, knowing that this time before the storm was when the preparations integral to the success of any skirmish were finessed.

"Drink the beverage now, Olivia. There may not be time later." He took his own advice, welcoming the burn of the nutrient rich soup he'd dispensed.

She drank, her gaze never leaving the screens before her, yet he knew she was aware of him and his actions, the same as he was of her.

Time passed, a slow molasses drip that tricked the mind and nerves.

His body now cooled, as his focus deepened on what was out there, and knowing their preparations were as complete as possible.

"Changing course. I've found an alternative location, one I think that will give us the time to cut and run away. We should be able to hold them off until the others get here." Her voice echoed in the silence. They'd prepared for this. He just hoped that the coalition forces were in place. The *Ishtar* and the *Morning* wouldn't make it in time. He'd already accepted that knowledge, but now everything depended on others. The loss of control ate at him from the inside out. "Sending you co-ordinates and details now."

The file blipped on his screen and he checked it over, giving a small grunt of agreement. She'd worked fast and found the best alternative possible. "That should do."

He felt the change in course as the ship heeled. "Checking all weapons systems." This was the most vital part of the mission. He had detected another five shuttles and several smaller craft on the horizon of the radar.

"Bogey count?"

"Thirteen, possibly fourteen. Five long-range craft, possibly armored shuttle. The rest smaller, likely fighters." Jod enabled the new system, an alert application that kept count of bogeys and flashed the updated count at the top corner of the screen. He would have liked it to be more accurate, but given the distances involved and the disparate sizes, it gave them an idea of the number of combatants they potentially faced.

"Entering atmosphere and venting." She arrowed the shuttle into the upper thermosphere and he watched as the red blue light glowed at the front of the shuttle. The flames flowed over the body of the craft, licking at the shield. Seeking anywhere it could find purchase, hungry for fodder.

They agreed she'd use the entrance to slow the shuttle, well aware that any craft following her would be slowed even more. Most of them wouldn't have the maneuverability and heavier plating to allow them to ride the layers of atmosphere.

The flames grew, the drag of gravity pulling them down, the shuttle was buffeted by the atmosphere, as they bounced. Olivia fought hard, using the manual navigation tools. Her whole body swaying as she fought the competing pressures while beads of sweat trickled down her hairline and soaked her grey ship suit. She'd never looked more amazing.

At this point, Jod was merely an observer. His training as a Warrior kept him still when his brain—working on a purely instinctual level—screamed at him to act. The knowledge that she was best able for the action that lay ahead sat poorly in his mind. He focused on what was yet to come. The opportunity to repay those who'd made Olivia's life so miserable, as well as being responsible for so many deaths and such widespread destruction.

Hardening his mind, Jod mentally prepared himself for what lay ahead. He'd protect Olivia. Whatever it took.

✪ ✪ ✪ ✪ ✪

Olivia fought the machine, the speeds at which she attempted re-entry requiring a different approach to anything she'd experienced. Before they'd left, she'd had time to meet with Jemma. The young woman walked her through the kinds of problems they might encounter. Olivia was amazed at the skill and abilities of the woman who railed against the requirement to rest and miss the—as she put it—fun.

"Leveling out at fifty-six thousand." Every ounce of skill and strength was absorbed with her task and she was peripherally aware of Jod's efforts as they dropped through the layers, watching for incoming unfriendlies and staying alert to the nuances of their shielding.

Once they dropped into the stratosphere, the clouds billowed, particles of ice skittered against the invisible barrier and she checked their power usage. They could run and hide long enough for their assistance to arrive.

"Jod, send an encoded message. Give the co-ordinates of the haven I located."

She waited and battled the craft, skimming and slipping through the updrafts.

Once more she checked fuel usage. She'd need to be careful, the drag had depleted them faster than she'd allowed for.

"Bogeys?"

"Less. Trying to lock onto how many. They're slippery though." Jod's voice betrayed the concern they both were coping with.

Time passed and she hurtled the shuttle through a ravine, almost scraping the edges. Skimming over a watercourse— splashing up a wave at some of the ships following.

"Another gone."

"Not enough Jod. Time check to assistance?"

He sighed, "maybe fifteen. We're running time down, but they're gaining on us. The acrobatics and constant changing are the only things that are keeping us ahead of them and out of range."

Fifteen. Enough, she theorized to get down on the ground and maybe hide. The location she'd selected initially was as defensible as any other on this planet.

But what if they had settled on it before they got there?

"Jod, can you find me a secondary landing location, in case the first is compromised?"

"Already done. I'll transmit the co-ords to your screen." The flash of incoming information caught her eye.

"When did you get time to do that?"

Jod smiled. "As soon as you sent me the first set of co-ords. Chowd suggested that we'd need a couple. I agreed, but not because he'd suggested it. A backup plan is essential to a warrior and guardian. I have one more as well, but it's not as safe."

She bit her lip. Not as safe? It wasn't as if anything about this whole thing was going to increase their security. After all, they were here to entice the rogues to come after her.

"Okay then. When we get down, you stay on board." In her own mind, his safety ranked as her number one priority.

"Negative. I'm your guard, remember? It's my job to keep you safe." She detected anger in his voice and had to admit, if the situation was the other way around, she'd be furious too.

"Jod..."

"No. We discussed this. Where you go, I go. Love means sacrifice. I'm not going to let you go out there, be taken prisoner and potentially used as a sex slave in a gilded cage. Olivia, you might be the bait, but I have no intentions of you being caught. Now, don't argue. Focus on flying and get us down safely."

Another buffet caught her attention, momentarily dismissing the argument as she flew back into the troposphere.

Once more she banked, her gaze settling on the ground in her viewer. She re-checked then plunged down toward the earth. It was wild, her body absorbing the G-force before she realigned the ship again, hand sweating on the joystick.

"I'm going to take a flyby. What's the status of those on our tail?" For a moment she released a hand from the control, slicked away the sweat that threatened to blind her.

"As expected we've got less than three minutes. Numbers increased to twenty. The extras have just entered the atmosphere. They want you badly Olivia, but they won't get you."

His hands ran over his console. Olivia knew he was recalibrating shield harmonics, preparing the automated systems to lock on should things get any more dangerous than they already were. With that many craft on her tail, she hoped they'd installed the improved multi-acquisition firing program.

Her clothes clung to her skin, drenched with sweat that cooled her fevered body as she worked the stick, pulling against the gravitational tug. She swayed in time with the deep loop, heading for the location they'd earmarked, aware that this brought her closer to those following. Olivia depressed the voice control on her left. "Close the front viewer and revert to all screens."

"Screens engaged."

In silence the black cover slid across the front of the shuttle, cutting out the bright light, leaving them both illuminated by the red and green flashing lights.

"Cabin lights thirty percent." She started as Jod gave the voice command to the shuttle's system.

"Acknowledged."

"I'm going VTOL for landing."

Jod grunted his acknowledgment as they hovered for an instant over the spot.

"Once we leave the ship, you stick by me." He released his straps with a snap as they touched down, the ship giving a gentle thud. "Exit via the priest hole in the base. Suit up."

He was off, tugging on the tactical suit he'd insisted they should wear.

The Ru'Edan technology was far superior to the humans but not built for a woman. She fought the covers but tugged them up ignoring the pouches in some areas and tightness in others.

Once garbed, he thrust a laser rifle into her hands, clipped a munitions belt to her waist and thrust the helmet onto her head.

"I've already activated the personal shielding. It won't give us unlimited protection, so be smart. Stay aware and alive."

He pierced her with his gaze.

She read his concern and nodded. "I'll follow your orders, Jod. Let's get out of here."

They both knew the shuttle sitting out in the open made them an easy target. It was exactly what they needed to draw the Rogues to their location.

"What if they don't take the bait, Jod? Then what?"

"There's enough of them to make the statement. I'd lay

odds they think you're alone and ripe for the taking. Now, stop talking and let's get out of here."

He lifted the grating below the crew seating and they slipped down, into the space between the cargo bay and walls of the ship. The plating threw off frigid waves from the atmosphere they'd flown through but she didn't care. Her body was warm and her endorphin levels remained high.

At the bottom, Jod stilled her, removing the small section of plating they'd retrofitted for easy opening. In his hand he carried a tiny device, capable of showing what waited beyond, swiveling silently at three hundred and sixty degrees. "Clear." She heard his whisper and exhaled.

The trapdoor sprung open and he climbed down first, feet touching the ground inaudibly then reached up and helped her. He carefully closed the plating and in silence, he indicated the small brush-like plant she'd landed beside and they crouched, half running half crawling behind it.

She glanced to the ground; pleased the rocky surface left no footprints. When she glanced back, he gripped her hand and tugged.

She followed.

Just beyond the brush was a cave.

They only had a few feet to go when the sound of the first pursuer echoed, the whine a discordant shriek.

Jod and Olivia reached the mouth of the cave and dove in. Their part in the mission was done. Now, they just needed to stay hidden and safe.

"You're sure they won't be able to detect us?"

She kept watch, gazing beyond the cave.

"No. The temperature control damps the heat signatures so no one will see us. Then the skin of the suits carries a series of tiny cameras, allowing the reflection of what they would normally see.

Olivia wasn't so sure the technology was as brilliant as Jod told her, but she'd been wrong before and was more than willing to let it be so again.

She held her breath, waited for the craft to settle on the ground as Jod employed the personal shielding he'd carried off the ship. In theory, if they found them, it would allow them to remain safe against just about anything. *Except ion cannons and torpedoes.*

She gulped as one by one the rogues disgorged from their ships, banding together. The groups formed one massed regiment.

Olivia licked her lips, but they were dry—like sandpaper.

Her fists clenched, knuckles white as she stared.

They advanced and she shrank back, Jod's hand on her shoulder, keeping her grounded as she faced her fears.

The closer they surged to the shuttle, the greater the chances of disclosure.

"Has enough time passed?" She had leaned as close to Jod as she could so only the merest whisper was required.

"I don't know."

The rogues inspected the shuttle, before one tried a shot from a plasma rifle, ducking as the shielding flung back the pulse of light.

Another tromped back to his ship and she heard the crackle of his demand that she surrender through the tiny headpiece.

Every action took time and she hoped, prayed and implored the gods to look kindly on their petition for just a little more time.

Suddenly, a flash of light erupted. The rogues scattered, heading for ships as the coalition forces emerged from hiding.

The rattle of guns, banging and crashing filled the air, smoke, thick enough to choke on wafted.

Chaos.

Jod pulled her close—safe in his grasp while beyond rogues battled Ru'Edan and humans, fighting together.

She squeezed her eyes shut, burrowed into his embrace and shook.

A rumble began, the dirt and rocks of their cavern shifting.

"We have to get out of here." Jod released her, his hand reaching for the tiny shield generator then pushed her out as the cavern where they'd sheltered collapsed. Debris rained down, cloaking her in sudden choking darkness.

She coughed once. "Jod?"

He didn't answer and a resultant spike of fear impaled her. "Jod?"

She leaned down, hands scrabbling at the rocks, tugging and digging, tears flowing.

The suit couldn't protect her hands, the tender skin abraded and tearing.

Olivia's attention was now consumed by the need to find her mate, the sounds of fighting melted from consciousness. *Jod. Please be alive.* The refrain ran through her head, over and again. The touch of a hand on her shoulder made her jump, and swing around.

"Where's Jod?" *Chowd.*

"How did you get here?" She gazed at him wildly, then shook her head. "Never mind. He's in there and we have to get him out, now!" She turned back, resuming her frenzied digging.

Chowd picked her up, dragged her away and she yowled. Screamed and fought him.

"Just a minute." He pressed the communicator on his jacket. "Locate Jod and transmit direct to sick bay."

"*Got him. Transmitting now.*"

She whirled on her half brother. "I need to be with him."

He grasped her hand. "In a moment. There's one more thing first. We have to ensure the success of the mission, Olivia."

Chowd's words slashed at her. Couldn't he see? "Olivia, Jod's going to be fine, but this is all for nothing if you don't complete the mission."

His words bit deep and she sucked in an unsteady breath, well aware that though Jod would never say it, her inability to finish would dog them forever. She closed her eyes for a second, looking for the well of strength hidden within herself then nodded. "What do you need me to do?"

Chowd smiled and tugged on her helmet that she removed. "Good work, Olivia."

Olivia squared her shoulders. "Where? What do I need to do?"

"Follow me. We need to deal with the head of these rogues, then you can go to Jod."

She nodded, stumbled but followed Chowd past the shuttle to the heavily guarded knot of assembled rogues. They glanced at her as she sneered at them. More than one seemed amused at her approach.

Not for long.

A shuttle flew in, landed without kicking up a cloud of dust and Olivia couldn't help craning her neck. It took an amazing pilot to manage that. The squeak of the gangplank captured her attention and she watched an older Ru'Edan male emerge from a shuttle, his long robes brushing the ground.

Jod's father. Senator Svan'Er. A moment of doubt assailed her but he reached out, a smile on his face. "Welcome Olivia Sur Banden. Before these assembled, will you take a vow of fealty to the Ru'Edan?"

It was a test. It had to be. Olivia shook her head. "I will not."

He frowned and more than one rogue snickered at her answer. But it didn't concern her. It's what they'd agreed on before the mission had been compromised.

A tall male, tightly packed followed by a woman packing serious weaponry strode off the shuttle. She knew him too. Admiral Elphin.

"Olivia, my dear. I'm so pleased to finally meet you." The Admiral grasped her hand, gave it a tiny squeeze of solidarity. "You are ready to pledge allegiance to the Federation?"

She shook her head. "No. Neither of you alone is capable of ensuring the safety of this universe."

The woman behind Elphin winked at her and for a moment she was startled then grinned.

Chowd turned her to face him. "My sister, Olivia. You're

quite right. As my first act as Ambassador to the Coalition of Ru'Edan and Alliance Governments, I'm authorized to accept your allegiance to this newly formed body."

"About time." Chowd grinned at her quip, but she inhaled deeply. "I pledge that I will do everything I can to ensure the success of this Coalition. Further, I ask that you deal with these Rogues here present. Ensure they are tried before an assembly of their peers. Let them be accountable for their actions."

Now they remonstrated as she turned to them, gazing out over the faces of those before her. More than one screamed 'traitor' but she simply watched until silence once more reigned.

"I never wanted this. I wanted peace. You hunted me down and allowed me no freedom to decide. You would have enslaved me and many others as you've done in the past."

Now she whirled away, heading for the shuttle. "Olivia, wait." The woman who'd followed Elphin from the shuttle called and she stilled, wanting nothing more than to see Jod. To know he was alive.

"What?"

"I'm taking you to the *Ishtar*. Jod's there." The woman, Kera, slipped a locator into her hands, pressed her badge and stated, "two for immediate transition to surgi-tech."

✪ ✪ ✪ ✪ ✪

Her arrival in the surgi-tech wing was anticlimactic. Jod was sitting up, railing against Elara who refused to release his restraints until he settled. That she didn't understand how terrified Olivia would be was clear, as she shook her head, lips firmly clamped together, so that fine white lines radiated.

"Until I'm satisfied that you've got no more dust in your lungs, you're not going anywhere."

The quick *tap tap* of steps brought him swinging around.

An instant of vertigo assailed, but the sight of Olivia, her face strained and pale both worried and in equal parts settled him.

He gave a cough and she hurried to the bed. "Why are you restrained?" She looked over her shoulder and Elara sighed.

"He's a terrible patient. He would have transmitted if I'd released his hands. He's got some inhalation issues and needs time. And rest. Thankfully in terms of physical injuries, he'd been in a pocket, so while there's bruising and spraining, he's got no broken bones."

Jod growled as Olivia sagged against him. *Thank the Stars*," she whispered then leaned down to kiss his brow.

Elara chuckled, leaned over. "Now I can release you. She's here, safe and sound and Kera is waiting just beyond. I sent her a quick report with instructions to bring Olivia here at the first available opportunity."

Elara unclasped one then the other restraint. "But, you are to stay here until I'm sure you're suffering no ill effects. Olivia, make sure he behaves." With a small laugh, the Surgi-Tech left the cubicle.

Alone, Jod slid his hands around Olivia, needing to be assured she was finally here, with him: Alive and well.

"What happened? Elara said I was transmitted from the cavern."

"It collapsed. You pushed me out and when I could finally see, you were..." Her voice broke and she hugged him tight. "I couldn't see you. You didn't answer and I was so scared."

She pulled away as he coughed again and glanced to her hands, caked thick with blood and dust. "What happened? Let me call Elara." He reached to press the call button but she stopped him.

"No, Jod. I tried to dig you out. I couldn't get through the rock, then Chowd appeared and had you transmitted." He smiled at her. "How did they do that?"

She leaned forward as he gave a choking laugh. "I have this." He held out the remains of a locator and smiled. "I had one embedded when I signed onto the Warrior. We'll get one for you too." He sighed, relaxing for the first time in hours. "Now, what's happening with the rogues?"

"They're all rounded up, or if not all, then enough to make the statement. Those that may have got away no longer have support. They should scatter far and wide now but their opportunity to regroup is destroyed."

He pondered her words; aware that the lack of satisfaction stemmed from knowing Olivia was no longer tied to the shuttle and crew. That she could leave at any time she chose. That knowledge froze him to the core.

She opened her mouth and he reached up, placed his hand gently across her lips.

"Olivia?"

She opened her eyes. "Yes?"

"I love you. Will you be my Life Partner?"

Her gaze narrowed. "Your asking me now, while you're confined to Surgi-Tech and I'm grubby?"

He waited for her to shake her head, his spirits dropping. He'd made a misstep. Chosen the wrong time, location. He closed his eyes then opened them as he felt the whisper of her breath against his lips.

"Of course I will." Then she kissed him.

Epilogue

Olivia grimaced at herself in the mirror. The formal attire of an Ambassadors wife hung heavily on her. At least Jod promised she wouldn't need to wear it often. The long skirts swished around her ankles.

Besides, this was a momentous occasion. The official agreement of the formation of the Coalition and all those important to its creation would be in attendance: Duvall and Mellissa, Jemma and Raven, Chowd and Meredith. The Senator and Life Partner—Jod's mother. The Admiral and Kera. And the Heads of State and Houses.

Celebrations were being conducted on every planet of the Federation and Ru'Edan worlds.

At the conclusion of the ceremony, Jod's sisters would be formally inducted into the Admiralty.

The door opened and Meredith, Jod and Chowd strode in. "You look amazing, Olivia. I don't get anything half so fashionable to wear."

Meredith clasped Olivia's hand, the formal Admiralty suit highlighting the tiny bump she caressed with her other hand.

"I'm not so sure it's me. I'd rather your attire."

Chowd laughed. "A woman who's not interested in clothes. Jod, I think my sister is one of a kind."

"Indeed." The sparkle in his eyes, when he glanced at her warmed her thoroughly. Once the officialdom was finished, they'd gather on the *Ishtar*, for a family celebration. They'd all played significant parts in the creation of this new coalition. Soon they'd be sent on their separate ways, but for now...

Jod held out his arm and she took it, watching as Chowd and Meredith did the same.

A moment of memory impinged. The fear she'd felt when she first met him, terrified he'd come to take her as a slave for the rogues. This event to her signified the ending of that life.

Oh, when she'd become Life Partner with Jod, it had given her a new life to look forward to. But with the scourge of the Rogues done, finally she could embrace it.

Excitement fizzed in her veins. "Let's go. I want to be there early so we can see better."

They all laughed. "As my consort wants." He kissed her softly on the lips sealing the agreement.

The four stepped through the door and into a new universe.

THE END

About Imogene Nix

Imogene is published in a range of romance genres including paranormal, science fiction, and contemporary. She is mainly published in the UK and USA due to the nature of her tales.

In 2011, Imogene Nix was born at the Bondi ARRA (Australian Romance Readers Association) Conference. Returning from the conference enthused, Imogene sat down and worked tirelessly for three months culminating in the book Starline. This book became the first in the Warriors of the Elector series. In fact, she has completed six entire series. Imogene has successfully been contracted for twenty-five titles and self-published three others under this pseudonym. She has also completed another three and is, like many of her contemporaries, seeking homes for these books—with at least one likely to be self-published once ready.

Imogene is a member of a range of professional organizations, including Romance Writers of Australia (where she holds a committee position as the Public Relations). She is also a member of Romance Writers of America, FFP (Fantasy, Futuristic, and Paranormal) Chapter of RWA (US), Australian Romance Readers Association (ARRA), Science Fiction Romance Brigade (SFRB), Dark Siders Down Under (the Australian Paranormal, Fantasy, and Futuristic Chapter of RWA), Erotic Writers of Australia, and Queensland Writers Centre and most recently Romance Writers of New Zealand.

Imogene's Website: www.imogenenix.net
Reader eMail: imogene@imogenenix.net
Newsletter: eepurl.com/cp-bZD
Books by Imogene Nix

Books by Imogene Nix

<u>BLOOD SECRETS</u> (*TOTALLY BOUND PUBLISHING*)
1. The Blood Bride
2. The Illuminated Witch
3. The Sorcerer's Touch

<u>CELTIC CUPID</u> (*TOTALLY BOUND PUBLISHING*)

1. Blame The Wine
2. A Stranger's Embrace
3. Revenge On Cupid

<u>REUNION</u> (*BEACHWALK PRESS*)
1. War's End
2. The Assassin
3. Executing Justice

<u>THE PLAN BIOCYBE</u>
Tangled Webs (Sex Love Aliens 1)
Covert Webs (Sex Love Aliens 2)
A Bar In Paris
Hesparia's Tears
The Chocolate Affair
Tomorrow's Promise
False Webs
A Sapphire For Karina
Falling In Love Again

<u>WITH SUZI LOVE</u>
Self Publishing: Absolute Beginners Guide